P

HAMPSHIRE COUNTY LIBRARY

WITHDRAWN

Get **more** out of libraries

Please return or renew this item by the last date shown.

You can renew online at www.hants.gov.uk/library

Or by phoning 0845 603 5631

 Hampshire
County Council

C015719820

KT-362-225

DANIELLE RAMSAY

Blind Alley

MULHOLLAND
BOOKS
HODDER

First published in Great Britain in 2013 by Mulholland Books
An imprint of Hodder & Stoughton
An Hachette UK company

First published in paperback in 2014

1

A CIP catalogue record for this title is available from the British Library

ISBN 978 1 444 75482 7
eBook ISBN 978 1 444 75483 4

Typeset in Plantin by Hewer Text UK Ltd, Edinburgh
Printed and bound by CPI Group (UK) Ltd, Croydon, CR0 4YY

Hodder & Stoughton policy is to use papers that are natural, renewable
and recyclable products and made from wood grown in sustainable
forests. The logging and manufacturing processes are expected to
conform to the environmental regulations of the country of origin.

Hodder & Stoughton Ltd
338 Euston Road
London NW1 3BH

www.hodder.co.uk

To the memory of Jack Ramsay

'There is no hunting like the hunting of man, and those who have hunted armed men long enough, and liked it, never really care for anything else.'

Ernest Hemingway

Chapter One

He watched her as she came outside. She couldn't see him – he had made sure of that. He sat back in the dark and waited. It was the anticipation of what was about to follow that he savoured more than the event itself. He licked his bottom lip. The location was perfect. Rundown and deserted. If anyone heard anything they wouldn't get involved. People here minded their own business. She couldn't have chosen a better place for what was about to happen to her. *If only she knew . . .*

He smiled to himself. He clenched and unclenched his hands as mentally he walked through the various scenarios he had meticulously planned.

Trina McGuire pursed her bright red lips and sucked on her tab as her cold, hard eyes scanned the shadowy street corners. It was second nature for her. A silver saloon car turned slowly off Saville Street West down onto Borough Road, casting its harsh beam over her. Blowing out smoke seductively, she looked in the direction of the driver. The silver car was now parked directly opposite her with the engine idling. The driver's face was in shadow but she knew he was watching her. Before she had a chance to walk over, he drove off. She was no fool. She was aware that the glare of his headlights had done her no favours. The roots of her long, straggly, bleached-blonde hair and the uneven fake-tan smears on her arms and legs would be all too visible.

I

'Fuck you!'

She was getting too old for this game. And she was cold, despite it being mild for late October. She wrapped her thin, bare arms across her low-cut vest top in an attempt to keep warm.

She rested her back against the wall and listened to the dull thump of U2 on the jukebox inside as she smoked. Anything to calm her nerves. She had never known the streets to be so dark and quiet. Business was virtually non-existent. Even the Ballarat pub was empty apart from the hardcore regulars. She shivered again. She could feel the small, prickly hairs on the back of her neck standing up. She didn't know what it was, but something felt wrong. Maybe it was just her nerves getting the better of her, but she couldn't shake the feeling that someone was watching her. She glanced up and down the badly lit street. She couldn't see anyone. *Or could she?*

'Fuck this!' she muttered as she threw away what was left of her cigarette.

She turned on her three-inch red heels, about to go back in.

Before she had a chance to realise what was happening, he had already dragged her into the alley behind the pub where the rubbish bins were kept. A large leather-gloved hand covered her mouth, preventing her from screaming. Panicking, she struggled to get free but it was futile. He had the upper hand. He was at least six foot one and built like a Rottweiler on steroids.

Suddenly his other hand was tearing at her vest top. He found her breasts and started twisting and pulling at them roughly.

She felt physically sick. She wanted to vomit as his hand mauled her. But she knew that no matter what he did to her she had to keep focused. Her mind was racing. She was trying to process what was happening to her and at the same time trying to figure out how to get free.

Was he a punter? No ... no. She'd been roughed up before but this was different. He was different ...

Then it hit her. The news. It had been all over the news. There was a rapist in the area. *Shit! Shit! Shit! How could she have been so stupid?*

The police had put up photofits of the bloke throughout the local pubs. There was even one pinned by the toilets in the Ballarat. He had attacked three women in the past two months. And from what she'd read in the local paper that evening, the third one had been hurt pretty badly – enough for the poor cow to need reconstructive surgery.

Shit ... shit ... shit ...

Tortured thoughts tore through her mind.

She was confused. She was sure he had only struck in Whitley Bay. She had been relaxed about the story because this was North Shields. How wrong could she have been?

She had to get away from him. Fight ... Anything to stop him hurting her ...

She used all her strength to prise his hand from over her mouth. Her long manicured nails snapped and split as she scratched and tore to no avail at the gloved hand. If she could scream it might be enough to scare him off. Desperate, she took her chance and bit as hard as she could through the leather to the flesh underneath.

His reaction was sudden and swift. He raised his knee and rammed it as hard as he could into the small of her back to make her let go.

It had the desired effect.

She was too winded to realise what was about to happen.

The first blow was a surprise. It split her nose clean open. She heard the sickening sound of snapping bones as his fist connected with her face, followed by the hissing of escaping air and blood. She was stunned. She had no chance of protecting herself against what was to follow.

The second punch was harder than the first. It smashed into her face with such force that her left eye socket imploded. Her head snapped violently backwards as her teeth ricocheted off her bottom lip, bursting it open like a swollen dam. Her legs gave way beneath her as everything went black.

Minutes passed as she lay on the ground, her body consumed with a blinding agony. Nothing made sense. All she knew was that she hurt so badly she was certain she would die. Slowly, the hazy fog started to lift. She remembered that she'd been attacked. He had dragged her into the perilously black alley behind the pub. She was aware that she was lying on something cold and hard – the ground. She must have collapsed after he'd punched her.

She could feel the panic overwhelming her.

She looked around in the darkness for him.

Where are you, you bastard? Where the fuck are you?

Her left eye had swollen shut and her right eye was nothing more than a slit. But it was enough to see the glow of a cigarette in the blackness by the large waste bins.

She realised with sickening clarity it was him. That he hadn't finished with her – not yet.

'Where is he?' he asked, throwing his cigarette butt away.

His voice was seamless and flat, devoid of any emotion.

It was this that scared her. It was the voice of someone capable of murder.

Her mind spun as she tried to figure out who he was after.

Realising he wasn't getting anywhere with her, he decided to jolt her memory. He walked over and bent down.

She waited, expecting him to hit her again, but he took her by surprise when he started caressing her bare thin legs with his gloved hand.

She trembled as he touched her gently. He slowly moved his hand further and further up her legs until it was under her skirt.

She tried to struggle, to get his hand away from between her legs. But he had her pinned down.

'I said, where is he?'

He stopped caressing her. His hand had become a ball of tension, waiting to explode.

She attempted to shake her head.

4

It wasn't the answer he wanted. He rammed his fist as hard as he could between her legs.

The pain was unbearable. She was certain she would pass out. Instead she retched.

He stood back and watched while she vomited, until eventually only bile was left. His stomach was turning at the sight of her. Vomit combined with blood trailed down the seeping, swollen mess that was her face.

'Nick. Where is he, you fucking slag?'

He was starting to lose his patience.

The question jolted her.

'What?' she mumbled through swollen, bloodied lips.

But the word she uttered made no sense.

Irritated, he bent over her, bringing his face close to hers. She was terrified. The look in his eyes told him he wasn't just going to rape her – he was going to kill her.

'No . . . please . . . no . . .'

But the words were inaudible. The only sound was a gargling, hissing noise.

'I said, where the fuck is NICK, you stupid bitch?'

He rammed a hand deep under her ribs to make sure that she was lucid.

She gasped in agony.

When she managed to breathe again, she mustered all the strength she had and spat at him.

Blood, vomit and spit hit his face. He took a tissue out of his jacket and wiped his cheek. He then took off the jacket and rolled up the sleeves of his shirt.

'Maybe it's time to teach you some manners,' he suggested as he began to unzip his trousers.

She tried to get up but her body refused to move. She willed herself to make a run for it. But something was wrong. Her legs wouldn't work.

Move . . . come on, Trina . . . Fucking move, girl! Move it before it's too late!

Desperate, she tried shuffling backwards on her elbows, dragging herself towards the entrance of the alley.

He was more than ready. He had been anticipating this moment for some time. He took his time stretching a condom over himself. He knew he couldn't take a chance with this disease-riddled bitch. He kneeled down and grabbed her by the legs as she tried in vain to scramble away from him. He leaned over and flipped her onto her stomach.

She groaned in pain at the sudden, violent movement.

Her reaction had the desired effect. It made him even more excited. He pulled up her faux leather skirt, exposing her black thong.

She attempted to struggle but was unable to move under the crushing weight of his body. She felt him yank her thong to one side before he forced himself into her. The pain was excruciating. But it was more the humiliation that hurt. Hot, furious tears slipped down her face as he succeeded in violently thrusting himself deep into her. One hand restrained her head, forcing her damaged face into the hard concrete, while the other held his phone as he filmed what he was doing to her.

She couldn't breathe. Dirt filled her bloodied mouth as she choked and gasped, desperate for air.

She could feel her body beginning to convulse as the lack of oxygen took effect. She prayed for unconsciousness. She was lucky. She blacked out before he started to really lose control.

Once finished with her he felt nothing but disgust and contempt. He gave her lifeless body another hard kick. Nothing. Satisfied, he picked it up and dumped it into the pub's industrial waste bins where it belonged.

Fucking bitch. Deserved everything she got. He had bigger problems than some has-been prostitute. He still had to find Nick Brady. And when he did . . .

He smiled at the prospect. He had what he wanted safe in a plastic bag: evidence that he had dealt with her. He felt no remorse. She was a used-up prostitute who was better off dead. No one would miss her.

He threw the business card with her name scrawled on the back into the alleyway before turning to walk back to his car. He doubted the police would be able to identify her. Not in the condition he had left her in. But he was more than happy to point them in the right direction. After all, he had a job to do and he had to be sure that the police didn't fuck everything up.

Chapter Two

Six days earlier:
Saturday, 19th October: 3:07 a.m.

Hidden in the shadows, he waited as she staggered on ahead of him. She made a sudden turn off the road into the alley behind the boarded-up Avenue pub, her body lurching from one side to another as she did so. She seemed oblivious to the fact that the streetlights were out in the alley. Too drunk and too intent on getting home to care. He followed, making sure he didn't get too close.

She stopped.

He pushed his body flat against the wall, obscured by blackness as he held his breath and waited.

Had she seen him? No ... He was sure of that. She had no idea that he was there. Or of what was about to happen.

'Shit!' she cursed, nearly falling over as she bent down to undo the straps on her black heels.

Successfully removing them, she yanked her dress up and crouched down.

He watched with stirring excitement as she relieved herself.

She was different. His tongue snaked slowly across his bottom lip as he thought about touching her. If he was honest, it was her tattoo that aroused him. It fascinated him.

Unlike with the others, he had waited for this moment – religiously following her movements on Facebook and Twitter. Even tonight she had updated her status:

'Out to get as drunk as I can. Are you up for it?'

8

He was 'up for it' all right. And if it was trouble she was looking for, she was heading in the right direction.

He studied her with a predatory interest as she managed to somehow pull herself up without tumbling forward. She even managed to drag her dress back down. Not that she needed to do that; he would soon be ripping it off.

He double-checked his jacket for condoms. Two weeks of watching her. Fantasising. Planning. Now he was ready, he wanted to savour every detail.

He had his phone with him so he could film her. Not that she could object, given the state she was in. She was lucky he'd been keeping an eye on her. Her friends – if you could call them friends – had abandoned her. Left her dangerously drunk outside the Blue Lagoon nightclub while they went on somewhere else.

It couldn't have worked out better for him when she decided to walk home – alone at 2:51 a.m. through the dark, empty streets of Whitley Bay.

Had she not watched the news or read the papers? Obviously not.

The police hadn't taken him as seriously as he wanted. But after tonight all that would change. She was the one. The one that was going to make the headlines. Her name – Chloe Winters – would soon have the following she craved. She wanted to be famous and he would be the one to give her that, and more.

He would make her newsworthy.

He playfully fingered the Stanley knife safely hidden in his jacket pocket for later. What he was going to do to her would take time. He would make sure it was slow and deliberate. The pain would be delicious. He could feel himself getting hard as he imagined the knife slicing neatly through her delicate, pale flesh.

He was ready to make a move.

He crept up behind her.

Hearing someone, she spun round. She froze for a second as she tried to register who was behind her – and why. Even through the hazy blur of drunkenness she could tell that something about him was wrong. She started to edge backwards, away from him. He scared her. It was his eyes. Something was wrong with the way he was staring at her.

Instinct took over.

She made a move and ran as hard and fast as she could.

But he was too quick. That, and she was too drunk to have ever stood a real chance of escaping him.

With no real effort he caught hold of her and rammed her hard up against the alley wall. He then used his body to pin her against it. He knew she could feel his hardness in the small of her back. He pushed it against her, wanting her to know how excited she made him.

He could hear her breathing – short, shallow gasps of air like a wounded animal. She was really scared now. He liked that.

He grabbed a fistful of hair and yanked her head back. He knew it hurt. He wanted it to hurt.

She cried out from the pain. Stinging tears blurred everything around her. She started whimpering.

He breathed in her fear. He could smell it on her skin, emanating from her pores.

'Shhh . . .' he whispered in her ear, enjoying every delectable whimpering sound she made.

Her eyes were desperate. Filled with terror at what was happening to her.

He knew that she couldn't breathe. He could feel the panic rising up from within her pathetic body as she struggled desperately to prise his hand off her face. It was useless. He completely overpowered her.

He had trained for this – worked out at the gym for hours on end. Pumping weights and then working on his cardio. It wasn't just his body he had taken care of – he also had a place prepared. He had thought of everything. He needed to be certain that nobody would find them. Let alone disturb him. What he had planned for her would take time. Lots and lots of time.

Chapter Three

When Chloe woke up, it was to more than just a hangover. She tentatively opened her swollen, bloodshot eyes. Her head was pounding as if it was going to explode. The searing pain was unbearable. She tried to remember how many tequilas she'd drunk. Simple answer – too many. She squinted at the dots of grey light dancing in front of her eyes.

FUCK! Oh fuck it hurts!

She quickly closed her eyes, unable to cope with the pain that the light caused. This had to be the worst hangover ever.

It took her a few more minutes before she realised that she was cold. Bitterly cold. She could feel an icy breeze caressing her goose-pimpled skin. Moaning in discomfort, she turned over. Her face hit something hard and wet. Shocked, she attempted to sit up.

Oh fuck ... fuck ... fuck ...

The pain in her head exploded. She had no choice but to gingerly lie back down and wait for it to ease. Her breathing was shallow and erratic – her head objecting to even the slightest movement.

She didn't know how much time passed as she drifted in and out of consciousness. When she eventually came round, it was to an unfamiliar reality.

Stunned, then panic-stricken, she held her breath as she realised that she had no idea where she'd spent the night. The shafts of light snaking through the boarded-up window barely penetrated the shadowy gloom of the room. But it was enough for her to make out that she was lying on a grim concrete floor covered in rats' droppings. She looked around and saw that the room was littered with broken bottles amongst other debris. A filthy, urine- and blood-stained mattress lay next to her. It stank. As did the room. The smell was cloying – suffocating.

Shit! Shit! Shit! Where am I? Where the fuck am I?

She knew something bad had happened even before she caught sight of her body. She was naked. Her black dress and underwear were missing. But that was the least of her concerns. Someone had . . . someone had . . .

Oh God! What did he do to me?

She started sobbing as sordid images flashed through her mind.

No . . . God, no . . . Her tied up on the mattress – face down. Someone was watching her . . . filming her. Filming what he was doing to her.

She suddenly remembered *him*. His face. His smell. The knife . . .

No . . . please . . . no . . . Don't let that be real . . .

She started to scream. Louder and louder. Anything to block out the horrific images flashing through her head.

She wanted to die long before she remembered the full extent of the sadistic injuries he had inflicted upon her.

Sunday, 20th October: 9:33 a.m.

He watched the film again on his desktop computer. It was his best work yet. She had been worth the trouble. He smiled to himself as he uploaded the sadistic, brutal rape onto YouTube. There was a group of them who followed one another's work. He was certain they would appreciate this one as much as he did. He watched as it uploaded, already anticipating the comments it would elicit.

Suck my dick, you bastards!

He heard banging and clattering below him. Loud and intrusive.

Fucking keep quiet, you bitch!

He never once took his eyes off the computer screen. He refused to have her break his concentration. His dark, predatory eyes narrowed to slits as he tried to control his anger. His nostrils flared with irritation as the relentless noise continued below.

What the fuck was she doing down there?

He switched to another window on the computer screen.

It was a live-feed of a dark, gloomy room. He scanned the debris, searching for her. It did not take him long before he found her. She was chained to the floor in the corner of the room. Waiting . . . waiting for him.

Chapter Four

Friday, 25th October: 9:01 a.m.

Brady sighed. Regardless of how often he read the victims' files, they still made no sense. His head was pounding. He had hoped that it would ease up, but instead it had intensified. He opened a drawer, took out some painkillers and swallowed them back with a mouthful of bitter black coffee. He grimaced in disgust. It was cold.

He checked his phone: 9:01 a.m. He had been sitting in his office, mulling over every nuance of the case for over an hour now, in the vain hope that he would have more to say to his team. He had scheduled a briefing for 9:30 a.m. Twenty-nine minutes left and he still had nothing.

Shit . . . shit . . . shit.

Brady knew he was missing something obvious.

But what? What couldn't he see?

He ran his hand through his long dark hair.

He was tired. He'd hardly slept last night – tortured by the fact that they were no closer to catching the serial rapist. It was the rapist's latest victim – Chloe Winters – that had really got to Brady. Ordinarily, he would have said that she'd got under his skin. But given the sadistic injuries she had suffered at the hands of her attacker, the irony made him feel physically sick.

Three young women had been raped in the last two months. With each victim the rapist's violence had escalated. So much that Brady was certain that if they didn't stop him, his next victim wouldn't just be raped, she would be tortured to death.

His boss, DCI Gates, was breathing down his neck for results. It was understandable; Brady would be exactly the same if he was in Gates's position. Not that he ever would be; he was under no illusions. Promotions always bypassed Brady. He was still surprised he'd succeeded in making it to the level of Detective Inspector.

But Brady knew who he was indebted to for his rise to DI. And it definitely wasn't Gates. Despite Brady delivering against targets, albeit at times by the skin of his teeth, Gates had made it clear that he didn't consider him anything more than some maverick cop from the wrong side of the tracks who would inevitably end up like his ex-colleague and friend, Jimmy Matthews. A bent copper who'd found himself in a segregated wing of a maximum security prison, doing time and being protected from the criminal element he'd once policed.

It was Gates's boss, Detective Chief Superintendent O'Donnell, that Brady thanked for believing in him. O'Donnell had known Brady when he was a wayward teenager looking for trouble on the poverty-stricken and crime-infested streets of the Ridges estate in North Shields. Streets that O'Donnell policed when he joined the force as one of Northumbria's first black coppers. It was O'Donnell's perseverance with Brady that had steered the teenager away from a life of crime and into a job that was the antithesis of everything he had ever known. Brady owed everything to O'Donnell; without him, Brady would have ended up on the other side of the law. But he knew that he had earned his promotion the hard way. It wasn't down to nepotism. It was down to sheer bloody hard work and doggedness. And, perhaps, a few unconventional methods thrown in for good measure. But he got results. Results that got noticed and finally rewarded. However, Brady knew that he had climbed as high as he could in the police force. There was only one direction he could move now, and that was down.

Brady irritably pushed his hair back from his weary face. He was wasting time. He was sitting musing about his dead-end career instead of coming up with something that would appease Gates and keep the scavenging rats from the door. In other words, the press: in particular, Brady's personal snitch, the hardened hack Rubenfeld.

Someone had kindly left a copy of last night's *Northern Echo* on Brady's desk. It was now in the wastepaper bin where it belonged. Brady's headache had kicked off as soon as he saw the vitriolic attack on the front page. Worse still, Rubenfeld had written it.

Rubenfeld sold papers; and lots of them. He was known for his scathing investigative articles, which typically dominated the front pages. And at the moment, Rubenfeld had his poisoned pen poised against the Northumbrian force. Or, to be more exact, Whitley Bay police station.

Rubenfeld was stirring up a public frenzy with the fact that the police – or Brady to be precise – had still not caught the serial rapist.

The problem was, the nature of the third victim's attack made great headlines. It was gruesome, sadistic and worryingly original. The third rape had taken place less than a week ago, and Brady and his team had done everything in their power to withhold the nature of the victim's injuries, just as they had with the first two victims. The less the public knew about the case, the better. However, someone, maybe a member of hospital staff or someone who knew the latest victim, had passed on details about the attack to Rubenfeld, who had wasted no time turning them into headline news. Money was a very persuasive tool to get people to talk. Rubenfeld knew it and abused it. But whether or not Rubenfeld had any idea how much he had compromised the investigation by publishing information that the police had held back from the public was a moot point: Rubenfeld had no loyalties, especially where Brady was concerned.

Now that the *Northern Echo* had published the extent of the victims' injuries, there would be a public outcry against the police for not having apprehended such a dangerous criminal. But Brady, as Senior Investigating Officer, had done everything in his power to try to find him. All the relevant information they had on the rapist had been fed into HOLMES 2: the police computer intelligence database. Given the seriousness of the crimes, it was a crucial tool in the search for the rapist's identity. It processed masses of information from police forces across the UK and cross-referenced it, making sure that no vital clues were overlooked. Gone were the days when it would take weeks, if not months, for an investigating team to collate information in a bid to track down a suspect.

The Major Incident Room, where the investigation was being coordinated, had been set up in the largest room available. Brady had a team of officers assembled there processing all the information they had on the three rapes, including whatever they had received from the public. Anything that Brady thought relevant was added into HOLMES 2. But as yet they had nothing. Nothing that would bring them closer to finding their man. The rapist had developed a style of his own, a modus operandi that Brady had never come across before. Nor had any of the other forces in the UK. It appeared this rapist was home-grown. Troublingly for the investigation, Brady was certain he was gaining confidence with each new victim, perfecting his inimitable trademark.

Brady was worried; worried that he might not be able to solve this case. It wouldn't be the first offender to elude him, but that was no consolation. Gates wasn't the only one who wanted results – Brady would give anything to put an end to the sick, twisted bastard who had raped and assaulted these young women. He had made a promise to the most recent victim, Chloe Winters. He had given her his word that he would get the man who damaged her so horrifically she would never be the same, let alone look the same, again. Brady did not want to break that promise but he wasn't quite sure how he could fulfil it. That was his fear: that this man was one step ahead.

It was no real surprise to Brady that he was feeling low. This investigation had been going for two months and they were no further forward. It was what they called a 'runner' – never a good word in a Senior Investigating Officer's book. The worst part of it was that they were waiting for the rapist to strike again. Anticipating when and who he would attack next.

Brady had already accepted that it would be impossible to replicate the high of intercepting an international sex-trafficking ring in the North-East of England. Since the success of that case, his superiors had expected him to deliver as quickly on this investigation. Six months ago Brady had managed to expose a lucrative business deal set up between two Eastern European brothers and a local North-East gangster. The Eastern Europeans, known to special intelligence as the Dabkunas brothers, had eluded the police. No trace of them had been reported in the UK since their illicit activity had been uncovered. It was now widely accepted that they had gone to ground in Europe. As for Ronnie Macmillan, the local gangster who had gone into business with the Dabkunas brothers, he'd found himself in Durham prison. Even Gates had been impressed with Brady. His exposure of the group had resulted in the Northumbrian force basking in media glory.

But the accolades had been short-lived. Very much yesterday's news. Today was a radically different story.

Chapter Five

Suddenly, there was a loud knock at the office door.

Brady looked up. 'Better be good,' he called out.

He was not surprised when Conrad opened the door.

'Sorry, sir, but I think you'll want to know about this,' Conrad said as he walked in.

'Go on,' instructed Brady.

'A woman was admitted to Rake Lane hospital in the early hours of this morning, sir.'

'And?'

Conrad cleared his throat. 'She's in a really bad condition from all accounts. She was beaten up last night and left for dead. She's spent the past six hours in surgery. Internal bleeding, a punctured lung and emergency surgery to her face.'

'Where?' asked Brady, frowning. His head felt like it was going to explode.

'Sir?'

'Where was she attacked, Conrad?'

Brady put Conrad's uncharacteristic obtuseness down to the fact he'd only just returned to work after a significant period of sick leave.

'The lower part of North Shields leading down to the docks. She was found in an industrial bin at the back of the Ballarat pub. If it hadn't been for the landlord's two Rottweilers kicking up such a fuss when he let them out in the back alley before going to bed, she'd definitely be dead.'

Brady massaged his throbbing temples as he thought about it.

'Ballarat pub isn't a great area to be hanging around, is it? At least, not for a woman.'

Conrad knew exactly what his boss was insinuating.

'We don't know whether she was working or not, if you get my drift, sir.'

'Look, I'm not being funny, but doesn't North Shields have its own Area Command? This is clearly out of our jurisdiction. We've got a briefing in about twenty minutes and I have a hell of a headache from trying to figure out what I'm going to say to DCI Gates afterwards,' Brady said.

As far as he was concerned the conversation was over.

It felt as if he had been sitting behind a desk for months now. Staring at files ... whiteboards ... witness statements ... following false leads like the one Conrad had just brought to him. But, crucially, not out there running this bastard down. He stood and walked over to the large window. His leg had stiffened up and he found himself limping slightly from the old wound in his thigh. His office was on the first floor of the old Victorian building that was Whitley Bay police station. The room was large enough to have an old leather couch in front of the window for the odd occasion when Brady didn't make it home. He prised the dusty Venetian blinds open and looked down at the street below. It led out to the centre of the small town. It was late October, which meant that it was typically overcast and grey. The rain and biting wind had been almost continuous now for six months. Spring had been a week of blazing sunshine at the beginning of May, and then the temperature had plummeted. It had remained that way since. Climate change had a lot to answer for when it came to the bleak drizzle that constituted seasonal change in the North-East. Gone were the scorching hot summers of the seventies. Now all they got were flash floods and hailstones. Brady wasn't surprised that an estimated 5.5 million Brits permanently lived abroad. That was almost one in ten of the UK population. Not that he could blame them.

Brady scanned what he could of the street; it looked normal. Whatever 'normal' meant. However, at night it was a different story. The small, rundown seaside resort had a dark underbelly to it. And somewhere out there a sadistic rapist waited. He was upping his ante – the question was, why?

'What day is it, Conrad?' Brady asked, his back to Conrad.

'Sir?'

'Friday. The answer is Friday. Which means that we're going to have another weekend of watching and waiting to see if he strikes again. It's exactly seven days since he last attacked and given the fact that his cooling-off period is lessening, I would say he'll be starting to look for another victim.'

Brady turned around.

Conrad was silent. He rarely spoke unless it was necessary, but Brady knew there was something wrong. He could read it in Conrad's face. His narrowed eyes and tightly clenched jaw always gave him away.

'What aren't you telling me, Conrad?'

'The victim was raped, sir.'

The news didn't surprise Brady – sex workers were at high risk of sexual and physical assault purely by the nature of their job.

So far, the rapist had only ever attacked in Whitley Bay in the early hours of a Saturday or Sunday morning. And so far, he hadn't attacked prostitutes.

'And ...' Conrad faltered. He knew what would be going through his boss's mind; that it couldn't possibly be their suspect. But there was something about the injuries that this victim had sustained that leaped out when Conrad learned the details. He'd made quite a few friends during his police training days; one of them was stationed at North Shields. They still got together for drinks every other week – mainly to gripe about their bosses and the impossible tasks they were asked to perform. Conrad hadn't needed to update her on the serial rape case. After the third victim, it had made national news. But Conrad had told her the gruesome details that had been held back from the press. His friend contacted Conrad as soon as she could after being called out to the new crime scene. The victim had suffered an unusual wound that was startlingly similar to the one found on the third rape victim. When she told Conrad, he knew it was something he couldn't ignore.

'Go on,' Brady prompted.

'From the update I received, it appears as if this new victim was hurt in the same way Chloe Winters was.'

'You're absolutely certain?'

'Yes, sir.'

'So why didn't you say so when you first walked in?'

'I was trying to, but . . .' Conrad faltered.

Brady wasn't listening.

He grabbed his beat-up black leather jacket from the back of his chair and snatched his phone and car keys from the desk before turning to Conrad.

'Come on. What are you waiting for?

Brady was worried that his deputy had returned to duty too soon after his injury. So he made a point of doing whatever driving was required. Conrad had been off for six months after being shot in the left shoulder during their last major investigation. Despite the months of sick leave, Brady was certain he shouldn't be back at work. More so when he saw Conrad grimacing in pain when he thought no one was looking.

Brady hadn't known whether Conrad was going to make it after he had been shot; let alone ever be fit enough to return to work. No one at the station had been more pleased than him when Conrad had reported for duty that Monday at 7:00 a.m. Conrad was irreplaceable. Something Brady had had no qualms in telling Gates when he tried to assign a replacement. But the last thing Brady wanted was Conrad causing long-lasting damage to himself because he'd returned to duty early. Conrad had an unfailing sense of loyalty to him, and Brady knew that Conrad would have felt obliged to return to work as soon as he could to help catch the serial rapist – especially once he found out what the sick bastard was doing to his victims.

'You ring Harvey and tell him what's happened. We need a copy of everything North Shields CID have on this case,' Brady said as he opened the office door.

'Do we have the authority to do that, sir?' asked Conrad, following Brady out.

He was worried about protecting his friend. The last thing he wanted was her getting into trouble for disclosing information on one of their cases to another Area Command.

'We do if this woman turns out to have been attacked by the suspect we're looking for,' Brady answered. 'Tell the team we'll reschedule the briefing for later.'

His mind was racing. Images of Chloe Winters' injuries flashed through his head. He'd never seen injuries like that before . . . and he'd prayed he never would again.

Chapter Six

Nothing could have prepared Brady for this: nothing. He swallowed hard. He could feel the bile rising up from the back of his throat.

Conrad was standing by his side looking the way Brady felt. His face was ashen, drained of any blood.

A machine bleeped irritably in the corner by the patient's bed. A constant reminder that death was still lingering behind the scenes, waiting. A plastic tube snaked out of the victim's mouth, held in place by tape as the machine regulated her breathing. It was an understatement to say she was in a bad way.

Brady tried to hold his breath. He hated the smells in hospitals. Partly the benign antiseptic that clung to the air. But it was the smell of approaching death and festering wounds that made him want to gag.

Brady had already blagged his way past the uniform stationed at the door. He knew they didn't have a lot of time before the detective in charge of the case turned up asking questions. He knew he shouldn't be here. As did Conrad. At least, not without the appropriate authorisation. But Brady didn't have time for such polite civilities. He just wanted to discreetly satisfy himself that this victim hadn't been attacked by the rapist Brady's team were trying their damnedest to hunt down. After Conrad had mentioned the nature of her injuries, Brady felt they had no choice but to pay a visit. The problem was, he hadn't expected the victim to be in such a critical state.

'Do they have an identity yet?' Brady asked.

He was aware that Conrad had contacts in North Shields police station. Even though they all worked for the same force, each Area Command tended to look out for itself. They had targets to meet, which in effect meant they were in competition with one another. Not that anyone would ever admit it. But Brady knew that the Senior Investigating Officer in charge of this case wouldn't be happy that he and Conrad were here poking around.

'Not that I know of.'

Brady nodded.

He couldn't take his eyes off the victim. Whoever had done this to her had wanted her dead. That much was clear. But why?

'Do me a favour, Conrad, will you? Go and have a chat with the uniform on the door. I want to get a look at this wound to see whether it's like Chloe Winters' injuries. The last thing I need is someone walking in.'

'Sir?' Conrad asked, unsure whether they shouldn't be getting a doctor or nurse to show them the wound.

Brady didn't have to look at Conrad to know that his eyes would be narrowed and his jaw clenched as he struggled with the concept of breaking the rules. Conrad liked to play everything exactly by the book. Brady, on the other hand, was prepared to take risks if he felt the outcome justified it.

'You heard what the doctor said. They don't know whether or not she'll regain consciousness, considering the trauma to her head. So, under these circumstances, I'm sure she won't mind. I suggest we do exactly what we came here to do. To see if this is the same sick bastard we're after. But looking at the state of her, I'm not so sure it is.'

'I don't understand, sir.'

'This is overkill. Whoever did this to her was angry. Very angry. It smacks of something personal,' Brady explained.

He forced himself to look at the swollen, distorted mess that had once been her face. The broken, weeping skin was discoloured, black and purple. It was hard to tell what she should look like. Her nose had been smashed beyond recognition. It was in a cast. As for her eyes, they were buried beneath engorged, weeping flesh that had been sewn together with ugly black stitches.

Her straw-like, bleached blonde hair was matted with clumps of rust-coloured blood and dirt.

Brady felt a pang of sadness as he looked at her.

She was once someone's daughter . . . maybe still is . . .

He shook his head. Thoughts of the young women the Dabkunas brothers had held captive and tortured – some to death – suddenly consumed him.

'Sir?' Conrad's face was etched with concern as he looked at his boss.

'It's nothing . . . just . . .' Brady's voice faltered. He swallowed. His throat was so dry it felt as if razors were lodged at the back.

Why the hell was it still affecting him like this?

But Brady knew the answer. It was simple. They were still out there – the Dabkunas brothers. And that meant they would be trafficking other young women. He couldn't help making the comparison with this poor woman, fighting for her life because some punter or pimp had decided to get heavy with her. Used and abused by all around her, she hadn't stood a chance. And Brady was well aware of the irony of two coppers standing in this small, private room without authorisation. It was out-and-out mercenary, and the fact that he acknowledged it did not make him feel better about it.

Brady had already made a judgement call. That was his job. He knew she was a sex worker. The clothes she had been found wearing, now in a Forensics laboratory, said as much. As did the area her body had been dumped in. It was a no-man's land at night. A stone's throw away from the Ridges, it was an area of dodgy, unlit street corners and flats above rundown shops. Anyone hanging around that area was looking for trouble. And if not, it sure as hell would find them.

But Brady had already noticed the tell-tale tracks from heroin or crack cocaine use up and down her badly bruised, stick-thin arms.

'Take a closer look at her, Conrad. She's a prostitute with a heavy drug addiction. You see her arms? And I don't mean the fact that she's severely underweight – I'm talking about the injection marks.'

It was hard not to be taken aback by the results of life on the streets. It was cruel, and Brady knew it. The evidence was there in front of him. The team had found it extremely difficult to come up with a 'type' that the rapist targeted. But Brady was absolutely certain that this woman in front of him would never have ticked whatever twisted boxes the rapist used. The first thing to strike him was that she was too old; the rapist liked his victims young. They were all in their early twenties and looked like 'normal' women, not some fashion designer's idea of heroin chic. And right then, staring at a skeletal heroin addict, Brady had no understanding how something so sickening could be sold as desirable.

He breathed out slowly. He was absolutely certain that she hadn't been attacked by the man they were after. But there was one question going through Brady's mind: why would she have a similar wound to Chloe Winters? Brady knew the rapist was escalating with every new victim. Chloe Winters was testimony to that worrying fact. But Brady could not convince himself that the serial rapist they were looking for was responsible for the carnage suffered by this victim.

He stared at her, willing her to wake up and tell them who'd done this to her. But he knew it wasn't going to happen any time soon, if at all.

'Give me a few moments, will you?' Brady asked. He wanted to get it over with as quickly as possible.

Conrad nodded, relieved to be dismissed.

Brady waited until Conrad had left the claustrophobic room before walking over to the victim. He felt like a predator. Yet another man on the take.

He steeled himself as he stood by the head of her bed. Her face was a bloody mess. Distorted beyond human recognition. Whoever had wanted to hurt her had done an excellent job.

Brady's eyes drifted down her arm, ignoring the ugly tracks and bruising, towards the gauze dressing that covered the open wound. He knew that she was scheduled for more surgery. She needed a skin graft, but the doctors were waiting to see whether she was going to survive the attack. If not, surgery would be unnecessary.

Deciding he had no choice but to look, Brady gently pulled back the single sheet covering her lower left arm. He waited, half expecting her to wake up and ask him what the fuck he was doing – but she didn't stir. He could see the thick wad of dressing covering the inside of her wrist. Preparing himself, he pulled the dressing back.

He tried not to react to the grisly sight. The entire skin on the inside of her wrist, running four inches up her inner arm, had been removed. Raw flesh, sinewy veins and muscle were left exposed. Brady took out his BlackBerry and photographed the wound. He was well aware that this was against protocol but he had no choice. He needed to make sure this wasn't the handiwork of their serial rapist, who delighted in removing skin from his victims as keepsakes – or trophies.

The first rape victim had been lucky – if that was possible. She had been raped and stabbed repeatedly in both breasts. Nothing else. But it was enough. The rapist had grown more confident by the second victim and had removed the right nipple and the skin surrounding it before stabbing both breasts. Neither of the first two victims had tattoos, unlike the third victim. But it was the effects of his cruel, sadistic knife that had left the third victim's skin looking like a patchwork quilt after the surgeon had cut and grafted skin over the extensive, open wound. Chloe Winters had had an elaborate tattoo, an intricate sketch of a wolf's head. It had covered her right breast and chest leading up to her neck. This time he had taken time to peel off the entire skin from her breast and across her chest. After the removal of the tattoo he had then repeatedly stabbed what was left of her right breast and had then turned his attention to her left one.

Brady had seen enough before-and-after photographs of Chloe Winters' breast for it to be permanently scarred on his mind. He had also paid a visit to Fusion, the tattoo studio she'd used. Brady knew as soon as he saw a picture of the tattoo who the artist was: it took someone highly skilled to design and then tattoo a piece of work as beautiful as the wolf's head. The tattoo artist was the owner of Fusion – Dan Ridgewell. He was an imposing figure of a bloke, someone clients knew not to mess with – built like a brick shithouse, he kept himself fit by body-building and boxing. However, it was not just his muscle-bound body that would intimidate your average blue-rinse Sainsbury's shopper, it was the fact that every inch, and that meant *every* inch, of his hard, muscled body was covered in tattoos. Some good, some not so good. But every one was a testament to life; his life, which by all accounts had been a damned difficult one.

Despite the flattened nose and inked skin, Dan Ridgewell was a good-looking bloke. Admittedly in a thuggish kind of way. But he had a charm about him that young women couldn't resist. Whether it was his intense dark brown eyes, or his thick black hair, naturally tanned skin and roguishly handsome features, or his easy-going manner, something worked in his favour. And from the ex-wives and girlfriends dotted around the country, maybe a little too well.

Brady had soon found out that there was more to Dan Ridgewell than his threatening, tattooed body. That he actually had an A-Level in literature and a penchant for philosophy; an enthusiasm that he tended not to share with the majority of his clients, who were barely literate. Second and third generations on benefits with no hope of a job – at least not one that was legitimate. They were blighted by the location of their birth: North Shields. Home to high unemployment, teenage pregnancies, drugs and inevitably crime. Brady knew it well. After all, it was where he was born. But he'd been lucky. He'd managed to crawl out of the rat-infested alleys and had put as much distance

29

as he could between himself and the crime-ridden streets he once called home.

Brady had asked Dan Ridgewell if he knew anyone who had a tattoo fetish to the extent of actually removing them. Dan had laughed, until he realised Brady was deadly serious. He reminded Brady that he was in the job of putting ink into someone's skin, not removing it. But he did concede that 'we get all kinds of dicks in here. It's hard to know which ones really are nutters, like, compared to the ones who make out they are, if you get my drift.'

Brady had encountered some of Fusion's clientele and at times found the hardcore misogynistic comments so easily thrown between the blokes shameful. But as Dan had pointed out when Brady raised this, it didn't make them rapists.

Brady carefully replaced the gauze dressing over the ugly wound. He had seen enough. The serial rapist they were after had a breast fetish. However, this victim's breasts had not been mutilated. Nor was the removal of the skin on her wrist as clean and professional as the damage suffered by the second and third rape victims. On Chloe Winters' body, the assailant had shown the depths of his skill. What had surprised Brady and the team – one of the few details that hadn't been disclosed in yesterday evening's *Northern Echo* – was that her tattoo had been carefully cut out, leaving behind an odd, startling effect. It would have taken time for the rapist to do it. But from what Chloe Winters had told the police, she had spent forty-eight hours held hostage, chained to a concrete floor. She had no memory of being released. It was a taxi driver who had found the unconscious, naked girl lying in a back lane and called the ambulance and police. When Chloe came to, she had no idea how she'd ended up there, or, more crucially, where she had been raped and tortured.

Chapter Seven

A knock at the door startled Brady. It was swiftly followed by Conrad sticking his head from behind the door.

'Sir? We've got to make a move.'

Brady nodded.

'Yeah . . . I'm coming, Conrad.'

Just then something caught his eye. Something he had missed before. Brady bent down and gently swept her matted hair back out of the way. He could see it now. The two small, faded tear droplets that had been inked onto her neck below the left ear using good old-fashioned biro. Crude and lacking finesse, they had stood the test of time. She had ironically predicted her future – one filled with lousy decisions and painful repercussions.

Brady felt winded as he stared at her. He took time now to look at the horrific injuries she had sustained. Her face had been obliterated. Whether she would get some skilled plastic surgeon to put it back together again, Brady seriously doubted. After all, she was just some throwaway prostitute. Someone who had ended up with the wrong punter in the wrong alley, at the wrong time of night.

It all made sense now. The straw-like bleached blonde hair. The fake-tanned skin, the scrawny body covered in tracks – deep, permanent scarring from heavy needle usage.

'Sir!' Conrad hissed, his face strained with urgency.

Brady didn't respond. He couldn't look at Conrad until he got himself together. He needed to get a handle on the situation before he told Conrad and the SIO in charge of the investigation that he knew her. That he could formally identify her.

31

'Sir? We've got to go!' Conrad insisted, desperation creeping into his voice.

Brady gave her one last look, his dark, normally gentle eyes betraying him. They were filled with anger and a need for revenge.

Then it hit him. The wrist; the skin that had been cut out. He knew what had been there. It was a tattoo. But not any tattoo – this one meant something to him as much as it meant something to her. She had inked into her wrist four letters in large, black, gothic script – NICK.

Nick was Brady's younger brother, and the woman lying fighting for her pathetic life had loved him once, and, Brady presumed, still did. Few people knew Nick in the North-East. After all, as a teenager he had relocated to London and assumed a new identity: rumoured to have killed a member of another rival street gang, he had disappeared, fast. Brady knew he hadn't done it; that he had been framed. But it had given Nick no other alternative. He left two people behind that day: Brady and his girlfriend. She would go on to live a life pitted with misery, pain and disappointment. Never quite recovering from Nick's decision to abandon her so easily, leaving her to rot in the very decay and futile existence that he had run from as hard as he could.

Shit . . . shit . . . shit.

Brady's head was reeling. The facts sinking in.

It was her. But why? Why the fuck would someone do this to her?

Then Brady got it. He felt winded from the realisation.

Nick . . . This is connected to Nick.

Brady had seen assaults like this before. Henchmen hired to beat up someone close to the person they actually wanted, but for whatever reason could not track down. To prove that they were serious, the hired killer would take something identifiable from the victim. Such as a finger with a recognisable ring. Or an ear with an earring. But this assailant had taken the skin with Nick's name on. What better way to show that you mean business than someone else's skin.

One person came to mind and that was Johnny Slaughter. This was his style. An East End London gangster who had a score to settle with Nick.

There was one other person who would know what was going on and that was exactly where Brady was heading.

'What's wrong?' Conrad asked as Brady walked past him.

Brady ignored him and carried on down the corridor. Conrad ran after him, shaken by the sudden change in his boss.

'Did you recognise her?' Conrad asked.

'Look at the state she's in, Conrad. Not even her own mother would be able to identify her. And before you ask, whoever tried to kill her is not our rapist.'

'Why remove a piece of her skin then?'

'Fuck knows! Maybe some crazy bastard read that article plastered all over the *Northern Echo*'s front page last night and decided to emulate the rapist. But it's not him. It might have gone unnoticed by you, Conrad, but our serial rapist has a penchant for his victims' breasts. That isn't the case here. Also, the removal of the skin is too careless. Then there's the fact she was attacked in a back alley behind the Ballarat.'

'Just like the first two rape victims,' argued Conrad.

Brady shook his head. Ordinarily he would have shot Conrad down for making such a glaring mistake. But he knew he wasn't up to speed on the first two rape cases. This was his fifth day back on the job and to be fair he had walked straight into a major serial rape case. One where the latest victim had been abducted, raped and mutilated over a period of two days. She had been found on the same morning that Conrad had decided to come back off sick leave. If Conrad had returned hoping to gradually ease back into the job, he had been bitterly mistaken. The station had been thrown into pandemonium with the discovery of Chloe Winters and it had been Conrad's misfortune to walk straight into it.

'Not like this, Conrad. Think about it. Both places that the rape victims were attacked were deserted. He knew that there was very little chance that someone would interrupt him. The first victim, nineteen-year-old Sarah Jeffries was attacked eight weeks ago in the early hours of Saturday morning. He stalked her Conrad. Followed her as she made her way home alone. When she reached Whiskey Bends he came up from behind and dragged her into the back alley behind the boarded-up building. No one was around. The rapist guaranteed that by the timing and location.' Brady paused for a moment.

'Sir?'

'Nothing,' Brady replied, shaking his head. 'The second victim, Anna Lewis, was also followed on her way home from a night out in Whitley. He waited five weeks before his second attack. She, like the first victim had taken a familiar short cut home. She had cut through another derelict eyesore – the High Point Hotel on the seafront. This time he had been waiting in the shadows of the empty car park for her. Again, no one was around, Conrad. No late night stragglers, no inquisitive residents. He forced her into the grounds at the back of the boarded-up hotel where he bound and gagged her. This time he took longer with her. Maybe he felt more confident? After all, he had already done it once before and had succeeded in not getting caught. Anna Lewis was subjected to his sexual assault for over an hour. He finished off by carefully removing her right nipple and the surrounding skin. Not the work of a man in a hurry is it, Conrad?'

'I don't follow, sir?'

'Location, Conrad.' Brady sighed as he looked at him. 'Think about where the third victim, Chloe Winters, was found.'

'You mean the alleyway next to that boarded-up building on the sea front?'

'Yeah, the Avenue pub. Really popular in the eighties. But like Whiskey Bends, it's been derelict for decades now. Just like the High Point Hotel. All three crime scenes are isolated areas. Deserted. No one goes there. In other words, the ideal location to rape and mutilate someone without getting caught

34

– especially the first two locations. As for the third crime scene behind the Avenue pub, perfect place to dump a body and then disappear.'

The team had already assessed all CCTV footage but were no further forward. Brady assumed from the first two witness statements that the rapist had followed them on foot. Neither of them had reported hearing a car approaching them or driving off after they had been attacked. As for Chloe Winters, Brady was certain he had used a vehicle. How else would he have taken her to wherever he had held her captive for forty-eight hours? And, how could he have dumped her unconscious, naked body on the Monday morning?

Brady turned to Conrad.

'But the attack last night? No, the Ballarat pub was still open with a few regulars inside, which meant that whoever did this to her didn't have a lot of time. It's rushed. Heavy-handed. Exactly like the removal of the skin. Our rapist savours what he does, Conrad. The sick bastard enjoys every inch of their skin in a way unimaginable to me. One thing he does not do is rush. That's why he chooses derelict and abandoned locations. It gives him time to do what he wants without the fear of being caught. The attack on this woman couldn't be more different. The alleyway in which she was raped and left for dead was behind the Ballarat pub – a working pub. Christ! The landlord even lives above the premises with two Rottweilers. If I didn't think it was such a crazy idea I'd suggest he wanted to get caught. No, Conrad. It's not the same man.'

Conrad didn't bother arguing with Brady. He'd worked with his boss long enough now to know that when he had a hunch about something he was usually proven right.

Brady reached the ICU's double doors. He pressed the buzzer to open them. He needed to get out. He felt sick. He hadn't felt like this since he had feared that Nick was working for the unscrupulous Dabkunas brothers. At the time he had struggled with the belief that his own brother was prepared to jeopardise their relationship, not to mention Brady's career. That had been six months ago. But the same feeling of dread and foreboding had come back – tenfold. It felt as if a bomb was going to detonate. The question was when?

'Come on, Conrad, I need a cigarette.'

Conrad dutifully followed Brady through the maze-like, sterile white corridors to the revolving glass doors that led out of Rake Lane.

'I still want copies of all the reports connected to this attack on my desk ASAP. I don't care whose bollocks you trample over to get them. For all we know there might be something in there that could be of some help.'

Brady paused as he lit a cigarette. He realised his hands were trembling.

'Shit!' he swore after inhaling. It felt good. Too good.

He was trying to give up smoking. Had been for the past five days. It was all part of the reformed Brady. If he was honest he had made a pact with God. Not that he really believed in God, but his Catholic upbringing came in handy on rare occasions. While Conrad had been in surgery, Brady had made a pact that if he managed to pull through and returned to work, he would quit.

Brady had even given up rolling his own cigarettes. He had duped himself into believing it was healthier, when in fact he ended up smoking more. Unlike a pack of cigarettes, you could easily smoke twenty roll-ups in a day without even realising it. And if it had been a particularly stressful day, that number doubled. At least with a pack, Brady knew exactly how much he was smoking. Until now, he hadn't opened the pack that he had bought on Monday. Admittedly, both his arms were covered in nicotine patches. And his mood had been so dark that most of his team had done their utmost to avoid him.

Conrad was about to tell him that he wasn't allowed to smoke on hospital grounds, let alone at the entrance, but Brady was already walking away.

Conrad watched his boss. Six foot two, lean with muscle; long dark hair with swarthy skin and a permanent five o'clock shadow, Brady couldn't have been more different from Conrad if he'd tried. Clean-shaven, short blond hair, an impeccable wardrobe – this summed Conrad up. Dark tailored suits and expensive, handmade English brogues, accompanied with a crisp white shirt, cufflinks and a carefully selected silk tie. Conrad's appearance counted for something. He was very much the new face of CID. Whereas Brady was still the old school of policing in a beat-up jacket that had seen better days, skinny black jeans, black T-shirt and black leather boots. Conrad admired that about his boss. The fact that he refused to be compromised; whether in the way he looked or how he carried out an investigation, he had conviction.

Conrad knew Brady held the rank of DI because he was damned good at his job. Admittedly, he was unorthodox at times, but he still managed to get there in the end, regardless of the way he looked. And luckily for Brady, he managed to pull off the unkempt, dishevelled, 'couldn't give a fuck' look even as a Detective Inspector.

Conrad inwardly steeled himself. Something told him that he better get back into shape and fast. He was going to need his wits about him; especially now Brady was on to something. What it was, he had no idea. But if he knew his boss, it meant trouble – big time.

Chapter Eight

Brady pulled up as close as he could get to the crime scene.

'Sir?' Conrad asked, unsure why they were here. One answer came to mind, and it was one he didn't like. This was only his fifth day back and things were starting to take a familiar turn for the worse.

'Two seconds. OK?'

Brady slammed the car door, not giving Conrad a chance to argue.

He headed towards the police tape that sealed off access to the Ballarat pub and the back alley behind it. A large white Mobile Incident van and numerous other vehicles belonging to the forensic officers examining the crime scene blocked off most of the street.

Brady could see that Ainsworth's team had placed three-inch plastic A-frame evidence markers along the path leading into the alley behind the Ballarat pub. The SOCOs had also placed stepping stones of forensic platforms for the team to walk on. It was Ainsworth's way of preventing contamination of any evidence that might have been left at the crime scene.

Brady took in the location. It was the ideal place to hurt someone. The alley would have been dark, aided by the over-grown bushes and hedges that separated the entrance of the back lane from the houses that ran down the embankment towards North Shields quayside.

Brady knew that DI Bentley would have instructed officers to bang on all the doors to see if the residents had heard anything. He knew it was a waste of time. Even if someone knew something they wouldn't talk for fear of repercussions. This was the lower end of North Shields, populated by hardened scum who would have stabbed a dirty needle in your eye before you even realised it.

Brady nodded as he approached the two uniformed officers blocking the entrance into the cordoned-off street.

'DI Brady,' he stated.

'Sir,' answered one of the officers.

The officers may have been stationed at North Shields but they both recognised Brady as the SIO in charge of the serial rape case. Brady had a certain unconventional look for a copper, let alone one of his rank, that preceded him.

He watched as one of the officers recorded his name in the crime scene log. The log list would stay active until the last person left, which would typically be Ainsworth, the Crime Scene Manager.

Brady knew he had to tread carefully. Word would get out fast that he was sniffing around. The last thing he wanted was trouble – especially not with DI Bentley. He was a hard-faced bugger at the best of times and if he thought Brady was trying to poach one of his cases then it would be all-out war. He guessed that Bentley would be assuming that this assault was linked to the ever-growing drugs problem poisoning the dregs of North Shields. Simple maths: a drug-addicted prostitute found beaten to within an inch of her life. Bentley would no doubt assume that she was assaulted because she owed money to her supplier. But Brady knew different. This had nothing to do with drugs; he was sure of it. Nick was at the forefront of his mind. He was certain that someone had beaten her up to get to him. The question that was torturing Brady, was why? Nick's connection with her was firmly rooted in the past.

Or was it?

Brady watched as the white-clad figure of Ainsworth, the Crime Scene Manager, walked over. He had worked with Ainsworth on numerous cases. He was a short, portly, cantankerous man with a receding head of curly grey hair and a large, jowly face that had been ravaged by too many years on the job. He also had an infamous, fiery temper, which he defended as a legacy of his Gaelic roots. Despite his biting tongue, Brady would be the first to admit he was fond of Ainsworth. Some of the Crime Scene Managers he had worked with made it quite clear that they didn't like coppers near their crime scene – regardless of whether they were Senior Investigating Officers.

Brady had heard talk that Ainsworth was due to retire soon and hoped this wasn't the case. He had a dark, sick sense of humour; though it was hard to tell he had one at all during his daily rants at whoever had got in his way. Despite his reputation for being irascible, he was damned good at his job. Nothing excited Ainsworth more than a call in the early hours telling him his team were needed to attend a suspicious death. But he wasn't that different from the rest of them. Whenever a call came in, anyone in the job would be lying if they didn't admit to feeling the same surge of excitement and anticipation at what lay ahead. The only exception was when a suspicious death involved a child. In those situations every copper felt a sense of dread. Regardless of how often you dealt with a serious crime like that, you never got used to it.

'You'll be needing a suit before you trample all over my crime scene, Jack,' Ainsworth greeted him in his usual brusque manner. 'Help yourself. There's plenty in the van over there.'

'Thanks, but that won't be necessary. I just wanted a word.' This was Bentley's crime scene and the last thing Brady wanted to be accused of was pissing over another man's investigation.

'All right, then. I assume, knowing you the way I do, Jack, that Bentley has no idea that you're here?'

Brady ran his hand through his dark hair uncomfortably as he looked across at two young female SOCOs walking out from the cordoned-off alleyway. Both pulled down their white face masks to talk freely. One of them was carrying a plastic evidence bag. She held it away from her body as she laughed at something her colleague had said. Her bright green eyes sparkled with mischief as she said something in response. Brady recognised her immediately as Fielding, a new recruit on Ainsworth's team. She was the new breed of SOCO, a recent graduate from Teesside University. Basically, they were cheap to employ. Cheaper than a copper who had been in the force for years and had specialised in photography, like Ainsworth. It wouldn't be long before he retired, and he was doing what he could to train up the graduates so he could leave the force knowing they'd be capable of continuing in his absence.

Brady wondered what they were laughing about. And what was in the evidence bag. That was the real reason he was here. He wanted to know what Ainsworth and his team had found – if anything.

Fielding turned, as if conscious of Brady watching her. Surprised that he was there, her face suddenly flushed.

Brady had run into Fielding on an investigation a year earlier. She had made it quite clear that she wanted more than a professional relationship – even insisting Brady took her number so he could call her. It never happened. The investigation Brady had been in charge of got in the way. That and his unresolved feelings for his ex-wife, Claudia.

Fielding held Brady's eye for a moment then turned back to her colleague, acting as if she didn't know him.

Brady breathed out slowly.

'No good looking at them, Jack. My SOCOs are off-limits where you're concerned. Last thing I want is my staff transferring because of you,' Ainsworth joked light-heartedly. He instantly realised what he had said; but it was too late.

If it had been another bloke, Brady would have laid him out flat. But this was Ainsworth and Brady knew he'd simply let his mouth run before putting his brain into gear. Ainsworth might have had one hell of a temper when someone was screwing up the job, but the last thing he could be accused of was being callous – at least not where Brady was concerned.

Anyone with a pulse in the Northumbrian force knew about Brady's brief affair with DC Simone Henderson. She had been a junior copper stationed at Whitley Bay. Their regrettable one-night stand had resulted in her transferring to the London Met to get as far away from her commanding officer and the ensuing gossip as possible. But unfortunately, that wasn't the end of it. She had ended up a casualty in an undercover investigation gone wrong. It had cost her more than Brady could bear to think about. She was still recuperating from her horrific injuries six months on. Brady was uncertain whether she would ever fully recover or accept the cruel hand that life had dealt her. She still refused to see him, in spite of his numerous attempts. He knew that she had remained in the North-East, despite hearing that the Met had offered her a post. However, the fact that she could no longer talk meant that she would never be a copper again. And from what Brady knew of Simone, behind-the-scenes admin work wasn't for her. She had loved her job with a passion. But the case she had been working on had become more of an addiction – one she had paid a high price for.

Brady knew from the look of regret in Ainsworth's small black eyes that he was really sorry about his reference to Simone Henderson.

'Look . . . Jack . . . I didn't mean anything when I—'

Brady stopped him. 'Forget it. I have.'

Neither spoke for a moment.

Ainsworth was the first to talk. His way of making amends. 'You know, I've clocked up more years on the force than I care to remember. And now I'm being replaced by young kids who don't know shit about policing. Civilians who walk in as Crime Scene Officers with nothing more than a degree in forensic science. You know I was a copper first for twenty years? Specialised in photography, which is how I ended up being a Crime Scene Manager. But once a copper, always a copper. Big bloody difference between having experience behind you and coming in as a civilian with some fancy qualification.'

Brady simply nodded.

'You know the two I'm training up just now?'

'They seem to know what they're doing,' Brady said as he watched Fielding and her colleague.

Ainsworth shot him a sceptical look.

'That's because I'm breathing down their necks all the time. They even expect me to wipe their bloody noses for them! It's all about budgets. They're a damned sight cheaper to employ than the likes of me, but it comes at a price. At least when you've come through as a copper you've got a nose for when something isn't quite right. Civilians wouldn't know a hunch if it kicked them in the guts. Christ knows what crucial evidence they're going to miss when I'm not around to tell them what to do.'

Brady couldn't disagree. TV programmes like *CSI* had glorified forensic science, leading to huge interest in the profession. However, the reality of the job was far removed from the sexy image portrayed on TV.

'You know this job involves a lot more than just photographing and bagging up evidence. A hell of a lot more!' Ainsworth complained, the sadness in his eyes stronger than the anger in his voice.

Brady didn't answer. He knew Ainsworth was right. Times were changing, and not for the better. The overall police budget had been drastically slashed by the government, which meant that the cheapest option had to come first. Instead of training up coppers to be forensic officers, as they had done in the past, it was cheaper to employ civilians. Even the police laboratory used for forensic analysis no longer existed. Instead, the work was outsourced to the cheapest company, and cheap didn't necessarily mean good.

Worryingly, that was just the start of it. The public were completely unaware that highly qualified CID officers were now reduced to working in uniform because of the budget cuts. The choice was hard: take a demotion or lose your job. But some officers had lost their jobs anyway when the depleted funds demanded it. Brady had personally known quite a few officers who, when re-interviewed for their current posts, didn't quite make the grade and were now unemployed.

'You know something?' Ainsworth said.

'Maybe you're getting out at the right time?' Brady suggested.

Ainsworth laughed.

'Yeah . . . maybe I am,' he answered, shaking his head at the prospect of his looming retirement.

Brady watched Ainsworth contemplate what the future held for him. He had been there himself after he'd been shot. Not sure whether he'd be able to return to work. He'd realised that without the job, he had nothing. The sad fact was that his life was the job. It meant everything to him.

'Anyway, at least I've still got a job, unlike some, eh?'

'Yeah.' Brady inwardly prepared himself. He needed to ask a favour. That was the reason he was there.

'Look, Ainsworth . . .'

'Exactly what is it you want?' Ainsworth asked.

'I need to know what you've found,' Brady answered.

Ainsworth shook his head.

'You know what you're asking?'

Brady looked away uncomfortably. Disapproval lined Ainsworth's face.

'Shit, Jack! You know this is Bentley's investigation. If you have a query, you should be going to him. Not turning up here asking me about the evidence.'

'I know . . . but . . . I wouldn't ask you if it wasn't important. You know me better than that.'

'All right, all right! Just keep my name out of it. Understand?'

Brady nodded. 'Thanks.'

'Yeah . . . yeah. You owe me, Jack.'

Ainsworth sighed as he rubbed a hand over his face.

'We've collected the evidence you'd expect at a crime scene of this nature. Blood, hair and skin samples. We haven't found the victim's bag or any other personal belongings – that is assuming she had some with her. But we did find a business card. It's smeared in blood and there's a thumb mark on it, but it's not a print. Looks like whoever made it was wearing gloves.'

Brady nodded, feigning disinterest. But inside he could feel the adrenalin coursing through him. He needed to see that business card. Now.

'Can I see it?' Brady asked.

Ainsworth paused for a moment as he thought about it.

'All right, but that's it, Jack.'

Brady nodded. He watched in anticipation as Ainsworth went over to the Mobile Incident van. He returned a minute later carrying a sealed evidence bag.

'Thanks,' Brady said as Ainsworth handed it over to him.

Brady knew Ainsworth's beady eyes were on him, scrutinising his reaction to the bag's contents. He tried to keep the muscles in his face relaxed and casual. But it was difficult. More so when he recognised the business card. It was for a nightclub in Whitley Bay. He knew it and the owner very well. Too well.

He turned the card over. Just as he thought. On the back was a name scrawled in black ink – Trina McGuire. The name of the victim lying fighting for her life in Rake Lane hospital.

His mind was reeling. He had been praying this wouldn't be the case. He looked at the words, wondering if someone was trying to set the owner of the nightclub up. It wouldn't have been the first time someone had attempted to frame Martin Madley, and Brady was sure it wouldn't be the last.

Ainsworth cleared his throat.

'Is this what you were looking for?'

'Not really . . .' Brady answered. 'But thanks anyway. I owe you.' He handed the bag back, conscious that his hand was trembling. Not that Ainsworth had noticed – luckily. His eyes were fixed dangerously on one of his SOCOs.

'What have I told you? The platforms are there for a bloody reason!' he barked.

Brady watched as the poor sod nearly jumped out of his white forensic suit.

'Bloody idiots! I'll be wiping their arses next!'

'You're a cantankerous old bastard, you know that?' he said with a slight smile.

'Yeah . . . yeah . . . You've got what you wanted, now clear off and let some of us do some real work, eh?'

Brady didn't need any persuading. He turned and headed back under the tape towards the car.

He had one thing on his mind. Or should that be one person? Martin Madley. He took his mobile out and scrolled through the numbers. He pressed dial. Then he waited. Finally Madley answered: 'Yeah? This better be good.'

'I need to see you.'

'I'm busy.'

'Tough shit. I'm serious. I need to see you ASAP,' Brady demanded.

The phone went dead.

'Fucking bastard!' Brady muttered.

Madley had left him no choice. He would have to pay him a visit. But something was wrong; felt wrong. That wasn't like Madley. He'd never hung up on Brady before – they had too much history between them for him to blank Brady.

Unless . . . he really was involved. But why Nick?

That was the problem. Brady knew exactly why he would be after Nick.

He quickly discounted the thought as he went over to the car and jumped in.

'Did you find what you wanted, sir?' asked Conrad.

Brady didn't answer. He was too busy lighting a cigarette.

'Not exactly,' he finally replied after inhaling deeply.

He switched on the engine and pulled off, his mind racing.

Who would be after Nick? And why was Madley's business card left at the crime scene? Coincidence?

Brady's problem was that he didn't believe in coincidences. He had no choice but to ask some questions – whether Madley liked it or not. And he needed to get to Madley before DI Bentley and his team started making their own enquiries.

Chapter Nine

Brady had dropped Conrad back off at the station with a list of orders that would keep him too preoccupied to worry about Brady's whereabouts. He was now parked up on Brook Street trying to ring Nick. He had already called the landline only to find it had been disconnected. Brady's second attempt at calling him on his mobile had also failed. But at least it had cut to voicemail.

'Nick . . . Look, something's happened to Trina McGuire and I'm not sure what it's connected to or who, but you need to call me . . .' Brady paused. He then hung up, deciding it would be better to tell Nick in person what had happened to Trina than leaving the gruesome details in a message.

Brady lit another cigarette and wound down the window. The car was parked facing the promenade and the North Sea. It was a miserable, bleak late October morning, which reflected Brady's mood perfectly. He was angry and disappointed with himself for smoking. He had gone through hell for the past four days, or ninety-three hours and thirty-four minutes – not that he was counting. And for what? To give it all up as soon as something came along and threw him off course? But this wasn't just any something. Very soon DI Bentley would join the dots and realise that the woman lying critically ill in Rake Lane hospital was Trina McGuire: former lap dancer, full-time prostitute, mother of teenage offender Shane, and ex-wife of well-known low-life thug, Tony McGuire.

Not that Bentley could connect anything to Brady. He was a copper and Trina McGuire was a prostitute. There were no links between them. No one on the force, apart from Chief Superintendent O'Donnell, was fully aware of Brady's troubled background, or the fact he had a brother. Or that his brother had once had a relationship with the victim. Brady's ex-wife, Claudia, was the only other person who knew that he had a brother. And Claudia had never seen a photograph of him, let alone met him. She only knew Brady had a brother from accessing court documents about his mother's murder at the hands of his father. She had mentioned it in passing, hoping Brady would talk about him. It had had the opposite effect.

Brady drew heavily on his smouldering cigarette as he watched two scavenging seagulls fighting over last night's leftovers; a pool of lumpy vomit and half a portion of curried chips dumped on the pavement by some considerate lout staggering home with a belly full of beer and greasy food. Brady wished his life was as simple as fighting over last night's slops.

Disgusted, he threw his cigarette out and wound the window up. He had no option but to pay Madley a visit and ask him what the fuck was going on. Whether he would be accommodating was another matter entirely. Since the sex-trafficking investigation six months ago, Madley had been remote with him. Brady didn't know whether it was because he had put away the notorious North-East gangster and businessman Ronnie Macmillan, or if it was because his brother, Nick, had dangerously overstepped the mark with Madley. But something had caused the rift between them.

If Brady was brutally honest, he knew the reason – Nick. That was why he was here. Nick had successfully infiltrated a dangerous, international, elitist group known as the 'Nietzschean Brotherhood'. But in the process he had double-crossed Madley.

They were a covert organisation virtually impossible to penetrate. Even SOCA (the Serious Organised Crime Agency) were still struggling to ascertain information on them, let alone break into their ranks. This powerful organisation communicated through encrypted chat rooms and websites. They were untraceable for a very good reason. Somehow Nick had managed it. But at what cost?

The members of this group were wealthy men who could afford to buy whatever they wanted; including a girl's life. Membership was merely 100 grand a year. Any extra perks came in at figures that would astound the average person. But the organisation offered a unique service; an exquisite catalogue of girls ranging from as young as the client wanted to twenty-five years old. Whatever creed or nationality a client desired, they provided it – at a price.

Brady's first introduction to this nefarious organisation was six months ago when a headless female torso washed up on the beaches of Whitley Bay. The victim had been branded with the letters 'MD' and a symbol of a scorpion. Brady later found out that the letters 'MD' were in fact initials and stood for the brothers Marijuis and Mykolas Dabkunas – her owners. The victim had been decapitated, but first she had been raped by a group of unknown men. One of whom had placed a captive bolt pistol to her temple and pulled the trigger. Allegedly, it was the ultimate sexual high for some of these men: raping a girl while her body convulsed as she died.

Brady and his team had never found the men responsible for her brutal murder. But he had managed to break up the international trafficking ring run by the Dabkunas brothers and their new business associate, local gangster-cum-businessman and estranged brother to North Tyneside's Mayor Macmillan, Ronnie Macmillan. And against the odds they had uncovered the decapitated victim's identity; Edita Aginatas, a young Eastern European woman trafficked into the UK by the Dabkunas brothers. Brady had even succeeded, with the help of Trina McGuire, in securing the release of Nicoletta, another sex-trafficked victim who had been given as a goodwill gesture by the Dabkunas brothers to Ronnie Macmillan.

But it had all begun with his own brother, Nick; an ex-SAS bodyguard who hired himself out to people with problems that they couldn't take to the police. Nick had been hired by the Lithuanian Ambassador to secure the release of his kidnapped daughter. Nick delivered, but in the process he had risked his friendship with Madley and his relationship with Brady. Worse still, as a means of gaining the trust of the kidnappers – the Dabkunas brothers – Nick had had to carry out an appalling crime. One that Brady still found hard to accept. Nick had followed orders and dumped the savagely mutilated body of Simone Henderson in the Gents in Madley's nightclub. He had then made an anonymous call to the police. In other words, he had acted on behalf of Ronnie Macmillan and the Dabkunas brothers in their attempt to silence an undercover copper and stitch Madley up as punishment for not going into business with them, or at least having the courtesy to sell up to them.

During the investigation it had taken Brady all of his inner strength to hold on to the belief that his brother wasn't corrupt. It wasn't until the end of the case that Brady was informed of the facts by Nick – off the record. Nick had delivered as promised. The Lithuanian Ambassador's daughter was safely returned to him. The sex-trafficked victim and a missing local sixteen-year-old girl who had also been lured in by the Dabkunas brothers had been freed. Brady had been highly commended by his superiors for the outcome.

The only people who knew about Nick's covert involvement were Brady, Madley and the Dabkunas brothers. Both Madley and the Dabkunas brothers had a score to settle with Nick. Madley for the fact that Nick had betrayed him – undercover or not, he had brought the police to his door. Then there were the Dabkunas brothers, whose whereabouts were still unknown. Brady was no fool. He knew that no matter how long it took them, they would hunt Nick down for his betrayal. Whether they would employ the likes of Johnny Slaughter to do their bidding, Brady wasn't sure. After all, the Dabkunas brothers were still in hiding and, Brady presumed, would be for a long time to come.

But Brady needed answers. And there was only one person who would know what was going on. Madley.

Brady banged loudly on the locked doors of Madley's nightclub, the Blue Lagoon. He knew Madley was inside. He had seen Gibbs's imposing figure standing at the first floor window looking down at him as he had walked up to the club. Gibbs was Madley's right-hand man. He did anything and everything that Madley ordered him to do and he did it with pleasure. The Afro-Caribbean was a forty-six-year-old retired professional boxer, who still had the impressive physique of a brick shithouse. His thick, knotted black and silver dreads and the large diamond drilled into his front tooth were as legendary as his fists.

Brady looked up and caught Gibbs's eye. It was as cold and impassive as ever. Brady gestured for him to come down and open the door. Gibbs didn't move. Furious, Brady proceeded to bang on the glass door as loud as he could. Before he actually smashed his way through, someone came and opened it.

It was another of Madley's men. Tall, wide and ugly, with the charm of a testosterone-fuelled gorilla on steroids. He was dressed in the same uniform as all Madley's men; a black suit and tie with a white shirt. Nothing fancy or in your face – that was Madley's domain – but just enough to give the required effect of meaning business.

'We're closed, so fuck off!'

'I need to see Madley,' Brady replied. He didn't scare easily. Not that Madley's men worried him. Their barks were worse than their bites. Apart from one new recruit, the man Brady called Weasel Face. He had come up from London and was trouble. It wasn't the Glock 31 semi-automatic pistol that he carried around under his cheap, synthetic Burton's suit. No, it was his thin, sinewy body and small, hungry, darting eyes that told Brady to be careful. He walked like a man on the edge, pumped full of adrenalin, waiting for trouble.

'Yeah? Do I look like I give a fuck what you want?' the man answered with a sneer, revealing cracked and missing teeth.

Ugly didn't come close.

Brady noticed his flattened nose bore a long, jagged scar across it, which trailed down his left cheek. Not that it surprised Brady. Nothing about Madley's men surprised him. Madley surrounded himself with the best in the business. They looked the part and did as instructed – no questions asked. Loyalty was unconditional. Brady didn't know what Madley offered them in return but he knew that they were prepared to go to prison in order to protect their boss.

But this new face in front of him was local.

'What's your name, mate?' Brady asked.

'None of your fucking business, "mate"!' came the sneering reply.

'Mine's Detective Inspector Brady,' he said, flashing his ID card. 'And when I say I want to see Madley, I mean now!'

'I couldn't give a shit if you were the Queen stood in front of me. I said we're closed, so FUCK OFF!'

He went to slam the door shut but Brady was too quick. He threw the full weight of his body against the glass, throwing it back into the new recruit's ugly face.

It had the desired effect. Madley's employee was too preoccupied to even bother about the fact that Brady had walked past him.

'You fucking bastard! Look what you've done!' he said, cradling his nose.

'You should be more careful, pal,' Brady said as he pushed past him.

It was then he noticed they had an audience.

'Hey, Carl. How's business?' Brady asked as he walked over to the club's bar.

Carl, the one-eyed Mancunian bartender, shrugged. 'Same shit as always.'

'Get me a fucking bag of ice. Now!' growled the black-suited thug. He had both hands over his nose as he tried to stem the blood.

Carl ignored him and continued methodically cleaning the bar. It was already spotless – not that Brady would be the one to point this out.

Brady liked Carl. He liked his attitude. He wasn't intimidated by anyone. Including this new, bald thug who thought he could throw his weight around. Carl might have only been in his early twenties but he had a way about him that made him appear much older than his years. He was handsome, there was no disputing that. Never short of female attention. He was tall and fit, with tousled curly dark blond hair and designer stubble. Always impeccably dressed in dark, well-cut suits, crisp white shirts and sharp shoes. Everything about Carl spoke volumes. He was also one of Madley's most loyal employees: barman, receptionist and prime look-out – he did it all, no questions asked.

'Coffee?' Carl asked Brady.

'Yeah, why not?' he answered.

'Hey! What the fuck is your problem? I asked for a fucking bag of ice!' the new recruit demanded. His hands and shirt cuffs were now covered in blood.

Brady watched as Carl politely continued to ignore him as he walked over to the coffee machine. A minute later he came back with an espresso.

'Thanks,' Brady said, taking the small coffee cup.

'You fucking little Mancunian shit. Just wait until Madley hears about this.' He grabbed the tea towel Carl had left on the bar and pressed it to his face. He flashed Brady a look that told him this wasn't over, before turning and heading towards the Gents.

'Who's the pet Rottweiler?' Brady asked.

'A new bouncer. Well, not so new now. He's been here for a couple of months. He's turned out to be a bit of a dick, though,' Carl explained.

'I reckon that's got to be the understatement of the year,' Brady answered.

Carl raised his head and looked Brady straight in the eye.

'Yeah . . . well, you know me. I'm paid to be polite,' Carl said. His face remained as expressionless as always.

Brady sipped his coffee. It had a kick like a mule to the bollocks; just the way he liked it.

'Is that little runt from the East End still working for your boss then?' Brady asked.

'Last time I heard, he was. Why?'

Brady shook his head. 'Nothing.'

But he was concerned. Now that things had settled down, he couldn't figure out why Weasel Face would still be on the payroll. Madley was obviously still worried. Brady just didn't know why.

Brady realised that Carl might have looked as if he was busy wiping down the bar when in truth he was weighing him up. He drained his coffee. It was time to make a move. It was obvious that Carl wasn't going to talk. Whatever was going on, Brady would have to go and ask Madley himself.

'Great coffee, thanks,' Brady said.

'Anytime.'

Brady turned to make his way towards the back of the club.

'Madley's indisposed right now. But if you want to leave a message I'll make sure he gets it,' Carl said.

The look in his eye told Brady it was time to leave.

'Thanks for the offer, but no thanks. I need to see Madley personally,' Brady answered.

Carl didn't reply but his silence said it all.

Brady shrugged it off. He had no choice. He needed to talk to Madley. He headed towards the stairs ignoring his gut feeling that maybe he should have taken Carl's advice. That he should just leave a message and disappear – fast.

Chapter Ten

Brady climbed the stairs leading up to the first floor and Madley's spacious office. Directly above, on the second floor, were his lavish private quarters. Not that he needed them; he had a house rumoured to be worth a million on Marine Avenue in Whitley Bay and a palatial farmhouse in the middle of the wilds of Northumberland. Life had been good to Madley.

Brady reached the first-floor landing, anticipating a cold welcome. But he was surprised. No one was there. He was expecting to face another clone of the black-suited gorilla who was fixing himself up in the Gents. He walked along the corridor to Madley's office door. He thought briefly about knocking and decided against it. Better to just walk in.

'What the fuck?' someone said as Brady entered.

Weasel Face, who had been standing behind the door, stepped in front of Brady, blocking him.

But it was too late. Brady had already seen them. Two businessmen sitting on a leather couch with their backs to him. Neither one even bothered to turn and look at Brady. Whoever had walked into the room uninvited was inconsequential. A minor irritant to be dealt with in the alley at the back of the nightclub.

Madley was sitting across from them on one of his antique leather couches. His phone was ringing on the desk set against the back wall. A continuous, intrusive dull whine.

'Get that, will you?' Madley ordered, making a point of ignoring Brady's sudden intrusion.

Gibbs nodded and walked over to the phone. He picked it up, listened and then hung up. Brady assumed it was Carl with the warning that he was on his way up. Gibbs caught Brady's eye. It was an unblinking stare devoid of any emotion or even recognition. He walked over to his boss, bent down and whispered something to him.

Madley simply nodded.

Brady noticed a thirty-year-old bottle of Talisker on the table with two tumblers, both filled with a liberal measure of whisky. Madley, however, was drinking coffee. Not that Brady was surprised. It was only 11:00 a.m. Madley looked relaxed, casual. But the glinting coldness in his brown eyes told Brady immediately that he wasn't welcome.

Brady had known Madley for as long as he could remember. They had shared a childhood, if it could be called that, in the war-torn, crime-ridden streets of the Ridges. Both had chosen a life of crime: Brady fighting it, Madley living it. The police had been after Madley for years but he was elusive. Rumour had it that he didn't owe his extravagant lifestyle to the two nightclubs and hotel he owned. Revenue was good, but not good enough to afford Madley the life he led. The simple answer was drugs. Madley was the drugs baron and mafia lord of the North-East; at least, that was the word on the street. The closest the police had come to Madley was arresting two of his henchmen for dealing in Class A drugs and carrying firearms. Neither man talked, despite being offered more lenient sentences in exchange for information. Brady didn't know whether these men were working for themselves or someone else. Nor did he want to. He had once asked Madley about the rumours and Madley had appeased him. He had sworn to Brady that he wouldn't deal in that kind of shit and Brady had believed him. If the alternative was true, then Brady would have to distance himself from Madley. But Brady was certain he knew Madley well enough to know that he wouldn't deal in drugs.

Madley stood up, smiling apologetically at his guests as he did so. He made a point of smoothing down his black Armani suit and slightly adjusting his Italian, handmade silk tie before turning and walking over to Brady. Each step was measured as he weighed up the consequences of Brady's intrusion. Madley was the same age as Brady and a few inches shorter. His frame may have been slighter than Brady's, but that meant nothing. Madley could take down anyone. There was no question about it; his reputation preceded him. Not that Brady had ever witnessed anything. If he had, he would've had no choice but to act upon it – friend or no friend. But Madley had morals – of a sort. Like Brady, he had been raised a Catholic and would call upon his faith if the need arose. When his barman Carl had his eyeball ripped out by some-one punching him with a car key over the bar, Madley had looked after him. He had made sure that Carl was treated to the best medical care money could buy. As for the man who'd attacked Carl, Brady had heard talk that he'd ended up paying for what he'd done. Not that Madley's name had ever come into it.

'Jack?' Madley asked as he approached Brady. His voice was polite and controlled but his eyes said something entirely different.

'Martin,' Brady nodded at him. 'Do you mind calling your guard dog off?' He gestured at Weasel Face.

'What did you fucking say?' Weasel Face demanded in a thick Cockney accent, his blue beady eyes challenging Brady. He made a point of flashing the Glock 31 he had concealed under his cheap Burton's jacket.

'I said why don't you get the fuck off my planet?'

'I'll fucking—' Weasel Face began, but Madley's hand on his shoulder swiftly silenced him.

Brady watched him squirm under his boss' touch. There was something about Madley's unnerving calmness that could put the fear of God into even an on-the-edge, dangerous hired gun like Weasel Face.

'Why don't you let me handle this?' Madley said as he bent towards his employee's ear, not once taking his dark eyes off Brady. His voice was barely audible; low, unobtrusive but chill-ingly menacing.

Brady had known Madley too long and shared too much history with him to be intimidated. Brady knew where he came from, no matter how much Madley tried to pretend otherwise. He may have smoothed the edges off his rough North-East accent, refining it to suit the company he now kept, but they both knew his roots. The designer suits, tanned complexion and golfing afternoons might have fooled everyone else, but not Brady. He knew Madley better than anyone in that room. Which was the very reason he was there.

Brady watched as Weasel Face stepped away to lick his wounds. He shot Brady a look that said it all. He would wait for the day when it was just him and Brady. And then he would show Brady who was boss.

Brady gave Weasel Face a 'fuck you' look.

'Outside. Now,' instructed Madley.

Brady knew he'd overstepped the mark. But he didn't care. He needed to hear from Madley what the hell was going on.

Just as he was about to walk outside, he watched as one of the businessmen turned and said something to his associate. Quietly laughing at whatever his partner sitting next to him had said, he leaned over and picked up his whisky tumbler.

He wondered who they were and why they were in Madley's office. Both had kept their backs to him, making it impossible to identify them. But it was clear from the way they held themselves and their expensive taste in suits that they had money.

'Jack,' Madley said. It was not a question, more an order.

Distracted, Brady nodded. He was trying to see if he recognised the other man. But all that Brady could make out was the back of his head and his wide shoulders.

Brady realised that Gibbs was assessing the scene from the window. Thick, swollen biceps folded across his overly pumped, wide chest. Brady could see the buttons on the white shirt beneath his black suit jacket straining from the bulging muscle beneath. He gave Brady a jerk of the head. A subtle prompt to make a move – or else.

Brady ignored him. He had dealt with worse and survived.

'Why don't you introduce me to your friends, Martin?' he said, keeping his eyes on the two men on the couch.

Brady watched as the blond businessman abruptly stood up and walked over to the window towards Gibbs. He kept his back to the room as he said something to Gibbs that Brady couldn't hear, not that he was meant to. Gibbs nodded and then unfolded his arms and looked over in Madley's direction. It was clear that Madley's guest was uncomfortable. More, pissed off by Brady's unwelcome presence. He was obviously hiding something – his identity.

But before Brady could walk over to him, Madley had him by the arm and was dragging him out of the room into the corridor.

Madley waited until the office door closed behind them before speaking. 'What the fuck do you think you're playing at?'

'Who is he?' Brady asked, ignoring both the question and Madley's furious expression.

'None of your fucking business, that's who.'

'Looked a bit edgy to me . . . as if he's hiding something. You should be more careful who you do business with,' advised Brady.

Madley lost control. He pushed him hard against the wall and shoved his arm tight under Brady's throat. He might have been shorter but he had the upper hand; always did when it came to a fight.

'What the fuck are you doing here? You're a fucking copper, Jack! Bad news and bad for business. My business.'

'Christ, Martin! What's got into you?' wheezed Brady as Madley jabbed his arm even harder into his windpipe.

'Fucking you, that's what!'

'All right, all right . . .' Brady gasped, struggling to breathe.

Madley let him go.

'Better be fucking good, otherwise—'

Madley didn't need to finish the threat for Brady to know what he meant. Nick had already caused a lot of bad blood between them. In Madley's Machiavellian world, loyalty counted for everything. It was what kept a six-inch knife from being lodged in your shoulder blades as soon as your back was turned. Madley relied heavily on his men and he paid tenfold for that loyalty. But Brady's younger brother Nick had double-crossed Madley, in spite of their long-standing friendship. Despite leaving the North-East, Nick had never lost touch with Madley – until his involvement with the Dabkunas brothers.

'Trina McGuire,' Brady offered.

Madley's face remained expressionless. The name clearly registered but not in the way Brady had expected. He waited, expecting some trace of guilt but there was nothing.

'You have to be fucking with me. This is about some has-been, drugged-up prossie?' Madley asked, unable to keep the exasperation out of his voice.

'Yeah, Martin. This is about the woman we both grew up with; the one we both wanted. Remember those days? Or are you so far up your own arse that you have no memory of where you fucking came from?' Brady knew he was pushing Madley. But at that precise moment he couldn't give a damn.

Something about the men in Madley's office worried him. His gut was telling him that whatever dealings they were discussing would bring trouble to Whitley Bay.

Madley's eyes narrowed dangerously.

'Some of us succeeded in putting as much distance as possible from shit like that. You should try it, Jack. Especially with you being a copper and all. I'm sure it doesn't look too good, a man in your job fraternising with the very scum you're supposed to be banging up.'

Brady held Madley's menacing stare. He knew exactly what Madley was referring to; he had barged his way into Madley's office, potentially screwing up whatever deals Madley was trying to secure. But who the hell were they? And what exactly were two well-to-do businessmen doing with the likes of Madley? His mind kept coming back to one answer: trouble. Whether they were looking for it or bringing it didn't matter. For a moment Brady wondered whether they were involved in trying to set Madley up for their own gain. In Madley's dark world every business deal could potentially be his last. It was the nature of the beast that those around him wanted to usurp him. Why not? After all, Madley's business dealings made him a very wealthy man. Who wouldn't want a part of that?

'You want to explain to me what happened to her?' Brady asked, trying to keep the anger out of his voice.

He was doing his best to keep his cool. The last thing he wanted was to lose it with Madley. They had too much history between them and Brady, if he was brutally honest, owed Madley. If it hadn't been for him looking out for Brady and Nick when their father got banged up for the murder of their mother, they would never have survived the countless foster homes they were dumped in throughout North Shields. Madley had always been a constant in their lives. No matter what, he had been there. Whether it was breaking some little bastard's nose for taking the piss out of Brady or his brother because of their father, or skipping school for the day to mess around down at St Mary's lighthouse, he was always there. Brady looked at Madley and wondered what had happened to them. They had never allowed anything to spoil their friendship, even their wildly different choice of careers.

'What? She's some fucked-up druggie who does tricks to get her next hit? Is that it?'

'You know it's fucking not!' Brady fired back.

'For fuck's sake, Jack! What do you want from me? What's got you so wound up you barge in here after how long? Eh? How long has it been? You haven't given a shit about what was happening in my life until now. Are you here as Jack, or are you here as DI Brady?'

Brady turned away.

'That's what I thought.'

'I have never once come here as a copper. Never,' Brady said, looking Madley in the eye.

'So what the fuck are you doing barging into my office? Eh?'

'I told you. I needed to talk to you about Trina McGuire,' answered Brady.

'Then why don't I believe you?'

Brady looked at Madley. He tried to hide the hurt he felt but knew that his eyes would betray him. He dragged a hand through his hair to compose himself.

'You walk in pretending that this is something to do with some screwed-up prossie, when in fact you're trying to poke your nose in my affairs. What have you heard, Jack? Who's been talking to you, because I'd like to put them straight.' Madley's voice was calm, controlled again, without the hard North-East inflection.

'Nothing . . . I've heard nothing on you.'

Madley stared at Brady, weighing him up. There was menace in his eyes. Something Brady had rarely seen directed at him.

For some reason Madley backed down. Maybe because Brady couldn't hide the hurt he felt at Madley's accusations. He sank back against the wall, exhausted, and waited for Madley to talk.

He knew from Madley's defensiveness that he'd already been informed about Trina McGuire. Brady had no idea who could have told him.

Unless . . .

Brady didn't want to think about that – not yet.

'Does Nick know?' Madley asked, the coldness gone from his voice.

Brady shook his head. 'I can't get hold of him.'

'Why does that not surprise me?'

Brady looked at Madley. He knew that Madley would never trust Nick again; not after what Nick had done to him.

'How did you know about Trina?' Brady asked.

'Contacts, Jack. It's all about looking out for one another. You should know that better than anyone.'

63

Brady didn't answer. He knew it was a direct reference to Nick.

'So explain to me why you think I would have answers about who did this to Trina?'

Brady shrugged.

'I know you better than you know yourself. You're hiding something.'

'Let's just say I have a bad feeling that this was aimed at Nick,' Brady answered.

Madley thought about it.

'What makes you say that?'

'I can't tell you,' Brady said.

Madley nodded, accepting that as a copper there were things that Brady couldn't disclose.

'Who do you think would know that Trina was Nick's girlfriend before he left the North-East?' Brady asked.

'Christ, Jack! How many years ago was that? Fuck knows! Depends who has a score to settle with him, doesn't it? Money can buy you any kind of information as you well know.'

'Will you ask around for me?' Brady knew he was asking a lot from Madley; more so given that he hadn't been to see him for months. Madley's anger at Nick had been directed at Brady too, which had resulted in him keeping his distance.

Madley gave a non-committal shrug. 'I'll see what I can do. In return I don't want to see your face here again. Understand? It's bad for business.'

Brady looked Madley in the eye. He was searching for some kind of reassurance that their friendship, which had lasted over thirty years and survived their polarised lifestyles, hadn't run its course. Perhaps having a copper as a friend was too much of a liability for Madley. Maybe it had always been inevitable and they had been fooling themselves that it could continue. Or Nick's betrayal had been too much for Madley to swallow.

Brady respected Madley's wishes. There was nothing more to say. He turned to leave, not wanting Madley to see the pain in his eyes.

'Jack? Remember, Nick's pissed off a lot of people. Including Johnny Slaughter. From what I've heard he's still after him. And then there's those bastards he got caught up with—'

Without turning back, Brady muttered: 'Thanks.'

He could have forewarned Madley about the card for his nightclub the Blue Lagoon that Forensics had found. But he didn't. Brady had never crossed the line and passed on information to Madley. He was worried that Madley was in trouble. That someone was setting him up, but Brady was powerless to say anything. He knew that DI Bentley would do a good enough job of informing Madley. It seemed they were both playing their cards close to their chests. Brady was under no illusions – Madley knew a hell of a lot more than he was admitting. He had known him long enough to know when he was lying. The question was, why?

Chapter Eleven

Brady returned to the station. He was in a foul mood. His run-in with Madley had affected him more than he wanted to admit. That and the fact that he still couldn't get hold of Nick. His conversation with Madley had made Brady realise he had no one he could really depend on. Not any more. He rarely talked to Nick, let alone got the chance to see him in person. But Madley had always been there for him. Someone who really knew him, like Nick. Understood his background. And now? Brady thought of Trina McGuire – a drug-addicted prostitute who had once been the most beautiful girl to walk the streets of North Shields. She'd been filled with the promise and optimism of youth, only to have her naivety literally knocked out of her. Life could be shit depending on the streets where you grew up. It was a postcode lottery. Trina was a fine example of that.

Brady sighed heavily. He needed to get his head together. He had more pressing things to worry about, including trying to make some headway with the serial rape investigation that had developed into a 'runner'. Not good for his career, team morale, or the hundreds of young women who should have the freedom to go out drinking in Whitley Bay at the weekend without worrying about some twisted, sadistic rapist on the loose.

He got out of the car and slammed the door. He took a deep breath before walking over to the station. The air was thick and heavy with a sea fret. He could literally taste the sea salt in the air. He climbed the steps, avoiding the dog-piss-covered ramp that DCI Gates had built as part of his new PC policy. It was his way of showing the public that Whitley Bay police station did not discriminate against the disabled criminal. Not that it had ever been used as intended – yet. But Brady was certain that with the draconian cuts the current government was making to disability benefits, the ramp might end up being useful. Slashing benefits to those in dire need could result in people turning to crime just to survive. And he wasn't talking about the second and third generations who knew nothing but a life on benefits, he was talking about the most disadvantaged in society being easy government targets. Unfortunately, it would be the police force with its ever-decreasing budget that would have to pick up the tab for the government's solution to the country's debt.

Brady opened the heavy wooden double doors that led into the station. The smell of stale urine from too many drunken louts dragged in to sleep it off in the cells hit him. Nora, the station's cleaner, did her best but it was an uphill battle. The old Victorian green-tiled corridor had seen better days, as had the building, which was decrepit with flaking walls and maze-like corridors. But Brady wouldn't have it any other way. Even the out-dated basement cafeteria with its cracked sixties red laminated tables and wrought-iron bars on the windows had an allure for him. The place was reassuringly familiar; not surprising given how many hours of his life he had spent there.

Particularly after his marriage to Claudia had broken down. Brady had sought solace in his work. Even the rumours that had done the rounds about his alleged affair with Simone Henderson, the cause of his failed marriage, didn't stop him from working extreme hours in a bid to avoid facing his wrecked home life. He couldn't even count the number of dark, lonely nights he had spent in his office drowning in a bottle of scotch, unable to go back to an empty house. That period in his life was a blur now. At the time it had been a drunken blur, which was why he could barely remember any of it.

Brady dismissed thoughts of the car wreck his life had been back then. That was over twelve months ago. He was trying to get his life back on track. He had had no choice after news had filtered through to him that Claudia and her boyfriend, DCI James Davidson, had moved in together. Not that it should have surprised him. They'd been together for over six months. They co-headed a groundbreaking new Human Trafficking Centre in Newcastle that equalled Sheffield's. And now they lived together. It had been Tom Harvey, a long-standing friend and colleague, who had delivered the news in his usual blunt, insensitive way. Brady had not reacted to the blow. But it had taken everything in his power to act nonchalant. It was only when he was alone that he allowed the news to sink in.

DCI Davidson was everything that Brady hated. He was a tall, muscle-bound, ex-military Ross Kemp lookalike who had swaggered into the Armed Response Unit on the back of his hands-on combat experience in Iraq and Afghanistan. He was good looking in a macho, arrogant kind of way, with an arsenal of war stories that mere mortal men would kill for. Not that Brady could take that away from him. The man had balls and plenty of them. Anyone who risked their life in a war against fundamentalist insurgents, who used dirty guerrilla tactics, was a hero in Brady's books.

However, Brady's problem with Davidson was down to one simple fact: he was a self-confessed player with a reputation that a dog would be ashamed to own. Not that Brady could talk, but the last thing he wanted was Claudia being played.

Brady breathed in deeply as he prepared himself for what lay ahead. Given the morning he'd already experienced, his expectations for the rest of the day were low.

He pushed open the second set of doors to be greeted by the desk sergeant on duty, Charlie Turner. He was a short, rotund, balding man who looked as if he should have been forced to retire years ago. However, despite appearances, Turner was still a few years off retirement. The desk sergeant raised his unruly, spidery white eyebrows at Brady. It made no difference. Brady still couldn't make out the small, dark brown eyes hidden by Turner's sagging, heavily creased eyelids. But the act was enough to know that Turner, in his own paternalistic way, was warning Brady that something was wrong.

'Well, well, bonny lad! What have you done to get Gates so fired up, eh?'

Brady feigned surprise. 'I'm still breathing?' he answered with a wry smile.

'Better watch yourself, Jack. I'm being serious. Gates is livid. Conrad's been getting it in the neck. So God knows what he's got in store for you given the fact that that poor sod has just returned to work!'

'I'm sure after what Conrad's been through he can handle getting a bollocking from Gates.'

'Bloody hell! Why do you take such delight in winding Gates up? You know if he had his way you'd have been demoted to the streets of Blyth years ago,' Turner said, wizened, craggy face scowling at Brady.

'Who have you been talking to, Charlie?' It was a line Brady knew off by heart. It was one of Gates's popular threats when Brady pissed him off – which was often. But how Turner knew it was beyond him.

'I may be getting old but some people don't realise I still have my wits about me. I overheard Gates discussing your latest antics with O'Donnell earlier.'

'Is O'Donnell still here?' Brady asked, taken aback. He realised it must be serious for the Detective Chief Superintendent to have paid a visit to Whitley Bay police station.

'No, you just missed him. Maybe it's a good thing. He didn't look best pleased when he left.'

'Shit!' Brady muttered. He didn't like the idea that Conrad had got it in the neck because of him as much as he didn't like the thought of Gates running him down to O'Donnell.

He was aware that turning up at Rake Lane hospital and visiting a victim of a crime that he hadn't been assigned to investigate was not such a good idea. Not to mention his unauthorised visit to the crime scene afterwards.

'Thanks, Charlie. I owe you one,' Brady said. He needed to get hold of Conrad before Gates realised he was back in the station. The last thing he wanted was to be hauled into Gates's office without an update from Conrad of what had been reported against Brady – if anything.

'You owe me more than one, bonny lad,' corrected Turner.

'Yeah . . . yeah,' Brady replied, walking away.

'You'll miss me when I'm gone, Jack Brady!'

'If you're right, looks like I'll be going long before you retire,' Brady called back light-heartedly before taking the stairs.

It was unfortunate timing. He ran straight into DCI Gates. He soon lost his jocular mood. The look on his boss's face was enough to tell him he was not impressed with Brady's attitude.

'My office. Now!' ordered Gates.

'Sir?' Brady asked. It was a precarious move, but before he went in front of Gates's firing squad he wanted to know exactly what he was being shot for. He needed to be certain it was connected to DI Bentley's case and not some other monumental 'fuck up' he had no idea about.

Gates was roughly Brady's height and build, but right now he was using the advantage of being three steps up to tower over Brady. He was an imposing man at the best of times. He might have been ten years older than Brady but he was physically fitter, and he knew it. Everything about Gates was regimented and controlled.

'Don't try and be clever with me, Jack. You know exactly what this is about. My office, and I mean now!'

'Yes, sir,' answered Brady, accepting that he was about to get bollocked.

Chapter Twelve

'Sit,' ordered Gates when Brady entered his office.

Brady closed Gates's door, then did exactly as instructed. Now was not the time to push Gates. Brady may have been a lot of things but he wasn't an idiot.

Gates kept his back to Brady as he stood looking out of his office window. Something he never did. The atypical behaviour told Brady he was in trouble. The question plaguing Brady was what kind of trouble? He kept his mouth shut and his head down while Gates collected himself.

'Would you like to tell me what the fuck you're playing at?' Gates finally asked. He turned and looked at Brady. His eyes demanded an explanation.

Brady tried to think of a believable answer. He knew that he was in deeper trouble than he first anticipated. Gates rarely cursed. Which meant that when he did, something or someone had seriously angered him.

Gates sat down and waited. His intelligent eyes were filled with an unnerving coldness.

'All right, since you don't seem to understand my question, let me rephrase it for you. Why would you pay an unauthorised visit to one of DI Bentley's victims?'

Brady started to clear his throat but Gates silenced him.

'Do you know DI Bentley?' Gates asked, his voice as chilling and damning as his eyes. Again, he made it quite clear he did not expect an answer. 'No?'

'I can explain, sir,' Brady began, but Gates's expression told him if he wanted to leave in one piece he better keep his mouth shut and take what was coming to him.

He did the only thing he could do in the circumstances; he inwardly readied himself for the verbal whipping that Gates was intent on unleashing.

'So, explain to me why DI Bentley knows so much about you and your exact whereabouts this morning? Forgive me if I'm mistaken, but don't you have your own investigation to deal with, let alone make some headway on? Or what? Is it that after two months of being in charge of your case you've decided you've had enough? Because from where I'm sitting you're not exactly delivering, are you?'

Brady sat perfectly still and waited for Gates to continue. He did his best to hold Gates's scathing stare, but it was proving difficult. The problem was, there was some truth in what Gates had said. He was getting nowhere with the rape case, which had resulted in him taking desperate, unorthodox measures. He had gone along in good faith believing there was a chance that Trina McGuire had been attacked by the man he was trying to apprehend. Admittedly, he should have gone to Gates and asked for authorisation so as not to tread on anyone else's toes – Bentley's in particular.

Gates leaned forward on his desk. He narrowed his eyes slightly as he weighed Brady up.

'I don't like getting it in the neck from North Shields Area Command because of your reckless behaviour. Understand?'

'Yes, sir.'

'So, is Bentley's case connected to our investigation?'

Brady took his time. He was absolutely certain that it wasn't the same perpetrator who had attacked the three girls in Whitley Bay, but he was unsure whether Gates was trying to trip him up. That maybe he knew something that Brady should have known.

'No, sir,' Brady answered.

'Why?'

'Different MO.'

'How?' asked Gates, interested. 'From what I've been told it's exactly the same MO.'

Brady shook his head.

'No, sir. Initially it sounds as if it is, but when you compare Chloe Winters' injuries to this recent victim they're very different.'

Gates nodded for Brady to elaborate.

'Well, sir, whoever attacked Chloe Winters knew what they were doing. It was a skilled hand. The removal of her tattoo was an intricate business. He took his time. Last night's attack was rushed. There was no thought or care taken when her skin was removed. If we get the photographs of her injuries we can make comparisons to Chloe Winters. I'm certain you'll find that a different blade was used. Then there's the breast fetish. He makes a point of focusing on his victims' breasts. This isn't the case with last night's assault. Also, whoever attacked the victim last night seemed to know her. It was overkill. He couldn't control his anger. The level of violence smacked of something personal. The problem we have is whether the victim will ever be able to tell us who did this to her. She's in a really bad way.'

'Why rape her and remove her skin in exactly the same way as your third victim? It doesn't make sense,' Gates asked, making a point of ignoring Brady's comment. 'From what Bentley's gathered the assailant actually removed a tattoo from her wrist. Seems more than just coincidence to me, DI Brady.'

Brady was surprised that Gates knew this detail and wondered whether Trina McGuire had talked. Or maybe someone who knew Trina had talked to the police. Brady was sure that Bentley would be turning to his informants to get what information he could on her assault.

'The *Northern Echo* has a lot to answer for, sir.' It was a simple answer. But it was the truth.

Gates sighed heavily and sat back in his chair. He clasped his hands under his chin as he considered what Brady was implying.

'So let me get this straight. You think someone read that article and decided to assault this woman in the same manner as Chloe Winters? But why?'

Brady shrugged. 'I don't know, sir. Do they have an identity on the victim yet?'

'Yes. Seems she's a prostitute. Works the area where she was attacked. Trina McGuire. Do you know her?' Gates asked, watching Brady's reaction to his question. 'Used to work at The Hole in Wallsend before it got closed down.'

Brady tried not to react.

'I know her from having dealt with her son, Shane McGuire. He's been in and out of here so often that I'm surprised he hasn't taken up residence.'

Gates nodded. But he didn't look convinced.

'That's the only reason you know her?'

Brady nodded. But he was a lousy liar and he was certain that Gates knew he was only telling him part of it.

'What's DI Bentley's take on her attack?' Brady asked, trying his best to change the conversation.

Gates stared intently at Brady.

'Well, Jack, this is why I wanted your views on this assault. It seems you and Bentley are in agreement. Bentley is as convinced as you are that this has nothing to do with your serial rapist.'

'I see, sir,' answered Brady. He tried to sound as nonchalant as possible, despite the fact he had a sickening feeling that Gates was leading him straight into a trap. 'What's Bentley's take on her assailant then?' It was an obvious question and Brady had no choice but to ask it.

'He believes that her assault is related to the drug dealer she owed a substantial amount of money to. From what Bentley has found out, she was behind in her payments. Seems that the dealer wanted to make an example of her. Put the word out on the streets that this is what happens if you don't pay up. Bentley's not sure whether this dealer was her pimp as well.'

Brady looked at Gates. He knew exactly where this was heading and he didn't like it. He was just waiting for Gates to throw a name into the ring – Madley's.

'So Bentley believes that her attack was directly related to money she owed?' Brady asked.

'Yes. From the intelligence he has on this drug dealer it's his style.'

Brady sat back. He could see Bentley's reasoning. It made perfect sense – not that Brady wanted to accept it.

'So, her attack is a warning shot. I understand that. Especially given the gravity of the assault she suffered. It looked like the handiwork of some street thug. Clumsy and heavy-handed with a touch of sexual sadism mixed in for good measure. By all accounts she was left for dead?' Brady asked. Inside he felt sick to his stomach, despite the casualness in his voice.

Gates nodded.

'So, what we have is an assailant copying the Whitley Bay rapist, no thanks to the *Northern Echo*, in the hope of throwing the police off. Very clever and great timing. To strike on the night when the nature of Chloe Winters' attack is headline news.'

Gates didn't say anything. Instead he watched Brady.

Brady tried to keep his face as blank as possible

'You talked with Ainsworth, I gather?' Gates asked. But it was more of an accusation than a question.

'Yes, sir.' Brady knew the direction this was heading, and there was no way he could stop it.

'I assume you wouldn't have missed the opportunity to find out if there was any incriminating evidence left behind at the crime scene?'

Brady steeled himself. Gates was about to deliver a hard blow.

'The card for Madley's nightclub, the Blue Lagoon. I take it Ainsworth showed you?'

He could feel himself sweating. The police had never been able to finger Madley. Not even come close to getting anything on him. But now? Brady couldn't believe it. Or, if he was honest, he didn't want to believe it. He nodded at Gates, unable to trust himself to answer without betraying himself.

'Well . . . looks like Bentley's got something on Madley. I just hope for your sake that you really were interested in Bentley's case because of the similar MO and not because of Madley.'

'Of course, sir,' answered Brady.

Gates stared hard at Brady. Cold and detached.

'Good. I'd hate to think that you were trying to protect someone here. Or even forewarn them.'

Brady wasn't surprised that Gates knew his connection with Madley. After all, Jimmy Matthews had come clean that he had been in Madley's pocket. Feeding him whatever scraps of police intelligence he had in order to wipe out significant gambling debts. Brady had never quite figured out how Matthews could afford his lifestyle on a modest copper's salary. The answer was easy once you realised he was on Madley's payroll.

'I don't know what you're getting at, sir,' Brady said, knowing that he was playing a dangerous game.

'Don't take me for an idiot. You know exactly what I'm saying. But by all means sit there and pretend you don't.'

Brady didn't answer him. It took all his effort not to break eye contact. He was furious at what Gates was daring to imply. He knew a few corrupt coppers, such as Matthews who was currently banged up in Durham prison. But Brady wasn't one of them. He had never crossed the line with his friendship with Madley – not once. So for Gates to sit there accusing him of being bent was wildly unfair and, crucially, unsubstantiated.

'What I'd like to know is why would DI Bentley's victim be asking to see you?'

Brady sat back. He was absolutely stunned.

'She's regained consciousness?'

'That's what I've just said. Before you showed up, DI Bentley said that she was awake. But she's refusing to talk to him or his officers. Instead she asked for you, which obviously surprised him. But what surprises me is that you've just sat there and told me you don't know her.'

Brady was temporarily speechless as he tried to figure out how the hell to get out of Gates's snare.

'I take it you have nothing to say in your defence, Detective Inspector?'

Brady cleared his throat first. It felt so dry he didn't know if he would be able to get the words out. 'I didn't tell you that I knew her because she's an informant. I wanted to protect her identity. Trina McGuire is someone I've had contact with over the years. But it has always been in a professional capacity and I have never compromised her safety.'

Gates remained impassive. Whatever Brady was selling, Gates clearly wasn't buying.

'I don't like being lied to, regardless of whether she's your informant,' Gates replied.

Brady realised that he had no choice but to tell Gates the truth, or at least part of it. He still had to protect his brother Nick's identity.

'Trina McGuire worked with Nicoletta. She was the one who gave me the information on the Dabkunas brothers and Ronnie Macmillan. If it wasn't for her, Nicoletta wouldn't be alive – let alone in protective custody.'

'So why didn't you mention her name in your report when the investigation was over?' Gates asked. His eyes were filled with distrust as he waited for an answer.

Brady breathed in. He hadn't expected this when he walked into Gates's office. He had assumed he was going to get a bollocking – understandably. But the last thing he had expected was to walk into a spider's trap; the more he tried to free himself the more enmeshed he became, and all the while Gates sat back watching him squirm.

He tried again to explain himself: 'I didn't want her to end up in the witness protection system, sir.'

It was an honest response. If she had been a witness the judiciary system would have used and abused her for its own ends.

Once they'd finished with her she would have been thrown like a piece of rotting meat to a pack of wild, snarling dogs. The world that Trina McGuire inhabited was unforgiving and if it had become public knowledge that she'd snitched to the police then she would have paid a high price for it – her life.

Trina McGuire had worked for Ronnie Macmillan at the Ship Inn – or the Hole as it was known locally, for obvious reasons. It was a notorious strip joint which stood alone in a deserted no-man's land against the backdrop of a shipping industry that was long gone. The Hole had been left to rack and ruin once Ronnie Macmillan had gone down for his part in the sex-trafficking ring. It now sat abandoned like the River Tyne and the disused docklands behind it. Gone were the ships and twisting sky-high cranes that had dominated Wallsend; a small town once known globally for its thriving shipping industry. It was better known now for its ever-increasing dole queues and crime figures.

Gates waited. He still wasn't convinced.

'If I'd disclosed that she was one of Ronnie Macmillan's women we both know what would've happened to her. She'd have ended up on the bottom of the Tyne and I can guarantee that the only people to know she was dead would've been the ones who'd dumped her body in there. I didn't want that on my conscience.' Brady looked at Gates. There was nothing more he could say. It was up to Gates to decide whether he believed him or not.

'All right.' It was dismissive and abrupt. 'I want two things from you. Firstly, I will inform DI Bentley that you'll be paying a visit to Trina McGuire. If you are the only person she'll talk to then I want you there. Anything to help Bentley's team get who they believe is responsible. And understand this, Jack.' He paused as he stared hard at Brady. 'You will tell Bentley every-thing she tells you. Are we clear on this?'

'Yes, sir.'

Inside, Brady felt physically sick. He was being asked to get a witness statement from Trina McGuire – regardless of the consequences for her. But this was no straightforward state-ment; Bentley wanted it to finger Madley. To name him as her drug dealer and the man responsible for ordering the savage beating.

Why the fuck was your card there, Madley?

Brady couldn't get his head straight. It was clear to him some-one was after Nick. That they had beaten Trina McGuire up to get information and as a warning.

But who? Who would do that? Fuck ... not Madley? Surely not Madley?

Brady's mind darted all over the place as he tried to make sense of what was happening. He knew that Madley wouldn't have been stupid enough to have left a calling card. Unless – Brady thought of the henchmen that Madley surrounded himself with, not exactly the sharpest pencils in the box. The more Brady thought about it, the more it made sense. He could imagine one of Madley's men screwing up like this. But not Gibbs or Carl. Madley trusted these two men and there was a reason why; they never made mistakes.

Then who? Unless ... unless Madley had been set up?

For whatever reason Brady couldn't shake his hunch that Madley was in trouble.

'Good. I'm pleased you understand the significance of what you're being asked.'

Gates leaned forward again and started keying something into his computer. He wasn't even looking at Brady as he spoke: 'I want you and your team doing everything in your power to apprehend this rapist. Two months is a long time. Too long. I want him caught and I mean now.'

'Yes, sir.' There was nothing else Brady could say.

'Every new detail or information you get on this case you bring to me. I want to be updated every hour if need be. From where I'm sat, Jack, it looks like you need to be managed. Whether you've lost your edge or you've decided to sit back on your laurels after the success of your last investigation I don't know and to be perfectly honest, I don't care.' Gates stopped typing and turned to face Brady. 'Either you shape up and start delivering or I hand your case over to Adamson. We haven't got the budget to support dead weights around here. Not any more.'

Brady winced. It felt as if Gates had punched him in the stomach.

He wondered whether Gates had already run this by Chief Superintendent O'Donnell. He knew that the force were cutting back on officers – they'd already had a number of casualties of the police budget being slashed left, right and centre. They already had DI Adamson at Whitley Bay station – Brady's nemesis. He knew that Adamson, who was Gates's protégé, would take great delight in taking the 'runner' that Brady currently had on his hands and dramatically turning it around.

Gates had already turned back to his typing.

'Sir? How is Bentley so sure that this attack on Trina McGuire is connected to Madley? I mean, a card with details of the night-club recovered at the crime scene isn't exactly conclusive evidence against him. It could have been left by anyone.'

'Except it wasn't. I don't believe in coincidences Detective Inspector. Do you?'

Brady didn't, but he wasn't going to admit that to Gates.

'Sir?'

'For God's sake, Jack. Can't you see I'm busy?' Gates snapped.

Brady ignored his outburst and continued. He had no choice.

'What if this is connected to Ronnie Macmillan? She worked for him. Maybe word has got back to him that she talked to me? And there's the—'

But before Brady could finish, Gates abruptly cut him off. 'Enough! Ronnie Macmillan is in Durham prison where he belongs and his Eastern European business associates have dropped off the radar. They've gone. It's over with. End of story. Now get out there and do what you're paid to do for a change.'

Brady pushed his chair back and stood up. It was clear that Gates thought he was trying to protect Madley. That he was coming up with ridiculous theories to throw Bentley off the scent. But nothing could be further from the truth. Brady had a really bad feeling about Trina McGuire, who had done this to her and why.

Brady reached the office door but before he had a chance to walk out Gates spoke again.

'DI Bentley has been watching Madley for some time now. Every move has been scrutinised. Madley's been branching out of Whitley Bay for a while. He's built himself quite an empire and got some powerful business associates along the way.'

This caught Brady's attention. He thought back to the two well-heeled businessmen in Madley's office. It was obvious they hadn't wanted to be seen there. Whatever deal was being brokered they wanted their identities protected.

'He's known in North Shields, Wallsend and even Newcastle,' Gates continued. 'Rumour has it, he's even got connections in London. He has an army of street dealers throughout the North-East who work for him while he sits back in his office keeping his hands clean. But not any more. Bentley has some intelligence on him which means he could be going down for a long time.'

'How can DI Bentley be so sure about Madley?' Brady asked, unable to keep quiet. This was news to him. He accepted that Madley was involved in various shady business deals and that he had a reputation for looking after his own. But as to running some major drugs cartel in the North-East? Brady found this hard to accept. He had heard the rumours. But that was all he believed them to be – rumours. The Madley he had grown up with had values and an unerring sense of loyalty, which was why they had remained friends. Brady wasn't a fool. If he really believed that Madley was corrupt he would have no time for him – regardless of the past they shared.

'He has his sources. Not everyone is in Madley's back pocket, Jack.'

Gates had made his point. He turned back to his work.

Brady's eyes flashed with fury at this comment. He clenched his fists tight as he resisted the urge to tell Gates exactly what he thought of him. Now wasn't the time. It could wait.

Unceremoniously dismissed, Brady walked out of Gates's office feeling like he'd had the worst kicking of his life. He had to try and salvage what career he still had left. He had to get his priorities straight. He had to forget about Madley and whatever he'd got involved in. Madley was not Brady's problem now. He'd made that quite clear earlier. And as for Nick, he was more than capable of taking care of himself. Had proved that countless times before. Brady was the one who seemed to have a problem holding things together.

He breathed in deeply. He needed to keep his head down and make some serious inroads into the serial rape case. But first he would do as Gates had ordered. He would visit Trina McGuire – but he would be damned if he would hand anything over to DI Bentley. He would not have her sacrificed for the sake of another copper's career.

Chapter Thirteen

Brady stuck his head out of his office door. 'Conrad!' he shouted.

He was waiting for Conrad. Had been waiting for him for the past few minutes.

'Sorry,' Conrad called out as he came running up the corridor. 'Got caught up with something.'

'Yeah? Well, we haven't got a lot of time. And we have even less now,' Brady replied. 'Have you got the photofit of the rapist?'

'Yes, sir,' Conrad answered, gesturing to the file in his hand.

'Good. That's something.'

Brady started walking off down the corridor. He was losing the day. It was fading fast and he'd got nothing done. He'd spent the last hour chasing down DI Bentley so he could lick his arse. It was on these occasions that Brady hated the job. He'd apologised for trespassing on Bentley's investigation. And then been forced to listen to Bentley's crap as he went on and on. Luckily, Conrad had walked in, giving him the perfect excuse to get off the line. The upshot of the conversation was that Brady had agreed to visit Trina McGuire and to divulge everything she said to him. In fact, Bentley had had the bright idea of Brady walking in with a hidden tape recorder. Not that she would notice. Given the extent of her injuries he would be surprised if she could even move, let alone raise her head to look out of the swollen slit that was her good eye. The other one had been operated on to repair the bones that had been ruptured during her attack. The doctor had explained that she had suffered both an orbital frontal bone fracture and a direct orbital floor fracture. In other words, something like a baseball or a fist had been rammed so forcefully into her face that they had been worried she was going to suffer brain damage.

Brady would find out soon enough how well Trina McGuire was recovering. That was where he was heading – straight to the hospital to interview her. Bentley had assured him he would be there to meet him and, of course, brief him before he went in. And to make sure that he understood how to operate the tape recorder to avoid the obvious – Brady 'accidentally' switching it off. Brady hadn't bothered to go into the rights and wrongs of taping an interview without the interviewee's consent. He decided to let Bentley figure out the legal implications of that one. The problem was, Brady had to show willing. He had a lot to prove here – primarily that he was not a bent copper on the take from Madley. If there was any doubt in Gates's mind, or Bentley's, Brady had to do everything asked of him – he had no choice. If he refused, he could be seen as hiding something. Which of course he was – Madley's connection with a brother no one knew he had.

Brady was worried that if Bentley had a surveillance team watching Madley, they'd seen him turning up at the Blue Lagoon that morning. There was nothing Brady could do but wait. It wasn't as if he had done anything wrong. He hadn't forewarned Madley about the evidence found at the crime scene that pointed, whether Brady liked it or not, to Madley's club and ultimately Madley.

'Sir?' Conrad called out as he tried to catch up.

'Come on, we can't keep DI Bentley waiting.'

He had better things to do on a Friday afternoon than be played by Bentley. He had, as Gates had so kindly pointed out, a serial rapist to catch. It was now seven days since his last attack and they were fast approaching the weekend. The rapist had been consistent in his attacks – all three had taken place in the early hours of either a Saturday or a Sunday. The last thing Brady wanted was to get a call in the early hours telling him another woman had been attacked. Or worse, getting the news

Monday morning that someone had been reported missing after going out drinking. Considering the rapist's last attack, where he held his victim for over forty-eight hours, Brady was prepared for this behaviour to be repeated and, if anything, extended. Practice makes perfect. Troublingly, Brady had the distinct feeling that their suspect was still perfecting his MO.

Brady hadn't been in the mood for talking. Consequently the short drive to the hospital had been torturous – mainly for Conrad. Brady swung the car into the car park.

'Great!' Brady said. 'Fucking great!'

The car park was typically full.

'Why don't I wait here until a space becomes available? Then I'll join you inside,' Conrad suggested.

'The only reason I'm here is because DI fucking Bentley wants to piss all over me.'

Conrad didn't answer. He knew his boss was right. Bentley would be livid on two counts. Brady had walked into Bentley's investigation without even having the respect to ask first, and to add insult to injury, the victim was refusing to talk to anyone but him.

Brady breathed in deeply for a few seconds. He needed to calm down. In fact he needed a cigarette but he knew that was not an option. He didn't have time to smoke and he was supposed to have quit. He wanted to get this over with as quickly as possible so he could get back to his team. He had a briefing that had been postponed and a team that were sitting around waiting for instructions.

'All right, you park up and join me. But be as quick as you can, I don't trust myself to keep my mouth shut.'

'I'll be there as soon as possible, sir,' Conrad answered.

Without another word, Brady switched the engine off and got out the car.

Conrad knew Brady was being serious. That he really was worried in case he said something out of line. It was stating the obvious to say that his boss was stressed.

Brady hadn't told Conrad what Gates had said, but his silence spoke volumes. That and the fact that he was now doing someone else's bidding. That wasn't like Brady. Whatever trouble he was in must be serious for him to be suddenly following orders. More so, when it was someone of the same rank giving them.

But Conrad knew that it had to be connected to Gates's talk with Brady. Before his boss had returned to the station, Gates had hauled Conrad into his office demanding to know his whereabouts. Conrad hadn't needed to feign ignorance to protect his boss. He genuinely had no idea where he'd gone. All he knew was that it was connected to the sexually assaulted, beaten woman in Rake Lane hospital. Not that he said this to Gates. Conrad knew where his loyalties lay and that was firmly with his boss. There had been times, countless times if he was honest, when he had questioned his boss's unorthodox approach. But now Conrad knew to just leave him to it. Brady always delivered. Not necessarily in the way that his superiors would approve of, but he always came through – until now.

Gates had questioned, or to be more accurate, interrogated Conrad about the serial rape case and exactly where they were with it. But Conrad was well aware that Gates was indirectly asking whether Brady was up to the job any more. Two months was a long time for the investigating team to have no concrete leads. This was the reason Conrad had come back a month earlier than recommended. He'd heard rumours about Brady's performance – or lack of it. DI Adamson was doing a great spin job of running Brady into the ground. Throwing questions around as to why Brady had made no headway with the case. He had managed to infiltrate and bring down an international sex-trafficking ring, yet he couldn't find a rapist terrorising the streets of Whitley Bay. But Conrad knew, as did Adamson, that the Northumbrian force was scheduled for further cuts. Conrad kept his ear to the ground. Adamson, who had a cut-throat attitude to climbing the corporate ladder, had already been promoted from DS to DI, walking straight into Jimmy

Matthews's office. It was no surprise. He was Gates's blue-eyed boy; he could do no wrong. So when it came to the choice of downsizing the number of senior officers at Whitley Bay station, Conrad was absolutely certain that Gates would back Adamson. When it came down to the wire, Whitley Bay did not need two Detective Inspectors.

Brady's success in intercepting the sex-trafficking operation and the conviction of Ronnie Macmillan was yesterday's news. What mattered now was that Brady was failing to deliver on a case that affected local people. This was not an unseen crime involving foreign women and girls who didn't even speak English. Instead, this was personal – it targeted the very people who paid their taxes and rightly expected the police to keep them safe in return. And Brady was failing them. The *Northern Echo* had done a good job of stirring up public fear. Britain had become a blame culture. And at this precise moment Brady was being blamed for failing to protect the streets of Whitley Bay.

Conrad slid across from the passenger seat into the driver's. He switched the engine on, kicked it into gear and sat ready to pounce as soon as a space became free. He caught sight of Brady as he reached the hospital's main entrance. He looked like a man walking to his death. In his hand he clutched a file, which held a photofit of the Whitley Bay rapist. But they both knew that it was not about Trina McGuire recognising him and helping with their investigation. It was about her furthering Bentley's career. Conrad watched, feeling responsible. If only he hadn't taken the news about the attack to Brady then his boss wouldn't be in this position. He should have known better. He knew Brady better than anyone, knew exactly how he would react. How had he not anticipated that it would go so wrong? Maybe he had come back too soon.

Chapter Fourteen

Brady forced a smile as he approached DI Bentley. Bentley on the other hand did not even pretend to be civil.

He was clearly pissed off.

Brady looked at Bentley. He'd seen him countless times before and had made a point of avoiding him. The man was in his mid-forties and surprisingly good looking – something he was known to use to his advantage. He was precisely the same height as Brady. But that was where the similarities ended. Bentley's cropped, sandy-coloured hair was rapidly receding but it somehow added to his strong cheek-bones and jaw-line. However, it was his startlingly light blue eyes that caught people's attention. They had a profound intensity about them; as if they could see straight into your soul. Bentley made a point of pulling down the crisp, white cuffs of his shirt. He was impeccably dressed and he knew it. He was a man with taste – expensive tastes. His dark suit had been tailored and it looked the part. He was used to being treated with respect. And he wore clothes befitting a man of his rank. It was clear from his dismissive glance at Brady's attire that he couldn't understand how Brady had made it into the police, let alone to Detective Inspector.

'Why you, Brady?' Bentley asked. His voice was deep and deliberate. 'Why the fuck would she want to talk to you?'

'You tell me.'

'Don't fuck around with me.' His delivery was slow and threatening.

The uniform guarding Trina McGuire's private room made a point of staring rigidly at the blank wall ahead. But his young face was flushed with embarrassment.

Brady resisted saying anything. Better that than saying something he would regret.

Where the fuck are you, Conrad?

He needed Conrad here. His deputy was good at these situations, unlike Brady.

'She does know that you want the conversation recorded? Otherwise, I'm not sure this is entirely legal.'

Bentley looked for a moment as if he was going to grab Brady and throw him back against the wall. It was clear that he wasn't used to being challenged. Least of all by someone like Brady. But Bentley reined it in.

'I don't give a shit what you think. I don't trust you, Brady. And I certainly don't trust you to tell me what it is she'll only tell you. The fact she can't say it to either myself or a member of my team makes me highly suspicious.'

'Maybe she's asked to talk to me because she knows I'm not some judgemental, career-obsessed copper who wouldn't piss on her if she was on fire,' Brady said. 'Trina McGuire is more than just a beat-up prostitute. Far more than that.'

'My heart bleeds. What are you, her fucking probation officer?'

Brady resisted telling Bentley to go fuck himself. But unfortunately, the 'fuck you' look in his eyes spoke volumes.

'Unless you want me to report you to your boss for obstructing a major drugs investigation, one that's been approved by Detective Chief Superintendent O'Donnell himself, I suggest you do what I ask,' Bentley advised in a relaxed tone, letting Brady know that he had him over a barrel.

Without a word, Brady took the small Sony tape machine and turned and walked down the corridor to Trina McGuire's room. Better that, than smacking Bentley in the teeth.

'Sir,' the young uniform said, immediately stepping out of Brady's way.

He didn't need to have witnessed the altercation between the two senior officers to know that Brady was ready to punch someone and he wanted to make sure he was well and truly out of shot.

Brady braced himself. He needed to get rid of the anger he felt at Bentley's bully-boy tactics before he went in to see Trina McGuire. He knocked tentatively on the door before opening it. She was clearly not in a position to answer but he at least wanted her to know that someone was walking in.

'It's DI Brady, Jack Brady,' he greeted her as he closed the door behind him. His voice was low and respectful.

She didn't respond.

Brady's fingers nervously gripped the recording device he was holding. In his other hand he held the file with the photofit of the serial rapist. The only thing going through his mind was that this whole Bentley set-up was farcical. He couldn't believe he was actually doing this, but then he had no choice.

But the last thing he wanted was for her to talk. Not if she was going to implicate anyone close to him. He would rather have that information off-the-record and deal with it in his own way. Apart from Chief Superintendent O'Donnell, no one on the job knew that he had a brother. Let alone a brother who was an ex-SAS private bodyguard. Brady was certain that Trina wanted to disclose some information about Nick. He knew she would do anything to protect him – including asking to talk to Brady. He needed to know what kind of trouble Nick was in first, then he would figure out what to do.

He walked over to her.

The tubes had been removed from her throat, which was a good sign. But her face was a brutal mess. It looked worse than it had when he'd seen her earlier with Conrad.

Brady sat down in the visitor's chair by the head of the bed. He dragged his hand back through his hair nervously as he looked at her. She appeared to be asleep. But he couldn't be too sure as one of her eyes was hidden behind bandages and given the puffiness of the other one, it was difficult to tell whether she could even see.

He cleared his throat before speaking: 'Trina, it's DI Jack Brady. I was told that you wanted to talk to me about who did this to you?'

She moaned slightly in response as she attempted to turn her head. He realised that she could see him – just.

He placed the recording device down on the bedside cabinet. She caught sight of it, which was Brady's intention. If Bentley wanted their conversation recorded then so be it. But Brady was not going to hide it from her.

He took a minute to compose himself. He didn't know what to say to her. He knew that the last thing she would want was his pity. She still had some pride. But she was in a desperate state and it killed him to have to be the one to witness it. He was grateful that Nick was not here to see it – or Nicoletta. He didn't know what she would make of the woman who effectively risked her own life to save her lying in intensive care beaten to within an inch of her life. Trina McGuire had had a cruel life that had failed to deliver anything but misery and pain. She had been used and abused by everyone and the last thing Brady wanted to do was add to the list.

He cleared his throat again. The dry air in the room catching the back of it.

'Trina, I've brought a photofit of a suspect and I would appreciate it if you could take a look and see if this is the man who attacked you.'

She automatically turned her head away from him. It was clear that she was not going to identify her attacker for fear of reprisals. After all, he had already left her as good as dead.

Brady frowned as he dragged his hand back through his hair again. He assumed that she had read the article in yesterday's *Northern Echo*, which had named him as the SIO in charge of the serial rape investigation. It was a good ploy. It gave her a credible reason for talking to him instead of DI Bentley. But

Brady was certain that this had nothing to do with his investigation. Instead, he believed that he was only here because she had crucial information that could affect Nick.

'Trina? If you could just look at it for me? Please?' Brady asked as he held it up for her.

Nothing.

'Trina?'

'It's not him,' she croaked without looking at it.

Brady noticed the tears sliding out of her bloodshot eye.

'Take another look. Just to be absolutely certain,' Brady suggested. His voice was low and gentle as if he were talking to a child.

Trina McGuire shook her head.

'Trina? Please?'

She turned her head in his direction. Her look was of abject resignation. The feistiness that Trina McGuire was known for was gone, replaced by a depressed acceptance. Whoever had done this to her had kicked out whatever fight she had left.

Brady held the photofit up in front of her in a last-ditch attempt at getting her to look at it. She automatically closed her eye.

'Trina?'

More tears slid down her battered face.

'It looks like him. But no . . . it's not him,' she answered, her croaky voice barely audible.

'What do you mean?'

'He was tall and shaven-headed like the bloke in your photo. But it's not him.'

'Trina, are you certain it wasn't him?'

'Yes,' she whispered as she turned her head to the wall.

'Trina? Can you take another look at his face?'

She refused to look.

'Can you give me more of a description?'

She shook her head.

'It was too dark. It happened too fast. He grabbed me from behind. I . . . I . . . couldn't see . . .' she faltered.

Brady waited a moment to let her get her thoughts together. He hated doing this to her. She had already been through enough without him interrogating her as if she were the guilty party.

'Look, Trina . . . I'm really sorry about this. About what happened to you . . .' Brady was unsure what to say without sounding trite. 'But I need to know more than you're telling me. You say that the man who attacked you looks like the suspect in the photofit? Is that correct?'

Trina nodded weakly.

'But what makes you so certain it wasn't him?'

'He was older. Older than the rapist you're looking for.'

'How old was he?'

She stared at the ceiling as she thought about it.

'I dunno? Maybe in his mid-thirties? It was dark. Too dark to really tell.'

Brady wasn't surprised that she didn't identify her attacker from the photofit. He was certain that it wasn't the same man as the one responsible for the series of rapes in Whitley Bay. But what did shock him was that she described her attacker as physically similar to the serial rapist – apart from being older.

'Trina? Are you absolutely certain that it's not the same man?'

'Just go, will you. Leave me alone,' Trina replied.

Brady waited.

'Go!'

'Trina, you asked to see me. Remember? You had something you wanted to tell me?'

'Yeah? Well I was mistaken. Just leave, will you?'

Brady didn't understand why she had asked to speak to him if she didn't want his help.

'All right, Trina, I'm leaving. OK?'

Brady stood up and picked up the Sony tape recorder. He switched it off. He wasn't sure what Bentley would make of it.

Not that he cared. It looked like they had both lost out here. Neither one of them had anything. Whether Trina McGuire could actually help either of their investigations was another matter.

'Look, if there's anything you remember, just ask for me.'

Brady put the recording device in his pocket and turned to leave.

'He . . . he wanted Nick,' Trina began.

Brady stopped and turned back.

'What?' He realised that she had been waiting for him to turn off the tape before she would talk.

'He wanted me to tell him where Nick was . . . That's why he did this to me,' she said, raising her bandaged wrist.

'Nick's name. I had the tattoo done after . . . after . . . You know. Everything he did for me . . . for Nicoletta and the other girls.'

Brady was speechless. He realised that his gut feeling had been right; that her attack had been connected to Nick. But the reality made him feel as if he had been punched in the stomach. He felt physically sick that someone could do this to her because of Nick – his own brother.

He looked at her. He didn't know what to say. Part of him felt guilty that her attack was connected to his brother. And part of him felt a great sadness at the unrequited love she still clearly felt for Nick. So much so she had ended up at the hands of some maniac who had a score to settle with him. But her loyalty was unquestionable. If she had known where he was, she would never have said. Brady knew that even if he asked her about Nick, she wouldn't talk.

'Why? Why hurt you like this?' Brady asked.

She looked up at him and attempted to speak but nothing came out.

'Here . . . have some water,' Brady said, offering her the half-filled tumbler of water on the bedside cabinet.

She nodded gratefully as he gently guided the straw into her lips so she could drink.

When she was finished he put the plastic tumbler back on the bedside cabinet beside the plastic container of lukewarm water. There were no flowers or get well cards on the unit. Not that Brady had expected there to be, but for some reason the starkness still affected him.

'Trina? What has Nick done for someone to hurt you like this?'

He had no choice but to ask, despite dreading the answer.

She looked at him. She was scared. But Brady didn't know whether her fear was for Nick's safety or her own.

'I don't know. I don't know what he's done.'

A chill went down Brady's spine. It was the first honest response he'd had from her.

'But you've got to warn him. Warn him before he gets to him. What he did to me is nothing compared to what he said he would do to Nick.'

Brady nodded. It was the best he could do because he couldn't guarantee he would be able to warn him. He still couldn't get hold of him and right now, Brady wasn't entirely sure whether that meant they'd already found Nick. And if they had ... then ... Brady couldn't bring himself to think about it.

He made a move to leave. He knew he'd run out of time. Bentley was no fool. He would be timing how long Brady had been in there against the length of the recording.

Before he left there was one final question he needed to ask. He needed to be absolutely certain before he walked out.

'The photofit. Are you absolutely certain this was not the man who attacked you?'

Without looking at him, she nodded.

'It's not him.'

'What about your attacker? Clothes, smell? What about his voice – was he local?'

'I ... I don't know ... It was dark and ... I couldn't see him properly.'

'Trina?'

She looked at him.

'Did you know him?'

Brady watched as she turned her head away. But before she did there was no mistaking the fear in her eyes.

There was nothing he could do about it. No amount of persuasion was going to make her talk. Whether she actually knew her attacker was a moot point. If she did, she definitely wasn't going to say anything. Whether it was fear for her own life or Nick's, Brady couldn't say.

The only detail that she did divulge troubled him. Was she playing him? Trying to throw him off the scent of who had actually attacked her? It was an easy out to simply state that her attacker looked similar to the man they were after apart from one crucial detail – his age.

Brady came out of the room and walked straight into Bentley.

He threw the tape recorder at him. Bentley caught it with ease.

'Enjoy,' Brady said as he walked straight past him.

'Did she mention Madley?'

'It's all on the tape,' Brady answered without turning back.

'Did she ID the photofit?' Bentley asked.

Brady looked at him, unable to hide his disdain. 'No.'

'Pity. I reckon we would've made a good team. Maybe she'll open up to me when I interview her later. I'm pretty good with her sort. She lives by a different set of values. You've just got to give her an incentive to make her talk.'

Brady resisted the urge to wipe the smug expression off Bentley's face. Instead, he turned his back on Bentley to leave. If he didn't, he wouldn't be responsible for his actions.

Conrad suddenly appeared at the bottom of the corridor.

'Thank fuck!' Brady muttered under his breath.

'You took your time,' Brady said when he reached him.

Conrad was about to reply but after seeing Bentley he decided against it. He waited until they had left ICU before talking.

'Is everything all right, sir?'

'Couldn't be better,' Brady answered.

'Did she say anything?'

'It's not what she said, Conrad. It's what she didn't say.'

Conrad frowned at Brady's cryptic remark. But he knew not to ask what he meant. Brady would tell him in his own time – if at all.

Chapter Fifteen

It was late afternoon. Brady was keenly aware that the day hadn't unfolded as he had planned. He was now about to go into the briefing that had been scheduled for that morning. He had let go of all thoughts of Madley and his brother, Nick. He had other things on his mind now. But what troubled Brady wasn't what Trina McGuire had said. It was the look of fear in her eyes that had betrayed her. The question going through his mind was did she know her attacker? And if she did, why wasn't she talking?

Brady walked into the Incident Room. It was a large bright room that could comfortably hold up to thirty officers if required. Despite the two substantial sash windows, the over-head fluorescent light was switched on to counteract the grey drizzle outside. The daylight had evaporated, replaced by a shadowy bleakness. It was October so what else did Brady expect? A large whiteboard dominated one wall. It was covered in photographs and Brady's scrawled writing. Desk stations had been set up at one end of the room where the team were able to sort through whatever information and leads came in. A phone rang out bleakly on one of the desks but the call was lost amongst the light-hearted banter being traded around the table. The team were relaxed – too relaxed in Brady's mind. They were sitting drinking coffee or water around the large conference table in the centre of the room. As yet, they hadn't noticed Brady. The atmosphere was casual as talk turned to the weekend and arrangements they had made, or were going to make. No one seemed bothered about the reason they were there. Instead they had already checked out. It was a late Friday afternoon; yet another day had slipped away and they were still no further forward with the investigation.

Brady slammed the door of the Incident Room. The banter immediately ceased. He hadn't intended to shut it so forcefully but it had the desired effect; he now had everyone's attention.

'I'm sorry about the delay,' Brady apologised as he walked over to the table. 'I'm sure you all had better things to do than wait around for me.'

The atmosphere in the room suddenly changed. It became awkward and stifling.

Brady caught Dr Amelia Jenkins's eye. He could tell that she knew something was wrong. After all, she had been his shrink for a while. That had been eighteen months ago when his life had unravelled, plummeting downwards at a breakneck speed. Claudia, his then wife, had caught him in bed with his junior colleague, Simone. Not that he had realised at the time. She had literally walked in and then out of his life. The following night he was shot in the thigh, too close for comfort to his balls, on an undercover drugs bust in North Shields. To say he had issues was putting it mildly. So, he was assigned the police shrink to help him get over the car wreck that his life had become.

Amelia Jenkins had spent the first six weeks after Brady had been shot trying to sort his head out. He had insisted all he needed was a couple of bottles of scotch and a divorce lawyer but she wanted to try the more professional method. In the end she gave up. She was into the 'talking cure' – which had become a problem given Brady's refusal to talk.

Amelia had originally worked with the force as a forensic psychologist. But for some reason she had turned to practising clinical psychology instead. Brady presumed something had shaken her to her core. But Gates knew Amelia from old and had asked her to work on an investigation. Surprisingly, she had agreed. That had been over a year ago and she was still here.

Brady needed to talk to her. Go over Trina McGuire's reaction to the photofit of the rapist. It didn't make sense to him and since she was the team's forensic psychologist he wanted her take on it. But from the evidence he had seen, Trina McGuire's attack wasn't the handiwork of their rapist.

Brady watched, momentarily mesmerised, as Amelia tucked her sleek, black, razor-sharp bobbed hair behind her ear. It refused to stay and obstinately fell back against her flushed cheeks. She was only in her early thirties, with a career that was going somewhere – and fast. Added to that, she had a fatal combination of intelligence and uniqueness about her. But that was what scared Brady. He was attracted to Amelia, there was no doubt about that, but at the same time he didn't want to risk their professional relationship. Or was he making excuses? He wasn't sure whether it was because he still had feelings for Claudia. Or maybe it was the fear that whenever something good came into his life, he inevitably destroyed it.

Amelia's dark, almond-shaped eyes studied Brady. She frowned slightly. She knew from the look in his eye that something was wrong. Lately, she had spent a lot of time with him. Whether it was because Conrad had been off on sick leave and she had been an easy replacement, she couldn't say. However, in that time she'd got to know him quite well. Not as well as she would have liked. But she was still hopeful that he would take her up on the drink she had suggested. That was six months ago and she was still waiting for an answer.

Brady turned from Amelia and looked around the table at the rest of his team. There was only a handful of them. But it was enough. He trusted every one of them.

His eyes fell on Tom Harvey, the oldest member of the team. He was not the kind of Detective Sergeant to waste time with small talk. Still unmarried, despite some desperate attempts, and fast approaching his late forties. He was an average looking, stocky bloke who dressed in a dark M&S suit with a pale blue shirt and matching tie. His light brown hair was cropped short in an attempt to minimise the spreading flecks of grey. His jaw was severely shaven with telling razor nicks. But he was getting old. It was hard not to notice the widening waist-line or the double chin that had developed over the last year. Harvey's downfall, like a lot of coppers of his generation, was the pub. He liked a pint. Or if Brady was honest, Harvey liked more than one pint. He had an unquenchable thirst and a reputation for always being the last man standing at the end of a night. But Brady had known Harvey for years now and still had a lot of time for him.

His gaze drifted over to DC Kodovesky, who was sitting next to Harvey; she was the youngest member of the group and Harvey's partner. They made a good team. A fact that still surprised him.

Kodovesky kept herself to herself. Unlike Harvey, she did not socialise with the other coppers. She was the new generation – clean-cut and career obsessed. She came in, did the job and then went home. Always the first one in and the last one out. Brady admired her dedication and determination. She knew where she wanted to be, which was sitting behind the DCI's desk. Her long black hair was pulled back in a tight ponytail. She never deviated from this harsh, perfunctory look. It was the same with her clothes. Professional yet practical: a black polo neck top with black pinstriped trousers and low-heeled black boots. In all the time she had been stationed at Whitley Bay, Brady had never known Kodovesky to wear a skirt or make-up. Not that she needed either. But he knew she was making a point. After all, she was a woman in her late twenties trying to make a career for herself in a male-dominated police force. Consequently she had more to prove than her colleagues. Brady assumed this was why she always had an air of detachment about her. It was simply a case of self-preservation in a testosterone-fuelled environment. She had heard about the reason for DC Simone Henderson's sudden transfer to the Met. They all had. And the last thing Kodovesky wanted was to repeat Henderson's mistake. Kodovesky was too professional and too aware of the potential repercussions for her career to let herself fall foul of becoming involved with a colleague, especially a senior officer.

Brady's eyes glanced over to Conrad, sitting opposite Kodovesky. He was very much the male version of Kodovesky, a few years on. He was clean-cut, handsome and dependable. His life was the job. So much so that Brady worried about him. Conrad kept whatever personal life he had to himself. Brady knew part of it. But that was only because he had worked with Conrad for so long. At times, private calls inevitably ended up being overheard. Brady had picked up a couple of clues about Conrad's private life. It was enough for him not to ask about it. Better that Conrad came out and told him than to speculate. But there was no one else that Brady would have assigned to him. Conrad was Conrad and in Brady's eyes he was irreplaceable.

Brady turned to Daniels and Kenny, the other two DCs making up the team. Both in their early thirties. Unlike Conrad and Kodovesky, they were not graduates. Nor were they focused on fast-tracking. The two of them enjoyed the job, but not enough to let it take over their lives. Their talk revolved around three subjects outside work: football, drinking and women. In that exact order. In all the time Brady had known them it had never varied. Not once. They were Geordie blokes and proud of it.

Daniels was well-built at five foot eleven – a testament to long hours at the gym. Good looking in a hard way, with his hair shaved so close to his scalp that you could only just make out that his hair was sandy blonde. He had hazel eyes that were normally filled with mirth, and a strong, determined jaw. Women liked him and he knew it and abused it.

He and Kenny were inseparable: best mates on the job, best mates off. Kenny was tall, with short, curly dark brown hair. His face with his deep-set, mischievous brown eyes was already heavily lined. What he lacked in looks he made up for by being a comedian. Brady would constantly find himself telling Kenny to rein it in. But he knew that Kenny's macabre sense of humour was his way of dealing with the atrocities that they faced. Not that Kenny was unusual. Brady knew a lot of coppers and scenes of crime officers who wouldn't miss the opportunity to come out with a sick one-liner at the expense of the deceased. But Brady was in no doubt that being a copper suited Kenny.

As it did every person on the team.

Brady was aware that no one was speaking. The air was tense. Even DC Kenny and DC Daniels were motionless. Both averting their eyes from Brady's penetrating gaze.

As were DS Harvey and DC Kodovesky.

Even Conrad was studying his coffee.

'All right. Who's going to tell me what's wrong?'

Conrad looked up at Brady.

'You might want to take a seat,' Conrad advised.

'Why?'

'It's about Trina McGuire,' Conrad explained.

The look on Conrad's face was serious.

Brady took a seat, fearing the worst. 'Go on,' he instructed not taking his eyes off Conrad.

'I think you should watch this first, sir,' Conrad recommended. 'I've just recorded it.'

He turned and switched on the flat screen TV against the wall.

It took a moment for Brady to register what Conrad wanted him to watch.

'What the—' Brady stopped himself short before adding 'fuck'.

It was Bentley. And he was on the local five o'clock news being interviewed about the attack in North Shields the previous night.

'What has this got to do with us?' Brady asked as he turned on Conrad.

'Just listen,' Conrad advised. His tone was calm and non-combative, despite the fact that Brady probably looked as if he wanted to punch some sense into him.

'Turn it up then,' Brady instructed. Not that he actually wanted to hear to it. But he obviously had no choice.

He listened as Bentley gave a brief about Trina McGuire's attack. He named the location and the approximate time of the attack. He obviously didn't disclose the victim's name. But he did say something that made Brady sit back, winded.

'Rewind it! I said rewind it, Conrad!' barked Brady.

He was trying to control the anger coursing through his body as it rewound, aware that all eyes were on him.

Conrad pressed play and waited.

'We are looking into the possibility that this attack might be connected to a series of sexual attacks that have taken place in Whitley Bay over the last two months. Obviously we are treating this very seriously and are liaising with the investigating team dealing with the previous rapes.' Bentley paused for effect as he looked straight into the camera.

Brady felt for a moment as if Bentley was looking straight at him. Mocking him.

He cleared his throat before continuing: 'A silver saloon taxi stopped briefly outside the Ballarat pub. He waited for a minute or so before driving off down Borough Road. This was witnessed by our victim at approximately at ten thirty p.m. yesterday evening. Shortly afterwards she was subjected to a brutal and violent sexual attack in which she has sustained significant injuries. This taxi driver might have seen something that could help with our enquiries and we would appreciate it if he could come forward. If anyone has any information please contact my team at—'

'All right, switch it off,' Brady ordered. He had seen more than enough.

Conrad did as instructed.

'When did you find out about this?' Brady asked.

He was pissed off. Brady did not like being the last to be informed. More so since he was the SIO in charge of the team.

'I just got a call five minutes ago about it,' Conrad answered sheepishly. 'Otherwise I would have told you in private, sir.'

Brady sat back in his seat. He couldn't believe what Bentley had just done. He had no authority to make such a statement. Let alone to make it public. He tried to compose himself. He had no choice. He had a team of people sitting here waiting for his take on Bentley's public territorial pissing.

'I don't know what the fuck Bentley is playing at, but our rapist didn't attack Trina McGuire,' Brady said. It was an honest statement and he believed it.

But he could tell from the reaction on his team's faces that they weren't so sure. Brady had to accept that Bentley was very convincing. He was a charismatic speaker – not that Brady had personally experienced it – and he used his charm arsenal, in particular his expressive, startling, bright blue eyes to great effect. The stylish suit, the strong, trustworthy, handsome features and the deep, slow voice worked a treat. At least it had done on Brady's team. And if Bentley had convinced them that Trina McGuire had been raped and assaulted by the same person they were supposed to be tracking down, who knows what the public, let alone Brady's superiors would make of it. In particular, DCI Gates.

Chapter Sixteen

Brady pushed his chair back and stood up. He was too agitated, too wound up to remain seated. He got up and walked over to the whiteboard. Details of all three rape victims were laid out bare. Brady cast his eye over the victims' oblivious, smiling faces. He then studied the photographs of the crime scenes where the first two girls had been raped.

The first victim, Sarah Jeffries, had recently returned from a three-month trip travelling across Thailand, Indonesia and Australia. She was a petite girl for nineteen with no weight to her. Whether she was naturally underweight or travelling had taken its toll on her body, Brady wasn't sure. But he knew one thing – she was the ideal first victim. They knew from all three victims' statements that the rapist was tall, at least six foot, and muscular. Sarah Jeffries' small-framed body didn't stand a chance. But if there was one small mercy, at least she was the first victim, which meant that she didn't suffer the extent of injuries endured by the following victims.

The rapist had seized his opportunity as she had drunkenly made her way home at 3:00 a.m. on a Saturday morning after clubbing in Whitley. For whatever reason she had ended up walking home alone. It was as she had turned up by the boarded-up eighties pub, Whiskey Bends, that he had grabbed her and dragged her into the back alley behind the disused building. It was the ideal location to attack someone – dark and deserted. He had bound, gagged and blindfolded her before raping her. He had then stabbed her nine times in her breasts.

Sarah Jeffries, like Anna Lewis, was certain that she had not heard a car. She was convinced he had followed her on foot and had waited until she was walking past Whiskey Bends before making his presence known.

The latest that Brady had heard was that Sarah Jeffries had quit her job as a trainee hairdresser. She was nineteen and terrified. Her life had stopped. Brady hoped that it was only temporary. But he knew that the only way he could help her was to catch the bastard that had destroyed her life.

It was not until the second victim had been attacked five weeks later that they realised they had a serial rapist on the loose. Same MO but the violence had radically escalated. Anna Lewis' attack had lasted substantially longer and was more brutal than the first. She had been assaulted during the early hours of a Sunday morning as she had been walking along the Promenade towards Cullercoats after a night out celebrating a friend's birthday in Whitley Bay. By her own admission she had been drunk. Too drunk to realise what was about to happen. It was as she walked through the unused car park of the abandoned High Point Hotel, a short cut home she had taken countless times before, that the rapist had attacked. At 3:30 a.m. he was guaranteed no witnesses. He had overpowered the tall, heavily built twenty-three-year-old and dragged her round to the back of the deserted building. It was in the shadows, hidden from passersby or prying residents, that he had raped and mutilated her. This time he had not only repeatedly stabbed his victim through both her breasts, he had also taken with him a trophy. A souvenir to remind him of her – her right nipple and the skin surrounding it.

He had left her tied, bound and blindfolded. Bleeding profusely and in shock, she had somehow made her way out from the back of the empty hotel grounds in an attempt to get help. Luckily, an early morning jogger had found her. Once she was discharged from hospital, Anna Lewis' parents had insisted on her staying with them for the foreseeable future until the police had caught the man responsible. Not that Brady could blame them. They had relocated to the Outer Hebrides to get away from the crime-ridden streets of the North-East. Anna, who had been training as a legal secretary, had chosen to remain behind. Now that choice had been taken from her.

Then there was Chloe Winters. To date she was the third and, if Brady had anything to do with it, the last. He had made a promise to all three victims that he would catch the serial rapist. But it was Chloe Winters who had really affected him. What had happened to her was horrific. Beyond anything he had ever seen. And he never wanted to see anything like it again.

Brady glanced at the photographs of the alley where the third victim had been found. Her unconscious and badly mutilated body had been dumped unceremoniously in the back lane behind the eyesore that was the dilapidated and unused Avenue pub.

Details of each victimology had been scrawled on the board. Nothing tied the three victims together. The first victim was petite with medium length curly blonde hair, the second tall, heavy set with short, spiky black hair. Then there was Chloe Winters, medium height and build with long, straight dark blonde hair. It wasn't even as if they all had tattoos. Chloe Winters was the only victim to have one. As far as Brady could make out they were not a 'type' – all very different from one another. Apart from their age. All three victims were comparatively young. If he did have a 'type' then that was it.

They still had no idea where the rapist had held Chloe Winters captive for over forty-eight hours. This troubled Brady. He had somewhere to hide her. She would have screamed out in pain when he tortured her. So why had no one heard anything?

His eyes rested on Winters' breast where the rapist had carved out her intricate tattoo. It had been a labour of love, leaving a startling outline of a wolf's head and wide, roaring teeth where her skin should have been. It was sadism, not the personal rage and anger that had been meted out against Trina McGuire.

So why had Bentley put his neck on the line by claiming there could be a connection between Brady's case and Trina McGuire's? It was clear to even the untrained eye that the same hand wasn't responsible for removing the skin from Trina McGuire's wrist. Her attacker had followed to the letter the article written by Rubenfeld. The *Northern Echo* had reported that the third rape victim had had a tattoo on her body cut out, which had left her requiring extensive skin grafts. But what the article didn't mention was the fact that the offender had actually spent time cutting out the outline of the wolf's head and not just hurriedly slicing the skin around the tattoo, which is what had happened to Trina McGuire.

Brady's thoughts were abruptly interrupted by a cacophony of ringing as Conrad's mobile rang at the same time as two of the phones on the desks began to screech shrilly.

'Answer it,' Brady instructed.

Conrad looked at him. He was unsure which phone Brady wanted silencing.

'The one in your hand, Conrad.'

He then turned to Kenny and Daniels. 'You two, take those calls. Whoever it is, tell them you'll get back to them later and bloody get those phones redirected through to the front desk. You should know to do that when we have a briefing.'

'Sorry sir,' Kenny answered as he scrambled to his feet.

He was quickly followed by Daniels who hared over to his desk.

Brady dragged a hand back through his hair. His head felt as if it was going to explode. The headache from earlier that morning had returned with a vengeance as his mind struggled with the implications of Bentley's public revelation.

Had Trina McGuire identified her attacker from the photofit they had of the Whitley Bay rapist? If so, why hadn't she identified him when Brady showed her the image? It didn't make sense. None of this made any sense.

Brady watched Conrad's expression become taut as he listened to the voice on the other end of his phone.

'Yes, sir,' he answered. 'No, sir. Yes . . . Yes, let me see if I can get hold of him.' He put his phone on mute before turning to Brady.

'Sir? It's Bentley.'

'Tell him I'm busy. If he wanted to talk to me he should have done it before he decided to tell the world we don't know what the fuck we are doing!'

Kodovesky and Harvey suddenly busied themselves with various files in front of them. Even Amelia made a point of checking her emails on her phone.

Conrad's jaw was clenched tight as he looked at Brady.

'Sir?' he asked.

'Actually, give me the phone,' Brady said. 'I'll do it myself!'

Conrad resisted the order. The last thing he wanted was for Brady to lose his head and consequently his job. This was exactly what Bentley wanted. Brady had walked all over Bentley's investigation and now it was payback.

'Phone. Now!'

'I don't think—'

'I'm not asking you to think, Conrad. I am asking you to do as I ordered.'

Brady put out his hand for the phone.

Conrad reluctantly handed it over.

'How do I work this bloody thing?'

'You press that button there, sir. Takes it off mute,' Conrad instructed as he shot Amelia Jenkins a look that implied he needed her to intervene before Brady did something he would regret.

'Jack? Let me deal with this,' Amelia suggested.

Brady's face said it all.

'Please? I need to request all the forensic reports and statements anyway. And I am the forensic psychologist on this investigation so if DI Bentley has any questions concerning our offender I'm sure I can be of assistance. And equally, I think it would be a good idea if I give him my opinion on Trina McGuire's attacker.'

'A little bit late for that, don't you think?' Brady pointed out, unable to keep the caustic tone out of his voice.

'Maybe not. At least, let me try,' she said, getting up from the table and walking over to him.

Brady resisted but he could see from her expression that Amelia was not going to back down. Dr Amelia Jenkins had a way of getting to him. She had a knack of looking too deeply into his eyes and searching – for what, he didn't know. But she was doing that now. That was partly why he had never looked directly at her when they had had their shrink sessions eighteen months before.

'Jack?' she prompted. Her brown eyes held his stubborn gaze.

'Fine. Do it your way.'

He handed the phone over.

Her dark red lips broke into a smile. 'Thanks.'

She turned her back on Brady and headed for the door.

He watched her as she walked away from him. She was wearing one of his favourite outfits – a light-grey cashmere fifties-style dress. She wore it with a thick black belt that accentuated her narrow waist and full hips. Even her black high heels had been chosen with care to perfect her look.

'Yes. Hello, DI Bentley? This is Dr Jenkins.' She paused as she listened to his response. 'No. I'm afraid that DI Brady is tied up right now. But I'm really pleased I've got the chance to talk to you . . . Yes . . . Yes—' Amelia's charming, professional voice disappeared as she walked out into the corridor.

'I'm sorry, sir,' Conrad apologised once Amelia had closed the door to the room.

'Forget it, Conrad.'

'No, I should have known about the turn Bentley's investigation had taken before he went to the press.'

Brady gave him a half-hearted smile.

'Conrad, you've just got back from sick leave for Christ's sake. This is my problem. All right? I've just got to figure out how to deal with it – without losing my temper!'

'Yes, sir,' answered Conrad, relieved that there was no bad feeling between them. He still felt responsible for suggesting to Brady that there could be a connection between Bentley's rape victim and their case. He agreed with Brady that Trina McGuire's attack only bore a crude resemblance to their serial rapist's handiwork. There were too many inconsistencies for it to be the same offender. He was now worried that Bentley was just out to cause trouble for Brady. After all, hadn't Brady walked into Bentley's case without authorisation? Maybe this was Bentley's way of paying Brady back.

Chapter Seventeen

It was Amelia Jenkins who broke the silence.

'That's sorted. DI Bentley will be sending everything he has on Trina McGuire's case ASAP,' she said as she came back into the room.

It took her by surprise that no one was talking.

She gave Brady a questioning look.

He ignored it.

Amelia sat back down opposite him.

'Did he say what led him to believe that Trina McGuire's attack could be connected to ours?' Brady asked, curtailing the cynicism in his voice.

Amelia nodded, surprised by his cold, interrogative tone. 'Same MO,' she answered as casually as possible.

'Says who?' Brady said, unable to keep the incredulity from his voice.

'Bentley.'

'That about sums it up then.'

'He did say that he tried calling you this afternoon to run this past you but couldn't get hold of you,' Amelia said. 'He was profoundly apologetic about you hearing about this second-hand so to speak.'

Brady's expression told her he didn't buy it – not for one second. He knew she was trying to smooth things over between him and Bentley. But it was too late for that.

'Did Bentley say if McGuire positively identified her attacker from the photofit of our rapist?' Brady asked.

He needed to know what Trina's game was – if any.

'I did ask him that,' Amelia replied, refusing to drop eye contact with him. Despite the unusual sternness in his eyes. 'He said Trina McGuire stated that her attacker looked similar to the suspect in the photofit.'

'And that was good enough for Bentley to go on the news and suggest that she's been raped by the same man who's attacked three women in Whitley Bay?'

'That, and the MO,' Amelia reminded him. 'But remember, Bentley never actually committed himself. He just said there's a possibility it could be the same offender.'

'Yeah, how could I forget that crucial detail? Maybe the same way Bentley crucially forgot our serial rapist's MO. Whatever fancy way Bentley tries to dress it up, Trina McGuire's injuries are very different from the ones sustained by our three victims.'

He knew he was being belligerent, but he couldn't help himself.

So, Bentley, what the fuck happened to pinning Trina McGuire's attack on Madley?

Brady couldn't figure it out. He knew he was being played. But to what end?

Amelia studied him.

As did the rest of the team. The spat between the forensic psychologist and their boss had not gone unnoticed.

'Why are you so convinced it's not the same offender?' Amelia asked.

Her voice was as level and calm as always. Nothing seemed to unnerve her. Not even witnessing Brady acting in this way.

'How long have you got?' Brady asked as he looked her in the eye.

She held his gaze, her eyes filled with genuine concern.

Brady wasn't sure whether the concern was for him or the team. Nobody knew at that moment whether the case would suddenly be assigned to Bentley's team at North Shields station. After all, he had been the one to make a very public press release.

'All night, if need be,' Amelia answered. And she meant it.

She turned to the rest of the team. 'I don't know what the rest of you think, but I'm prepared to work through this until we have something more conclusive.'

No one voiced an objection, but Brady was certain that inwardly they would be cursing the sudden loss of their Friday night. Their shift was supposed to end at 6:00 p.m. Exactly the time the briefing was scheduled to conclude. Not that Brady would have been clocking off then. He already had plans to stay most of the night to go over the victim statements and forensic reports to see if he'd missed anything. But the difference was that he was the acting officer and as such, it was expected that he put in over and above the hours detailed in his contract.

Brady was grateful to Amelia. She had a way of steering people and getting them to agree to something that ordinarily they would have opposed.

'Thanks,' Brady said, the relief evident in his voice. 'Chinese take-out's on me later. And if we manage it, a couple of rounds at the Fat Ox.'

But Brady knew he was being hopeful in suggesting that they might be finished before last orders. There was a hell of a lot he needed them to do. And the first thing was putting as many holes as possible in Bentley's theory that the Whitley Bay serial rapist had strayed into North Shields – his territory. Brady knew that Trina McGuire had not been attacked and raped by the same suspect his team were trying to apprehend. She had her own reasons for wasting Bentley's time. But the last thing Brady wanted was the public being misinformed. There were two rapists out there – not one. And they were very different. The public needed to know that for their own safety. Brady wasn't interested in Bentley, or his reasons for the course of action he had taken. Maybe Bentley still believed that the assault was a drugs-connected crime. Perhaps this was his way of disarming Madley. Or maybe it was simpler than that? Maybe Bentley had a score to settle with Brady and this was all a ruse.

Whatever Bentley's reasons, Brady did not want to see Trina McGuire's attacker have the opportunity to disappear. Let alone strike again.

Chapter Eighteen

'All right, Conrad,' Brady began.

Conrad looked at him. He already had his notebook out ready to take whatever Brady threw at him.

'I want everything that Bentley has on the Trina McGuire case. And I mean absolutely every little detail. I know Bentley promised Amelia that he'll pass what he has on to her but I want you on top of this. I've already requested this information twice and for some reason I still haven't received it. What about your contact at North Shields, are they actually part of Bentley's team?'

Conrad nodded. 'Yes, sir.'

'Good. Use them if you can. We need to make sure that Bentley's not fobbing us off with filtered information.

'I want photographs of Trina McGuire's injuries. In particular, photos of the injury to her wrist and inner arm. I want them sent with the photographs of Chloe Winters' injuries and Anna Lewis' to Jed ASAP. I need those images digitally enhanced and back to us tonight. And tell him I don't give a fuck that it's late Friday afternoon – this is urgent.'

Jed was Northumbria's computer forensic officer. He was one of the best. But slashed budgets had seen his workload double.

'As soon as he comes back with the images I want them sent across to whichever forensic scientist is available to us. And tell them I need a quick turnaround on this now Bentley is involved.'

Brady was certain that Trina McGuire's wounds were different. But it would take a forensic scientist specialising in knife wounds to ascertain if it was the same perpetrator, or the same implement. Even knowing whether the wounds were carried out by a left- or right-handed person was crucial.

Conrad nodded. 'Will do, sir.'

'Daniels and Kenny,' Brady began. He watched as they prepared themselves for the worst. 'You two are going to be revisiting the CCTV footage from the nights the victims were attacked and in particular the evening Chloe Winters was abducted. Check every piece of footage, particularly along the Promenade where the clubs are,' Brady instructed. 'Anything, and I mean anything, no matter how incidental, you report it to me.'

Kenny suddenly folded his arms and slouched back against his chair at the magnitude of the work they had been given.

'But we've been through that CCTV footage three times already,' Daniels complained, unwilling to accept their fate.

Brady's dark expression said it all. He was not impressed at having his orders queried.

'If it takes you ten more times analysing that bloody footage, you'll do it. Understand? This isn't the bogeyman we're dealing with here. Or some bloody ghostly apparition that just materialises out of thin air, attacks our victims and then evaporates. He's there in those tapes. He has to be. We're just not seeing it.'

Despite the sullen, pissed-off look in his eyes, Daniels kept quiet. He knew not to push Brady. They all did.

This was the job – sitting around and checking records, CCTV footage, cross-referencing details. The majority of the time it was downright time-consuming and boring. If Kenny and Daniels had joined the force thinking it was going to resemble *The Sweeney*, they were sadly mistaken.

Brady finally turned to Harvey and Kodovesky.

'I know we've already done this but I want you two to go over the information we have on the bartenders and bouncers in the clubs and pubs in South Parade and the Promenade again. In particular, I want you to focus your energies on the Blue Lagoon nightclub. We're missing something. These attacks have spanned two months now. Even if it's something as coincidental as a bouncer or bartender starting work within the last year, inform me. The last thing I believe in is coincidence. The problem we have is that our offender is right here – in Whitley Bay,' Brady said as he jabbed the table with his right forefinger. 'He's right under our noses but for some reason we're not seeing him. So, it's time to up our game and put the pressure on. Starting with the Blue Lagoon.'

Conrad couldn't contain his surprise at Brady's request.

It hadn't gone unnoticed by Brady, but now was not the time to explain his decision. Not here in front of the rest of the team.

If Bentley was investigating Madley, Brady would make sure that his team trampled all over his career-enhancing, under-cover operation. He knew that was guaranteed to piss Bentley off. And there was nothing he could do about it. Brady was merely chasing up his own leads. Then there was the business card advertising the Blue Lagoon left at the crime scene where Trina McGuire was attacked. That was something that troubled him. Whether Madley was being set up, Brady had no idea. But that was the least of his concerns right now.

But this wasn't just about pissing off Bentley. Brady needed to publicly cover his back. He did not want any allegations levied at him that he was biased. That he was protecting Madley. He had no choice but to make sure the same, if not even more extensive, checks were carried out on the Blue Lagoon staff.

'You're not serious are you, Jack? This will take us all week-end,' Harvey said, taken aback.

Conrad shot him a look.

'Sorry, I mean, sir,' Harvey corrected, as he stared straight at Conrad.

Brady knew that old habits died hard. Harvey and Brady had shared the same rank for years and during that time had developed a strong friendship. It'd felt odd for both of them when Brady had become the boss. But over time they had got used to it and found a way of balancing their friendship with the imbalance in their professional relationship. Not that Harvey would have wanted Brady's job. He had made it clear that he didn't want the politics or the responsibility that came with it. Brady understood his reasons. He would not wish his job on anyone. Especially at this precise moment.

He sighed heavily as he looked at Harvey.

'Look, I hate to state the obvious but we're running out of time. It won't be long before he attacks again. So we need to do everything we can to try and find him. And if that means working through this entire weekend then that's what we'll do.'

'So, you really think Bentley's got it wrong? That the rape last night isn't connected to the ones we're working on?' Harvey asked, confused.

'Yes. Which is why I just said we're up against the wire here because I guarantee that he'll strike for a fourth time any night now.'

Harvey didn't look convinced. Whether it was the fact that it was the end of a long week and he just wanted to go home or Bentley's public stunt had persuaded him otherwise, Brady was unsure.

'Despite what DI Bentley has said, Trina McGuire's rape couldn't be more different from our three victims,' Brady said as a means of appeasing Harvey. 'What do you think, Dr Jenkins?'

'I'm sorry, I can't comment yet. I'm not up-to-date on her case,' Amelia answered. It was honest and direct.

Brady nodded. He should have known better than to ask her to offer an opinion when she hadn't been fully briefed.

'OK. Forgive me if I'm not as eloquent as Dr Jenkins here but I'll give it a go. There are three main types of rapes committed: power, anger and sadistic rape. Nicholas Groth, a leading expert in this field, states that fifty-five per cent are power rapists, forty per cent are anger rapists and five per cent are sadistic rapists.' Brady paused for a moment as he caught Amelia's eye. It had momentarily thrown her. She looked both surprised and impressed at what he'd just said.

Brady cleared his throat before he continued: 'I would say that Trina McGuire's assailant was clearly an anger rapist. An anger rapist is about physical brutality. This kind of rape is based on conscious anger and rage. The rapist's intention is to hurt and debase his victim and he'll do this through verbally abusing her, beating her and then, finally raping her. Always remember, this is not about sex. It's about absolute debasement and humiliation. Sex is a weapon that the rapist uses to defile, degrade and humiliate his victim. This is precisely the kind of rape that Trina McGuire was subjected to.' Brady stopped for a moment, expecting questions. But there were none.

Brady nodded. 'OK. With regards to our other rape victims we are dealing with a sadist. He eroticises power and anger, taking great pleasure in his victims' suffering as he tortures them. The sadistic rapist often has a bizarre or ritualistic trait, which we clearly see exhibited with the three rapes we have here. In particular with the last victim, Chloe Winters. Sadistic rapists have a penchant for mutilating their victims' sexual areas. All three victims' breasts were mutilated. This isn't the case with Trina McGuire,' Brady said, looking at Harvey. He was intentionally labouring the point so that his team were under no illusions that the two investigations were actually linked.

'Chloe Winters also had most of the skin on her upper chest removed.'

Some of the team shifted their eyes over to the whiteboard to photographs of the victim.

'The skin removed from her right breast had been tattooed some months earlier. As you know we have taken statements from the owner of the studio where Chloe Winters had the work done and we ran checks against his two employees and his clients. But nothing unusual came up.'

'Conrad was telling me that Trina McGuire had skin removed from the inside of her wrist and lower arm,' Harvey said.

Brady looked at him. Tom Harvey was like a dog with a bone once he got an idea in his head.

'You're right, Tom. But the difference is our offender exhibits both sexual mutilation and ritualistic qualities. As for Trina McGuire, I hardly think her lower arm constitutes a sexual area, do you? Unless you have some strange fetish that you want to share with us?' Brady asked.

'No, sir,' Harvey muttered as he tried to ignore his burning cheeks.

Kenny and Daniels couldn't stop themselves from bursting into laughter.

'I always wondered why all those Internet dates you've had never worked out,' Kenny sniggered with a cruel glint in his eye. 'What? You don't know your arse from your elbow, eh? Or is it, you don't know their bits from their tits?'

'Thanks, Kenny. I think we've got the picture,' Brady interrupted before the conversation slipped even further.

Amelia shot Kenny an acerbic look that told him to grow up. But it was lost on him as he sat elbowing Daniels.

'Did Trina McGuire have a tattoo removed as well then?' Harvey asked, attempting to move the conversation on.

'Yes,' Brady answered. He had no choice but to be honest. Bentley had already found out that the skin cut from Trina McGuire's wrist had been tattooed.

'What was it?' Harvey questioned.

Brady could see it in his eyes. He was still belligerently hanging on to the hope that there could be some merit in Bentley's assertion that Trina's attack could be connected.

Brady shrugged. 'I don't know.'

It was easier to lie. If Brady had told the truth then awkward questions might be asked – especially if Bentley and his team had no idea that the tattoo was NICK – his brother's name. Whether Trina McGuire had told them, or would tell them, was her call. He knew that she was protecting Nick, so he highly doubted that she would inform them the actual identity behind the name tattooed on her wrist. Too many questions would be asked.

'Focusing on what we do know, all three of our rape victims had been bound and blindfolded before he tortured them. Same MO with all three. But we see evidence with Anna Lewis, the second victim, that he's actually starting to develop his technique in preparation for the third victim – Chloe Winters. He held her captive for forty-eight hours during which she was subjected to—' Brady stopped and shook his head. The torture that she had undergone was sickening.

He looked around the room. The air was heavy and still. No one was laughing now – rightly so.

'The rapist used some type of instrument or foreign object to damage or penetrate the victim's skin,' Brady explained as he walked over to the whiteboard.

He pointed at the multiple photographs of Chloe Winters' injuries.

'You see here,' he asked, pointing at the carnage that had been exacted on her breasts. He tried not to flinch at the gruesome photographs. Brady didn't like to think about the time she had spent in surgery. 'He did exactly the same to the first two victims with what we think could be a screwdriver. Chloe Winters suffers the same injuries but he then takes it up another level by removing a significant portion of the skin on her right breast and the area above.'

'Why, sir? Why actually remove the skin?' Kodovesky asked, frowning.

'Good question. And I don't know the answer. I can only assume that the tattoo disgusted him and he wanted to remove it,' Brady answered.

'Or,' interrupted Amelia, 'perhaps he took it as some kind of a trophy. He clearly focuses on the victims' breasts. This is the area he stabs and cuts. He would have taken great pleasure in hurting Chloe Winters to this degree. Both physically and mentally. He has actually removed a piece of her. Something unique to her. No one else would have had that tattoo in that particular place.'

Brady nodded. 'Good point. We know that he blindfolds his victims while he tortures and rapes them, which is characteristic of a sadistic rapist. And that's why we've had such a problem getting an accurate photofit. As you all know this image' – Brady pointed to a copy of the photofit he had shown Trina McGuire – 'is the best we could come up with given all three victims' descriptions. The problem we have is that the victims were intoxicated when he attacked them, and before they got a chance to see his face they were blindfolded. The main similarity between the descriptions of the attacker is that he is tall, shaven-headed and in his mid-twenties.'

'And you definitely think he works in the area where the victims were attacked?' Harvey asked. 'If he's an opportunist, why not just cruise the streets until he finds a young woman that's easy pickings? It's not hard in Whitley Bay at the weekend. You know the problem we have with stag and hen parties getting bladdered down here. Then there's the hardcore locals who go out every Friday and Saturday night. It wouldn't be hard to pick up a girl too drunk to even know her name.'

Brady walked back over to the large conference table. He poured himself a glass of lukewarm water before answering. He needed to clear his throat.

'He is definitely an "opportunist" who works in Whitley Bay at the weekend. He's clever, Tom. Which is why we haven't caught him yet. He's part of the milieu. He's comfortable there. Knows it.'

Harvey frowned at this comment.

'He's part of the physical or social setting. He's watching the victims. I've already said he's not got a type and that his choice of victim is opportunistic but what I mean by that is that all three were regular drinkers in Whitley Bay at the weekend. Heavy drinkers by all accounts – the high alcohol levels in their blood samples shows that. Also, all three victims said that this wasn't the first time they had found themselves walking home alone. Yes, they all regularly got taxis, but on the odd occasion they would find themselves with no cash, separated from their group of friends – whatever. I firmly believe that his assaults are deliberate, calculated and pre-planned. He's already chosen his victim. Now all he has to do is wait until the opportunity arises to attack them, and to be able to do that, he has to be in the same vicinity biding his time for his moment to strike. He's not a fool, he doesn't take risks.'

'So, if I'm not mistaken, there's one common factor here,' Conrad interjected.

Brady turned to Conrad. He knew exactly what he was going to say. It was his next and final point.

'Go on,' Brady encouraged him.

'Well, sir. Based on information we've got from the victims themselves, their friends and the social network sites they used, they . . . well . . . liked to party.'

Brady nodded. 'Yes, like a lot of kids their age who go out drinking at the weekends, Conrad. The only difference is, someone out there is watching them and waiting for the right opportunity to enact his sadistic fantasies.'

Amelia looked at Brady and then turned to the rest of the team: 'The problem we have here is that for some sadistic rapists, the ultimate satisfaction is gained from murdering the victim. What happened to Chloe Winters is just the beginning for him. I think his next victim might not be so lucky – not that "lucky" is the right word considering what the victims have suffered.'

Brady thought of Chloe Winters. She was a twenty-year-old fine art student studying at Newcastle University. The operative word here was 'was'. Her ordeal was unimaginable. She had been tortured at the hands of a sadistic rapist. Whether she would get over something so horrific was debatable. And he was certain that Bentley's publicity stunt would have terrified her into thinking that the rapist had struck again. This time leaving his victim for dead.

No one said anything. Amelia's comment weighed heavily in the air as the team dealt with the knowledge that if they didn't catch him soon, the next time he struck they could be dealing with a murder investigation.

Chapter Nineteen

Brady took a drink of water as he looked around the rest of the room. He resisted the urge to dismiss them. They had their orders. But it wasn't enough. He needed the team to be trying to get inside the rapist's head. They needed to understand him, to think like him to stand any real chance of apprehending him.

Silence.

'Why those three particular girls?' Brady said, gesturing to the girls' faces on the whiteboard.

The first victim had been attacked two months ago. She had only been nineteen – his youngest victim to date. Blonde, petite and full of life. Sarah Jeffries had travelled for three months before returning to Whitley Bay to continue her hairdressing apprenticeship at Thatch in Whitley Bay. That had all disintegrated after her attack. The mental scars were even deeper than the physical ones. It was very much a hate crime. There was no doubt in Brady's mind that they were dealing with a misogynist. The second victim, Anna Lewis, couldn't have been more physically different from the first. But like Sarah Jeffries, she was vivacious and enjoyed socialising. That was before she had been attacked. Now was an entirely different story.

Brady thought of the third victim, Chloe Winters. Her life would never be the same – she would never be the same.

Brady sighed. It was torturous. They were no further forward. It was the same old ground that he kept covering.

'And you definitely don't think that Trina McGuire is connected to our case?' questioned Amelia.

Brady dragged a hand back through his hair and looked at her.

'No, they're not linked.'

His eyes told Amelia he was 100 per cent behind his conviction, despite Bentley's press call stating the exact opposite.

'You'll see for yourself when Bentley gives you the information he has so far. But I guarantee that her attack was about pure frenzied rage and anger.'

Harvey shot Brady a quizzical look. 'But isn't that the same as the assaults on our three victims?'

'No. They're very different. The assailant effectively left Trina McGuire for dead. His rage was out of control. It was overkill. Christ! He obliterated her face, Tom,' Brady said, shaking his head, the image of what he had done to Trina McGuire too much to bear. He tried to block it out of his mind before continuing. 'I would say that he knew her. He wanted to destroy her. To kill her. Why? I don't know. But he did.'

He turned and looked over at the photographs on the white-board. 'Whereas the man who carried out those attacks planned every small detail. He took his time. He deliberated every slice of the blade. Enjoyed every moment with his victims. Yes, he hates them. These are very much hate crimes fuelled by his rage at women. But it's a cold rage. One that he nurtures and to a certain degree can control. Otherwise we wouldn't see him escalating with every victim. We wouldn't witness him perfecting his MO. Instead, we would be looking at three identical frenzied attacks.'

Brady studied Harvey's face. He didn't look convinced.

'Whoever attacked Trina McGuire couldn't care whether she lived or died. The crucial difference here is that our serial rapist wants his victims to live. He wants them to live with the permanent reminder of what he has done to them. He removed Anna Lewis' and Chloe Winters' skin as trophies so he would always be connected to them. And them to him.'

'But—'

Brady stopped Harvey before he had a chance to raise an objection.

'Whoever cut out Trina McGuire's skin hasn't taken it as a trophy. He was simply copying what he'd read in the *Northern Echo* yesterday evening. If it really was our serial rapist then he wouldn't have so savagely destroyed her face and body, leaving her for dead. He would have raped her and then mutilated her breasts. But crucially, he would have then left her to live with the effects of what he had done to her. He's proud of what he does, Tom. And if he gets the chance to strike again there's a high probability that he will kill. But if he does, it will be carefully exacted and not carried out in some frenzied, blind rage like the assault on Trina McGuire.'

Brady sighed. He was tired. Tired of the whole damn case. He dragged his hand back through his hair as he looked around the room.

Silence.

It was heavy and awkward. He had laboured the point. He knew it. But he had no choice. He needed to make sure his team were clear that there was no connection between the attack last night and the serial rapes that had taken place over the past two months. They had no time to waste – especially not when there was a chance that their man was already out there, looking for his next victim.

Amelia nodded at Brady then looked over at the victims' faces.

'All right, if we eliminate Trina McGuire then we're still looking at three rapes that took place within the jurisdiction of Whitley Bay and all at the weekend,' Amelia said, considering Brady's idea that the offender worked the weekends near where the victims had been drinking. It made perfect sense.

'All three victims were highly intoxicated and had decided, for whatever reason, to walk home alone after the clubs and pubs had closed. Perfect combination for someone looking for a woman to sexually assault. I would say he watched them. All three. This is no coincidence. I think you could be right. I think he could have a job which enables him to watch them and then strike when the opportunity arises.'

'So, you're now saying that he works locally?' Brady asked.

'I still think we should be looking at someone who works away during the week. A blue-collar worker in his mid-to-late twenties. Returns home at the weekend and for whatever reason holds down another job. Maybe as a barman or a bouncer in a club?'

Brady nodded at her. All three victims had said that they ended the night of their attack in Madley's nightclub, the Blue Lagoon.

'Either one is the ideal job. It would allow him to watch his chosen victim over a period of time. He might even already be in a relationship. If he is, he's dissatisfied. He feels powerless. Emasculated even.'

'Why?' Daniels asked.

Brady watched him closely. Just to make sure he and Kenny weren't trying to wind Amelia up. But his question seemed born of genuine curiosity.

Amelia looked across at Daniels and shrugged.

'It could be to do with his relationship with his mother. Some researchers have suggested in the case of rapists, parental cruelty, sexual frustration, as well as over-stimulation or even seduction are key factors that influence the rapist's personality and criminal behaviour.'

The look on Daniels' face was enough for Amelia to realise that she had lost him.

'OK. You must have seen or heard of Alfred Hitchcock's *Psycho* with Norman Bates, and Thomas Harris' *The Silence of the Lambs* character, Buffalo Bill?'

Daniels shot Kenny a wry smile.

'Yeah, but you can't believe what you see in a film, Dr Jenkins.'

'That's where you're wrong Daniels,' she replied. 'Both Norman Bates and Buffalo Bill were inspired by one of history's most notorious and gruesome serial killers, Ed Gein. He was born in 1906 to a submissive, alcoholic father and more significantly a dominating, religious mother who preached to him and his elder brother about the evilness of women. She did everything in her power to discourage sexual thoughts and desires in Gein. When his mother died, Gein developed an unhealthy obsession towards the female anatomy, as well as a growing fascination with the Nazi camps and human experiments. Gein went on to dig up graves and experiment on the bodies; it's believed he even dug up his own mother. When the police searched his house they found his mother's heart in a pan on top of the stove. As Gein's experiments developed they became more and more gruesome and even included cannibalism. His desire to turn into a woman led him to make breasts with human skin and wear them. To perfect a sex change, he believed that he would need fresh bodies and so he began a killing spree. When the police finally caught him they found human skin, lips and female genitalia used as pieces of jewellery and art to decorate the house.'

Daniels laughed. 'That's some crazy bastard!'

Brady shot him a look that was enough to make him rein it in.

'I'm sorry. I mean that's just sick. Surely you're not suggesting that the rapist we have in Whitley Bay is like this Gein character?'

'No. I'm not saying that by any stretch of the imagination. We have a rapist on our hands. Gein wasn't a rapist. He didn't have sexual intercourse with his victims because he said "they smelled too bad". The point I was making was that your formative years as a child are crucial and there are countless cases of serial sadistic rapists and murderers who were controlled, dominated and humiliated by their mothers. Some rapists and killers have even blamed their sadistic impulse on their mothers' exposing them to inappropriate sexual behaviour. Bobby Jo Long killed women who he said reminded him of his own mother – he described his victims as whores and sluts. According to him, his mother had sex with men in the same bed and room that he shared with her until he was thirteen years old.'

Daniels looked visibly sickened by Amelia's matter-of-fact revelation. As did the rest of the team. Amelia was surprised by their reactions; she was certain that she had already given the team background information on what would lead to someone becoming a rapist. There were multiple kinds of rapes and she had gone through them all: statutory rape, spousal rape, rape of children, gang rape, power rape, prison rape, war rape, corrective rape, anger rape and sadistic rape. But Brady had been right, the team were dealing specifically with a sadistic rapist.

Amelia slowly breathed out and looked around the table at their weary faces. Whether it was because it was late on a Friday afternoon and they all had better things to be doing than going over old ground or if they were sick of the case and the fact that they were not making any real progress with it, she couldn't be sure. But clearly whatever she had previously told them, they had forgotten.

'The rapist you're after would have begun to exhibit mild to moderate social maladjustments such as temper tantrums, fighting, truancy, theft before going on to develop more deviant behaviour such as torturing animals and starting fires. That kind of extreme behaviour would be more fitting with the sadistic rapist that we have here, who has the potential, given the fact he gains sexual gratification from hurting his victims, to go on to murder.'

'Yeah, but we're dealing with a rapist here. Not a murderer,' Daniels objected.

'At this point we are, but who knows what he'll do when he attacks again. Because he *will* attack again, unless he's stopped. And with every rape his sadism is escalating. It's only a matter of time.'

Daniels didn't look convinced.

'Rapists tend to be young, with eighty per cent under the age of thirty and seventy-five per cent under the age of twenty-five. Many come from lower class backgrounds and most choose victims of their own race. So we're looking for a white, lower-working-class male in his mid-to-late twenties. Most stranger rapists, like this offender, plan their attacks and most have histories of violence. One in three has a prior record for a violent crime and twenty-five per cent have been before the court for rape.'

Brady already knew these statistics and had carried out countless checks and cross-references to see if he could spot the unknown offender in the system. He had failed to see him. Despite the profile Amelia had given the team, they still had very little to go on. And as for the photofit, it could easily match half the men in the North-East under the age of thirty. They needed something more. More than general details that just led them down multiple blind alleys. And the last thing he needed was Bentley confusing matters.

Brady sat back down. He stretched his hands behind his head, leaned back in his chair and waited for Amelia to finish lecturing Daniels and the rest of them.

'But if that's the case, and he has a history of violence, why haven't we found him in the system yet?' Daniels asked.

Amelia slowly shook her head. Her dark brown eyes fixed on Daniels.

'You tell me. That's your job. Mine is just to give you guidelines on the type of offender you're looking for, which I've done.'

Brady knew that tempers were rising. The team were feeling demoralised. They were over-worked, under-paid and in dire need of a weekend off. But that wasn't going to happen anytime soon. Brady needed them all working through the next couple of days. He turned to Daniels. He looked as Brady felt. Disgruntled and sick to the stomach. It was Friday and Brady assumed he had a date lined up that night. Instead he would be dealing with this 'runner'. A case that had them all frustrated and ready to start turning on one another.

Brady watched Amelia as she collected her thoughts. She was reassuringly calm and collected – unlike Daniels. She looked across at the whiteboard and shook her head.

'I'm sorry if that was too much information. But I want this sick bastard caught as much as you do,' she said. It was heartfelt.

The room breathed a collective sigh of relief. The briefing was over. Chairs were scraped back and files shuffled as the team gathered up their belongings.

Brady watched them. They looked tired and sick to the stomach. They all had a long, arduous weekend ahead of them. But Brady had no alternative. He was literally watching the clock count down, waiting for the rapist to strike again. He needed to find him before that happened. And if that meant keeping his team back, so be it.

Chapter Twenty

A couple of loud knocks on the door of the Incident Room preceded the door being thrown open.

Brady turned around to witness the desk sergeant, Charlie Turner, come rushing in. He looked unusually flustered.

'Sorry, Jack,' he said, out of breath.

'What's the problem, Charlie?' Brady asked.

This was atypical. Turner rarely left the front desk. And Brady couldn't remember the last time he had looked so flustered.

'Get your breath back then tell me,' Brady suggested.

Turner nodded as he licked the spittle from his bottom lip.

'Getting too old to be running up those damned stairs,' he wheezed.

Brady caught Conrad's eye. He looked as concerned as Brady felt.

'I tried calling you but obviously you're not answering and you redirected all your calls down to me . . .' Turner paused, still playing catch-up with his breathing.

'Yeah, I know. Sorry about that. We just didn't need the distraction of phones ringing,' Brady apologised.

'No . . . no problem. But an urgent call came in,' Turner explained as he raised his long, wiry, white eyebrows.

Brady could see the worry in his small, beady eyes.

'What's the call?'

'It's from Chloe Winters, Jack,' Turner began.

The room around him suddenly went deadly quiet.

'She . . . she saw DI Bentley's interview on the news and said that she needs to talk to you. That it's urgent. She had tried getting hold of DI Bentley but couldn't get through so she rang you.'

'Why the hell would she ring Bentley? She knows that I'm investigating her attack. That if she has any problems or remembers anything to talk to me or a member of my team.'

'Calm down, Jack. The poor lass is terrified because he attacked again last night.'

Irritation flashed across Brady's face, but he did his utmost to keep quiet about how irresponsible and unprofessional Bentley's interview had been – proven by Chloe Winters' reaction.

'Why did she ring Bentley first?' asked Brady.

'Well, it's quite straightforward,' Turner answered, feeling unfairly under attack. 'She said that he described a silver car at the crime scene shortly before the fourth victim was attacked.'

'It's not his fourth victim. It's entirely unrelated,' Brady corrected. He knew he was being pedantic but he at least needed the desk sergeant to be up to speed – especially if they were going to be besieged by however many calls from the concerned public regarding last night's attack.

'Yes . . . yes. Whatever you say,' answered Turner, frustrated that he couldn't get the information out that he needed to. 'The car—'

'What about the car?' interrupted Brady.

'She says she recognised the description of the car.'

'What? Why the hell didn't you say that when you walked in?'

Turner shook his craggy head at Brady. 'I was trying to,' he muttered, but Brady had already turned his back on him. There was frustration mixed with affection in Turner's watery eyes. He had known Jack Brady for years; had watched him develop into the Detective Inspector he was now. He knew when he left he would miss him dearly. Whether Brady would notice when he had gone, he wasn't so certain. Without a word, Turner left Brady to it.

Brady looked at Kodevesky. She was already standing up, waiting for his order.

DS Kodovesky had been the officer who had dealt with Chloe Winters and the other rape victims – understandably. She was a woman and the last thing a rape victim needed was some burly male copper asking them questions about one of the most traumatic experiences they would ever experience.

'Get on the phone to her. See if what Turner said is true and if it is, see how she feels about making a statement. Is she still in Rake Lane?'

'No, sir. I was informed she was discharged late this morning,' Kodovesky answered.

Brady was surprised by this news. Given the severity of her attack he had assumed she would have been kept in for longer. He wondered whether the dire state of the NHS was the driving force behind freeing her hospital bed rather than an expedient recovery.

'See how she is first. But if she's agreeable, you and Amelia visit her at her parents' home.'

Kodovesky simply nodded.

Brady turned to Amelia. 'You don't mind do you? I know it's a Friday night and—'

'I don't have plans,' Amelia interrupted. 'So no, I don't mind. It would be good to feel as if I'm doing something more than just talking at everyone whenever we have a briefing.'

'You know you do a hell of a lot more than that,' Brady corrected.

'Really?' Amelia asked. 'Sometimes I'm not so sure.'

Brady looked at Amelia, not knowing what she wanted from him.

'Right, sir, I'm ringing Chloe Winters now,' Kodovesky told her boss, unintentionally breaking up the conversation. She had her mobile pressed to her ear as she walked to the other end of the room.

Brady watched her as she talked. He couldn't hear the conversation; all he could do was wait. It was pointless trying to read Kodovesky's face to glean what was happening. It was typically expressionless. She had a professional look that never betrayed her emotions – no matter how difficult the job at hand. She finished her call and walked back over to Brady.

'She did call, sir. And yes, she recognises the description of the silver car.'

Brady didn't say anything. He waited for Kodovesky to tell him what was happening next while he absorbed what this new development meant.

'She actually wants to come into the station to make a statement. As long as I'm present during her interview.'

'Is she up to it?' Brady asked, surprised.

'She suggested it,' Kodovesky said.

'All right, bring her in,' Brady instructed. 'And thanks, Kodovesky.'

'What for, sir?' she asked, her voice as neutral as the expression on her face.

'For saying whatever it was you said to convince her to come in.'

Brady knew that she must have persuaded Chloe Winters to talk to him. She had developed a good relationship with her. She trusted Kodovesky. The key was making the victim feel as if they were not being exploited, and convincing them to believe in the judicial system. Convictions of offenders charged with rape or another serious sexual offence had increased in the last year, which was encouraging. The Crown Prosecution Service statistics showed that 63.2 per cent of cases where someone was charged with rape had resulted in a conviction, up from 62.5 per cent the previous year. This was good news for the victims and the police. But it was still a difficult process getting a victim of rape or sexual assault to report it. The figures were still demoralising when research showed that 473,000 women and men in the UK suffered a sexual assault every year but only one in twenty came forward, resulting in only 54,000 sexual offences recorded annually. It was understandable why victims were so reluctant to come forward. Even when they did, it was incredibly difficult for them to relive the humiliation, pain and even guilt they felt. Reporting it to the police was just the first step of a difficult process. Brady appreciated everything that Kodovesky had done to reassure and support Chloe Winters, as well as the first two victims. Whether Kodovesky realised how invaluable she was on this investigation was something Brady couldn't answer. She kept her cards very close to her chest. To the extent that it was difficult to tell what she was thinking most of the time.

Kodovesky nodded. Without comment she turned and left.

'Do you still want me to go with her?' Amelia asked Brady.

Brady nodded. 'You might glean something from her that she wouldn't necessarily feel comfortable mentioning in front of me.'

'All right. That's if Kodovesky hasn't already left.'

Brady watched as Amelia quickly gathered up her belongings and headed out the door to catch up. He wondered whether she would actually get anything useful out of the victim on the way back to the station. His mind turned to the silver taxi that Bentley had mentioned. He wondered whether it was relevant, and why Chloe Winters hadn't mentioned it before.

Chapter Twenty-One

It was now after 7:00 p.m. Brady had been waiting to interview Chloe Winters. She had arrived at the station fifteen minutes before but wanted time with Kodovesky to compose herself. Brady would give her all the time she needed. This was on her terms, not his. Brady was just relieved that she'd volunteered to come in with this new information – information that Bentley would have wanted first.

Suddenly there was a knock at his office door.

'Yeah?' Brady looked up from the files on his desk. He'd been familiarising himself with Winters' original statement.

Amelia Jenkins walked into the room.

'She's ready if you are,' Amelia informed him.

'Thanks,' Brady said, pushing his chair back and standing up. 'What do you think?' he asked her.

'I would say she's telling the truth, Jack. Initially, I was concerned she could have been suffering from false memory syndrome, which wouldn't be surprising given the traumatic ordeal she suffered. I was curious as to whether it was a reaction to having seen Bentley's news interview and wanting to do everything in her power to help find her rapist, who she now thinks has struck again. When Bentley mentioned the silver car, it was something tangible to cling on to. More than we've had throughout the entire investigation,' Amelia stated.

Brady looked at her face, realising that this was not an attack against him and the team. It was just an observation. But it was correct. This could be the team's first real lead. They'd had countless phone calls since Bentley's news stunt. All false leads

– so far. Brady had uniformed officers staffing telephones to check out the reports from the public relating to the silver taxi. Whether anything concrete would materialise, Brady was unsure.

'What about DI Bentley? Has he got any leads yet on the car?' Amelia asked.

'Not as far as I know. I'm relying on Conrad for updates as I don't think Bentley will be that forthcoming with me.'

'I'll give him a call later, shall I?'

'Feel free,' Brady answered, but it was clear from the tone of his voice that he resented even the idea of her calling Bentley.

'Come on, Jack,' Amelia said, frowning at him. 'We're all in this together. Same intention. To get whoever is hurting these women. Does it matter who gets the result as long as we get one?'

It took a moment for Brady to digest what had just been said. He couldn't believe she would even have the audacity, let alone insensitivity to say it. Bentley was a self-obsessed dick who was currently intent on fucking up Brady's investigation for his own gain. It had nothing to do with Trina McGuire, or the first three rape victims. So of course it bloody mattered. It mattered to him more than he was willing to admit.

'I've got to go,' Brady said. His face said it all as he walked towards his office door. He held it open. A sign for Amelia that her professional words of wisdom were not needed, and more to the point, not appreciated.

Kodovesky sat beside Chloe Winters. They had been in the small, claustrophobic interview room for ten minutes now. The air was tense and heavy, filled with expectation and resentment – both emanating from the victim. Expectation that Brady and his team would find the rapist with the new information she had; resentment that after so long they still hadn't found him. Brady had been shocked by the physical change in Chloe. Her appearance told people to look the other way. That she had nothing

– was nothing. Her long, dark blonde hair was scraped back from her face in an unruly, straggly ponytail. She wore no make-up. Instead, her face was uncomfortably naked – the pain etched for all to see. Her eyes were bloodshot and puffy, and her skin blotchy from crying. Brady assumed that Bentley's stunt would have brought everything back. Brady knew that the effects of her attack would always be there with her. A constant worry and unease in the background that she could never quite drown out. But Brady was sure that hearing the news second-hand on the TV that the rapist had struck again would have thrown her straight back to the night he had tortured and raped her.

She was a victim; there was no disputing that. Whether Chloe Winters could turn this around and become a survivor was as much down to Brady and his team as it was to her. If they could catch the man who had so damaged her, both physically and mentally, it would change things. She could rest assured that he would not finish off the sadistic, torturous game he had started with her and she could perhaps move on and rebuild her life.

If Brady hadn't known it was her, he wouldn't have recognised her. She looked like she had lost nearly a stone since her attack. It was as if she was shrinking in front if him. Physically disappearing. Not that Brady was surprised by this; every victim had a coping mechanism, and Chloe Winters appeared to be starving herself to death. Whether it was the 'old' Chloe she was punishing, he didn't know. Or perhaps she was removing every trace of her old self so her assailant would never recognise her, would not target her again. All Brady knew was that the physical result of what had happened to her, let alone the mental effect, was unsettling even for a copper like Brady who had seen it all.

The photographs of Chloe Winters prior to her attack could not have been more different. Her hair had been sleek and long, cascading freely down her shoulders and back. Her make-up had been flawless but precise. She had worn her clothes with ease and pride – she had a good body and had not been ashamed to show it.

That was then. Now she wore a large, baggy burgundy Hollister hoodie that hid anything from below her neck. Brady didn't know whether this was a reaction to the brutal stab wounds and the scars that covered her chest from the countless skin grafts she had undergone. He had no idea whether they'd taken. Nor was he in a position to ask. He was treading as carefully as he could. His eyes glanced down at her small, bony fingers, clutching onto Kodovesky's hand as if she feared that without her, she would drown. He noticed that her nails had been chewed and bitten well below the tip.

Brady breathed in deeply. He caught Kodovesky's eye. She was waiting for him to take charge. To finish off what he'd started. He looked at Chloe. But she had her head down. Throughout the interview she had refused to look him in the eye. Her answers had been directed at the table or the bottle of water beside her hand. Not that he could blame her. He represented everything that scared her to the very core of her being – he was a man who wanted something from her. He knew how to change the dynamics. How to get her to trust him and society again. That was by apprehending the man who had done this to her. But whether Brady would be able to do that was another matter entirely. To do it, he needed her help.

'Chloe? This taxi you mentioned? It was definitely a silver car?'

'I already told you that,' she answered, an edge to her voice.

It was anger. Brady took that as a good sign. Anger was better than defeat. And she had every right to be angry with him. In her eyes, Brady and his team had betrayed her. She should have been forewarned that the rapist had struck again, instead of hearing it on the news.

'I know you have, I just need to be clear. So it was a silver car. Definitely a taxi?'

She nodded without looking at him.

Brady could see her grip tighten around Kodovesky's hand.

'Do you know what firm the driver worked for?' Brady asked. His voice was gentle and unobtrusive.

'No. I saw the markings on the side and the taxi sign on top but I didn't recognise the firm,' she answered.

'When you say you didn't recognise the taxi company, is that because it wasn't a local taxi?'

'No . . . I don't know. I just didn't register it. You know? It's a taxi, like? They all look the same late at night.'

Brady took 'late at night' as a euphemism for being drunk – extremely drunk.

'Yeah, I know. I wouldn't be able to recognise one firm from another. Not if it just pulled up beside me,' Brady replied.

He waited for a response. Nothing.

'You rang East Central taxis on that night?' he asked.

'You know I don't remember that. I've already told you,' she replied, her voice thick with accusation at him for forcing her to repeat it again. Forcing her to experience the waves of humiliation and guilt that came with going over the same old ground.

'I know . . . I'm sorry. I just wondered whether it could have been an East Central taxi?'

Brady knew that the dispatcher who logged her call at 2:53 a.m. on Saturday, 19th October hadn't actually sent a taxi out. That Chloe Winters had been so drunk that the dispatcher hadn't been able to make sense of her request. The team only knew about it because they had traced every call made from and received by the victim's mobile phone in the vain hope of finding something connected to the offender.

'OK,' Brady said, collecting his thoughts. 'You say that this taxi pulled up beside you when you started walking home, yeah?'

She nodded.

'And this was just outside the Blue Lagoon nightclub?'

Again she nodded, without looking at him.

'He pulled up beside you, wound the window down and asked if you needed a lift somewhere?'

'Something like that. I can't remember exactly, you know?' she said, turning to look at Kodovesky.

Kodovesky nodded in return.

'And you said no. Why, Chloe? You'd already tried ringing a taxi to get home so why wouldn't you get into one when it turned up?'

For the first time in the entire interview, she raised her head and looked directly at him. Her bloodshot eyes were narrowed and filled with distrust.

'Because he creeped me out. OK?'

Brady looked at her, willing her to expand on what it was about the driver that so unnerved her.

She shrugged as if in response to Brady's questioning silence.

'You know? There was something about him. His eyes . . .' she frowned as she tried to recall the driver. 'I can't remember what he looked like. It was dark and all. But there was something about his eyes. They scared me. Just creeped me out like I said.'

'What colour were his eyes? Can you remember?' Brady asked.

'Brown,' she answered. 'Dark brown.'

'Anything else about his face? His hair?'

'It was dark. He was in his car so I couldn't really make anything out. Apart from his eyes . . . I didn't like the way he looked at me. You know?'

Brady nodded in appreciation. 'Yeah, I know.'

He gave her a moment to compose herself.

Then, accepting that the interview was over, he cleared his throat.

'That's great Chloe. Look, if you remember anything else about this taxi driver let us know. Doesn't matter what the time is, just call either DS Kodovesky or me. You've got our numbers haven't you?'

Chloe Winters nodded.

'Is it him? I know DS Kodovesky said it's not him. The attack last night. But the news report said it could be?'

'It's not him, Chloe. The attack is very different. I know we said they were similar but actually there's some subtle differences. Differences that only we and the man who attacked you know about,' answered Brady, giving it his best shot. But he wasn't so certain it had worked.

'But she had been raped, right?'

'Yes, unfortunately she had been raped.'

'Then why did DI Bentley say that they were similar?'

Brady steeled himself. 'I think last night's assailant had read the article in the *Northern Echo* earlier that evening. This is only supposition, but I believe he took what details had been printed about your attack and applied them. But it was clear that he was just copying what had been printed, otherwise the victim's injuries would have been more in keeping with yours.'

'What exactly happened to her?' Chloe Winters asked.

'I'm afraid I can't divulge that information, Chloe. But believe me when I say that last night's attack is totally unrelated to yours.'

Chloe Winters nodded slowly as she digested the news. She looked Brady straight in the eye. Her face was filled with anger and incredulity. The anger was clearly directed at Brady.

'So that means there's two violent rapists out there? One who's copying the other? All within a three-mile radius? You can't be serious. I still can't sleep at night after what he did to me because I'm so scared that he'll find me again. But now . . .' She shook her head as she stared at Brady, tears of both fury and fear welling up in her eyes. 'Now what?'

Brady hadn't thought about it that way. And why would he? He was only interested in solving his own case. Not worrying about the cold, hard reality – they now had two dangerous rapists at work. Both exhibiting murderous tendencies.

Chapter Twenty-Two

Brady sat in his office. He took a slug of cold, bitter black coffee. It had been on his desk since before the interview with Chloe Winters. Kodovesky had returned her to her parents' home and was now with Harvey, working on identifying and eliminating all the bar staff who worked in Whitley Bay at the weekend. They were starting with the Blue Lagoon. It was a task that Brady did not envy. But it was a necessary one. Something told Brady that the rapist worked in Whitley Bay. That he knew the place better than anyone, and that he was in the ideal location to watch his victims and wait for the right moment to strike. He was clearly clever – otherwise he would not have been able to elude the police for so long. Kenny, Daniels and Conrad were busy analysing hours and hours of CCTV footage from the night that Chloe Winters was attacked. They were looking for the silver taxi.

Brady had already had Bentley on the phone wanting to know what Chloe Winters had wanted to say. Brady had downplayed it. The last thing he was going to do was give Bentley crucial information. He needed to give his team time to see if they could find anything. Brady had also told Conrad to try and get hold of the CCTV footage, if there was any, of the silver taxi that Trina McGuire had seen shortly before her attack.

Before Bentley had the chance to cut the line, Brady had challenged him about why he had suddenly changed direction when he had been so sure that Martin Madley was responsible for Trina McGuire's assault. Especially since Bentley had questionable evidence – the Blue Lagoon business card with the victim's name scrawled on the back. However, Bentley was as forthcoming as Brady had been with him. He had simply stated that the victim had identified her attacker from the photofit of the serial rapist. That in itself was enough for him to follow it up.

Brady slowly drank what was left of his coffee. It didn't matter that it was cold. He just needed some caffeine to help clear his head before giving Daniels and Kenny a hand looking through the CCTV surveillance tapes. He wanted to know whether this silver taxi had been around the nights the first two rape victims were attacked. If not, maybe Chloe was clutching at straws and it was false memory syndrome. After all, McGuire's rape had been committed by a different offender altogether – one who seemed to be trying to emulate the Whitley Bay serial rapist based on the scraps doled out in the *Northern Echo*.

Brady had already had word back from Kodovesky that Sarah Jeffries and Anna Lewis had no recollection of a silver taxi on the nights they were attacked. Whether they had been too drunk to notice, or Chloe Winters had remembered wrong, Brady couldn't be sure.

He dragged a hand back through his hair. He needed to wake himself up. He was tired and running on empty. That, and he was in dire need of a cigarette. But he was fighting the urge. Not that successfully. He'd lost count of how many nicotine patches he had plastered to his arm.

He looked at the time on his mobile: 10:55 p.m. He was ravenous, which was no surprise. He hadn't eaten since last night. He had planned on getting a bacon stottie from the cafeteria that morning, but events got in the way. The team had ordered a Chinese take-away in after 9:00 p.m. at Brady's expense. Not that it had counted for anything. When he'd made his way to the Incident Room, half an hour after the food arrived, every carton had been stripped bare. Aside from two bags of cold prawn crackers that no one ever ate. Everyone had blamed Tom Harvey. Of course, Harvey wasn't there to defend himself. But considering Harvey's rapidly expanding gut, Brady wouldn't have put it past him to polish off every last morsel. Tiredness made people hungry, which was no doubt why Brady's stomach felt as if he hadn't eaten for a week.

Brady stood up. He needed to keep working. He had no choice. If there was a chance that the silver taxi was connected somehow, Brady had to make sure his team found it.

'Seen anything yet?' Brady asked, yawning.

'Nothing,' Conrad answered, rubbing his eyes.

Brady turned to Daniels and Kenny. 'What about you two?'

'Nope, nothing,' Daniels said.

'Same. Zilch,' Kenny added as he stretched his hands behind his back.

'All right, let's call it a night,' Brady said. It was after 2:00 a.m. and everyone was exhausted. It was no surprise they hadn't found anything yet. They were all beat.

'Back here seven a.m. sharp. We continue where we left off with these tapes. OK?'

'Yes, sir,' Conrad replied, grateful that Brady had given them a couple of hours respite.

The best Brady got from Daniels and Kenny was a combination of tired yawns and groans of exhaustion.

Brady watched the three of them get up and shuffle out of the room. Amelia had gone home hours ago. It had seemed pointless keeping her back. As for Kodovesky and Harvey, Brady was about to ring and tell them to call it a night. But before he had a chance, Harvey beat him to it.

'Yeah? Tom, I was just about to call you,' Brady said, leaning back in his chair. He closed his eyes and massaged them. His vision was blurred from scrutinising too many hours of surveillance tape.

'Yeah . . . yeah,' Brady muttered as he listened.

It suddenly struck him what was being said. He opened his eyes and sat forward.

'Run that by me again?' he demanded.

'Ahuh, yeah . . . yeah. Shit!'

Brady listened.

'I know we can't ignore this, but my hands are tied until the morning.'

Brady massaged his temples as Tom argued with him.

'Bloody hell, Tom! I want to arrest him as much as you do. But there's nothing I can do right now. All right? Go home, get some sleep and we'll bring him in for questioning in the morning,' Brady instructed. He then cut the call, not giving Harvey a chance to argue.

It was 3:01 a.m. precisely. Despite Harvey's objections he needed to clear it with Gates first. The last thing he was about to do was call Gates at home at this Godforsaken hour. The suspect could wait. His team needed to rest – including Brady. He lay down on the couch in his office and gratefully closed his burning eyes. He just needed a couple of hours and then he would be all right. Munroe wasn't going anywhere. After he had showered, changed into the spare jeans and white T-shirt he kept at the station for such occasions and polished off one of Dora's renowned canteen breakfasts, swigged down with a strong, black coffee, then he would see about bringing Munroe down to the station.

As Brady started to drift off, the only thought going through his mind was whether he would be overstepping the mark if he brought Jake Munroe in for questioning. Did they have enough on him to warrant it? Brady wasn't sure. Not now. He had been when he'd talked to Harvey. But maybe he'd been too tired to think straight. He'd worry about it in the morning. Brady yawned and turned over onto his side.

The next thing he knew, Conrad was standing beside him with his Che Guevara mug filled with steaming, black coffee.

'Shit! What time is it?' yawned Brady as he blinked. It was still dark.

'It's seven seventeen, sir. I left you as long as I could.

Daniels and Kenny have picked up where they left off last night and Harvey and Kodovesky will be here in the next thirty minutes. And this,' Conrad gestured at the mug, 'is from Amelia. She insisted on making it herself, telling me that you like it "strong enough to feel like you've been kicked in the balls by a mule". Especially first thing in the morning. Her words, not mine.'

Brady blinked blearily at Conrad as he swung his legs off the couch and attempted to sit up.

'Shit!' he muttered. His head was pounding and this time he didn't have the excuse of having polished off a bottle of whisky.

'Not the most eloquent of risers are we?' Conrad said.

'Fuck you,' Brady answered with a wry smile.

'Maybe this will help?' Conrad said, offering the mug to Brady.

Brady took it and attempted a sip. It was scalding hot.

'Seems things have changed quite a lot while I've been off sick,' Conrad stated.

Brady looked up at him and frowned. 'I don't follow.'

'Well, let's just say I always thought you liked the way I made your coffee, sir. You've never complained.'

Brady attempted another sip as he looked up at Conrad.

'Don't tell me you're jealous?' he asked, feigning surprise.

'No, sir,' Conrad answered in a flat tone. It was his way of signalling that the conversation was over. That and his clenched jaw told Brady that he had hit a nerve.

'Where is our forensic psychologist this fine morning?' Brady asked.

'She's looking over Jake Munroe's prior convictions. Seems he's got quite a few.'

Brady nodded as he took another sip.

'All right, I need to get showered and change into some fresh clothes. Do me a favour will you? Can you get me one of Dora's bacon stotties from the canteen and another coffee to wash it down with?'

'Will do.'

'Just leave it on my desk. I want everyone ready for a briefing at eight a.m. sharp. Then we'll see about bringing Jake Munroe in for questioning.'

Chapter Twenty-Three

Brady had just finished the bacon stottie and coffee that Conrad had left for him. It was 7:50 a.m. and he had a ten-minute briefing scheduled before ordering Munroe's arrest. The team had already assembled there – even Harvey and Kodovesky were waiting.

Brady walked into the large conference room. The energy couldn't have been more different from the briefing yesterday. Sunlight streamed through the two large Victorian windows, defying the Venetian blinds that tried to block the light out. It was a rare sight. Especially after the miserable summer they had endured.

'Good to see you all and thanks for reconvening so early. It was a long day yesterday, so I'm impressed to see you back here looking refreshed and eager to get started.'

Kodovesky and Harvey were hanging on Brady's every word. He knew what they wanted. What they were secretly hoping for – to interview Munroe once he'd been brought in. But Brady couldn't let that happen. Under different circumstances he would have given them free rein. But not today. And definitely not with Jake Munroe. Brady had managed to spend five minutes going over his history of prior convictions and it made for an ugly read.

'Firstly, I've got to thank Harvey and Kodovesky for putting in all those hours last night. I know you had four uniformed officers with you, but between the six of you that was a lot of ground covered. And you found us a suspect – Jake Munroe.' Brady paused as he looked around the table. 'It's no surprise that you never found him when we first ran a check on all the employees at the Blue Lagoon after the first rape. He was on a two-week trial back then and hadn't yet been put on the payroll. If it hadn't been for you two turning up at the Blue Lagoon last night and actually realising that . . .' Brady broke off, acutely aware of how close they had come to fucking up. 'Anyway, we've got him now. Or at least we will do after this briefing.'

Everyone was hopeful that he was their rapist. Whether he was or not, Brady would soon find out.

'I'm sure you'll all be interested to know that Jake Munroe has a list of priors as long as my arm. Including three counts of rape and seven counts of aggravated assault.'

The air in the room became electric. Brady even had Daniels' and Kenny's full attention.

'He has a clear history of violence. So, not the kind of guy you want to piss off on a Friday night. But he is the type of bloke that you would want working for you as a bouncer. That's what he's been doing for the past two months. He's currently employed by Martin Madley as a part-time bouncer at the Blue Lagoon.'

Brady's eye caught Amelia's as she watched him talk. He knew she was already aware of all of this as she had been the first one to read Munroe's files.

'By his own admission, he only works from a Thursday to a Sunday night. He's originally from London. From what I can make out from his records he was released eight months ago so I assume he's relocated up here to start afresh. To date he hasn't been charged with any offences here.'

She seemed to take her time on deciding whether she should speak. When she eventually did she surprised not only Brady, but the rest of the team.

'Look, I don't want to dampen your spirits here. But I'm not so sure he's your rapist.' She looked around the table and then finally back at Brady. She'd done exactly what she had wanted to avoid – dampened their spirits. In fact she had soaked them.

'Look, I'm sorry, all right? But I'd rather be honest with you. That's why you pay me.'

'What makes you so sure it's not Munroe?' Brady asked.

From the tone of Brady's voice, Amelia knew he was pissed off with her. She should have told him this in private. Not shown him up in front of the team. But she hadn't had the opportunity to talk to him before now. She would be the first to admit that Munroe ticked some of the boxes. But not all of them. Obviously he needed to be brought in for questioning, but Amelia wanted to make sure that the team didn't get too excited.

'All right, I'll agree with you that his history fits perfectly. He's violent and he's a convicted sex offender. He relocated here from London two months ago, which ties in perfectly with the first rape. Also, he has the ideal job. Works in the heart of where these rape victims were drinking and socialising. He could watch them come and go every weekend. He finishes at two a.m., which again fits, as all three rapes happened later. He travels to London on the four days he's not working as a bouncer. What he does in London, who knows? But we do know that there haven't been any crimes reported there that fit with the rapes here,' Amelia said.

She looked around the room.

The feeling had gone from hopeful to out-and-out resentful.

'And those are the precise reasons we've brought Jake Munroe in for questioning,' Brady said, trying to keep the exasperation out of his voice.

'I know, Jack. I know exactly why he's a suspect.'

'So, what's your problem then?' Brady asked, his expression darkening. He didn't have time for whatever game Amelia was playing. This was not the time to suddenly backtrack.

'OK. I would say we're all in agreement that he looks like the photofit? Yes?' Amelia asked.

Everyone agreed in one way or another. Some made muffled noises that constituted a 'yes', others nodded. But no one looked

Amelia in the eye. They didn't trust the direction she was leading them in.

'I'd say that's fairly obvious,' Brady interjected.

He checked the time on his phone. He didn't have time for this.

'Look, Amelia. We've all got a lot to do so why don't you get straight to the point?'

Amelia looked at Brady, caught off-guard by his abruptness. She understood that tensions were running high. They all wanted Jake Munroe to be guilty. To put an end to this investigation. They were no different from her. Except that she believed he wasn't the Whitley Bay rapist and that they were in danger of conveniently making him into something that suited them.

'OK. My point is he's too old. Look at my profile. Think about what the victims said. We are looking for a suspect in his mid-to-late twenties. Yes, Munroe is tall, well-built and bald but he's too old.'

Brady tried to hide his surprise.

'That's it? That's your only objection to him? The fact he doesn't exactly fit your profile?'

'Or the victims' statements,' Amelia pointed out.

'So?' asked Brady. 'We get one small detail wrong. How old is he?' Brady asked, turning to Kodovesky and Harvey.

'Thirty-six, sir,' Kodovesky immediately answered.

'Thirty-six years old. What's the difference between thirty-six and his mid-to-late twenties?'

'There's a big difference, Jack. You can't make him something he's not,' Amelia answered. Her voice was calm and steady as she held Brady's dark gaze. 'All three victims categorically stated that he was in his mid-twenties. And given that they are all under twenty-three, to them anyone above thirty would seem old. Not one of them said their assailant was old, or even older than them. They all unknowingly came up with the same age – roughly twenty-five.'

Brady picked up the file in front of him. It contained a print-out of all of Jake Munroe's prior convictions.

'You've read these? All of these? Yeah?'

Amelia nodded.

'So you know that he has a history of violence and sexual violence. He came from an abusive background, raised by a single mother. She was an alcoholic and a prostitute. There's a hint that Munroe's father may have been a John. That Munroe was eventually placed in foster homes for his own safety because he was being sexually abused by some of his mother's clients. While he was in foster care he was known for torturing animals and abusing the other children in care with him. He was repeat-edly relocated to new foster homes because of his behaviour. Not surprisingly, he ended up in a remand centre for teenagers. And that's us just getting started,' Brady said, dropping the heavy file on the table for effect.

Amelia shook her head. She resisted the urge to applaud Brady's performance.

'Come on. He fits everything you described in your profile. Damaged by his mother, socially deviant as a child and a violent sex offender as an adult. What more do you want? Physically he fits our photofit and he's in the right location at the right time when these attacks took place. Or is that all coincidence?' Brady asked.

'He's the wrong age. It's like making a house out of a pack of cards. If one card is out of place the house falls down. Same deal,' Amelia answered with a tone of finality.

'Right, people,' Brady said as he turned his attention to the rest of the team. 'I appreciate Dr Jenkins' concern regarding our suspect, as I am sure you do.' He turned back to her. 'We'll keep an open mind when we interview him, Dr Jenkins. Just in case we're wrong.'

He intended it to appease her. But the sudden flush of her cheeks told Brady she had taken it the wrong way.

Despite her crimson cheeks and the flash of irritation in her eyes she simply nodded, then folded her hands on the table in front of her and waited for the meeting to conclude.

Even she had doubted herself and had spent over an hour evaluating the police files and social services reports. He did tick all of the boxes, apart from his age. If the team had purely been relying on her profile, she would have discounted it. Simply dismissed it as her mistake. After all, Brady was right. What was a couple of years? But this was more than a couple; it could be up to ten years' difference.

Brady looked at Amelia. She looked really pissed off. He thought about her reservations and understood that she was just playing safe. She was the forensic psychologist for a reason. It was her job to keep them grounded. To make them question everything. Could he be wrong? Brady wouldn't know until he'd interviewed Munroe. But first they had to arrest him.

'Conrad, did you get a copy of the taxi drivers working in the area? Both private and with companies?'

'Most of them,' answered Conrad. 'Still got a few to chase up.'

Brady nodded. 'Hand over what you have so far to Kodovesky and Harvey. I need you with me when I interview Munroe.'

'Yes, sir,' Conrad answered, mildly surprised.

He'd been expecting Brady to choose Amelia. She seemed the obvious choice given her qualifications and background. But then, after their slight disagreement perhaps it wasn't a good idea for her to be present while Brady interviewed the suspect.

Brady turned to Kodovesky and Harvey. 'I want you to bring Munroe in.'

'With pleasure,' Harvey replied as he pushed his chair back and stood up.

Kodovesky quickly followed.

Brady knew they'd been chomping at the bit from the moment Harvey had informed him of the suspect. They had found Munroe and it was their right to bring him in.

'When you get back I'll need the two of you to continue following up this lead about a silver taxi. Trina McGuire mentioned one pulling up shortly before she was attacked and then Chloe Winters made a statement last night saying something similar. What's the connection? We need to talk to this taxi driver. For all we know he could have seen both offenders without even realising it. It's crucial we track him down ASAP,' Brady ordered. He refrained from telling the team that they had to find this taxi driver before DI Bentley. He knew it wouldn't look professional.

Brady turned back to Conrad. 'Does Bentley's team have footage of the car yet?'

Conrad nodded. 'From what I've gathered they have, sir. They're analysing it now. As soon as I hear anything I'll let you know.'

Brady had a choice. He could request to see the CCTV footage himself. But then how would he explain his interest in their investigation? He had already blown Bentley off by stating in no uncertain terms that Brady's investigation wasn't connected to Trina McGuire's attack.

Brady decided to let it go. Bringing Jake Munroe in for questioning was the priority. Why was he worrying about a silver taxi in an unrelated case?

Chapter Twenty-Four

Brady looked Munroe straight in the eye. He was an ugly bastard all right, who was lacking not only in looks, but also in basic oral hygiene. Ugly on the inside and ugly on the outside.

'Fuck you!' He leered at Brady as if reading his mind.

'Yeah? I bet you wish you could,' Brady answered with a smile.

'You sick fucking bastard!' retaliated Munroe.

'Not as sick as you though, Munroe,' Brady said as he picked up the file in front of him. 'Let's have a look at your life shall we?'

Munroe turned and faced the uniformed officer standing guard by the door.

'Your DI's a fucking wanker. You know that darling?'

The young woman turned red. But she kept her eyes straight ahead, refusing to look at the suspect.

'She's not interested, Munroe. You're too ugly for her and too stupid,' Brady said.

'Fuck you!' Munroe spat. 'Where's the fucking copper who brought me in, eh? The one that's all legs and tits? Now I wouldn't mind being interrogated by her!' Munroe laughed as he sat back and folded his arms.

Brady resisted the urge to inform Munroe that if DC Kodovesky was interviewing him, his balls would have been nailed to the interview desk by now.

'Conrad, please tell me this next hour isn't going to be a repetition of the last thirty excruciating minutes, where the suspect uses the same profanity again and again? Tell me that he has a wider vocabulary than these two words?'

Munroe's response was to smile at Brady.

Brady was aware that he was clearly enjoying wasting their time.

'Do you recognise any of these young women?' Brady asked as he pointed to the photographs laid out on the table in front of Munroe.

The suspect bent his head down to have a look.

Brady could clearly see the six-inch gnarled scar running across the centre of his shaven head. It looked as if someone had planted an axe in his skull. Brady assumed that Munroe, whose muscle-bound body, thick-knotted neck and ugly face were intimidating enough by themselves, no doubt shaved his head so the scar was permanently on show.

Munroe raised his head and caught Brady's eye.

'Yeah, it's something, ain't it?' Munroe acknowledged, running a large hand over the scar.

As Munroe raised his hand to his head, Brady saw part of a tattoo on Munroe's lower right arm.

'What's the tattoo?' Brady asked.

'Black panther coming down my arm. Beautiful piece. Bit like me, eh?' Munroe said, laughing. He then proceeded to take his jacket off and to undo the cuff of his shirt to show Brady.

It was an intricate piece of art. Only a highly skilled tattoo artist would be able to pull off the shading and textures used to create the effect of the black panther. Brady knew immediately who had done it.

'Dan Ridgewell's work?'

Munroe looked at Brady, surprised he recognised the artist.

'How do you know him?' Munroe asked as he pulled his shirt sleeve down.

'There's only one tattoo artist in the entire North-East who could produce work of that quality.'

Brady cast a glance at Conrad. They had already questioned Dan Ridgewell, about the possibility that one of his clients could be connected to the rapes, after Chloe Winters' attack. After all, the rapist had removed the tattoo of a wolf's head from her body. Her tattoo had been inked in the same, distinctive style – black and grey with subtle shading.

'When did Dan do it?' Brady asked, trying to be casual.

'Oh, I dunno. Maybe two months ago?' Munroe answered, shrugging.

Brady silently did the maths. Two months ago was when Chloe Winters had gone to Fusion to get her tattoo. What was the possibility of Munroe waiting to get inked while Dan was working on Chloe Winters' body? Given the intricacy of the art, both clients would have had to make at least three appointments with Dan Ridgewell to complete the tattoos.

'So, do you recognise any of the young women here?' Brady asked again, watching Munroe closely for a reaction.

Brady pushed the photograph of Chloe Winters towards him and waited.

Munroe raised his head and looked at Brady, refusing to look. He had been in the game too long and knew exactly what Brady was trying to do.

'Nah, can't say I do guv'nor,' Munroe answered in a thick Cockney accent.

For the brief second that Munroe looked at Chloe Winters' face, Brady was certain he saw a flicker of recognition in his eyes. He knew that Munroe may have been ugly but he was far from stupid, regardless of what the pseudoscience, phrenology would have suggested. Developed by the German physician, Franz Joseph Gall in 1796, phrenology became popular in Britain in the nineteenth century. Munroe's wide face, sloping forehead and beady black eyes fitted perfectly with the pseudoscience's definition of stupid, untrustworthy, with a predisposition to criminal activities.

'Pretty girls. Yeah I'd fuck them if they're on offer. What are they? Tonight's entertainment, lads, eh?' Munroe asked, laughing at Brady and Conrad, still refusing to drop his eyes to look at them. 'I've heard about you coppers. Bunch of dirty fuckers you lot. Who was the dirty bugger who asked for sexual favours from prossies in exchange for not banging them up? Worked here didn't he? I read about it in the local rag. Go on, was it one of you lads? You—' Munroe turned to Conrad. 'Bet it was you. Bet you liked taking them up the fucking arse didn't you? You look the sort. Believe me, I've met plenty of your kind! You look all civil and polite sat there in your expensive suit with your posh accent and that look in your eye that you can't quite disguise. The look that says you're better than me. Better than this—' Munroe said grandly waving his arms around at the interview room.

He suddenly leaned in close to Conrad.

'But I know you. Believe me; I can smell it on you. Have you told your boss? Does he know?'

Conrad didn't flinch. He didn't move a muscle despite Munroe's bad breath and ugly grin.

Brady could tell that he was holding back. Conrad's taut, clenched expression said it all. But Brady knew Conrad wouldn't react. He was better than Munroe and he knew it. His problem was, it showed.

'He hasn't told you, has he?' Munroe asked Brady, smiling. 'Let's do a trade, you and I. I don't tell your boss about you and you let me go,' he suggested.

Again Conrad didn't react.

Munroe seemed to be enjoying this game at Conrad's expense. Brady decided it was time to intervene.

'The photographs, Munroe. Do you recognise any of them?'

'Nah,' Munroe said, now eyeballing Brady. 'Why?'

'You know why,' Brady answered, his voice level.

Munroe broke into a leer of a smile.

'Yeah, but I want to hear what happened to those girls. You know, the ones you said had been raped and tortured? I like a good story. Just make sure you don't skip the sex scenes.'

Brady didn't say a word.

'Ah, but you didn't tell me, did you guv'nor? But that's why I'm here, ain't it? I'm not stupid. I read about this shit in the papers. Were you going to surprise me and hope that I'd break down and confess? Well, fuck you!'

Brady felt sickened by the candid look of pleasure on Munroe's face. His smile was twisted and cruelly ugly. Fate had dealt him an unkind hand. One that it seemed Munroe had used to his own advantage. His smile was perhaps his most sinister aspect. It was intimidating – intentionally so – but there was also a coldness; a chilling coldness deep in his black eyes. They spoke of a darkness that made the hairs on Brady's back stand up. It felt as if he was looking at a man who had sold his soul to the devil. However, Munroe, unlike Christopher Marlowe's Dr Faustus, would not be dragged to hell screaming and fighting. He would be pushing Mephistopheles aside to get there first.

Brady thought about Amelia's objections regarding Munroe. He understood her problem with his age, but sitting where Brady was sitting, even she wouldn't be able to ignore the smell of blood on Munroe's hands and the naked, disturbing lust to hurt set deep in his eyes.

Munroe suddenly swiped at the photographs, knocking them onto the floor.

Neither Brady nor Conrad moved.

'So, when you worked in London as a hired thug, or should I say bodyguard, who employed you?' Brady asked.

Munroe scowled at him.

'Why?'

'Just making conversation,' answered Brady.

'John De Silvio. Why, what the fuck's it got to do with you?'

Brady immediately recognised the name. John De Silvio was an East End gangster otherwise known as Johnny Slaughter.

'So, was it De Silvio who recommended you to Madley?'

'Summat like that.'

Suddenly there was an abrupt knock on the door.

The young officer answered it.

'Sir?' she said as she turned back to Brady.

Brady got up. He couldn't help but notice the look of satisfaction on Munroe's face.

'About fucking time, too!' Munroe complained as he crossed his burly arms. 'You, what about you get me a cuppa, eh? You lot want to be treating me with some respect now my lawyer's here.'

Brady had no idea what was going on.

'I'll be back in five minutes to resume this interview,' he said, nodding at Conrad. His eyes automatically glanced up at the camera in the corner of the ceiling, which was filming the interview.

'Yeah? Is that when I get my fucking apology for wasting my time?'

Brady simply turned and left the room.

DCI Gates stood waiting in the corridor. The look on his harsh face told Brady it was bad news.

'Can I have a word, Jack?'

Before Brady had a chance to answer, Gates continued. 'Martin Madley's lawyer's here. Seems that on the nights in question, Munroe was working for Madley.'

'Can he prove it?' Brady asked. He couldn't believe it. Since when had Madley stuck his neck out for someone – let alone a hired thug like Munroe?

Gates nodded. He looked as pissed off as Brady felt.

'Surveillance tapes from the nights in question. On all three nights Munroe is seen on the Blue Lagoon's security tapes locking up. He then helps out behind the bar cleaning up and knocks off at about four a.m.'

'You're not serious?' Brady asked.

But the expression on Gates's face told him he was deadly serious.

Brady dragged a hand back through his hair as he tried to digest the information.

165

'No . . . no . . . I don't believe it,' he muttered, more to himself than his boss.

'Believe it. I've just had to sit through Madley's lawyer showing me the evidence. Unless Munroe has an identical twin, he physically couldn't have committed those three rapes, Jack.'

'They haven't been rigged, have they?' Brady asked. He knew Madley was capable of doing that. He had money, which meant he could employ the expertise capable of digitally altering times and dates on security tapes.

'It's been sent off to Jed to authenticate,' Gates said.

Brady felt like he'd been winded.

'You thought he was responsible?'

'All the evidence pointed that way. His job, his history of violence and sexual offences, two of which included rape and . . .' Brady faltered as he shook his head. 'He even matches the photofit.'

'That's not what Dr Jenkins has said,' Gates stated.

'Yes, I know,' answered Brady.

Gates waited, clearly wanting more.

'Aside from being older, he fits every other aspect of Dr Jenkins's profile, sir.'

'Irrelevant now, if he has a watertight alibi, don't you think?' Gates pointed out.

Brady kept quiet.

'Sort this mess out, Jack. And fast. I don't want any fallout. You understand? We've got the press crawling all over us as it is without you making us look incompetent. As soon as Jed authenticates the surveillance footage release him.'

Before Brady could argue, Gates had already turned and started walking away.

He stood for a moment trying to compose himself. He now had to go back and terminate the interview. Munroe would be entitled to have a private conversation with Madley's lawyer, who so happened to be one of the best – and most expensive – in the North-East. But Brady could not get rid of his gut feeling about Munroe. There was something about him; it wasn't just the look in his eye and his cocky, foul-mouthed attitude. It was something else, but Brady couldn't put his finger on it. There was one thing he was certain about. Munroe was capable of murder – he had already proven he was capable of rape.

Chapter Twenty-Five

Brady had spent the entire day chasing his own tail – to no avail. The upshot was Munroe had been released without charge. They had nothing on him. The surveillance tapes had come back kosher. Brady had talked to Jed, who had stated categorically that they hadn't been altered in any way. Brady had taken some persuasion, but Jed had indulged Brady's refusal to accept it; counteracting every argument until he felt he had no choice but to hang up on him and get on with some 'real' work. Madley's lawyer had also dropped the bombshell that on the three nights in question, Munroe had also driven Madley home after he'd locked up. Apparently both Gibbs and Weasel Face, Madley's bodyguards and drivers, had been given those nights off. So, not only did Madley provide Munroe with surveillance footage as an alibi, he threw himself in for good measure.

Brady didn't buy it. But there was nothing he could do. Madley was protecting Munroe, that much was obvious. But why?

He had rung Madley, of course. He wanted to know what was in it for him to risk everything for a hired thug with a history of sexual violence. Brady had never known Madley to willingly get involved with the police. He had too much to hide to want to attract attention to himself. But Madley had refused to take Brady's calls. So he'd decided to pay the Blue Lagoon a visit. But the doors were locked and the place seemed conveniently deserted.

Brady had then taken a detour to Fusion to talk to Dan Ridgewell. He wanted to check his records to see whether Chloe

Winters had been booked in on the same day as Munroe. Simple answer – she had. Brady asked if they'd talked. Ridgewell's answer had been: 'Fuck knows. It's a fucking tattoo studio not a fucking knocking shop, Jack!'

They'd stood outside while Ridgewell had a tab break. Brady had questioned him about Munroe and found out the East London bloke had quite a fierce reputation. No one messed with him. Not even Ridgewell, who had quite a reputation of his own and was built like a New Zealand rugby player. He had turned to Brady with a serious look and said: 'There's something in that mad fucker's eyes which tells you he wouldn't think twice about slitting your throat from ear to ear if the fucking mood took him.'

Ridgewell went on to advise Brady to steer clear of him. That he was one of Johnny Slaughter's boys. Or had been. These days he was under the protection of Martin Madley. Brady had refrained from telling him that he already knew. And it was these precise facts that worried him.

After they'd smoked another cigarette and chatted about Newcastle United's chances this season, Brady had thanked Ridgewell and left. He had headed back to the station hoping that Amelia would have already clocked off. He'd successfully avoided her since Munroe had been released. It was late on a Saturday night and the last thing he needed was Amelia gloating over the fact he had got it so wrong. But there was still something about Munroe that made Brady uncomfortable.

Brady took a gulp of black coffee. It was lukewarm. He sat back in his seat and put his hands behind his head as he looked out the windows. Dusk was settling outside. It unnerved him. Another Saturday night. Had he released a potential murderer and sadistic rapist back onto the streets of Whitley Bay? He couldn't be sure. It was that knowledge that was chewing him up inside. What had he done? Or, more to the point, what had he failed to do?

Someone knocked at the door, saving Brady from torturing himself with unanswered questions about Madley and Munroe.

'Yeah?' Brady called out.

Conrad walked in. He was carrying two unopened sandwiches and a bag of salted crisps.

He threw them at Brady.

'Dinner, sir,' he said. 'All they had left in Sainsbury's. Chicken salad and tuna mayonnaise.'

Brady gave Conrad a surprised look.

'What's this in aid of?'

'Felt bad about the Chinese last night. And with everything else that's happened today I knew you'd have forgotten to eat.'

'What makes you think I might be hungry now?' Brady asked, ripping open one of the sandwiches. 'By the way, much appreciated,' he said before taking a large bite.

Conrad was right. He'd been too busy beating himself up over Munroe's release to think about food. His hunger surprised him.

'I've got some news that might put a smile on your face.'

'Go on,' Brady said through a mouthful of chicken salad sandwich. He gestured for Conrad to pull up a seat.

Conrad did as instructed and sat down in front of Brady's cluttered desk. Rarely had he seen it cleared.

'The CCTV footage of the silver car. It was a Mercedes Benz C-Class saloon.'

Brady nodded.

'He's a driver. But not a taxi driver. Name's John Summerfield. He's Mayor Macmillan's driver.'

'What?' spluttered Brady, nearly choking on a piece of malted bread.

'Yes.'

'What the fuck is Mayor Macmillan doing in those parts on a Thursday evening, or should we not be asking that question?'

'Well, allegedly the mayor wasn't in the car. John Summerfield had decided to take a drive and found himself in that part of North Shields.'

'What, looking for sex?'

'By all accounts. It's taken Bentley some time to get this out of him.'

'So, I take it he didn't come forward with the information?'

Conrad shook his head.

'No, sir. They managed to trace the car from a partial registration they got on the CCTV. They were certain it was the car that Trina McGuire had seen – the time on the footage matched the time she said she saw it.'

Brady couldn't help but smile at this news. Mayor Macmillan's driver scouring the streets looking for sex. His smile broadened as he wondered whether Macmillan was actually in the back, hidden behind tinted glass. Nothing would have surprised him where Macmillan was concerned. Brady had given up watching him. He was a corrupt politician with an equally corrupt gangster brother banged up in Durham prison. He had been elected and re-elected as Mayor of North Tyneside. But the public didn't realise the kind of man they had representing them. The police and press were well informed of Macmillan's questionable past. Even Rubenfeld, the snitch who had written the damning piece on Brady's failure to apprehend the Whitley Bay rapist, couldn't sink his teeth into Macmillan, despite the fact he had a gangster for a brother and a prostitute for a sister. Macmillan had put a great deal of distance between his political career and the criminal element that were his family.

The problem Brady had with Macmillan was that he socialised with the right kind of people. Powerful people. Even his penchant for prostitutes, the younger the better, was never reported to the police, let alone in any of the papers.

Mayor Macmillan had even foiled Rubenfeld, who was a hardened hack. There were countless front-page spreads that Rubenfeld could have done on Macmillan aside from one slight problem – no editor would touch it.

'The greasy git has the right approach. He knows how to stop people talking. Money, Jack. Money!' Rubenfeld had often grumbled over one too many pints followed by countless whisky chasers. Most of the time at Brady's expense.

Brady knew that Rubenfeld was right. Macmillan had protection. Whether he paid for it or not, Brady had no idea. But there were quite a few powerful North-East businessmen, and even high-ranking police officers like Detective Superintendent O'Donnell, who weren't afraid to be seen publicly with him.

'And Bentley? What's his take on this?'

'Well, you know how it goes with Macmillan. There's nothing he can do. From what I've gathered, word came down from the top to not pursue it any further. That Mayor Macmillan's driver was in the wrong area at the wrong time. In other words, he got lost.'

'You're serious?' Brady spluttered.

Conrad nodded.

'What's his driver look like?'

'Short, fat and bald.'

'One out of three isn't bad, Conrad,' Brady said with a wry smile.

'He's definitely not our rapist, sir,' Conrad answered. 'If you saw him, you'd know what I mean. Guy would have a heart attack if his pulse got above forty.'

'Does Bentley think he could be connected to McGuire's attack?'

Conrad shook his head. 'They've got nothing on him.'

'Poor sod. I bet he's married. Yeah?'

'Yes,' Conrad answered.

'Imagine explaining that one to the wife? Bet he told her he was on some official mayoral business and there he is driving around in the mayor's car looking for a good time. So, has the rest of the team gone home as I instructed?'

'Not yet. That's why I'm here.'

'What? You're not here to bring me food and keep me entertained while I eat?' Brady asked, feigning disappointment.

His mood had lightened considerably after hearing about Mayor Macmillan's driver.

'Afraid not, sir.'

Conrad prepared himself. He didn't want to take his boss down another blind alley. Not after the fiasco with Trina McGuire's attack and then Jake Munroe. The press were dining out on the fact that the police had released a potential suspect. Conrad was already steeling himself for the scathing headlines in tomorrow's *Northern Echo*. He'd seen no need to bother Brady with the endless calls from journalists requesting information on why the suspect had been released and demanding developments on the serial rape case. The problem was that they had nothing new to give them – until now.

'You know we've been studying the CCTV footage from the nights when the victims were attacked? In particular, the night that Chloe Winters said she was stopped by a taxi driver?'

'Yeah. But this whole car business has been blown out of the water by Macmillan's idiot of a driver, surely?'

'No, sir.'

'You're telling me Chloe Winters was actually approached by a silver taxi? That it wasn't just a false memory induced by Bentley's press call?'

Conrad shook his head. 'We found it. Took all day and most of this evening. But we found it.'

He was clearly pleased with himself. It was a rare moment to witness.

'Got it on the CCTV camera from the Siam Bay restaurant as you turn off the Promenade onto Marine Avenue. That was why we couldn't find her before – we were looking in the wrong place.'

It was just the break they needed.

Brady breathed out. He resisted the urge to get up and hug Conrad.

'What made you broaden your search?' Brady asked.

'You, sir. You'd insisted that the rapist was there. He had to be. So if we couldn't find him that meant we were looking in the wrong place.'

173

'What have you got then?'

'A silver Passat pulls up beside her opposite the Promenade. She goes over to the driver's window. They talk. Then she turns and walks back the way she came.'

'Which direction?'

'Back along the Promenade past the Spanish City dome.'

'What did the driver do?'

'He sat and watched her until she disappeared. Then he appears to follow her.'

'Did he pull up beside her again?'

'No, sir. He takes a right turn up by Brook Street and then we lose sight of him when he reaches Oxford Street.'

'Do you have any other footage of the driver after that?'

'No. Unfortunately there's no cameras up Oxford Street. He could have turned off anywhere and parked up.'

'Yeah, and he could have picked her up as well.'

Brady thought about it for a moment.

'What about Chloe?'

'Nothing, sir. Same information that we had before – she turns up the alley behind the Avenue pub. That's the last we see of her for forty-eight hours.'

'We need this driver, Conrad. Registration details?'

'I can do better than that. Lee Harris, twenty-seven years old. Part-time weekend taxi-driver for East Central. No priors though.'

'Doesn't matter. I want him picked up and brought in for questioning. And I mean now! He was the last known person to see Winters before she was taken. I'd say that he's crucial to our investigation. Is he working for East Central tonight?'

'No. Their dispatch operator said that he'd called in sick earlier.'

'Harvey and Kodovesky are still here?'

'Yes, sir.'

'Good. I want them to pick up Lee Harris and bring him in to the station. We need to get an interview room sorted. But first,

I want to see this CCTV footage for myself,' Brady said, standing up.

'Of course, sir.'

'What about Kenny and Daniels?' Brady asked as he walked towards the office door.

'Still here.'

'All right. Let's see if they can find this Lee Harris' taxi in the CCTV footage from the nights the first two victims were raped. Now we know what car we're looking for, it shouldn't be that difficult to either eliminate him or implicate him. You're certain there's no previous convictions?'

Conrad shook his head. 'Nothing. Completely clean.'

Why did Brady not buy it? His gut was telling him that they could be on to something here. Before he questioned Lee Harris, Brady wanted to make sure that he ran a check on him personally. He wanted to be sure that nobody had missed anything. Not that he didn't trust Conrad. But the last thing Brady wanted was to screw up. Not again. Not after letting Munroe slip through his fingers.

Chapter Twenty-Six

It was now 1:33 a.m. Too late to still be at work. But things hadn't quite gone to plan.

'Where the fuck is he?' Brady demanded.

Conrad caught Brady's darkening expression as he walked into the office. He kicked the door closed with the heel of his foot. He stood still waiting for Brady to finish his call.

Brady nodded at Conrad, gesturing for him to put his coffee on his desk.

'I honestly don't know, Jack,' Harvey answered.

'What the fuck is his girlfriend saying?'

'Kodovesky's with her now. She thought he was working for East Central. She had no idea that he'd rung in sick.'

'You believe her?' Brady asked, unable to hide the scepticism in his voice.

He massaged his tired eyes as he listened to Harvey's response.

'What do you think? She's hysterical. Thinks something serious has happened to him.'

'I can give you serious. What about the police are after him as a suspect in a serial rape case? You've tried ringing him from his girlfriend's mobile and landline I take it?'

'What do you think, Jack? Of course we have.'

'And she seriously has no idea where he could be?'

'I've already said – she hasn't got a clue.'

Brady thought about what to do next.

'Stay put until he shows. OK? Because he will turn up,' he said. However, he didn't feel as confident as he sounded.

'OK, Jack. Your call.'

Brady cut the line and then turned to Conrad.

'Bastard still hasn't showed up,' Brady informed him as he walked over to his desk and picked up his coffee. 'Thanks by the way,' he said. 'Pity you couldn't have made it a pint.'

'Believe me if I could have done, I would, sir,' Conrad answered as he tried to stifle a yawn.

'Look, why don't you head off? There's nothing else you can do here. As soon as we get him, I'll let you know. OK?'

'Are you sure?' Conrad asked. Not that he needed much persuading.

'Yeah. We've got an APB out for his car so all we can do is wait it out. Uniform numbers have been increased tonight in Whitley Bay. They've all been briefed about him. So, everything's covered, Conrad. Go home.'

'Yes, sir,' Conrad answered, relieved. 'What about you?'

'I've got my bed sorted,' Brady said, gesturing with his head towards the beat-up old leather sofa positioned under the window.

Conrad didn't make a move to leave. Instead he looked at Brady. His face was filled with concern.

'Sir? What if . . .' Conrad faltered, unable to finish.

'What? What if he strikes tonight? What if he called in sick because he's busy trawling the streets waiting to attack his latest victim?'

'Yes, sir,' Conrad answered.

'I don't know, Conrad. I honestly don't know,' Brady answered. The reality of the thing scared the hell out of him. He dragged a hand back through his hair as he thought about what could be happening right now to some young woman. It was unbearable. Brady had uniform crawling through Whitley Bay in an attempt to scare him off – just in case he actually had decided to attack tonight. But was it enough? Who knew?

Brady's mobile rang. He looked at it – Claudia.

It took him a moment to register that she was actually calling him. He hadn't heard from his ex-wife in months. She'd made her point. She had moved on with her life. Unlike him.

Conrad waited, expecting it to be connected to Harris.

'If I hear anything I'll call,' Brady instructed.

'Yes, sir,' Conrad answered.

Brady watched Conrad leave before answering his mobile. 'Jack?'

'What's wrong?' Brady asked. It was direct and to the point.

'Oh, God, Jack. I . . . I didn't know who else to talk to . . .'

Brady waited.

He was trying to rein in the tumult of emotions he was feeling. Just hearing her on the phone was difficult. But he couldn't afford to get emotional. There was too much at stake – primarily his career. He had Lee Harris' whereabouts to worry about. So he didn't have time for Claudia and whatever mind-fuck games she wanted to play at this time of the morning.

'Jack? Are you still there?' Claudia asked.

Brady tried to ignore the fact that her voice sounded small and fragile. Desperate even. But she had DCI James Davidson to turn to, so why the fuck was she calling him?

'Yeah . . .' he muttered, reluctantly. It was the best he could do.

'I . . . I need to share something with you.'

Brady resisted the urge to say that they stopped sharing anything the day she gave him divorce papers. Instead he kept his mouth shut.

'God, you're making this awkward!'

'Look, Claudia. I'm busy, all right? I'm in the middle of working on a case.'

'What? At this time?' Claudia asked, incredulous.

'That's what I said.'

Neither one spoke for a couple of moments.

'Claudia? Why don't you just tell me why the fuck you've called?'

He heard her sigh. 'OK. But promise me you'll help?'

'How can I promise when I don't know what you want?'

'Christ, Jack! You can be so difficult.'

She sighed again. It took her a few more moments before she talked. Whether she was debating just hanging up on him, Brady couldn't say.

'It's about Nicoletta . . .' Claudia began.

She now had Brady's full attention. 'What's happened?'

'Everything . . .'

'For fuck's sake, Claudia! Stop playing games!'

'I'm not. It's all one big mess and I don't know what to do. Nicoletta's been denied residency, Jack.'

He suddenly sat back. He felt as if someone had punched him in the guts.

'You're fucking with me?'

'Would I do that?'

Brady didn't answer.

'We found out on Thursday morning. I've been doing everything in my power to try to get an appeal. But . . .'

Brady knew the way the system worked. It was highly unlikely the decision would be overturned.

'Do you know why she's been refused residency? I mean, they know, don't they? What she went through with those Dabkunas bastards?' He suddenly realised he was shouting. Not at Claudia, but at the situation.

'Of course they do. I'm trying, you know? I'm trying to do everything to keep her here. God, Jack, if she gets sent back they might get her—' Claudia's voice broke off.

'They' were the Dabkunas brothers. Brady didn't need her to spell it out.

'How's she taken it?' Brady asked.

'How do you think? She's terrified. Absolutely terrified about what will happen to her if she gets deported.'

Brady didn't know what to say.

'I promised her, Jack. I promised that I wouldn't let anything happen to—'

'*We* promised,' interrupted Brady. 'We both gave her our word.'

Brady was sure he heard a muffled voice in the background. He knew who it would be – DCI James Davidson.

'Look, I'll call you back when I get more news. Yeah?' she whispered.

With that she hung up.

The more Brady thought about it, the more he convinced himself that Claudia would be able to get the decision revoked. She had powerful contacts and he knew she would do everything she could to secure Nicoletta's residency.

It didn't take long before the phone call was overshadowed by other more pressing matters. There was still no sign of the suspect. Brady had ordered Kodovesky and Harvey home. He had other officers stationed at Harris' house for when he returned – if he did actually return. Brady was worried that he had run. That he'd got wind of the fact that the police were after him and he had just disappeared. Brady was under no illusions – their man was dangerous. He was clever enough to have eluded the police for two months. Would it surprise Brady if he had been waiting, expecting this moment? No. This was a situation he would have been anticipating for some time now.

Brady had already alerted the airports and ferries in case this was the scenario. It might have been over-reacting but the last thing he wanted was to be hauled into Gates's office to have his bollocks chewed off for not being proactive. The fact that Harris had disappeared and wouldn't answer his mobile was atypical according to his girlfriend. That was enough for Brady.

Brady stretched his arms behind his head and yawned. He was literally dropping from exhaustion. His eyes were so tired that he could hardly read the words on the screen in front of him. He was in the computer room running a search on Lee Harris: twenty-seven-year-old Caucasian male; residing at 28A Marine Avenue, Whitley Bay. Nothing had come up so far. Brady couldn't shake Amelia's profile. If this was their rapist, then he had to have had some prior convictions against him.

Something in the system, no matter how minor. Brady knew better than anyone that your average law-abiding citizen didn't wake up one morning and decide to commit a crime. Especially something as heinous and sadistic as these ones. There was always a history of criminal activity. A pattern that showed the gradual escalation. That was lacking here. Completely. And Brady didn't trust it.

He looked down at the photograph they had of the suspect. The police could access the DVLA and it was this photo Brady had released to the airports and ferries. The picture from Lee Harris' driver's licence was similar to their photofit. Apart from the fact that he had a thick head of black hair. But it had been issued six years ago. The similarity was good enough for Brady considering that the three victims who had put the photofit together had all been drunk when the rapist approached. The fact that they had any kind of photofit was a miracle. Brady decided to do some further digging later that morning. Something was missing. But he wasn't quite sure what. What he did know was that he needed to sleep. He stumbled back to his office, bleary-eyed and in need of eight hours uninterrupted kip.

He lay down on the couch and closed his eyes. Despite the fact he was exhausted he couldn't silence his mind. Too many questions were racing through it. He waited a few minutes but the noise in his head did not abate.

'Fuck it!'

Resigned, he got up and walked over to his desk. He yanked open the drawer and pulled out a bottle of whisky. It was a Talisker: a twenty-year-old single malt; distilled and matured on the Isle of Skye. It had been a gift from Madley. He looked at the bottle. It was Madley's favourite whisky. As he opened it, Brady knew it would be the last one he would ever receive from Madley. He poured a liberal measure into his Che Guevara mug. Then he walked back over to the couch and collapsed. He waited a moment before taking a drink. He wanted to savour it.

'To you, Madley,' Brady said, raising the mug in honour of his childhood friend. 'You fucking bastard!'

He took a much-needed gulp. He waited for it to burn the back of his throat as it worked its way down. It was smooth with a subtle kick – just like Madley.

You stupid bastard, Madley. What the fuck are you playing at?

Brady took another drink as he tried to put all thoughts of Madley to the back of his mind. He felt betrayed. He had never thought Madley would distance himself from him. But he had. It was indisputable. Brady had called him countless times. The result? Silence.

Brady sat back and attempted to relax. It was just him and a mug of whisky. No calls. No team needing to be told what to do. Just him in the dark waiting for . . . Waiting for what?

He glanced down at the mobile by his feet. He had left numerous messages with Nick in the vain hope he would get back to him. It wasn't just Trina McGuire's attack he wanted to talk to his brother about. It was Jake Munroe. After all, Nick had worked for, or to be more precise, against John De Silvio – AKA Johnny Slaughter. Munroe's old boss and the same man Madley had warned was after Nick. One of many men who wanted to take him down. Brady wanted to know whether Nick had had any dealings with Munroe. Brady still couldn't let go of the fact that there was something going on between Munroe and Madley. What, he didn't know, but he wanted Nick to reassure him.

He swigged back what was left in his mug and contemplated a refill. His head was still buzzing. What he wanted was that numb feeling that would enable him to switch off and fall asleep, even if it was only for a couple of hours. He decided on one more shot and then he would call it quits.

Brady woke up with a start. It felt as if he had suddenly been resuscitated. He gasped with a combination of pain and surprise as he opened his eyes. Dusty shafts of light danced in front of him. It took him a moment to come to his senses and realise that he was still in his office. Then it hit him. The blinding pain in his head.

'Fuck!' he groaned.

He closed his eyes again and dropped his arm down by his side as he braced himself against the excruciating pounding where his head was supposed to be. His hand accidentally knocked over the bottle of whisky that was on the floor.

He picked the bottle up. It was empty.

'Shit!' he cursed.

He had no recollection of finishing it. He had drunk over half a bottle. No surprise then that his head was exploding.

Brady winced as he attempted to look at the time: 5:33 a.m.

Preparing himself, he swung his legs around and sat up. It took him a moment before he felt he could actually stand. He needed painkillers, coffee and a tab. In that order. It was a perfect remedy for any hangover. He was undecided whether or not he would be slapping a nicotine patch on instead of smoking a cigarette. Maybe he would do both. Anything to stop himself feeling so crap.

He needed an update on the suspect. It was obvious they hadn't apprehended him yet. Otherwise Brady would've known about it. Then he would go home, get showered and dressed and make a point of bringing a change of clothes back into work.

First, he had to find some painkillers.

It took Brady less than an hour to sort himself out before heading back to his office where he was waiting for Conrad to show. His headache had finally eased off with the help of aspirin and copious amounts of black coffee. As yet, they had no news on the suspect. Brady was mentally preparing himself for taking what paltry scraps he had to Gates. He was also waiting for Amelia Jenkins. Admittedly, it was early on a Sunday morning. He had no idea when she would show up. He'd left a message on both her landline and mobile asking her to come in. But she hadn't answered. He imagined she had plans the night before. Why would she not? She was a clever, attractive woman in her early thirties who could get any man she wanted. The last thing Brady imagined her doing was sitting in on a Saturday night with a bottle of Pinot Grigio, an M&S meal for one and *X Factor* on for company.

Brady slowly breathed out. Thinking about Amelia Jenkins and some hot date was not helping his headache. But he did need her in ASAP. He wanted her opinion on Lee Harris. Jake Munroe was yesterday's problem. Brady was prepared to move on and accept that she'd been right about him. He had no choice. He had other priorities now. Not that Munroe didn't worry Brady. He did. It felt as if he'd let a dangerous animal loose back onto the streets of Whitley Bay, but without any concrete evidence against him, Brady had no choice but to go against his better instincts.

There was a knock at his door.

'It's open,' Brady called.

Conrad walked in.

'Sir.'

'Anything?' Brady asked without looking up. He was busy searching through what they had on the suspect, which was effectively nothing. The mortgage, council tax and water rates were all in his girlfriend's name. Lee Harris didn't even have credit cards. He had one bank account – a Co-operative cash account. No cheque books – nothing. But nor did he have any bad credit history. In fact he had no history.

'You know something, Conrad?'

'Sir?' Conrad asked as he walked over to stand in front of Brady's desk.

'Sit!' ordered Brady. Sometimes Conrad was too damned stuffy for his own good.

Conrad did as instructed.

'What are we missing here?'

Conrad didn't answer.

'I mean, this Lee Harris has nothing on him. So how the hell am I going to convince Gates that he's our suspect?'

'We have him pulling up to our third victim and talking to her. She refuses and walks away. He sits in his car for a few moments. Then he drives off in the direction she was heading. His car disappears. The victim disappears,' Conrad answered.

Brady shook his head.

'I wish it was that straightforward. But we're ignoring the glaringly obvious here – he's a bloody taxi driver. Of course he's going to be driving around. He's working. It's his bloody job!'

Brady dragged his hand back through his hair as he looked at Conrad.

'Christ, when Amelia finally walks in it will be the first point she picks up on. He's a taxi driver. He works weekends. He drives people home. He gets paid to do that. Shit! He probably saw Winters and pulled over worried about the state she was in. I mean, she was so pissed she couldn't walk straight. At one point she fell over. I've got no idea how the hell she didn't break something.'

Brady shook his head.

'I mean I've tried to make this work. I went through the surveillance footage from the nights of the first two attacks to be sure he wasn't there. But there's no sign of him. Nothing. All we have to go on is him stopping and seeing if our victim needed a lift home. Given the state she was in he comes over as more of a good Samaritan than serial rapist.'

'I agree, sir. She was exceptionally drunk. And yes, Lee Harris is a taxi driver. And it would be expected that he would be driving around the streets of Whitley Bay.'

'My point exactly.'

'Except, sir, he wasn't.'

'Wasn't what, Conrad?' Brady was not in the mood for games.

'Working.'

'What? Run that by me again?' Brady demanded, leaning forward.

'I checked the nights in question with East Central. On all three nights our suspect wasn't working. He cancelled the first one because of a scheduled holiday and the other two were due to illness.'

Brady sat back and absorbed the news. His mind was racing through what it meant.

'Not exactly in our favour then, is it?' Brady stated. 'He's on holiday or off ill on those nights. We know that all three victims were attacked as they walked home. The first two victims believed he followed them on foot. Neither one heard a car. But did he need a car, Conrad?' Brady asked as he looked at him. Before Conrad had a chance to answer, Brady continued. 'No. Why? Because he raped them where he attacked them. He didn't need to take them anywhere, unlike the third victim. With Chloe Winters he would have needed a car. He took her somewhere. He held her captive for forty-eight hours and then he released her. But on all three nights in question Lee Harris didn't show up at work. Why?'

Brady looked at Conrad. The look on his face showed he knew what Brady was getting at. That the reason he wasn't working on those nights was because he was busy stalking his victims before he attacked them.

'All right. Let's see what he has to say when we interview him. That is, if we get hold of him.'

'You think he's gone to ground?'

'What would you do in his situation, Conrad? You know the police are after you. If he's rung his work at all, he'll know that we've been asking questions about the shifts he's worked. And the three nights that the victims were attacked he wasn't at work,' Brady said. He looked Conrad straight in the eye. 'There's one thing I don't believe in, Conrad.'

'Coincidences, sir?'

'Precisely. And we haven't even got to the question of what the fuck was he doing cruising around in his taxi the night Chloe Winters was abducted and attacked, if he wasn't working?'

Chapter Twenty-Seven

'Sir? Sir?' shouted Daniels as he burst into the office.

Brady was at his office desk with Amelia Jenkins across from him, updating her on events. Lee Harris had replaced Jake Munroe on the list of suspects. But before Brady had even got a chance to hear Amelia's take on him the door had been thrown open and Daniels was standing there, red-faced and panting.

'Tell me there's a fire? Because that's the only reason I can imagine you would have for barging into my office uninvited.'

Daniels took a moment to catch his breath. He had just run up a flight of stairs in record time.

'I'm sorry, sir. I . . . I didn't mean to—'

Brady raised his hand to cut him off.

'Why are you here?'

'He's just walked into the station, sir,' Daniels said.

'Who has?' Brady asked.

'The suspect. He's just voluntarily handed himself over.'

'Lee Harris has?'

'Yes, sir.'

'Why didn't you say that when you walked in?' Brady demanded.

Daniels was speechless. He thought that was exactly what he'd done.

Brady turned to Amelia.

'I'm going to introduce myself to Mr Harris. Feel free to watch the interview if you like. Daniels will show you where the monitor's set up.'

'Thanks. I'd appreciate that,' Amelia said, standing up.

As she did so, Brady breathed in her delicate fragrance. It was some subtle but distinctive perfume. Which meant it was expensive. Everything about Amelia was expensive. Her education, her clothes, her jewellery and, Brady assumed, her taste in men.

He couldn't help but notice that she was not dressed in her usual attire. Instead she was wearing a pair of worn, faded jeans and a white shirt. It was a simple, casual look that suited her perfectly. He had initially been taken aback when she'd breezed into his office at 11:00 a.m. Not because she hadn't bothered to return his messages and tell him she was coming in. No. It was because she looked breath-taking.

'Something wrong, Jack?' Amelia asked.

Brady suddenly felt embarrassed.

'No . . . nothing,' he answered, unable to look her in the eye. Instead he turned and addressed Daniels: 'Get me Conrad will you? I want him in on this interview.'

'Yes, sir,' replied Daniels, relieved to be dismissed.

Brady headed for the door.

'Good luck,' Amelia said.

Brady turned back and shot her a questioning look.

'Why would I need "luck"?'

'Because no one voluntarily hands themselves over unless they're absolutely certain that the police will find nothing on them,' Amelia stated. 'Am I correct in believing that he has no prior convictions?'

Brady stood by the open door, not believing what he was hearing.

The suspect had just handed himself in, which meant that Brady could call off the search for him. He could also cancel the press release that was due to go out appealing to the public for information. Surely this was good news? It was good news for the team. For Whitley Bay police station and for Brady's career.

'What exactly are you getting at?' Brady asked as his expression darkened.

For whatever reason, Amelia had taken to opposing Brady at every turn of the investigation. It was a recent phenomenon that had kicked off when Conrad had returned from sick leave. But whatever her problem was, Brady wanted her to sort it – and fast. Otherwise he would have to ask Gates to have her assigned elsewhere. It wasn't good for morale for the team to witness them constantly at each other's throats. Nor was it good for Brady to have to fight her every inch of the way. He needed to feel that she was on his side instead of criticising every move he made.

'Think about it, Jack? The last thing you want to do is to go into that interview room and knee-jerk. Firstly, he has no criminal history. Secondly, he's willingly come in to help with your enquiries. Doesn't exactly fit the profile of the rapist. Nor does it sound like a man who has anything to hide.'

Brady didn't say a word but the look in his eye was enough for Amelia to know that she had crossed a line.

'Is that what you said to DCI Gates? That arresting Munroe was a knee-jerk reaction on my part?'

'No,' Amelia answered.

Brady could see the hurt in her eyes. He chose to ignore it. The accusation only hurt because it was true. She had stitched Brady up to his boss. There were no two ways about it. She'd been asked her opinion regarding the likelihood of Munroe being their rapist and she had used her 'superior' knowledge against Brady. Instead of backing him, and ultimately the team, she had used the opportunity to make herself look good. Brady had always known that she was interested in furthering her career – he just hadn't realised it would be at his expense.

'Just be careful. That's all I'm saying. I think you're walking into a trap here,' Amelia stated.

'Look Amelia, I appreciate your concern. But I've got a job to do,' Brady said.

'Think about it, Jack. Your suspect is a control freak.'

Brady paused, his hand on the door. But he didn't turn round.

'The crimes he's committed were highly organised. He left no DNA on the victims or at the crime scenes. He stalked his victims and then struck when it suited him. He blindfolded them and then tortured and raped them. The last victim he held for forty-eight hours. He then released her. Left her where she could be found. He could have killed her. Disposed of her body. But no, he lets her go,' Amelia paused, waiting for a reaction from Brady.

There was none.

'It's all about control. Don't lose sight of that. He's in control right now. Not you. He's the one who chose to walk into the station. That worries me, Jack. It should worry you too.'

Without a word Brady walked out of the office and straight into Conrad.

'Sorry, sir,' Conrad said, quickly moving out of Brady's way.

Brady ignored him and marched off. Better that, than throw a verbal punch at the wrong person.

Conrad looked at Amelia, who had joined him in the corridor.

'Why?' Conrad asked her. He had overheard the conversation. And what he'd heard he didn't like. He had known Amelia since they'd both been graduates and this was out of character for her.

'Because he needed to hear the truth.'

With that, Amelia turned on her heels and headed in the opposite direction to that which Brady had taken.

Chapter Twenty-Eight

If Brady was honest, he was taken aback. The suspect was not what he had been expecting. Amelia's warning about him kept going through Brady's mind.

Lee Harris was surprisingly good-looking. His driver's licence photo didn't do him justice. Harris was reminiscent of a young Brad Pitt. Everything about him said that he couldn't possibly be a suspect in a serial rape investigation. Jake Munroe – no question about it. But as Brady looked at Harris, he could understand why people would have a difficult time accepting that someone of his looks and charm could be connected to such sadistic crimes. His face was too handsome, with his dimpled cheeks and his gentle dark brown eyes.

Brady could imagine that few women would be able to resist Harris. He was extraordinarily handsome but seemingly without ego. He also had a way with him of putting people at their ease. Of reassuring them that everything was going to be all right. This was exactly what he was doing now. Reassuring Brady and Conrad that they had nothing to worry about; nothing to fear. He was here willingly because this was all a simple mistake – Brady's mistake. But Harris wasn't angry. Far from it. He was understanding, even sympathetic. After all, they had a serial rapist at large. And that was why he was here. To help them with their enquiries.

'So, you see why I came straight in?' Harris asked innocently.

Brady didn't answer.

Looking at him, he bore no resemblance to the taxi driver that Chloe Winters had described to them. Chloe had said that the taxi-driver had 'creeped' her out. But sitting opposite Harris with his disarming good looks and gentle manner, it was hard to believe that he could possibly creep anyone out. Brady didn't like the fact that there was a slither of doubt in his mind as to whether Harris could be their man.

Harris' response to Brady's silence was to relax back against his chair and give him an easy-going smile. It had the right balance of being friendly, but not over-friendly. Confident without being arrogant. If anything, Harris' whole demeanour was one of embarrassment and apology at wasting police time.

'I'm sure the two of you would have done the same thing in my shoes,' Harris said as he looked from Brady to Conrad, who was silently sitting next to him.

Brady was fascinated by him. He wanted them on side. In fact, he wanted more than that. He wanted Brady and Conrad to like him. Understand him. And ultimately, release him. He had refused his right to a solicitor – even the duty solicitor. Stating quite emphatically that he had no need for legal representation. He was here of his own free will.

Brady looked up at the surveillance camera recording the interview. He wondered whether Amelia was actually watching this; and if she was, what the hell she made of it.

Harris ran a long, strong hand over the couple of centimetres of black stubble covering his scalp. Few men could pull such a hard look off without looking intimidating. Harris, on the other hand, looked as if he should be a model on the front page of *Esquire* magazine. Not sitting in Whitley Bay police station being questioned as a suspected serial rapist.

He was dressed in a smart black suit and white shirt with the first two buttons undone. His attire added to the suave charismatic air about him.

Brady was aware that Conrad hadn't said a word.

'So Mr Harris—'

'Please, call me Lee, Detective Inspector,' Harris interrupted.

'So, Mr Harris,' Brady said as he looked him in the eye.

He gave Brady another friendly smile, which implied he understood. It was all right. Brady had to play by the books.

'You say that you spent last night driving from Newcastle to Gatwick airport and then back again?' Brady asked.

Harris shot him another winning smile as he slowly nodded. 'Yes. I did it as a private job. I made more money last night than I've done working for East Coast in the past month.'

'And who was this client?'

'Gareth Rochdale. Businessman. Absolutely minted.'

Brady nodded.

'And can he verify your whereabouts last night?'

Harris fumbled around inside the inner pocket of his suit jacket.

'There you go,' he said throwing Gareth Rochdale's business card down on the table. 'Great guy. I'm sure he would be happy to help. Only problem is he's on his way to the Bahamas right now. Some property deal over there,' Harris said. 'I'm due to pick him up from Gatwick when he lands in four days' time.'

'I see,' Brady said.

'Sounds like the kind of job that you'd be crazy to refuse, wouldn't you say?'

'Yes, sir,' answered Conrad.

'But an overnight job like that, you'd tell your girlfriend, wouldn't you?'

'Of course, sir.'

'So, why didn't you, Mr Harris?' Brady asked as he turned to face him.

Harris ran a hand over the stubble on his chin.

'I didn't want to worry her,' he answered.

'But that's exactly what you did,' Brady replied. 'She had no idea where you were. In fact, when you didn't return any of her calls she was adamant that you had been in an accident.'

Harris held Brady's gaze.

'And I feel really bad about that. But I didn't tell her because she'd have worried that I'd lose my job with East Central if they found out. Obviously they now know I lied when I rang in sick yesterday.'

'Yes,' Brady answered, thinking that was the least of Harris' problems.

'Look,' Harris said as he made a gesture of opening his hands. 'I'm here now. As soon as I found out that the police were looking for me, I came straight to the station. I could have gone home, explained myself to Lisa. But I didn't. I chose to come here.'

'How did you find out we were looking for you?' Brady asked.

'I rang East Central and talked to Eileen. I wanted to see if my shift was still available tonight or if she thought I'd still be off sick and had given it to one of the other lads. And that's when Eileen told me that the police had been in looking for me. Checking up on all the shifts that I worked over the past few months.'

Brady nodded. They had specifically instructed East Central not to say anything if Lee Harris got in touch. That they just had to tell the police he had contacted them. Brady assumed Eileen had helped Harris because she couldn't believe that someone like him could possibly be in trouble with the police.

'Do you shave your head, Mr Harris?' Brady asked.

'Sorry?'

'Simple question. Do you shave your head?'

Lee Harris looked at Brady. He gave him a slow, assured smile as he thought about it.

'No. I know it's short but I've never shaved it,' he answered with mild amusement.

Brady knew that he had seen the photofit of the rapist. They were plastered up all around Whitley Bay; including in the police station.

Brady thought about it. If it was dark, and you were a bit the worse for wear, would it be possible to mistake Lee Harris' aggressively short haircut for being bald? Maybe.

'So, when can I go?' he asked, breaking into a smile. 'I've got some apologising to do.'

'I wouldn't worry about that Mr Harris. Your girlfriend's on her way here.'

'To meet me?'

'No, Mr Harris. To see if she can corroborate your story,' Brady answered.

For a delicious moment, Brady noted that Lee Harris looked surprised. His charming, easy-going manner slipped. A flash of uncontrolled anger briefly betrayed him.

'I don't understand,' Harris said, quickly assuming his usual calm manner.

'The three nights in question that we asked you about,' Brady replied, looking at the dates on the notepaper in front of him. 'You said you were working. But East Central have already informed us that you didn't cover those shifts for various reasons.'

'Maybe? I can't remember,' Harris answered, giving Brady an apologetic smile. 'You know how it is. I work all week away and then I come back and work a weekend nightshift to pay towards a deposit for a house and our wedding next year. I hardly have time to sleep let alone make a note of what I do every day.'

'Even last weekend?' Brady questioned.

Harris shrugged. 'You know how it is? One weekend blurs into another when you're working night shifts.'

'Well, it's a good thing that your girlfriend is prepared to talk to us. Quite efficient, isn't she? I suppose as a doctor's receptionist she must be very organised. Anyway, she's offered to help us with our enquiries. I'm sure she has an excellent memory for dates.'

Brady called an end to the interview before Lee Harris had a chance to talk. He wanted to let the suspect sweat for a while. Then they might get some truth out of him.

He still had the CCTV footage of him talking to Winters

shortly before she was abducted. He was saving that vital piece of evidence until after he had talked to Lisa Sanderson; the girl-friend. He wanted her version of where Lee Harris was on the nights in question.

Chapter Twenty-Nine

It was now 6:20 p.m. Brady had left Harris to rot in a holding cell for the past six hours while he regrouped with his team. He had asked the Custody Officer if he could extend the twelve-hour holding limit to a further twenty-four hours. He was nowhere near ready to charge him – if at all. Luckily for Brady it had been granted, because he was in dire need of extra time. At this point they were in trouble. Serious trouble. It looked as if Harris could walk. Nobody wanted that; least of all Brady.

Gates had already been breathing down his neck. The press were crawling everywhere wanting an update. However, Gates was reluctant to release any details until they were in a position to press charges.

Amelia had surprised Brady by agreeing that there was a very strong possibility that Lee Harris could be there suspect. There had been a 'but' – of course. This was Amelia Jenkins after all. But she had raised what everyone else on the team were thinking; that the suspect, surprisingly, had no prior convictions. He had no history. If Amelia's profile was to be believed, he should have had some kind of charges in his past. But they had drawn a blank.

Then there was the fact that he was everything that you would not expect. Exceptionally good-looking, articulate, polite and even charming. Tom Harvey had made the obvious point: 'Why would he rape?'

This, of course, was like showing the dog the rabbit where Amelia was concerned. She had gone on to another one of her lengthy lectures about the fact that rape is not about sexual fulfilment; so Harris' good looks and charm were inconsequential. Harvey had made the fatal mistake of not seeming convinced, so Amelia had gone on to cite Ted Bundy as an example of a good-looking man who was friendly and charismatic and had no trouble in attracting female attention. Nevertheless, between 1974 and 1978, Bundy had managed to kidnap and murder thirty young women in the US. Amelia had pointed out that the only reason Harris troubled them was because, ordinarily, serious offenders tended to be very ordinary. The police dealt with them on a daily basis, so when someone like Harris strolled through the station doors volunteering to help the police with their enquiries, it was no surprise that people struggled with the concept of him being a serial rapist. If he was, why would he offer himself up?

Amelia may have been talking to the team, but the question had been levelled directly at Brady. He didn't have an answer.

Brady had concluded the briefing when news that Lisa Sanderson, Lee Harris' fiancée, had been brought into the station to be interviewed. But then the investigation took a turn for the worse. The suspect's lack of priors and his willingness to help the police with their investigation had been nothing compared to the bomb that Lisa Sanderson had dropped on them. She had provided a water-tight alibi for Lee Harris' whereabouts on the night of the first rape.

Afterwards, Brady had got Conrad to run checks against her information. It had come back conclusive – she was telling the truth. He had then updated Gates before informing his team. Deflated and discouraged, Brady had dismissed them for the evening. There was nothing else they could do. He had given Harvey enough money to buy them a couple of rounds in the Fat Ox and then an Indian in the Ahar in Whitley Bay. It was a good old-fashioned North-East Sunday night tradition – a couple of pints followed by a chicken tikka masala. The team were demoralised, so Brady had to dig deep into his pocket to try and lift their spirits. He needed them back in the morning in a better mood than when they had left. He had no idea what tomorrow would bring and that worried him as much as it did them.

The DNA swab that had been taken from Lee Harris had come back negative. No DNA evidence had been recovered from any of the attacks but he had been hoping that it would bring some prior convictions to the surface.

Brady leaned forward on his desk and held his head in his hands. He was certain that Lee Harris was their rapist. There was something disturbing about him. If you scratched beneath the surface you could see it. Brady had seen a flash of it. And it was enough to convince him that they were dealing with a psychopath. The problem Brady had was they didn't have enough evidence to charge him, let alone impound his car so Forensics could search it.

'Sir?' Conrad asked as he walked into his office.

Amelia followed behind him.

'Sorry, the door was open,' Conrad apologised.

Brady dragged his head up and looked at them. They both looked sheepish. Embarrassed that they had caught Brady out.

'I thought you two were heading out with the rest of the team for a beer and a curry?' Brady asked, trying to sound light-hearted. It failed.

'No. We thought you might want some company?' Conrad replied.

Brady looked at them. The last thing he needed right now was company. He was in a lousy mood. All he wanted to do was go home, open a bottle of wine or two and put some music on to drown out his shit day.

Conrad ignored the look in Brady's eye. It was obvious that he wanted to be alone. But given the day's events, that was the last thing Conrad was going to do.

He walked over to the beat-up leather couch and sat down. Amelia looked unsure. Brady's dark expression told her she was the last person he wanted to deal with on a Sunday night.

Especially at the end of a torturous day. But then there was Conrad who, loyal as ever, wanted to work through Lisa Sanderson's interview. He wanted to make sense of it. See if they could turn it around for tomorrow. But from the look in Brady's eye, it was clear that he wasn't in the mood for talking.

'I don't know about you two, but I need a drink,' Amelia suggested. It was her way of breaking the ice. She thought Brady looked like he could do with one.

He nodded. 'Yeah. I've got some scotch that I keep as an emergency.'

He stood up, walked over to his filing cabinets and pulled out a top drawer. Inside were six bottles of scotch – all unopened. These were Christmas gifts that he had filed away. This stuff wasn't the Talisker whisky that Madley drank. It was middle-of-the-road bottom-shelf piss. But under these circumstances it would do.

Brady picked up a blended malt and cracked it open.

'Do me a favour, Conrad, go fetch some mugs?'

Conrad jumped up and left the office.

There was an awkward silence between Brady and Amelia with Conrad gone. Brady busied himself with reading the labels on the other bottles of scotch he had stashed away, while Amelia hovered by the open office door waiting for Conrad.

They both inwardly breathed a sigh of relief when Conrad finally returned.

'Sorry, had to give them a wash first,' Conrad said as he walked over to Brady.

Brady poured a liberal measure in both mugs before turning to fill his own.

He then went back and sat down behind his desk.

'Cheers!' he said, raising his mug to Conrad and Amelia, who were sitting at opposite ends of the couch.

'Cheers!' mumbled Conrad and Amelia together.

Brady took a drink. It tasted like shit. But it was the best he had to offer.

He watched as Amelia winced at the harsh, burning taste. But she persevered with it, forcing herself to take another mouthful.

Nobody spoke. The atmosphere in the room was chillier than a walk-in refrigerator.

'So,' Brady began, deciding he had no choice but to get it over with: 'Lisa Sanderson?'

Amelia looked up at Conrad, unsure of who should speak first.

Conrad gestured for Amelia to answer.

'Well, she's an intelligent, attractive, twenty-two-year-old young woman. I wouldn't expect anything less from someone like Lee Harris,' Amelia stated.

Brady took another mouthful of Scotch as he contemplated Amelia's summary. It wasn't exactly what he wanted. But she was right. Lee Harris' girlfriend suited him in more ways than one.

She was petite with long, straightened blonde hair, pretty, delicate features and trusting bright blue eyes. Everything about her was charmingly innocuous. She was a doctor's surgery receptionist and consequently came over as polite, professional and courteous. She had never been in trouble with the police, or even been in a police station. She came from a good, respectable family, had a reasonable college education behind her and held down a responsible job. Lisa Sanderson was perfect alibi material.

Brady had spent two hours interviewing her. He had needed to because he didn't trust what she was telling him. In that time she never once wavered from her belief that this was all a mistake and that her fiancé was innocent. The problem Brady had was she really believed it. And she had the evidence to substantiate it. When Brady had asked about their six-month relationship, it was clear that to her Lee Harris was perfect – too perfect for Brady's liking. They never argued; he had never raised his voice to her and definitely not his hand. They socialised with friends together. He even got on with her parents. When Brady had asked about his parents and family, Lisa Sanderson had in all innocence answered that he had none. That for whatever reason he didn't talk about his past.

Brady had asked her about the three nights on which the victims were attacked – the three nights that Harris wasn't working. Unfazed by the question, Lisa Sanderson had simply worked the dates back on her mobile phone. She had answers for every night in question. And she was convincing, because she was so transparent. There was nothing about her that told Brady she was lying. Her face blushed when Brady asked about their sex life, which was nothing to write home about. She described him as a gentle, considerate lover. Brady could tell that she meant it. She wasn't just giving Brady some spiel that she had prepared in advance. This was heartfelt. According to her, Lee Harris wasn't interested in anything that strayed from the missionary path. When Brady had mentioned sadism, Lisa Sanderson's startled eyes had looked at Brady with a combination of horror and disgust that he could even suggest such a thing. Brady was bitterly convinced by her. Despite fighting it, he'd had no choice but to accept that Lisa Sanderson was telling the truth.

And this was before she delivered the *coup de grâce*.

She had remembered all three nights – in detail. But it was her alibi for the first night that had Brady foiled. It was physically impossible for Harris to be their man.

It had been two months ago, at the end of August. Harris had booked time off work. She remembered specifically because it had been a surprise: he had taken her to Paris for the weekend, where he'd proposed.

Brady had taken a moment in the interview room to compose himself after she had delivered this damning news. The possibility of Lee Harris being in Paris while simultaneously raping and mutilating Sarah Jeffries, the first victim, was nil.

The second night in question was Saturday, September 28th. Again Lisa Sanderson was unfazed. Harris had just moved into her rented accommodation that afternoon. She had smiled at Brady and confided that he had 'pulled a sickie' that night so they could celebrate their first night officially living together.

Brady had asked her if he left her at any point during the early hours of the Sunday morning. Her answer had been an empathic 'no'. That they'd slept together. She went to sleep with him. And she woke up with him. It was the same story for all three nights.

The third time he'd missed work had been over a week ago – Friday, 18th October. She had been really ill with flu. He had been so concerned he'd rung in sick himself so he could look after her.

Again, according to Lisa Sanderson, Harris never left the flat.

What troubled Brady was the CCTV footage of Harris' taxi early that Saturday morning when Harris was allegedly looking after her.

Brady had pulled no punches. He had told her that they had footage of her fiancé's silver Passat pulling up to talk to the victim in the early hours of last Saturday morning shortly before she disappeared. Lisa Sanderson had reacted as Brady had expected. She didn't believe him. She couldn't believe him because Lee Harris had been in bed with her. Brady had asked if she had an explanation as to why Lee Harris' car was caught on CCTV cameras in Whitley Bay. Her answer was simple – she didn't know.

And the problem was, neither did Brady.

Lisa Sanderson was the perfect alibi. Looking at her, Brady knew no court in the land would convict Harris; not with his fiancée giving evidence that he had spent all three nights with her. And crucially, when the first victim had been attacked the suspect had been in Paris proposing.

'And?' Brady asked Amelia.

'And what? Do you want me to say she was lying? That she is so infatuated by Lee Harris that she made the whole Paris scenario up?' Amelia fired back. She shook her head. They were all feeling it. The frustration.

'She's not lying, Jack,' Amelia added.

'I know she's not. That's what I don't understand,' Brady said as he looked at her.

But Amelia had no answers for him. There were none.

'You definitely verified the details she gave us on the Paris trip?' Brady asked, turning to Conrad.

He couldn't shake the feeling that this was all too convenient. That the suspect just happened to be in a different country on the night of the first attack. It felt like a cover-up to him. But Lisa Sanderson was so damned convincing. And the evidence was indisputable. If Harris was in Paris on the night of the first attack it was impossible that he could be their suspect.

'Yes, sir,' Conrad answered, unsure of why Brady was asking. He already knew the answer. 'Lee Harris booked a weekend trip to Paris through Thomas Cook's in Whitley Bay. Five thirty p.m. flight outbound on Friday, 30th August returning on Sunday, 1st September at seven p.m. that evening. Hotel was included in the package. I checked with the hotel in Paris and they definitely booked in.'

Brady nodded. He had heard it before but he'd been hoping there was something, anything to cast doubt on the alibi. But the only thing that didn't work was Lee Harris as their suspect. It physically couldn't be him. The question now was whether Harris was actually protecting the rapist? Because if Harris wasn't driving his car the night of Chloe Winters' attack, someone sure as hell was.

But who?

'All right, so what are we left with?' Brady asked.

'Who was driving Lee Harris' car?' Conrad suggested.

'Yeah . . .' Brady muttered. 'And so far, that's all we've got on him. That he's an accomplice.'

'Maybe. Maybe not? You might have to face the reality.'

Brady swilled a mouthful of scotch around as he contemplated Amelia's words. He swallowed it, savouring the numbing effect.

'Meaning?' he asked.

'Just maybe Lee Harris is innocent—'

Brady's face was enough to cut Amelia off.

She sighed, irritated. 'Look, just hear me out. OK?' She waited before continuing, just to make sure that Brady was going to give her a chance to speak.

'Maybe he lent his car to a friend because he was looking after Lisa Sanderson on the Friday night? Remember she said she had to get an emergency doctor's appointment on the Saturday because she was so ill?' Amelia suggested. 'Maybe this friend worked as a taxi driver that night earning some extra cash? I know there are rules and regulations but I'm sure this has been done before. Or maybe this friend was driving back from somewhere. We don't know. What we do know is that Lee Harris couldn't possibly have been driving that car.'

'So, we're looking for "a friend" of his now?' Brady asked with an unmistakable edge to his voice. He couldn't hide the fact that he was feeling more and more pissed off the longer the conversation went on.

No matter how hard he tried, he could not get rid of the gut feeling that Lee Harris was their man. There was something about him that Brady couldn't shake. No matter how hard he tried. Even being faced with a watertight alibi made no difference. If anything, his gut feeling increased.

'Well, you have nothing on Harris, Jack. I know you don't want to hear it but it's the truth. His girlfriend not only provided him with an irrefutable alibi for the night of the first rape, she even gave you the information to corroborate it. Which Conrad did,' Amelia pointed out.

Conrad cleared his throat. 'Actually, Kenny did the background check for me with the travel agents. I didn't personally do it.'

Amelia flashed him a look of irritation. 'It doesn't matter whether you delegated the job or not, Conrad. I'm just establishing the facts.'

'And the facts are crap!' Brady muttered.

Nobody responded.

'What about the fact that his face matches the photofit?' Brady pointed out.

'As did Jake Munroe's and God knows half of the men in North Tyneside!' Amelia protested. 'It's not a great image, Jack. It was based on the memories of three victims who were all blindfolded before they got a really good look at him. And who were all drunk. It's difficult to remember things clearly when you're drunk. Or at least as drunk as they were.'

'What? So you're saying it's the victims' fault that we've got a "one photofits all" image?' Brady asked, in the mood for a fight.

'Don't be ridiculous. Christ! I'm the last person to level that kind of accusation. You know my stance on rape. It doesn't matter if a woman is lying flat-out drunk and naked on the ground in front of a man, it doesn't give him the right to just take her. Regardless of the clothes she wears or the amount of alcohol she consumes, rape is rape.'

Brady took another drink. It wasn't what he was implying but it wasn't worth arguing the toss with Amelia over such a delicate subject.

'Christ, Jack! My point was just this – if you tried hard enough you could even make DCI Gates fit that photo,' Amelia explained as a way of calming the situation down. It was pointless them turning on one another because the day had not gone as they'd hoped.

Brady waited a moment. He thought it best to let the air settle before talking.

'So, the upshot is that we interview Lee Harris in the morning and see what he has to say about the CCTV footage of his car driving up to the victim?'

It was all they had on him.

Amelia looked Brady directly in the eye.

'I don't think you have an alternative,' she replied.

It wasn't what Brady had wanted. He needed to hear her professional opinion about Lee Harris. He wanted to know that he wasn't the only one struggling with the concept that in twelve hours' time they could be releasing a serial rapist back onto the streets. Brady accepted Lee Harris had an alibi but he was sure that if he had the time he'd be able to unpick it. But he was running out of time. All he could do was see what tomorrow would bring. At least they had the CCTV footage, which meant Harris still had some explaining to do.

Chapter Thirty

Monday morning came round faster than Brady had anticipated – or wanted. One minute he was lying in bed unable to sleep. The next, his mobile phone was vibrating around on the bedside cabinet like a Mexican jumping bean.

He had forced himself to get up. He'd showered, dressed, smoked two cigarettes and drunk a strong black coffee in advance of the day ahead. Anything to keep him calm. But it had failed. As soon as he walked into the station he knew it was going to be a bad day. But he had no idea just how bad.

'Brace yourself, bonnie lad,' Turner greeted when Brady showed up at work.

He'd barely got a chance to get through the doors.

Turner was standing behind his reception desk waiting for Brady to turn up.

'Good news I take it?' Brady questioned with a playful look in his eye.

Whether Turner meant it or not, his troubled expression said it all.

'What? It can't be that bad can it? Don't tell me I've been sacked but someone forgot to inform me?' Brady said, still half-joking.

But he knew from Turner's silence that now was not the time for messing around. Something was clearly worrying him.

'Go on then. Put me out of my misery,' Brady said, resigning himself.

'Well . . . there's no other way to say it, I suppose,' Turner said as he raised his spidery white eyebrows at Brady. He took a moment to lick his pale, thin lips before continuing: 'Gates has released Harris. He was let go last night.'

It took a moment for the words to sink in.

'What? You're fucking with me? Right?' Brady spluttered, not believing what he was hearing.

Turner apologetically shook his scraggy head.

'I wish I was, bonnie lad.'

'On what grounds? I still had to interview him! I'm scheduled to interview him in half an hour!' Brady said, staring at Turner in disbelief. For a brief moment he thought the old desk sergeant might have finally lost it.

'It was down to Harris' girlfriend. Seems her father plays golf at Tynemouth Golf Club with Gates. Small world, eh? Sanderson owns a large transport business. You see his name plastered over half the haulage trucks around here.'

Brady shook his head. Sanderson and his business were inconsequential. It was the action that Gates had taken that bothered Brady.

'What the hell authority has some haulage owner got over Gates?'

'Well, last night Lisa Sanderson and her father, accompanied by some top-notch solicitor from Newcastle, brought in the person who was driving Lee Harris' car while he was off ill last Friday night. Seems he lent his car to another taxi driver. Their car had packed up suddenly so they borrowed Harris' for the shift until they could get theirs back on the Saturday. So—'

'Wait a minute!' interrupted Brady. 'Why the hell wasn't I informed about all of this? Another suspect is brought in and I don't hear about it?'

'You're arguing with the wrong person, Jack. I'm only warning you. That's all,' Turner pointed out.

'Look . . . I'm sorry . . . it's just . . .' Brady shook his head. He didn't mean to take his frustration out on Turner. It was just that the news had thrown him. No. It had more than thrown him, it had completely shaken him to his core. How could Gates just step in and take over his investigation? Brady couldn't understand why Gates had failed to inform him of the night's events without giving him a chance to have some input. He had worked on the case for two months now. Two, long, hard months, for Gates to just walk in at the eleventh hour and fuck everything up.

Brady took a deep breath while he tried to clear his head.

'So why was I not informed?'

'Because Sanderson specified that he wanted Gates to clean this mess up. That this was his future son-in-law they had in custody. And from all accounts you had nothing on him. He had rock solid alibis for all three nights.'

'But what about this driver? Is he in custody? Has he even been questioned?' Brady asked, not really believing that he was having to ask the desk sergeant what the fuck was going on with his own investigation.

'She gave a statement. It was verified by East Central that she worked that night.'

'She?' Brady asked, unable to contain his surprise.

Turner nodded.

'Yes. She looked like she was in her early fifties. Times are changing. In my day you would never have seen a woman taxi driver. Not working those late shifts and having to pick God only knows what kind of fares . . .'

But Brady wasn't listening. He needed to talk to Conrad. But first he had a few choice words for Gates.

'Jack? Did you hear me?' Turner asked, concern etched all over his lined face.

'Believe me, I heard you, Charlie,' Brady acknowledged as he turned and headed for the door into the back of the station. 'Is Conrad in?'

'He's spent the past hour pacing up and down waiting for you.'

'So why the fuck didn't he call me?'

'Why do you think?'

Brady thought about it. Conrad didn't want to be on the receiving end when Brady heard the news – understandably.

'And Gates? Where is he?' Brady asked.

'His office. Wanted me to pass on the message that he wanted to see you as soon as you clocked in,' Turner answered.

'I bet he fucking did!'

'Remember. You didn't hear any of this from me, bonnie lad. OK?'

'You know me better than that. Anyway, thanks.'

Brady knew that Turner would get it in the neck for simply looking out for him. He had no idea how Turner got hold of his information; for a copper soon to retire he still had his finger on the pulse. And Brady appreciated that, more than Turner would ever realise.

Chapter Thirty-One

'Sit down, Jack,' Gates ordered. It was a polite but firm instruction.

'I'd rather stand,' Brady replied.

'I mean it. Sit down,' Gates repeated.

'No thank you, sir,' answered Brady.

Gates said nothing.

He leaned back in his chair and waited for Brady to speak.

Gates's dark brown eyes were now fixed unnervingly on Brady. They betrayed the cold, detached intelligence of a man who would never allow himself to be compromised. The fact that Brady had just walked into his office unannounced or invited infuriated him. But this was DI Brady's typical maverick style. For some reason he didn't think that the rules of the job or the etiquette that came with his rank applied to him.

Brady waited for Gates to address him. He was dressed in his usual black uniform. Brady looked at the lines on Gates's hard face, a testimony to his dedication to the job. His skin was covered in harsh, pitted acne scars, some partially hidden by a permanent five o'clock shadow, but there all the same.

Gates irritably pulled the cuffs of his expensive white shirt down past his black uniform, glaring at Brady while he waited for him to explain his intrusion. It didn't happen. Brady stood perfectly still, hands clenched tight by his side with his eyes firmly fixed on Gates. He was intentionally not speaking for fear that what he wanted to say might have him thrown in the cells for a couple of hours to cool off. Or out on the streets with his P45 in his hand.

Minutes went by like this. Both at a stand-off. Brady had already decided he could spend all day eyeballing Gates until he got the apology and explanation he deserved. And he wanted Gates on his hands and knees when he said it.

It was Gates who finally broke the silence.

'I take it you've heard, then?'

It was clearly a rhetorical question given the fact that Brady had just barged into Gates's office without knocking. His secretary had done her best to prevent him from walking in unannounced. But her best had not been good enough. Brady had simply ignored her pleas and protestations and thrown open Gates's door.

Brady just looked at Gates. The anger in his eyes spoke louder than words.

Gates slowly nodded. 'I had no choice, Jack,' he said.

His words hung heavy in the air. Brady refused to accept them.

'For Chrissakes! Your job was on the bloody line! That's why I didn't call you back to the station when all this erupted. I had Henry Sanderson and his Goddamn solicitor baying for your blood. If I hadn't managed to calm the situation down your name would have been plastered all over the news this morning. You know what you would have been waking up to this fine Monday morning? Eh? Not hearing second-hand from someone at the station that your suspect has been released without your knowledge. Christ no! You would have woken up to the Goddamn press camped outside your house and your suspension letter in the post.'

Brady stood perfectly still as he absorbed what Gates was saying. He still did not trust himself to talk. But the questioning look in his eyes was enough for Gates to continue.

'Lee Harris was released late last night on my orders, Jack. Mine. And I had no choice. We had nothing on him. Or should I say, *you* had nothing on him. Why the hell the Custody Officer granted you another twenty-four hours is beyond me. But I'll be having a word with him when he comes in later. You interviewed the girlfriend, I take it?'

Brady stiffly nodded.

'Well you know better than anyone that she provided Harris with an alibi for every night in question. And during the rapist's first attack, he was in Paris for the weekend. I mean, what more did you want?'

'I brought all this information to you, yesterday, sir,' Brady stated. His voice was heavy and thick with a sudden Geordie inflection. 'You were perfectly happy for me to hold him over-night and then question him in the morning about the footage of his car.'

'Yes, you did. But you fed me what you wanted. At no point did you let me know the full extent of it. I agreed to the suspect remaining in custody because you persuaded me he could be a threat to the public if we released him. That he could be protect-ing whoever was using his car on that night. Now I understand that you wanted to present the CCTV evidence to him this morning and ask him about it. But Harry Sanderson and his solicitor saved you the trouble. They actually brought the driver in person last night to end this fiasco. She gave a statement, which you can read when you're done. But it's solid. She works for East Central and borrowed Lee Harris' car because hers had broken down and he'd called in sick for the night. Very generous offer when you think about it. Hazel Edwards, fifty-two-year-old grandmother of two, needs the cash from her shift but her car's broken. So Lee Harris steps in to help. As Harry Sanderson had pointed out to me: "Hardly the behaviour of a serial rapist, is it?"' Gates stared hard at Brady. 'And before you get any ideas, Hazel Edwards is clean. She has a couple of prior convictions for shop-lifting. But that was over thirty years ago. So don't even think about her as a suspect or as an accomplice.'

Brady didn't comment.

'Even Harris' trip to London and back on Saturday night has

been verified. Gareth Rochdale happens to be Sanderson's business associate. He actually asked Harris to chauffeur Rochdale to Heathrow.' Gates looked at Brady. 'Christ, Jack! What more do you want?'

He stood absolutely still with his hands clenched tight by his sides. Maybe it was just the cynic in Brady but he had immediately picked up on the fact that Harris had lent his car out. Brady was about to ask whether he could have planned something and was using this Hazel Edwards as a cover-up but then the Paris trip foiled him. It didn't make any sense. There was something about Lee Harris that made him uneasy. Did that make him a serial rapist? That was another question entirely.

'Did this Hazel Edwards say that she stopped the victim?'

'She couldn't remember. She said that she's stopped countless young girls walking home alone late after having drunk a skinful in Whitley. She says she pulls over and offers them a ride. Rather they got in the car with a woman than some bloke tries to pick them up.'

'So she's not sure that she was the one driving the silver Passat saloon on the CCTV footage? She was shown that?' Brady asked.

'Of course she was bloody shown it. I dealt with it personally. Myself and DI Adamson sorted this mess out.'

Brady stared at Gates, trying to control the anger coursing through his veins.

DI Adamson was Brady's nemesis. It was a well-known fact around the station. Adamson couldn't stand Brady because he flouted the rules to get the job done. Whereas Adamson played everything by the book – Gates's book. Adamson had belonged to North Shields CID until he got promoted into Jimmy Matthews' job as Detective Inspector at Whitley Bay. Adamson was Gates's protégé; his blue-eyed boy. He could do no wrong – unlike Brady. Overall Adamson reminded Brady of a politician. In other words, he couldn't be trusted.

It appeared as if Gates had everything wrapped up. So why didn't Brady accept it?

'So, did she recognise the footage?' Brady asked, making an attempt to keep his voice steady.

'I already told you – no. She said that would have been just a typical night for her.'

'So why did Winters describe the taxi driver as male then, sir?' Brady persisted.

'I don't bloody know and at this point I don't bloody care! She was very drunk. She has admitted that herself. Even her friends said she could barely stand up. So I imagine all that happened was Chloe Winters simply assumed the driver was male. Most people assume that taxi drivers in the North-East are male.'

Brady didn't pass comment.

Gates could see from the look in Brady's eye he was looking for trouble.

'Let it go, Jack!'

Brady did not back down.

'I mean it, let it go. Be grateful that they haven't lodged a complaint against you. Sanderson's solicitor was talking about suing for wrongful arrest. Luckily, I managed to calm things down.'

Brady kept quiet. There was nothing more to say.

'A serious assault came in last night. I want you and Conrad to have a look into it,' Gates instructed.

'What about the rape investigation?'

'You're still working on it. Albeit by the skin of your teeth after this weekend. Two suspects dragged in and then released, one after the other. Doesn't look good, Jack, does it? Makes the police look incompetent. In particular, it makes my Area Command look incompetent. Get your act together, all right? And in the meantime look into that assault. Maybe some distance from this case will do you some good.'

With that, Gates checked his watch and picked up his phone. 'If that's all?'

Dismissed, Brady turned and left, not quite sure how it had switched from him wanting an apology from Gates, to Gates demanding that Brady apologise for just doing his job.

Chapter Thirty-Two

Brady was sitting in his office trying to get his head around what had just happened. He had Hazel Edwards's statement in front of him. It was enough. But not good enough. She had been vague – too vague – about whether she had seen the victim or not. Even after she had watched the CCTV footage. Brady was surprised that this hadn't jogged her memory, but apparently not.

He sat back in his chair and slowly breathed out. Maybe Gates was right. He was too close to the investigation. He had worked on it for too long. There was no end in sight. This weekend Brady had believed he'd be able to close the case. But no.

Brady was waiting for Conrad. He'd had a look at the report filed on the assault. It had happened in the early hours of the morning in a back alley behind Linden Terrace. Conveniently, a location without CCTV cameras. The victim had been found at around 6:00 a.m. by a dog walker. Brady looked at the photograph of the victim's injuries. To say he was in a bad way was putting it mildly. The attack was so violent that Brady could make out prints from the sole of a boot on the victim's face. Or what was left of his face. His skull had taken most of the kicks. It had split open in two places from the force of the blows.

Brady pushed his hair back from his face as he stared at the brutal images in front of him. This was Whitley Bay at the weekend. Sunday nights were the worst. The police spent most of Monday cleaning up after the louts who'd been drinking nonstop from Friday night and had found themselves banged up in a holding cell charged with glassing someone for no particular reason. It wasn't just men who were being arrested for these drunken assaults, disturbingly women were as well – regardless of age. It was a culture that Brady did not understand. Nor did he want to.

He closed the file in front of him. The last thing he wanted to do was work some 'rubbish' case, which in all probability was going to end up being a murder investigation given the critical state of the victim.

Brady knew him. His wallet had been left with his driver's licence and bank cards inside his jeans pocket. His name was Eddie Jones. A small-time drug dealer and thug. He'd been banged up more times than Brady could remember but he was a hardcore recidivist and as Jones had often said: 'Old habits die hard.' Every time he'd been booked for dealing or possessing, he would entertain the police with that line.

Brady thought bitterly about Jones' condition. It was ironic. The last thing he would ever snort had been his own brains back up his nose. Jones had either pissed off another dealer or had short-changed a client. Either way he had enough enemies to fill Newcastle United's St James' Park stadium. Gates was wasting Brady's time. Pissing him off for the sake of it. He already felt like shit without having to follow dead leads on a victim that most of the coppers in North Tyneside saw as a problem. Because that was what Jones had become: a major headache. Rumour had it that he'd been dealing at three high schools in the area. Easy money from easy pickings. Get them young and you have them for life. Brady hated the whole drug scene. It made him sick to the stomach. But most of all, he hated the drug dealers. So why the fuck had Gates thrown this at his door? Punishment? A reminder of who was boss?

He had already swallowed his pride and updated his demoralised team with the news that the suspect had been released without charge. Amelia had said she wasn't surprised considering the weight of his alibis. It did little to help the situation.

Brady had left them to lick their wounds. There was nothing else they could do for the time being.

He looked at his mobile. It was on silent but it was flashing red. He checked what had come through. It was an email from an unknown address. The title was 'YouTube Murderer'. The fact that it had been sent to his personal email address, not his work account, made him believe it was some scam. He opened the email. There was a short message, 'From a concerned friend.' And a web link.

Brady clicked on it. Ordinarily he would have ignored it, deleting it as spam. But something made him do the exact opposite. It was this decision that would change Brady's life – for the worse.

He watched curiously as the link took him to YouTube, unaware what was about to follow. A film entitled 'YouTube Murderer' started playing. Brady assumed it had been taken on someone's mobile phone. It had been filmed at night, which made it initially difficult to make out. But it didn't take too long before Brady realised what was happening.

'Shit!' he muttered, not believing what he was seeing.

Brady felt sick. He watched in horror as the film continued. But it was the last shot that threw him.

What the fuck?

Still holding onto his phone he got up and ran to his door. He yanked it open.

'Conrad? Conrad, where the fuck are you?' he shouted.

Brady had forwarded the email on to Jed to see if he could trace it. And so he could check the authenticity of the film. Not that Brady was disputing that it was real. They had Eddie Jones lying in intensive care with half his brains stamped into the back alley behind Linden Terrace. Someone had considerately filmed the victim being beaten until he lost consciousness. Then they'd uploaded it onto YouTube at 3:04 a.m. Eddie Jones at that time had still been waiting to be found. Currently, the police were trying to get the film taken down. But to date it'd had over a million hits worldwide. It had spread like a virus and there seemed to be nothing they could do to stop it. People were uploading it as a link on their Facebook accounts. It was like a domino effect: as it got taken down from one social network it got uploaded onto another.

It just confirmed in Brady's mind that people were sick bastards. It never failed to surprise him how far they would go to get their kicks.

'Tell me again?' Gates instructed.

'The assailant is Jake Munroe, sir,' Brady answered.

'You're definitely sure about that?' Gates asked as he scrutinised Brady. He had had enough fuck-ups these past forty-eight hours to last him a lifetime.

'One hundred per cent. I recognise the six-inch scar on his scalp. Then there's the black panther tattoo down his right arm, sir. Jed's managed to digitally enhance two clear images of both traits,' Brady answered.

He had printed them out and brought them to Gates.

For some reason whoever had filmed the beating hadn't taken great care to protect Munroe's identity. Munroe had worn a scarf around his ugly brute of a face. But his tattooed arm and his scarred skull were evidence enough to convict him.

There had been a lot of blood spilt at the crime scene. Enough for Forensics to have found bloodied prints. It seemed that the assailant had walked away with traces of blood and human tissue on the soles of his shoes.

Brady had a bad feeling about all of this. Jake Munroe wasn't stupid, despite his looks. He was clever and cunning. So why set himself up? Or had someone else set him up? If so who? Had the person who had filmed the brutal attack uploaded it on to YouTube and then sent Brady a link without Munroe's knowledge? But Munroe had people watching out for him. In particular, Madley.

Brady couldn't shake the feeling that he was walking into a trap.

That Munroe was simply the bait.

Gates cast his eyes over the images.

'All right. I'll go with you on this one. Bring him in,' Gates ordered.

'Yes, sir,' answered Brady. He refrained from adding 'again', certain that it would not go down too well. Maybe if they hadn't released Munroe on Saturday, Eddie Jones wouldn't be lying with half his brain missing.

'By the way, a call came in from Rake Lane. Eddie Jones has died from the trauma to his brain. He never regained consciousness.' Gates's delivery was matter-of-fact. No emotion.

Brady didn't expect anything less. Eddie Jones had become a serious problem for Gates. Now someone had taken care of him and saved the police a job.

Not that Brady felt anything either. However, he didn't think that anyone deserved to die such a brutal death – not even Jones.

'You're looking at a murder investigation now.'

'Yes, sir,' Brady answered. No surprise there, he thought. Especially considering the name of the film on YouTube. The word 'murderer' was a dead giveaway.

'Find Jake Munroe before he disappears for good.'

Brady did not need any more encouragement. He turned and left.

Chapter Thirty-Three

'Keep your mouth shut and just follow my lead. OK?' Brady said as he switched his car engine off.

'Yes, sir,' Conrad answered dutifully.

He wasn't looking forward to arresting Jake Munroe. And he was definitely not looking forward to doing it on Madley's premises.

'You sure we don't need back-up?' Conrad asked.

His face may have been blank but his eyes told Brady that he was worried.

'I know Madley, Conrad. He wouldn't take kindly to an Armed Response Unit kicking his door down. I'm sure that DCI Davidson would be willing to bring in his unit and show us how it's done but I think I'll give it a miss.'

Conrad looked at Brady, not quite believing him.

'You're serious, sir? It's just us?'

'Do I look like I'm taking the piss?' Brady questioned.

'No, sir,' answered Conrad.

Brady noted that Conrad didn't look too good.

He understood Conrad's reservations; Madley had quite a reputation. Most of it smacked of urban legend. But Brady had to concede that Madley was someone you did not mess with. Even he was worried about how Madley would handle him turning up to arrest one of his employees. Especially when Madley had marched into a police station armed with the best lawyer that money could buy to get Munroe released. That had been forty-eight hours ago. A lot had happened in that time.

Brady banged on the glass door of the Blue Lagoon. He could have gone in heavy-handed but that wasn't his style. They had already checked out Jake Munroe's flat on Edwards Road in Whitley Bay. Brady had gone armed with a search warrant that entitled him to kick the door down when Munroe failed to answer. They might not have found Munroe in the one-bedroom flat but they did find the boots that he'd used, wrapped in a black bin-liner ready to be thrown out. To Brady's eye they looked identical to the boots that had obliterated Jones' face. It had been a vicious, sickening attack.

Brady had bagged the evidence and taken it with him for Forensics to examine. He passed on instructions for the rest of Munroe's flat to be searched and for his computer to be brought in for Jed to analyse.

'You all right, Conrad?' Brady asked as he turned and looked at Conrad's pale face.

'Someone's coming, sir,' Conrad answered.

Brady turned back to the double glass doors of the nightclub.

One-eyed Carl unlocked the doors.

'DI Brady, is there a problem?'

'I'm looking for Jake Munroe,' he answered.

He had the feeling that Carl had been sent to stall them.

'I'm sorry, he's not here. I haven't seen him today. Monday's his day off,' Carl replied, his voice and expression as emotionless as ever.

The fact that two coppers had turned up in the late afternoon looking for one of their bouncers should have elicited more of a reaction. More so when it was Brady, and he had Conrad with him. There was one thing Brady never did, and that was mix business with pleasure. Not once had Brady ever brought the police to Madley's door. Today was the exception. That in itself should have had Carl asking questions. The fact it didn't bothered Brady.

Munroe was here. He could feel it. He could see it in Carl's eye.

Brady nodded as he looked past Carl. He was certain he could see movement at the back of the nightclub. He saw a flash of daylight, which suggested someone had just opened the emergency exit door. And Brady was sure that 'someone' would be Jake Munroe. Whether he had been hiding out at Madley's or Madley had promised to protect him, Brady didn't know – nor did he care. He just had to get hold of the bastard before he disappeared – permanently. He had already let him slip through his hands once. He would be damned if he let it happen a second time.

'By all means come in and wait to see if he shows. But I doubt he will,' Carl invited, as if on cue.

Brady turned to Conrad.

'Come on, Munroe's not here. Let's go check out the gym he uses.'

Conrad could see from the dark expression on Brady's face that something was wrong. He had no idea what had happened. But he had clearly missed something.

Brady waited until he heard Carl lock the doors behind them. He wanted to appear as casual as possible so as not to alert them to the fact that he knew Munroe had legged it out the back. The crucial question was whether he was doing a runner on foot or in Madley's Bentley, which was always parked around the back of the club. Brady knew it would be there. After all, it was impossible not to miss Martin Madley when he was standing at the first-floor bay window watching the proceedings below.

'How fast can you run, Conrad?'

'I don't know, sir,' answered Conrad.

'Well, you're about to find out. That bastard Munroe has slipped out the back of the club. You take the right along the Promenade and block off the back lane and I'll go up Brook Street and block him there.'

'What about assistance?' Conrad asked.

He didn't like the prospect of trying to single-handedly apprehend Jake Munroe. He'd been in the interview room with

Brady when Munroe was brought in at the weekend for questioning. He was a big bloke with a lot of muscle. This was muscle that Conrad had watched Munroe using without remorse on Eddie Jones. When he had finished with the drug dealer not even his own mother would have been able to identify him.

But if Conrad was waiting for a response from Brady it wasn't going to happen. Brady had already started running – and fast. Conrad steeled himself and then followed his boss's lead and headed as fast as could in the opposite direction.

Panting, he ignored his burning lungs as he sprinted round the corner of the Promenade up Ocean View. He then sped as fast as he could along the alley behind the Blue Lagoon nightclub.

'Shit!' he cursed.

Brady already had Munroe. Or to be precise, Munroe had Brady.

Conrad pulled out his radio and somehow managed to call for assistance in between gasping for air. There was so much adrenalin coursing through his body that he couldn't feel the pain in his shoulder. That would hit him later. His only focus was getting to Brady before Munroe finished him off.

Munroe didn't have time to raise his fist again. Conrad came in from behind with a rugby tackle. The force of Conrad's weight succeeded in throwing the brute off-balance.

Brady, who was already on the ground, took his chance and kicked out at Munroe's legs. It was enough. Munroe had no other option. He fell, face down.

'Cuff him!' ordered Brady as he pulled himself up. 'Bastard's under arrest!'

Conrad didn't need to be told. He was taking no chances. He already had the cuffs on Munroe and was busy reading him his rights. Not that he had any rights, lying face down in the gutter with Brady's foot pressed on the back of his thick bald head.

It took all of Brady's inner strength not to raise his leg and bring his heavy black boot smashing back down against

Munroe's skull. Brady had to remind himself that was what made them so different. Munroe didn't know when to stop.

Whereas Brady did.

'They're too tight, you fucking shit!' groaned Munroe as he attempted to raise his head. 'It's cutting my fucking wrists in two. And fucking get off my head you bastards! I can't breathe!'

Conrad's response was to give him a hard kick to silence him.

'Looks like my bad behaviour is rubbing off on you,' Brady said, attempting to give Conrad a wry smile. But his jaw resisted.

'Fuck!' he cursed as he raised his hand to it. 'I think that bastard's tried to break my jaw!'

Brady tried to move it but the pain made it impossible.

'Give him another fucking kick from me, will you? His balls would be a good place to start!'

But before Conrad had a chance to see whether Brady was actually serious, back-up arrived, blocking off both ends of the alley.

Brady took his boot off the suspect's head and stepped back. He knew it wouldn't look good. Despite the fact that Brady's face felt as if it had been rammed repeatedly against an iron girder, he couldn't be seen roughing Munroe up.

'Fucking typical! Too little too late. Where are the police when you need them, eh?' Brady joked as sirens screeched and officers scrambled to their aid.

'Thanks by the way,' Brady said as he took the pack of tissues from Conrad.

Brady took one out and dabbed at the cut above his eye.

He looked at Conrad.

'You know? For saving my arse just now. If you hadn't turned up, fuck knows what would have happened.'

Conrad didn't say anything.

Instead he watched as Munroe was dragged to his feet by two burly officers. Even they struggled between them to get the lout to stop resisting arrest.

'So, where did you learn to tackle someone like that?' Brady asked.

'Rugby, sir. Played for my school team and then at University,' Conrad answered as he made a point of watching Munroe.

Brady knew that Conrad didn't like to mention his background. Brady had no idea why that was. But then again, Conrad was not the only one who didn't like to talk about his background. Brady had spent years trying to put as much distance as possible between his present life and his former existence; with one exception – Martin Madley.

Brady looked at Munroe. What troubled him was that this guy worked for Madley. As if reading Brady's mind Munroe shot him a menacing smile, or a grimace to be exact. His small eyes were filled with malicious intent.

'This is just the beginning, Jack Brady. Mark my words,' Munroe shouted out.

'Fuck you!' Brady replied as he held Munroe's glare. It made his stomach turn to hear Munroe dare speak his name.

Brady turned to walk away. He had wasted enough energy on the ugly scrote without listening to any more of Munroe's bile. There would be plenty of time for that when he interviewed him back at the station.

'You see this? Eh? You see this fucking scar?' Munroe asked as he attempted to bend his head down. The two officers on either side of him yanked him backwards, bringing his head level with Brady's.

Munroe flashed him a cold, insincere smile.

'There'll be payback, Brady. Fucking payback!'

Brady gestured to the two officers restraining him to get him out of sight. He had no idea what Munroe was talking about.

Conrad turned to Brady.

'What did he mean, sir?' Conrad asked, frowning.

Brady shrugged. 'Your guess is as good as mine.'

Conrad didn't look convinced. Not that Brady was bothered. He had more important problems than appeasing his deputy.

He was worried. Worried that Munroe had something on him. Or on Nick. After all, Johnny Slaughter had accused Nick of fucking him over – as had Madley. Munroe had worked for both men. Coincidence? Brady seriously doubted it.

'Come on. I need to get cleaned up first. Then we'll see what Munroe has to say about Eddie Jones.'

Brady automatically looked over at the back of the Blue Lagoon. Madley's flash Bentley was parked up. He cast his eyes on the personalised number plate: MAD 1.

Madley was someone not to be messed with. But he'd given Brady no choice.

Chapter Thirty-Four

Eddie Jones' murder had now taken precedence over the serial rape investigation. Brady had spent the last two hours updating his team and issuing orders. He was going to nail Munroe's bollocks to the interview chair. But he wanted word back from the lab that Munroe's boots matched the prints Ainsworth's team had found. He also needed DNA evidence. Brady was in no doubt that part of Eddie Jones' face was entrenched in the grooves of Munroe's size eleven boots. Ordinarily lab reports could take weeks to come through. But Gates had ordered this evidence to be examined ASAP – regardless of expense. Northumbria's forensic laboratory no longer existed so it wasn't as if Brady could lean heavily on someone in the force. The work was now outsourced. It was another ingenious way of cutting costs.

Brady was also waiting for word back from Jed. They had Munroe's mobile phone and Brady needed to know whether the footage had been filmed on it and if so, whether he'd used it to upload the film. Jed also had Munroe's computer to examine.

'Sir?' Conrad said as he stuck his head round the door.

Brady looked up from his desk. He had been familiarising himself with Munroe's police reports. If he was honest, he was searching for something, anything, that could explain Munroe's threat. Whether the threat was from Madley or Johnny Slaughter, Brady had no idea. But he knew he couldn't bring this up in the interview.

'Dora in the canteen gave me this for you,' Conrad said as he walked over to Brady's desk. He was holding a bag of ice wrapped in one of the canteen's tea towels.

'How the hell did she know what had happened?' Brady asked as he took the ice pack.

He placed it against the left side of his jaw. For some reason Munroe had taken exception to that side of Brady's face. 'Fuck!' he cursed under his breath at the pain.

'You ought to get that seen to, sir,' Conrad suggested as he looked at Brady's bruised and swollen face. But it was the jaw that worried him. It had taken quite a few blows.

'Which part?' Brady questioned, attempting to laugh. He quickly regretted it. 'Fuck, that hurts!'

'My point, sir. I can take you up to A&E if you want? We've got time before the interview.'

'Do I look like I've got four hours to waste hanging around some Jeremy Kyle-style waiting room while half the scrotes who've been drinking all weekend drag themselves in to have an emergency liver transplant and shards of broken glass removed from their eyeballs?'

Conrad had forgotten that it was Monday. The weekend had passed in a blur. Half the population would have spent last night drinking in Tynemouth Front Street and down Whitley Bay's South Parade and the Promenade. It was a local tradition to get as bladdered as possible and sustain it over a period of three nights. Whatever happened in between would be stitched up or pumped out at Rake Lane hospital.

'Anyway, I've taken worse,' Brady assured Conrad.

However, even after a couple of prescription painkillers that he had saved from when he'd been recovering from the gunshot wound to his leg, it still hurt to move his jaw. The cut above his eye had eased. Brady had spent some time cleaning himself up in the station's Gents. Not the ideal place to deal with open wounds but it was better than nothing. It had stopped bleeding. That was good enough for Brady.

After the knocks and blows he'd received from his old man when he was growing up, Munroe's fist in his face was nothing more than an embarrassment.

But Brady's face was the least of his problems right now. He had something bigger and uglier to worry about – interviewing Jake Munroe.

Brady's mobile began to vibrate. He picked it up half-expecting another anonymous email from 'a concerned friend'. But this was not an email. Someone was calling him.

'Conrad, give me ten minutes?'

'Yes, sir,' Conrad answered.

'And chase up that bloody lab, will you? Gates has paid through the nose for them to expedite that evidence. Tell them I needed it yesterday!'

Conrad nodded and then turned and headed for the door.

Brady waited until the door was closed before answering the call.

'What the fuck do you want?'

'Come on, Jack. After what I gave you, this is how you talk to me?'

'What? A scathing front page attack inciting public hysteria?'

Rubenfeld laughed. It was a deep, throaty, gurgling laugh.

Brady cut the line.

'Fuck you!' he muttered.

His phone started buzzing again. Rubenfeld.

'Come on, Jack? What's your problem?'

'You!' Brady answered.

He was about to hang up but Rubenfeld knew how to keep Brady interested.

'What did you think of the "YouTube Murderer" then?'

'What?' Brady asked as his mind raced to think how Rubenfeld could have possibly got hold of this information.

Admittedly it had gone viral. But as yet, the public didn't know that the police had the offender in custody. DCI Gates was still arranging the Press Call. As the Senior Investigating Officer in charge of the investigation, it should have been Brady's Press Call. However, no amount of make-up could hide the mess that was his face. Gates had been quite sympathetic regarding Brady's injuries. After all, he had sustained them apprehending a suspect. But Gates had explained in no uncertain terms that the state of Brady's face would do more harm than good when it came to public confidence. Considering the dire outcome of the rape investigation, Gates wanted to use Munroe's arrest as a decoy. The press had been baying for blood for some time now. They had a serial rapist on the streets and so far, the police had no concrete leads. Gates was now going to do some damage control and throw them Jake Munroe.

It could work.

So what the fuck did Rubenfeld want from him?

'I don't understand,' Brady replied.

'I sent it to you, Jack. I thought you would have realised by now.'

'So why be cryptic with the "concerned friend" crap? You're only concerned about who's buying the next round.'

'Had to be careful. I can't use my work or personal email. So I sent it to you from one of those anonymous pay-as-you-go email accounts. There's a place in Northumberland Street in Newcastle if you ever need to use one,' Rubenfeld replied.

Brady wasn't interested in how Rubenfeld got his grubby hands on the footage or why he was acting as if MI5 were watching him. Nothing surprised him where Rubenfeld was concerned. Rubenfeld was always out for what he get could; either the big scoop that would make him, or the next best thing – alcohol and lots of it. If he had stepped on someone's toes on the way, that was his problem. Not Brady's.

'Thanks, but that was yesterday's news. No longer relevant,' Brady replied. It was cutting and to the point.

'Not so, my friend. I have something else that you might want. It's connected to the attack on that prossie on Thursday night?'

Brady didn't reply. How the hell had he found out that the

victim was a prostitute? Brady decided he was better off not knowing.

'Why don't you inform DI Bentley of what you have? Surely you know he's the SIO in charge of that investigation? You have your ear to the ground and your nose in the shit!'

'Come on, Jack. That article last Thursday didn't hurt your feelings did it? I thought you were made of tougher stuff than that,' Rubenfeld stated.

'Like I said, try Bentley.'

'Bentley's a fucking arse and you know it!'

Brady listened as Rubenfeld took a much-needed drink. He assumed he was in the pub. Exactly where Brady would have been if he had a choice.

'Come on, it's getting late and I've still got a hell of a lot to get through before the day disappears on me.'

'All right, Jack. I hear you. Look, I'm sending you a little something. You'll make better use of it than Bentley. That bloke doesn't know his arse from his elbow!'

'What do you get out of this?' Brady asked before Rubenfeld hung up.

'The biggest story of my career and a one-way ticket out of this shithole.'

With that, Rubenfeld was gone.

Brady placed his mobile phone down on the desk.

He didn't have the time or inclination for Rubenfeld's games. He had a murder suspect to interview.

Chapter Thirty-Five

But Brady didn't get very far. In fact, he didn't even manage to get up from his desk before another email came in. Again from 'a concerned friend' – Rubenfeld.

He reluctantly opened the email. Again there was a web link. The title of this one was 'YouTube Rapist'.

Brady braced himself for the worst. He clicked on the link and waited. He watched in disgust and repulsion as the film proved to be very much in keeping with its title.

He could feel his stomach contracting at the sadistic, violent scene being played out in front of him. Despite every inch of his body wanting to turn away, he forced himself to watch it to the end. This was personal. Too personal.

When it had finished he had no choice but to make his way to the Gents. Checking it was empty, he locked himself in a cubicle and proceeded to vomit up whatever contents he had in his stomach until there was nothing left but gut-wrenching bile. He waited a moment, body bent over the cracked bowl to make sure he'd got it out of his system. Tears were burning his eyes. He put it down to the force of the vomit coming up his throat rather than admitting the truth; that it hurt. It hurt so bad that he wanted to punch something – someone. He wanted to keep punching until the pain stopped.

Brady spent a couple of minutes bent over the washbasin throwing cold water over his face. He needed to calm himself down first before he did anything else. He made a point of not looking at himself in the mirror. Unsure whether he would like what he saw. This was connected to Nick, which ultimately meant to him.

Back in his office, Brady tried calling Rubenfeld back. He needed to know how the hell he had gotten hold of this material. But he didn't answer. Not that Brady expected him to. Rubenfeld would have already sunk his rat teeth into someone else by now.

Then he'd called Nick. Again no answer.

Where the fuck are you, Nick? I need you to talk to me. To tell me what the fuck's going on because I am way over my head here, bro . . .

Brady could feel his eyes burning again. He had to get control of his emotions. He had no choice. He breathed in. Deep, slow breaths. He needed to pull himself together. Think logically and not be blinded by emotion. Now was not the time. Later. But not now. He had to think about how he was going to interview Jake Munroe. How the hell he was going to question him about the evidence Brady had just watched. And if this centred around Nick, how the hell was he going to keep his name out of it?

You bastard, Madley! You fucking bastard!

Suddenly there was a knock at the door.

Conrad walked in.

'Sir, lab reports have come back. Good news. The boots we recovered conclusively match the footprints found at the crime scene. And the DNA found on the soles of the boots matches with the victim's,' Conrad announced, unable to keep the triumph out of his voice.

It took him a moment to register that something was wrong. 'Sir?'

'There's something I want you to watch, but I advise you to sit down first,' Brady said.

Without a word, Conrad did exactly as ordered. He had never seen Brady look like this before. There had been times when he'd witnessed Brady at rock bottom. But this? This was different.

While Conrad watched the film, Brady kept his head turned away. He couldn't bear to see what that animal had done to her. Not again. After all, this was a woman he had watched grow up. This was Trina McGuire.

236

He waited until Conrad turned to him. It took his deputy a moment to compose himself. At least he hadn't thrown up. But this was personal to Brady.

To Conrad it was just another rape and savage beating; another statistic.

'Why?' asked Conrad. His mouth was so dry that his voice was barely audible.

Brady shrugged. He felt the way Conrad looked. 'I don't know.'

He lied. Munroe had either taken orders from Madley or Johnny Slaughter. He'd been deployed to find Nick's whereabouts by any means necessary.

'What do we do now, sir?' Conrad asked.

'Get this sent off to Jed and then I inform DCI Gates.'

'What about DI Bentley? Isn't this his case?'

Brady looked at Conrad. He was a good bloke and an honourable copper; a rare breed. If he was not careful the Bentleys and Adamsons of the world would wipe their arses on him. Brady didn't share Conrad's sense of fairness.

'Bentley can go fuck himself.'

'Sir?'

'Who arrested Munroe? We did. Not Bentley. Admittedly it was for an entirely unrelated crime but we got to him first. Also, who has the evidence against him? Us.'

If Brady was honest the last person he wanted getting his hands on Munroe was Bentley. Munroe worked for Martin Madley and Bentley had convinced himself that Madley was the North-East's equivalent to Pablo Escobar: Colombian drug lord; narco-terrorist; cocaine trafficker; and politician. When Escobar was alive, his struggle to maintain power in the early nineties had resulted in Colombia becoming the world's murder capital. The murder rate was fuelled by Escobar giving money as rewards to his hitmen for killing police officers.

But Madley was no Escobar. Brady was certain of that. But that was where it ended. He had no idea what his childhood friend was involved in now. Not to mention why he had Munroe on his staff.

'Are you going to tell McGuire that we've caught her attacker?' Conrad asked.

Brady nodded.

'Once we've charged him. Then I'll tell her that Munroe will never touch her or another woman again. That he's going to be banged up for a very long time.'

Conrad looked at Brady. Neither of them believed what Brady had just said. It was wishful thinking on Brady's part. But if they didn't hold onto the belief that when they handed over murderers and rapists to the judicial system, that the offenders would be appropriately punished, then there would be no point in continuing in the job.

Brady thought of Munroe and his history of prior convictions. When he'd interviewed him on Saturday, Brady had been convinced that he was a dangerous individual. But would he have believed that Munroe was capable of such horrific acts of violence: especially the brutal attack on Trina McGuire? The answer was simple – yes.

Chapter Thirty-Six

The rest of the evening had not quite gone as Brady had planned.

Jed had come back with the unsurprising news that it had been the same mobile phone used to film both crimes. The mobile may have been unregistered but it had been on Munroe at the time of his arrest. Munroe didn't strike Brady as a stupid man. If anything, he had a chilling cunning about him. So the question Brady was struggling with was why would Munroe keep hold of incriminating evidence? He hadn't even deleted the films from the mobile. In fact why film it at all? Unless it was evidence to whoever was paying him that he had fulfilled his contract?

Then there were the boots he had used to stamp on Eddie Jones' face. Why leave them wrapped in a bin-liner by the kitchen bin? Why not dump them as soon as he left the crime scene? It didn't make any sense to Brady. It all seemed to point in one direction – Munroe wanted to get caught.

Jed had freeze-framed and then digitally enhanced images from both attacks that conclusively proved it was Munroe. He'd filmed Trina McGuire's rape and brutal beating with his left hand. He had used his right hand as a weapon. Exactly the same as when he filmed himself attacking Eddie Jones. The distinctive panther tattoo climbing down his right arm towards his hand was clearly visible on both pieces of footage.

Both films had been put onto his computer shortly after he'd left his victims and then uploaded onto YouTube. The police had tried everything to have the footage removed from the net. But it was proving to be impossible. YouTube had taken both films down. But it didn't end there; people had already downloaded the footage from YouTube onto their own pages. Both films had gone viral.

The press had heard about Jake Munroe's charges. The 'YouTube Murderer' and 'YouTube Rapist' would make the following morning's front pages. But Brady had remained true to Rubenfeld. He'd been given the front page scoop he wanted ahead of any other journalist.

Rubenfeld had refused to divulge his sources to Brady regarding the YouTube uploads. But it seemed that he didn't know everything. The hardened hack had no idea about the identity of the suspect. Jake Munroe's name came as a surprise to Rubenfeld. He had never heard of him before. But Brady was still left wondering who was giving Rubenfeld this information to pass onto the police. Or to be more precise – Brady.

Brady had so many questions he needed answering. But Munroe was refusing to talk. Not that he needed to; the incriminating evidence against him was enough for Munroe to have signed his own prison papers.

Gates was satisfied. He was quite content to let the court fathom Munroe out. As far as he was concerned, Munroe had committed these crimes alone and under no instruction. Case closed, target figures met. A murder and a brutal rape in one day was quite a coup for any station.

So why did Brady not feel the same sense of achievement? Because he knew more than Gates. He knew that Munroe was looking for Nick. That he had beaten Trina McGuire to within an inch of her life to extract the information from her drug-abused, bony body. And when it had failed, he had raped her. The final humiliation and the ultimate show of power.

But why beat Eddie Jones to death?

Brady was about to call it a night and take a walk down to the Blue Lagoon. The case was officially closed as far as Gates was concerned. But Brady needed to satisfy his own curiosity and try to put to rest any doubts he had about Munroe acting on Madley's orders.

The phone on his desk started to ring. Brady contemplated answering it. He decided against it. He'd had enough for one day.

Just as he stood up to leave, Gates walked in.

'Jack,' Gates greeted him.

'Sir,' Brady answered, unsure why Gates was making an impromptu visit.

Brady watched as he went over to the window. He was a tall and broad-shouldered man who walked with authority. He stood with his hands clasped behind his back as he looked out on the dark street. The last few stragglers from the weekend binge-drinking escapade were starting to make their way back to the Metro station.

Brady's window was open so he could make out the odd drunken shouts and catcalls drifting up from the town centre.

'I thought you'd like to know that Munroe has been remanded in custody,' Gates informed him. 'He left the station half an hour ago.'

He kept his back to him. It was rigid and proud.

'Which prison is Munroe going to?'

'All I know is that it's maximum security. Munroe's a danger-ous character, there's no doubt about that,' Gates answered.

Brady expected no less for Munroe.

'Anyway, I'm here to pass on Detective Chief Superintendent O'Donnell's praises. I'm sure he'll call you personally with his commendation. But needless to say he's impressed that you managed to solve two apparently unrelated crimes in the same day. He was even talking back to your coup last year when you broke up that sex-trafficking ring. He had some good words to say about you. My advice?' Gates turned round and looked at Brady. He waited for a moment as if weighing up what he was about to say: 'Forget about that fiasco with Lee Harris. I have. You stepped up today, Jack. I appreciate that. The mood around the station has lifted and that's because of you. And Conrad of course.'

Brady waited. He knew there was a 'but' coming: he could read it in Gates's eyes.

'A word of warning, though. The higher you climb, the further you have to fall.'

'I don't understand, sir.'

'O'Donnell's talking of promotion,' Gates replied.

Brady couldn't disguise the shock he felt. Firstly, he wasn't aware that a DCI's position was available and secondly, Brady was the most unlikely candidate for it.

'It's only talk, but I thought you should know. If people like DI Bentley get to hear what I've heard then you'll have to watch your back.'

Brady didn't answer. He hadn't given Bentley any consideration – until now.

'Just to forewarn you, I've heard that Bentley's furious that you closed his investigation. Not to mention you had a suspect for his case without informing him.'

'I didn't know that Munroe was definitely responsible for the rape and assault on Thursday evening, sir. And when we had conclusive evidence it was too late. Munroe refused to be interviewed and we had no choice but to charge him.'

'Don't bullshit a bullshitter. You and I both know you kept Bentley as far away from Munroe as possible. I know Bentley and he has a long memory, Jack.'

With that, Gates left the room.

Brady watched as Gates walked out, leaving the office door wide open. He stood for a moment, not quite sure what had just happened.

'So, where's Madley hiding?' Brady asked Carl.

He swigged back a mouthful of Peroni while he waited for an answer.

Carl was not that forthcoming. He simply shrugged.

'Eddie Jones?' Brady asked, changing the subject. He knew from the look on Carl's face that he would get nowhere asking about Madley. Carl was as loyal to his boss as Conrad was to him.

'Yeah. Little shit. Deserved everything he got and some,' Carl replied. There was a glint in his eye that told Brady that Eddie Jones was as popular with his own kind as he was with the police.

Brady raised his eyebrows. 'How so?'

Carl picked up Brady's empty pint glass.

'Refill?'

Brady nodded. 'Thanks.'

He watched as Carl walked over to the pumps.

'The amount of times I caught him selling drugs in here. He couldn't give a shit. Wasted half the time. And you know Madley's take on drugs in his clubs. He's worse than you lot.'

Brady broke into a smile at Carl's comment.

But he knew Madley had a very different reason for not liking people selling drugs on his premises. He had his own business to look out for and a fierce reputation to protect.

'Little shit was in here last night. Dealing coke and fuck knows what else. Got himself thrown out with a warning that Madley had had enough.'

'Is that why Munroe beat him up?'

Carl paused and looked at Brady. He cut the flow to Brady's pint glass. Despite the fact that it was half full, Carl simply threw it down the sink.

'Beer's off,' he said.

It was enough for Brady to know he had outstayed his welcome.

Chapter Thirty-Seven

Brady had gone home to mull over the day's events aided by a bottle of Rioja and a hastily thrown together stir-fry comprising the remnants of his fridge. In the background he had Radiohead blasting. He had the stereo on in the living room, which was at the front of the large terraced house. So it said something when he could still hear it in the kitchen at the far back of the property. The music was loud enough to drown out any complaints from the neighbours.

The house would be on the market soon anyway. He'd been here too long. It had taken eighteen months for Brady to accept the harsh reality that Claudia was never coming back. He had held onto their marital home in the vain hope she would return. It hadn't happened.

He turned the heat off under the wok before refilling his wine glass. Suddenly he had lost his appetite. He left the food and walked through to the lounge where the acoustic version of Radiohead's 'Creep' pulsated out of the state-of-the-art speakers on either side of the large room. It was sparsely furnished. Claudia had taken anything that hadn't been nailed down when she'd gone. He had been in hospital recovering from the gunshot wound when she'd cleared the house. Brady hadn't had the inclination to replace the furniture. He had simply bought what was necessary. The house had stopped being a home when she left. It wasn't the fact she had emptied it. The furniture was irrelevant. It was her he missed. He then thought of DCI James 'Wanker' Davidson and realised it was time to let go.

He walked over to the large bay window, letting the music soothe his irritable mood. He watched the slow, undulating waves of the blue North Sea. The house would sell. No question. It was part of an exclusive row of Victorian terraced houses that had been built on a cliff overlooking Brown's Bay, aptly named Southcliff. His expression was dark and brooding as he looked out at the calm water. Typically, when he wanted the sea to reflect his mood, it did the exact opposite. Normally the North Sea would be grey and heavy with thunderous waves crashing against the cliff forcing a shower of spray across the front windows of the house. But not tonight, mused Brady. Tonight it was the perfect picture of serenity.

He thought about Madley. Then Munroe. And finally Nick. His mind was in turmoil. Had Munroe been instructed by Madley to teach Eddie Jones a lesson? More than that: to film it and upload it for all to see what happens if you cross Martin Madley?

Then there was Trina McGuire. Was Madley after Nick? Did Madley have that much control and power over his henchmen that they would commit murder for him? Brady thought of the Colombian drug baron Escobar, who had paid his henchmen to kill anyone who got in his way. Was Madley any different?

Brady was woken by his mobile phone ringing. He groaned as he leaned over and checked the time: 9:23 a.m.

'Shit!'

He had slept longer than he'd intended. Not that it was a problem. He had left the office last night with the intention of taking the day off. After Gates's tête-à-tête regarding Bentley, Brady had decided the best thing to do was lie low for a few days. Let the dust settle and then get back on the job. He was exhausted anyway after the past few days. It was now Tuesday. He had been on the job since last Friday. It was no surprise he had slept so late. Anyway, if there was a problem he was sure Conrad would be on the phone.

Fuck! Phone!

Brady picked up his mobile and looked at the identity of the caller, expecting it to be Conrad. It was Madley.

Brady sat up.

What the hell would Madley be doing calling him?

It made no sense but there was only one way to find out.

'Yeah?' Brady answered. Short and succinct.

'You took your time. What were you doing? Busy trying to put a trace on the call?' Madley asked, laughing.

It was an insincere, cold laugh.

'What do you want, Martin? If I remember rightly you told me to keep clear of you and your business associates.'

'Come on, Jack. It's not like you to take things personally. You should know me better than that. Bad day at the office and I'm an absolute bastard to be around.'

Brady was not buying it.

The false camaraderie was made worse by the fact that Madley had done everything in his power to avoid Brady. Then there was the question of Munroe. It hung heavy in the air between them.

Madley had after all walked into Whitley Bay station with the best lawyer money could buy to ensure the release of his employee. An employee who then went on to murder one of Madley's small problems – Eddie Jones. Prior to that, he had beaten Trina McGuire so savagely that she was unrecognisable. Then he had raped her.

'It's not like you to be so sullen. Not after you nailed Jake Munroe. Two for one deal, eh? Good for you. Always knew you had it in you.'

Brady didn't reply. He didn't like the tone of Madley's voice or where the conversation seemed to be heading.

'I didn't realise what kind of bloke I had working for me. You can't get the staff these days. No matter how much you vet, something always comes up and bites you in the arse,' Madley mused.

Again, Brady remained silent. Whatever Madley was dangling, Brady was not biting.

'I thought we could have a chat like the good old days.'

'I haven't got time for this,' Brady replied.

'What? My company not good enough for you now, Jack? Is that it?'

Brady had no idea why Madley was goading him. It was out of character. At least where he was concerned. However, he had seen Madley in action before. He could be as cruel and ruthless as a cat playing with a trapped mouse.

'You can't hold me responsible for Jake Munroe's actions.'

Brady was about to speak. But Madley beat him to it.

'Anyway, you should be more interested in Ronnie Macmillan than Munroe. He's dead. Stabbed repeatedly in the neck,' Madley stated. It was chillingly clinical.

'What the—'

But before Brady could finish, the line had been cut.

His head was spinning.

Why the fuck had Madley called to tell him that? But he knew why.

Brady took a deep intake of breath as he steadied himself.

He felt nothing but relief. The bastard deserved everything he got – and more.

Brady suddenly thought of Ronnie's estranged brother, Mayor Macmillan. He wondered whether he knew and if so, what he had made of the news? Brady imagined that there would be an element of relief for him as well. After all, Ronnie Macmillan had the potential to damage a lot of people. From the day he had been arrested he hadn't talked. Brady thought about the obvious. Had someone silenced him before he found his voice?

Brady didn't even question how Madley knew such a fact. He had contacts everywhere; both on the inside and out. And he knew Madley was telling the truth. He wasn't a liar – never had been.

It didn't take long before Brady came crashing down. Madley's news took on a new dimension when Jimmy Matthews rang him. It had taken Brady by surprise, since Matthews was inside Durham prison.

'What took you so long?' Matthews hissed.

Brady realised from the heavy breathing that Matthews had his hand cupped around the mouthpiece. It was a survival strategy. If the other inmates knew he was talking to a copper, he would be dead. The fact that he wasn't already dead was a feat in itself. Most bent coppers who end up on the inside rarely come out the other end. Matthews had even had an attempt made on his life six months ago – a good old-fashioned biro in the neck.

'I was in the shower. How did I know you were going to call?' Brady answered.

Since Matthews's life-threatening injury, Brady had made a point of visiting him every two or three weeks. They shared a friendship that spanned twenty years. Most of that time had been served in the force together. All that had evaporated when Brady had been forced to arrest him. That was over a year ago and it had taken Matthews nearly dying for Brady to lose some of his anger and sense of betrayal.

'Jack, I need to see you. Now.'

'Come on, Jimmy. You're having a laugh. How would I get a visiting pass for today? It's too short notice.'

'I've already sorted it,' Matthews said, refusing to take 'no' for an answer.

Brady didn't need to ask exactly how Matthews had sorted it. Matthews had always been involved in various shenanigans, which is how he ended up as a bent copper. He just never knew when to stop.

'Bloody hell! I don't know . . .'

'Ronnie Macmillan's dead.'

'I know.'

'How the fuck would you know that? The place is in turmoil. It's in lock-down mode.'

Brady realised then that Matthews wouldn't be on the inmates' payphone. The inmates would all be locked in their cells. After all, Macmillan had shared the same wing as Matthews. Both of them had been segregated from the main prison population for their own safety. Macmillan, like Matthews, had enemies. It didn't matter that one was a copper and the other a gangster; both had pissed enough people off to warrant being attacked.

No. Matthews must be on a mobile phone. The guards wouldn't have known about it. Otherwise it would have been confiscated. Inmates had various ways of smuggling banned substances and objects into prison. Most of them came in through the back passage.

Brady realised in that moment Matthews must have been scared shitless to have risked ringing him on a mobile. Especially when every cell in his wing would no doubt be in the process of being searched. The guards would be looking for whatever weapon had been used to stab Ronnie Macmillan. That was, if they didn't already have it in their possession. A Self Honed Implement of Violence, otherwise known as a shiv, could be made out of anything found in a prison. Matthews had been attacked with a sharpened biro but toothbrushes, spoons, any seemingly innocuous object could be deadly.

'Who killed him, Jimmy?' Brady asked.

Brady wasn't an idiot. This was why Matthews wanted to talk to him. He was scared. There were two possibilities: either Matthews had killed Ronnie Macmillan; or the more plausible scenario was that he had witnessed another inmate kill him.

'That's why I need to talk to you.'

That was as far as Matthews got before the line went dead.

Brady listened to the dial tone.

Matthews had left him no option.

Chapter Thirty-Eight

Brady kept his head down. He still wondered what the hell he was doing in Durham prison: a maximum security prison at that. He had gone through the humiliation of having a body search. Nothing intimate. Otherwise Brady's reaction would have found him banged up alongside Matthews. But Brady could tell that the shit had most definitely hit the fan. The guards were on edge. No surprise. An inmate had been killed on their watch. Heads would roll – that was a given.

Brady had been taken through countless security gates until he reached the visitors' room. It was a large, soulless space filled with an air of desperation that clung to the dented tables and chairs. But primarily it clung to the occupants.

He could see Matthews sitting on his own in the corner. He looked nervous. Agitated even. Brady caught his eye. Relief filled Matthews's face.

Brady tried to hide his surprise when he sat down opposite Matthews. He looked like shit. He had dropped a lot of weight. His long hands drummed on the table nervously, while his eyes shone with a feverish madness as he surreptitiously looked around the large room. His brown hair was matted with a sheen of sweat covering his pale, clammy forehead. He looked like a man who was about to be shot.

'Hey, Jimmy. How you doing?'

'Cut the crap, Jack. I look like shit. I feel like shit,' Matthews answered as he stared at Brady's face. 'What the fuck happened to you?'

Brady automatically touched the left side of his jaw. It still ached like hell but at least it wasn't broken. And he could move it now without too much pain. The cut above his eye had started to heal. It was just the mottled bruising that made it look worse than it actually felt.

'Ran head-on into someone's fist. Repeatedly,' Brady said with a lame grin.

'Same old Jack Brady, eh?' Matthews stated. 'What is it about you not being able to keep out of trouble?'

Brady shrugged.

He waited for Matthews to tell him why he was here on his day off.

'Macmillan—' Matthews began in a low, conspiratorial voice.

Brady waited for him to finish.

Instead Matthews looked around the room.

'Macmillan?' Brady prompted.

'Do you know who had him murdered?' Matthews asked.

'I've got some ideas,' he answered.

Matthews looked at him as if he was an idiot. 'You have no fucking idea!'

'Do you know who did it then?'

Matthews nodded. 'Martin Madley.'

'Don't take the piss,' Brady hissed at him. 'Fucking Madley's not here is he?'

Brady sat back. He couldn't believe that Matthews still had it in for Madley. He wondered if he would ever let it go. After all, it was Matthews who tried to stitch Madley up – not the other way around.

'For fuck's sake! No one knows better than me Madley's not in here. But one of his men is!'

'Who?' Brady asked.

'Bastard named Munroe. Jake Munroe. Arrived late last night. Evil fucker.'

Brady felt winded. He tried not to let it show. He failed.

Matthews nodded at Brady's reaction.

'Yeah? Police charged him yesterday for rape and murder. He's inside for less than twelve hours and he's already butchered Ronnie Macmillan.'

'How do you know he did it?' Brady asked.

'Because I fucking witnessed it with my own eyes. That's how!'

'Did Munroe see you?'

Brady could understand Matthews's jittery state. Munroe would take great delight in slicing a bent copper's throat.

'Fuck no! Do you think I'd be sat here if he did?'

Brady nodded. 'What are you going to do?'

'What do you think? Keep my mouth shut.'

'So, why tell me?' Brady asked.

'Two reasons. If something happens to me, then you know who's responsible. And I wanted you to know that Madley was behind this.'

'What the fuck does Madley get out of silencing Ronnie Macmillan? Macmillan had no information on Madley. Madley refused to go into business with him if I remember correctly.'

'For a copper you're not very bright,' Matthews said, his voice thick with irritation.

Brady didn't say anything.

'Munroe turns up. Word is he's one of Johnny Slaughter's boys. He kills Ronnie Macmillan at the first opportunity that arises. No hesitation or deliberation. Stab! Stab! Stab! Macmillan's dead before he even knows it. But crucially, it's before Macmillan gets a chance to find out that Munroe worked for Madley. If Macmillan had known that, Munroe wouldn't have lasted an hour inside.'

Brady sat for a moment. He needed to make sense of what Matthews had just said.

'Why the fuck do you think Munroe let you lot catch him? He's a nasty fucker and he's clever. He could easily have eluded you. You should be asking yourself why didn't he? Why didn't he run? Why give it to you on a plate? The films on YouTube? The identifiable scar across his scalp? The black panther going down his right arm? Why give it to you by filming himself?'

Brady looked surprised that Matthews knew this level of detail about the case.

'Fucking hell, Jack! This isn't a Russian prison. We have TVs and computers in here. And I was a copper once, remember?'

Brady was silent for a moment. Matthews's eyes burned as he waited for Brady to speak. He was desperate for Brady to believe him.

'So you're saying that he wanted to be arrested and charged?'

Matthews nodded. 'Exactly.'

It made sense. Brady had already wondered why Munroe had left a bloody trail to his own back door. It smacked of stupidity. And Munroe was far from stupid.

'So he gets arrested. But who's to say he would end up in the same prison as Macmillan?' Brady asked. The odds of that happening were extremely low. Durham prison was not the only maximum security prison in the country.

'Given the severity of his crimes he had to be put in a prison with this level of security. And he's in the segregated wing for his own safety. Most of the inmates in here have watched the YouTube film of him raping that woman. A lot of the men in here are thugs. But they're not animals. Munroe wouldn't last in the main prison.'

Brady nodded. It all made sense. Apart from the coincidence of it being the same prison that held Ronnie Macmillan.

'I get it. But why Durham prison?'

'Munroe's charged but he's still awaiting trial. His court case will be heard at Newcastle county courts. After all, his crimes took place here. So what prison is close to Newcastle but offers the maximum level of security for someone like Munroe? Durham.'

Brady sighed as he ran his hand back through his hair. It was a lot to take in. And he was not quite sure whether it was mainly wishful thinking on Matthews's part.

'So again, this all comes back to Madley? Yeah?' Brady asked, still unclear as to why Madley would want Ronnie Macmillan dead.

'You're getting there. Yeah. Madley orchestrated this whole thing.'

'Why?'

'Remember DC Simone Henderson?'

Matthews didn't wait for a response. The dark look in Brady's eyes was enough.

'She was dumped by Ronnie Macmillan in Madley's nightclub as retribution for not going into business with him. With Macmillan it wasn't a question of whether you wanted to do something. If he asked, you did it. Madley really had no choice. So when he refused, Macmillan set him up. Dumped a copper who had been gutted and fuck knows what and then made an anonymous call to the police.'

Matthews waited for Brady to absorb what he had just said. Time was running out and he wanted to make sure that Brady understood the full magnitude of what was going on.

Brady thought back to Friday when he had called in on Madley unannounced. He had two well-heeled businessmen in his office. Both had kept their backs to Brady. But he was sure when one of them stood up and walked over to Gibbs that he recognised him. Albeit from the back. The more Brady thought about it now the more he was certain it was Mayor Macmillan. But why would a politician be sitting in a well-known local gangster's office? It hadn't made any sense. Now though? Had Madley and Mayor Macmillan been in this together? Brady knew that Madley was cut-throat and that if he saw an opportunity he would take it. The same could be said of Mayor Macmillan.

Ronnie Macmillan's his fucking brother though ...

Brady took a moment to try and accept that someone could want his own brother dead. But then again, this was Mayor Macmillan. He was a rising politician who would do anything to protect his political career. Perhaps Ronnie Macmillan's death was damage limitation? Who knows if Macmillan was preparing to strike a deal to have his sentence shortened if he talked? He had already been inside for six months. In all likelihood he would have been refused parole every time he'd applied for it. An indefinite life in prison could be a bitter pill to swallow – even for the resolute.

'So? Convinced?' Matthews asked with a gleam in his eye.

'Maybe … Or maybe someone else paid Munroe to kill Ronnie Macmillan. Madley wasn't his only enemy.'

'For fuck's sake. What more do you want?'

Brady stood up to leave.

'Watch your back, Jimmy. And keep that mouth of yours shut. OK?'

'Fuck you!'

Brady nodded at him. There was nothing he could do for Matthews. He was stuck in this hellhole with too much time on his hands.

'See you in three weeks,' Brady said before he turned to leave.

Matthews didn't respond.

As Brady walked across the room towards the guarded exit something, or to be precise, someone, caught his eye: Jake Munroe. Then he saw who Munroe was talking to. It was Weasel Face. Madley's right-hand man.

What the fuck? Why would that bastard be here?

Then it hit Brady. They were both from the East End of London. Surely they must have known one another? After all, the criminal world was not that big. There was a high probability that Weasel Face had also worked for Johnny Slaughter. At the time Weasel Face came up to the North-East, Madley had needed protecting, which was why the hired gun was here. Had Johnny Slaughter sent him up to help Madley out? Both gangsters went back together. Slaughter looked out for Madley and vice versa.

But maybe it's nothing to do with that. Maybe Weasel Face is here on business – Madley's business. Was he here to make sure Munroe

*had followed Madley's instructions and silenced Ronnie Macmillan?
At what price? How much had Madley paid Munroe? It must have
been a significant figure for a hit man to be prepared to spend time
inside.*

Brady put his head down and kept walking. He couldn't be
sure if they had seen him. If they had, they hadn't shown it. The
last thing Brady wanted was Munroe knowing that Jimmy
Matthews had been talking to him. If he found out, this might
be the last time Brady would ever visit Matthews.

Chapter Thirty-Nine

Brady had driven around for a couple of hours after his visit with Matthews. He didn't feel like going home. Nor did he want to go to the station. So he drove. In no particular direction, with no destination in mind. All he could think about was what Matthews had told him. That Madley had set this whole thing up, from Munroe's attack and rape of Trina McGuire to Eddie Jones' brutal murder. Munroe had even played the police when he copied details about the serial rapist printed in the *Northern Echo*. But he had tortured Trina for information on Nick. And then for his own sadistic pleasure he had raped her after removing her tattoo of Nick's name.

It was clever. Brady would give Munroe that.

Then there was Eddie Jones' attack. Both attacks were filmed by the assailant's own hand and then uploaded onto YouTube for the world to see. But more significantly, the police. Brady still wondered how much Munroe had been paid. The savage rape and murder were incidental, merely a cruel means to an end. The ultimate plan was to get inside Durham prison so he could kill Ronnie Macmillan. It was so crazy it was almost believable.

Apart from Nick. Why go after Trina for Nick?

This was Brady's and Nick's childhood friend. This was Madley. Would Madley really pay someone to torture Trina for information on Nick? Madley had made it very clear that Nick had stitched him up. After all, Ronnie Macmillan may have been behind setting Madley up with the police, but Nick had also played a part in it. So much so, Madley had made it very clear that if Nick ever returned to the North-East he would have him killed. Madley knew that it was nothing personal where Nick was concerned. That he was just doing a job. But it was a moot point. He had betrayed Madley. The reason why didn't matter.

Brady suddenly pulled off the Links Road and headed towards St Mary's lighthouse. He parked the car and cut the engine.

Why the fuck here of all places? Why come here?

But Brady knew the answer.

When he was a kid, he and Martin and Nick would skip school and spend tireless days down here. They would mess around in the rock pools, on the beach and race along the causeway from the lighthouse to the mainland trying to outrun the incoming tide. Brady had had a dark childhood. His memories of this place were the few happy ones he had.

So why does being here hurt so much?

Brady tried to silence his mind by turning his attention to St Mary's lighthouse. It was now a major tourist attraction for the small seaside resort. It was a leisurely stroll down from Feathers caravan site; still a popular destination with the Scots for their annual fortnight holiday, just as it had been since the fifties. The two council-owned car parks at St Mary's were positioned to take in the breathtaking curve of beach and cliffs that was Whitley Bay.

Brady looked straight ahead. The beauty of the place was lost on him. He couldn't see it.

He sighed heavily.

He had never contemplated leaving this place. Until now.

Maybe it was time for him to get out?

Brady sat back and thought about everything that had happened. It looked like he could be in line for a promotion. So why didn't he feel good about it? It was simple. He hadn't really solved Eddie Jones' murder or Trina McGuire's rape. Jake Munroe had effectively handed himself in. Was the end goal really to kill Ronnie Macmillan?

Brady couldn't even report what Jimmy Matthews had witnessed. If he did, he would be signing Matthews's death warrant. And Jimmy Matthews meant a fuck more to him than the likes of Ronnie Macmillan. The gangster had it coming as far as Brady was concerned. As for Jake Munroe, he was already banged up in a maximum security prison. What more could they do?

He spent the next two hours watching the dots of lights along the curve of the Promenade. He had ignored the cars that pulled in with their headlights flashing. St Mary's lighthouse was a local dogging spot. Not that the Tourist Information centre listed it as such. But it was well known amongst the locals that St Mary's and Gosforth park in Gosforth, a sought-after suburb outside Newcastle, catered for the non-dog walkers late at night.

Brady checked his mobile. It was 11:33 p.m. It was time to call it quits. He turned the engine of his black 1978 Ford Granada 2.8i Ghia. It growled in response. A deep, seductive reassuring noise. The car had been bought as a project. But it was Nick who had restored it, not Brady. Nick had been able to fix things since he was a young child. It had been a shell when they'd bought it nearly eleven years ago, but it was Nick's time and endurance that had rebuilt it to beyond its former glory.

At this moment it felt like the only connection he had with Nick was the car. He still couldn't get hold of him. He was starting to get worried now. After the spree of killings, Brady feared the worst.

He cast a glance back at St Mary's lighthouse. It looked serene, ghostly even; pale white against the blackness of the horizon. He put the car in first and pulled away in an attempt to leave his past behind in the rear view mirror.

Brady found himself back at the station. He couldn't stomach the idea of going home, where he would be tormented with thoughts about whether Nick was dead or alive. Or worse, being held captive and tortured. He couldn't exactly turn to Madley.

Brady assumed that when Madley had rung to tell him about Ronnie Macmillan, it was his subtle way of telling Brady that Nick was next.

Brady had his elbows on the desk and his head in his hands as he looked at the files in front of him. Anything to take his mind off what had happened in the past thirty-six hours.

He sighed.

Why was he doing this? Gates had pointedly told him to steer clear. That Gates had forgotten about the Lee Harris debacle and so should Brady. In other words, forget him as a suspect. So why could Brady not accept his boss's advice?

Because he's wrong. That's why.

Brady picked up his mug and took a mouthful of scotch. It may have been cheap, nasty shit but it did the job. He took another slug before putting the mug down.

He looked at the files again. It was staring him in the face. He knew it so why couldn't he see it?

He couldn't ignore his gut feeling about Lee Harris. He fitted Amelia Jenkins's profile, aside from having had no prior convictions. But why did that jar with him? He felt as if Lee Harris was leading the police, or to be more specific, Brady, down a blind alley. He couldn't put his finger on why he felt Harris was not who he claimed to be.

Brady looked at the facts in front of him. Hazel Edwards had driven the suspect's car. Lee Harris was still a suspect in Brady's eyes – regardless of Gates. The taxi driver had said that Lee Harris told her to park the car on Marine Avenue, outside his flat, and to post the keys through the door when she'd finished her shift. She claimed to have ended her shift half an hour before the CCTV footage had caught the silver Passat pulling up to talk to Chloe Winters. Neither DCI Gates nor DI Adamson had queried this statement. The fact that Lee Harris' fiancée had given him an alibi was enough. They had simply assumed that Hazel Edwards had got the time wrong. There was no need for another explanation. But if there was one thing Brady had learned in the job, it was not to assume. It was a dangerous tactic.

Brady thought about it. If Lee Harris hadn't been in Paris the night of the first attack, Brady would have suggested that he had used Hazel Edwards as a foil. That he had picked up the car keys while his girlfriend was sleeping and sneaked out.

It's not possible. He was in Paris that first night. Or was he?

But Conrad had checked it out.

Then it hit Brady. Conrad said that he had delegated the job to either Daniels or Kenny. He couldn't remember which one. Not that it mattered. Both could be equally useless at times.

What the fuck were you thinking Conrad?

Brady picked up his mobile. He searched for Conrad's number and pressed call.

It took Brady calling twice before Conrad picked up.

'Sir?' mumbled a bleary voice.

'Conrad, I need you here now!' ordered Brady.

'Where?' questioned Conrad, not fully awake.

Brady heard a voice in the background. He didn't ask.

'My office.'

He listened as Conrad covered the mouthpiece and mumbled something.

'Sir? You do know it's three a.m.?'

'Yes. Why?'

'Nothing. Right, I'll be there as soon as I can,' Conrad answered.

'Now would be preferable.'

Brady hung up.

He cradled his head in his hands as he thought about the possibility that they had let the suspect slip through their hands.

Where the fuck did he take you, Chloe?

It felt as if the answers were slotting slowly into place. Brady could feel it.

Chloe Winters had said that when she'd been held captive he had raped and tortured her over a period of hours. At some point she had passed out. When she came to he wasn't there. He didn't return for what felt like days. She had said that she'd been terrified that she would die in the dark, boarded-up room chained to the floor like an animal. When he finally returned, it was dark again. He had blindfolded her and raped her – repeatedly. That was all she remembered. Her next memory was waking up in hospital.

Brady sighed heavily. He took another drink as he thought through the facts.

What stood out was the fact that the suspect had left her for a significant period of time. Abducted on Saturday after 3:00 a.m.; tortured for hours; then he disappears. She's left. But for how long? Chloe Winters was sure it was for days. But in reality it could only have been forty-eight hours. Because Chloe Winters was found on Monday at 6:10 a.m.

What was so important that he left her for so long?

Brady thought about it. His fiancée was ill and had taken a turn for the worse on the Saturday. It was Harris who had called out the emergency doctor. It was obvious he wouldn't have left Lisa Sanderson, which would account for Chloe Winters being left alone for so long. Brady was sure that Harris hadn't expected his fiancée to become as ill as she had. The more he ran it through his mind the more convinced he was that Lee Harris had abducted Chloe Winters. He had then left her for a day before returning. He raped and tortured her again until she passed out. Then he dumped her naked body.

The crucial question was how did he manage to attack the first victim if he was in Paris for the weekend?

But Brady knew the answer – it was just proving it that was the difficult part. And that was why he had called Conrad in, regardless of the hour.

He was certain that Lee Harris had abducted Chloe Winters. That he had pulled over as witnessed on the CCTV footage and asked her to get in his car. She refused. He then followed her. He took her somewhere isolated. It had to be, otherwise he wouldn't have taken his chances and left her for hours before returning.

Brady had wanted to get Lee Harris' car impounded and forensically examined when he had been brought in for questioning. But his request had been denied by Gates. He had wanted something more conclusive than a hunch of Brady's before he applied for a warrant. Brady was certain that if there had been any DNA evidence linking Chloe Winters to the car, it would now be gone. Harris wasn't stupid. He would have had the car thoroughly cleaned inside and out. Whether he would have got rid of all the DNA evidence was a moot point. Brady had no reason to bring him back in. At least not yet. But the maths was simple. The victim had to have been driven somewhere when she had been abducted. And then driven back fifty-odd hours later. The silver Passat saloon was crucial.

Brady had already run a background check on Lee Harris. He didn't own any properties, nor did he rent a place to take the victim. A lock-up garage or workshop would have been ideal. But nothing was in Harris' name. At least, not that Brady could find.

When Chloe Winters had said that she'd been abducted near Brook Street, just off the Promenade, Brady had ordered all the derelict buildings in the area searched. It made sense. Chloe Winters had described the room that she had been held in as boarded up and derelict. Aside from the suspect she had heard nobody else. No dogs barking, people walking past – nothing. Apart from cars in the distance.

The old, derelict Avenue pub, which had been a Victorian hotel in its heyday, had been searched. Nothing. Brady had then turned his eye to the High Point Hotel – another eyesore that sat boarded up on the sea front. Again nothing turned up. He had then turned his focus on another building – Whiskey Bends. At least that was what it had been known as in the eighties. Decades later it was just another forgotten carbuncle. It may have been boarded up and whitewashed but it was still a blight on Whitley Bay.

Brady hadn't focused on all three discarded buildings by chance. The rapist had attacked each victim in the back lanes behind these derelict pubs. They were the ideal deserted locations. But that was where it ended. None of these buildings had been used by the suspect. So exactly where had he taken Chloe Winters? And why had nobody heard her screams?

Chapter Forty

'I don't give a shit whether you wake him up, Conrad. Ring him!' Brady ordered.

'Yes, sir,' answered Conrad.

Brady left him to it. He went back to his office, slamming the door behind him.

He needed answers and he didn't give a damn that it was 3:45 a.m. If one of his team had screwed up then he had a right to know. Brady's gut told him that that was the case.

Right now he had his hands full. He was looking up Harry Sanderson's haulage firm. It was located in the industrial estate on Scotswood Road, Newcastle. It was down by the River Tyne and a stone's throw away from Elswick council estate – Newcastle's answer to Beruit.

It was the ideal place to hold someone.

If Brady's hunch was right that was where they should be looking.

A knock at the door broke him from his thoughts.

'Yeah?' he called out as he looked up from the computer screen.

Conrad walked in. The sheepish look on his face told Brady it was bad news.

'Tell me Kenny didn't screw this up?'

'I'm sorry, sir. It's my fault. I should have followed it up.'

'Damn right you should have!'

'Kenny was correct though. Harris did book a two night stay in Paris leaving on the Friday, 30th August at five thirty p.m. and returning Sunday 1st, September at seven p.m.'

'But they didn't get on the Friday flight, did they?' Brady asked as he stood up from his desk. He was too agitated to remain seated.

Conrad shook his head. 'I'm sorry, sir.'

'Stop saying bloody "sorry" will you?' Brady exploded.

He needed to think. His next move had to be by the book. Otherwise Gates would have his bollocks nailed to the wall.

He looked at Conrad unable to disguise the incredulity he felt. He dragged his hand back through his hair as he thought about the implications. It made no difference.

'This is one monumental fuck-up!'

'I know. I'm sorry. I accept full responsibility,' said Conrad.

Brady marched over to the window and opened it. He needed some fresh air and he needed to keep his back to Conrad. Otherwise he was in danger of really losing his temper.

'Fucking hell, Conrad. What were you thinking?'

'I wasn't, sir.'

'At least you're honest. I'll give you that.'

He turned round and looked at his deputy.

'When did they fly?'

'Saturday at ten thirty a.m. They returned on the original flight they booked.'

Brady nodded. It made perfect sense.

So why had Lisa Sanderson said that they'd left on the Friday evening? Had she lied to cover Lee Harris? If she had, then she'd duped Brady because during her interview he was certain she was telling the truth.

'Do we know why they didn't get on the Friday evening flight?'

'They just didn't show up. However, Lee Harris must have known that in advance because on Thursday evening he booked two single seats flying out on the Saturday.'

'And he didn't cancel the Friday flights and change them to the Saturday?'

'No, sir.'

'Why wouldn't he cancel those flights?'

Conrad didn't answer. It was obvious.

'Call the team in. I also want some back-up organised. We're taking a road trip, Conrad. To Scotswood Road. Might need the Armed Response Unit with us though.'

'Sir?' questioned Conrad.

'I'm bloody joking! How long have you lived in the North-East now? Even you should have heard of Scotswood Road. One of the worst council estates in Newcastle is up by Scotswood.'

Conrad was still none the wiser.

'Elswick, Conrad. So when you see a sign for Elswick you avoid it all costs. Understand?'

'Perfectly, sir.'

'Little bastards would have your car stripped down to bolts as soon as the traffic lights turned red.'

Brady turned back and looked out the window.

The day was just starting to break. It was bleak and miserable with some drizzle; another typical day in the North-East. Brady hoped by the end of it he would have Harris banged up indefinitely.

'Conrad?'

'Sir?'

'I need you to run a check for me on Harris.'

'We've already done that,' Conrad answered, frowning.

'We missed something.'

'But he's got no prior convictions.'

'My point exactly.'

'I don't understand,' Conrad admitted.

'He has no priors as Lee Harris. But what if he changed his name by deed poll between the ages of sixteen and eighteen? What then?'

'Wouldn't we already know?' asked Conrad. 'We took a swab from Harris. Surely if he had priors, even under another name, his DNA would be in the system?'

'Depends how old he was when he was arrested. Remember that before 2004 DNA could only be taken from someone charged, not arrested.' Brady turned away from the window and started pacing the floor.

'How old is Harris?'

'Twenty-seven, sir.'

'In 2004 he would have been eighteen. Say he committed an offence and was arrested before then as a minor? If he wasn't charged then they wouldn't have taken his DNA.'

'What if he was arrested after 2004? Surely his DNA would be in the system, regardless of whether he was only arrested and not charged?'

Brady turned and looked at Conrad. 'Not necessarily. If he was just arrested there's a chance his DNA was destroyed. Remember that a large number of DNA profiles have been removed from the database because it was decided that there wasn't enough room to store profiles of people who'd been arrested but not charged. Either way Conrad, it doesn't matter whether he was arrested before or after 2004, there's a reason why his DNA isn't on the system.

'I'm sure we'll find that Harris isn't his real name and that he has quite an interesting history. One that his fiancée and her father know nothing about.'

'Yes, sir,' answered Conrad. He hadn't thought of that. It had never occurred to him to ask if Harris might have changed his name.

Chapter Forty-One

Brady and a team of officers were busy searching Sanderson's haulage yard. He had gone above Gates directly to DCI O'Donnell. He needed a search warrant granted and didn't trust Gates to approve the application. O'Donnell was different. He listened. Then he acted without hesitation. Brady knew that he had enough against the suspect to get a warrant issued for his arrest. Even Gates couldn't deny that. But Brady didn't want anyone dragging their heels and wasting time. He was acutely aware that Harry Sanderson and Gates played golf together at Tynemouth Golf Club. He was certain that most of the time would have been spent in the club's bar rather than on the grounds.

O'Donnell had sanctioned Harris' arrest warrant immediately, notifying the Met police. He was arrested at 5:01 a.m. by a group of burly officers kicking in the door of his digs. He was now in custody and in the process of being driven back up to the North-East.

Brady would worry about Gates's reaction to his bypassing his authority later. Right now he was more concerned with finding where Lee Harris had held and tortured Chloe Winters. When he walked back into that interview room he wanted to make sure that Harris, or James Hunter as he had previously been known, didn't have a chance in hell of walking out a free man. He wanted no fuck-ups this time.

'Nothing here, sir,' shouted one of the officers searching the yard.

It was 10:45. The search warrant had been hurriedly approved. It came with the territory of being a Detective Chief

Superintendent. Judges were more likely to act quickly for O'Donnell than someone like Brady.

'Fuck!' muttered Brady to himself. They had been here for two hours – and nothing.

They had searched all the offices and warehouses and even the haulage trucks. Brady had even had the dogs search amongst the crates on the off-chance that Harris had kept her in one.

Again, nothing.

'Sir,' Conrad greeted him as he joined him.

They were standing in the yard. All of Sanderson's employees had been interviewed. Brady wanted to know if anyone had seen Lee Harris hanging around the yard. No one had. It wasn't the news he wanted. However, he was sure that Harry Sanderson was more pissed-off right now that his future son-in-law had been picked up by the police and was in custody; as was his daughter.

'I don't get it, Conrad.'

Conrad didn't reply. He had no answer to give his boss.

They had both noticed the twenty-four surveillance cameras surrounding the premises. The haulage firm dealt with hundreds of thousands of pounds worth of goods on a daily basis. It was a given that security would be tight. Then there were the two security guards. Kodovesky and Harvey had already questioned them. They had never seen Harris on the premises. Brady currently had Daniels and Kenny searching the surveillance footage for any sign of Harris on that Friday night. So far, nothing.

He looked around the yard. It would have been impossible for Harris to bring Chloe Winters here. Brady had fucked up. There was no way he could have bypassed the security cameras and the two security guards undetected. It simply wasn't possible. And if Kenny and Daniels found no evidence of him on the security tapes then Brady was screwed.

He thought of what Gates's reaction would be to this news. Not good.

'Does he own anywhere else, Conrad?'

Conrad shook his head. 'No, sir.'

'These premises look new to me. Sanderson's office looked as if he had recently moved into it. Fresh paint . . . new carpet. What happened to his old premises? Because he's been in business for over twenty years . . .'

'I'll check, sir,' Conrad said as he took out his mobile.

Brady watched as he walked off.

What are you missing? What the fuck are you not seeing?

Then it hit him. He remembered that one of the paramedics had said something strange in their report. At the time Brady had discounted it. But the paramedic had clearly stated that 'Her hair and skin smelled of charred wood.'

Why had he not taken that seriously? Why had it not jarred at the time?

Brady didn't have an answer. He just knew that he had failed to see the obvious.

'Conrad?' Brady shouted.

He turned to Brady.

'I know what you need to look for.'

Conrad put his call on hold and waited.

'His old premises burned down.'

'On it, sir,' Conrad immediately answered.

Chapter Forty-Two

Two hours later they were searching through the burned remnants of Sanderson's original haulage site. It was conveniently close to the coast; two miles inland if that. No distance in a car. The haulage company was located on an industrial estate set back off Middle Engine Lane. The place had burned down over a year ago, so why had Brady not thought of it? He was kicking himself at his own stupidity.

He hadn't realised this place had belonged to Sanderson. Brady had heard that it had been intentionally torched. He had no idea why. But this place was called Douglas and Sons Haulage Company, which was why he hadn't made the connection. Brady assumed Sanderson had renamed his haulage firm to distance himself from the suspicion that someone had it in for him.

The condemned premises were surrounded by eight-foot high fencing and a padlocked gate. But it appeared that the heavy-duty padlock had been cut with bolt cutters and replaced with another. The keys Brady had got from Sanderson were useless. Once in, it didn't take the police dogs and their handlers long to find the room where Lee Harris had kept Chloe Winters. No surprise given the amount of blood and skin tissue left at the crime scene. Winters' scent had driven the dogs wild.

Lee Harris had been here recently. That was obvious. But no amount of industrial bleach could destroy the incriminating evidence. It was everywhere. The ground floor office had been used as a torture room. Harris had thoughtfully fitted a chain into the concrete floor. He had made sure that Chloe was going nowhere. A mattress had been left in the corner of the room. Again doused in bleach. Harris would no doubt have thought about pouring petrol over the mattress and setting fire to it. But if he had, the whole place would have gone up again bringing with it an investigation. It wouldn't have taken long for the fire officers to know it had been started intentionally and then the police would have started looking around.

Brady had left the room to Ainsworth's team. The less contamination the better. They would crucify Harris; he was sure of it. Every officer on this case felt sick to the stomach. Harris was a very disturbed individual. That much was clear from what they had found. Harris had presumably panicked. He had voluntarily come in for questioning but it hadn't quite gone as he'd planned. Without Lisa Sanderson, and her father's friendship with DCI Gates, Harris wouldn't have walked. Not if Brady had had his way. Harris had returned to the crime scene to try and eradicate trace evidence: blood, hair, saliva and semen. However, he hadn't been as clever as he'd thought. He had not anticipated the SOCOs using the chemical luminol and a portable UV light to reveal trace evidence that couldn't be seen by the naked eye. Ainsworth's team had their work cut out. It was gruesome.

Brady was looking forward to seeing Gates's face when he realised exactly what kind of sick, depraved kind of person he had released back into society.

Brady had just returned to his office after interviewing Lisa Sanderson. He needed time to unwind.

He sat down at his desk. It was late and he was tired. It hit him that he had had no sleep. That after he'd been to see Jimmy Matthews in prison yesterday he had driven around for hours. Otherwise he would have driven himself mad – literally. He had then wound up back at the station in the early hours of the morning. Anything was better than being at home alone. He had needed a distraction, which was why had turned his attention back to Lee Harris. Within eighteen hours that distraction had developed at an exponential rate. Lee Harris was now in a holding cell in the station's basement after being signed off by the Met police. Had been for the past six hours.

It was now 7:30 p.m. and Brady still had to interview him. But the forensic evidence they had against him was incontestable. Trace evidence had been recovered from his silver Passat despite his attempts at cleaning it. It was clear that he had transported Chloe Winters' body in the boot. Then there was the crime scene where he had held her captive for forty-eight hours. And Brady was only getting started.

He sighed heavily and took a drink of the cold coffee on the desk. Anything to keep awake. He couldn't believe what they had found at Lisa Sanderson's flat in Marine Avenue. Harris had sealed his fate by not dumping it all. Brady had questioned why, and the only answer he could come up with was that Harris, for whatever perverse, sick reason couldn't let it go.

Brady thought about his interview with the suspect's fiancée, or should he say ex-fiancée? It had been short and awkward. Harry Sanderson's lawyer had been present and had a knack of stopping Brady at every juncture. The upshot of the interview was that she had not knowingly lied about the dates for the trip to Paris. She argued that she had made a mistake when she had checked the dates for that weekend on her phone. Her mobile's calendar had flagged up both the Friday and the Saturday as the weekend trip to Paris. She had read the dates out and hadn't realised. She had even shown Brady the flagged dates on her phone at the time.

Sanderson had explained that they missed the Friday flight because Harris couldn't make it back from London in time. He changed the flights to the following day before he left London to avoid losing the tickets.

When Brady had informed her that Harris never cancelled the Friday flights and that he'd already booked two single fares for the Saturday earlier that week she was genuinely surprised.

Then taken aback and, finally, horrified. If her whole world had been in a state of collapse, it suddenly imploded at that point.

It had taken twenty minutes to calm her down. And another twenty to get her in a state where she could answer without the threat of needing to be tranquilised.

When Brady finally asked her if at any point she had realised her mistake with the Paris dates her answer had been no. Brady accepted it. It was an honest answer. The ground had been taken from beneath her; she had nothing to lose.

Her lawyer was good. He had argued that his client had been harassed at the time and had had no legal representation. In other words, she should never have been interviewed without a lawyer present. It was no surprise she would have been so shaken and shocked by the fact that her fiancée was being questioned over rape allegations. That it was an easy mistake to make.

He looked up as Conrad walked into the room.

'Tranquilisers?'

Conrad nodded. 'Exactly where she said they were, sir. In her bathroom cabinet.'

'Explains why she wouldn't have heard Harris leave the flat on the nights he raped his victims. Perfect alibi,' Brady said.

Why the hell had Lisa Sanderson not mentioned that when she had first been interviewed? More to the point, why hadn't Brady thought to ask if she was on any type of medication?

He had told Kodovesky and Harvey to search the flat that Harris shared with his fiancée, while he and Conrad had been at the crime scene. They had recovered a great deal of incriminating evidence against Lee Harris but they had missed the drugs. The tranquilisers were Lisa Sanderson's ticket out. It meant that her alibi for all three nights still stood. She had spent the evening with Lee Harris and had then gone to bed medicated up to her eyeballs. She wouldn't have heard a bomb go off with the strength of medication she was taking. So it was no surprise that Harris was able to come and go without her knowledge. As far as she was concerned, he had been with her all night. She went to bed with Harris and woke up with him. How would she know any different?

It was her lawyer who had raised the sleeping pills in her defence. Sanderson hadn't realised their significance. She had been taking them for so long that they were as much a part of her routine as cleaning her teeth before bed. But Lee Harris knew about them. He knew that she had had a bad fall horse-riding a few years ago and suffered from chronic back pain – she couldn't sleep without medication.

Harris lived at Lisa Sanderson's rented flat at the weekends and during the week he stayed in digs in London close to the construction site where he worked. They had confiscated his desktop computer from the flat in Whitley Bay and the Met police had picked up his laptop in his digs. Harris had made himself very comfortable in Lisa Sanderson's flat. He even had an attic room where he kept all his personal effects – including the surveillance cameras that he had removed from the crime scene. He had installed a camera in the room where Chloe Winters had been held so he could watch her live on his computer whenever he'd wanted. The door had a padlock on it so only Harris could enter. He had explained to his fiancée that he was worried about somebody breaking in and stealing all his computer equipment and personal belongings. For some reason, blinded no doubt by love, Lisa Sanderson had innocently accepted this arrangement.

Lee Harris' computers were now with Jed. Brady was certain that he would find everything Harris had stored; including the scenes when he had tortured and raped Winters. Harris was a narcissist and a control freak. He would have savoured being able to relive every cruel and sadistic moment. Even if Harris had deleted all the files after his brief period in custody, Jed was one of the best forensic computer scientists on the force so Brady had no doubts that he would find them.

Why hadn't Harris made a run for it? Brady couldn't say. Perhaps it was a combination of arrogance and the fact that his father-in-law had connections. After all, Lee Harris had already walked free once because of Harry Sanderson's money and social status. But that wouldn't have been able to protect him indefinitely. He was a sadist and a serial rapist. It would be very difficult for him to control the urge to attack again. Chloe Winters survived his attack; whether his next victim would have done was doubtful.

There was a knock at the door.

'It's open,' Brady called out.

Amelia Jenkins walked in.

'Congratulations, Jack. I don't how you did it.'

She stopped when she saw the state of him.

Amelia had not seen him since before Munroe's fists had redesigned Brady's face. She turned to Conrad as if expecting an answer from him.

She looked back to Brady: 'Christ! You look dreadful.'

'Thanks.'

'You know what I mean. I heard that Munroe had resisted arrest but . . . God that looks painful,' she said as she stared at his swollen jaw.

'It's nothing. Really. Munroe's old news.'

Amelia walked over and sat down in front of Brady's desk.

'Take a seat why don't you?' Brady offered.

'So, I hear that you've released Lisa Sanderson?' There was an unmistakable edge to her voice.

Brady nodded.

'Can I ask why?'

Brady turned to Conrad.

'Show her the evidence bag.'

Conrad did as instructed. The evidence had to be officially signed in and dated which was his next job.

'Christ! These would knock a rugby team out. And she was taking these on a daily basis?' Amelia asked, incredulous.

Brady nodded.

'For at least eighteen months.'

'How was she getting these prescribed? No doctor in their right mind would give her a repeat prescription. These are highly addictive.'

'She mainly bought them off the Internet. You know how big the illegal trade in pharmaceutical drugs is now. There's a lot of money to be made that way.'

Amelia turned the bottle over.

'Makes sense. Because how else can you explain having no idea that you're living with a serial rapist who just so happens to have a locked room in the attic where he keeps his trophies,' Amelia said. Her voice was thick with irony.

'Come on, Amelia. She had no idea,' Brady replied frowning at her.

He was surprised. This wasn't like her.

Amelia ignored Brady's comment and handed the plastic evidence bag back to Conrad.

'You better get that handed over, Harry. The last thing you want is losing Lisa Sanderson's alibi.'

Brady knew there was something wrong but he had no idea what.

'Go on Conrad, log it before it gets lost on the back of a shelf somewhere.'

'Yes, sir,' Conrad replied before leaving.

Brady waited until the door was closed before turning to Amelia.

'OK. What's going on?'

'I don't know what you mean,' Amelia answered, unable to look Brady in the eye.

'Don't bullshit me, Amelia. I know you well enough to know when something's wrong.'

Amelia looked at him.

'Let's just say that I'm not that impressed with myself. I should have done more with this investigation.' She shook her head and turned away.

'Like what? Lee Harris fits your profile perfectly. You did everything you could.'

'Did I?'

Brady didn't reply. He waited for Amelia to fill in the silence. If she needed to off-load he had time – plenty of it. Lee Harris was going nowhere.

He got up and walked over to the window to give her time to compose her thoughts. He lifted the old Victorian sash window up to let the cool October evening into the stuffy room. As he did so he looked down at the street below. He caught sight of Lisa Sanderson leaving the station. Fragile and vulnerable, led on either side by her father and lawyer. The world as she had known it had evaporated. She was now part of a serious investigation. She would be called to court and questioned about her knowledge of Lee Harris and his crimes. Every word, every reaction would be scrutinised. Her alibis would be ripped apart. She would become guilty by association. Whether it was the press who took that angle or some barrister, it was inevitable. Not that she had been charged. Not as an accomplice, or for withholding evidence, or even wasting police time. As far as Brady was concerned she was only guilty of being duped by Lee Harris. She was another one of Harris' victims. He may not have raped and tortured her. But Brady was certain the mental scars would torment her for the rest of her life. Especially when she found out Lee Harris' actual identity and what she had unwittingly been storing.

She suddenly turned and looked back at the station. He didn't know whether she had seen him. But he had seen her. Her pretty, perfect-featured face was pale and taut. Pinched even. Her bright blue, lively eyes had lost their *joie de vivre*. They were dull, filled instead with pain and recrimination. He wondered who the recrimination was directed at – herself or Brady?

After all, he was the catalyst. Brady was responsible for her life being destroyed. If Gates had had his way, Lisa Sanderson's day would have been very different.

'Why didn't I think of that?' Amelia asked.

Brady turned and walked back to his desk.

'Think of what?' he asked, sitting down.

'His bloody name. Why didn't I suggest that he could have changed his name by deed poll?' Amelia asked.

Brady knew the anger in her voice was directed at herself rather than at him.

'Because it didn't seem obvious at the time. Why did DCI Gates let Lee Harris walk? Why did I let it get that far in the first instance? I should have nailed him when I had him here on Sunday. But I didn't. Why did Kenny not check that they had actually got on the flight the Friday evening Sarah Jeffries was attacked? Why didn't I double-check that crucial piece of information myself? I even accepted that Kenny had contacted the hotel and verified that Sanderson and Harris had spent the weekend there. He'd checked with the hotel all right. Checked that they had turned up for the weekend. But he had missed one crucial detail. He didn't double-check what day they arrived. He didn't think to ask. The worst part is I had a gut feeling but I did nothing.'

Amelia looked at Brady, surprised by what he'd just said.

'But you turned it around. You did the impossible.'

'Really?' Brady questioned, his eyes filled with scepticism. 'You want to try telling DCI Gates that? I don't think he'll quite see it that way.'

Amelia frowned at him.

'Double-edged sword. I resolved this case against Gates's wishes. He released Harris without my knowledge. He then told me to let it go and move on.'

'What? From the case?'

'No. From my belief that Lee Harris was our suspect.'

Amelia didn't say anything.

Neither did Brady.

He might have closed the case. But at what price? He had committed career suicide in more ways than one. He had ignored DCI Gates's advice and then he'd bypassed him and gone higher to get the answer he wanted. He should have gone to Gates and shared the new information he had on Harris, instead of to O'Donnell. Gates would never trust him again.

Chapter Forty-Three

Brady was sitting opposite Lee Harris. The interview wasn't going well. The suspect was refusing to talk. He had taken his right to silence one step too far.

Brady wanted to grab him by the throat and force the answers out of him. But he knew that was out of the question. Instead, he tried his best to rein his anger in. They had enough evidence on this sick bastard to make sure he would never get the chance to hurt another woman again.

The Duty Solicitor, Harold Oliver, was next to the suspect. It was clear he had better things to do than waste a Wednesday night on Harris.

Oliver checked his watch and then shot Brady a questioning look.

'Can we speed this along Detective Inspector? It's clear my client isn't willing to talk to you. We've been here for an hour now. So can I suggest if you're going to charge him, you do that? Rather than wasting time?'

'In a minute. There's still some details I'm not quite sure about.'

Oliver folded his arms as he glared at Brady. He was an average-looking man in his mid-thirties who was only here for the money. He had a wife, a mortgage and expensive tastes in clothes. Simple maths.

Oliver leaned in towards Brady in an attempt to reason with him.

'Come on, Jack. Do we have to do this? I mean, Lee Harris won't even talk to me. What chance do you think you have?'

The look in Brady's eye told Oliver it might be a long night.

Infuriated, he sat back, realising he had no choice but to wait it out.

'So, James? It is James Hunter, isn't it?'

Harris shot Brady a relaxed, easy-going smile that told Brady he could stay here and sit this out for as long as it took.

Brady realised that Harris really couldn't give a damn.

'Why didn't you report your change of name to the Met?'

Again Harris didn't say a word.

'You've got quite a history as James Hunter, haven't you? I can understand why you'd want to forget about it. Don't blame you really. I mean . . . let's see . . .' Brady said as he picked up the file in front of him.

He turned to Conrad.

'You want to feel the weight of this file. James Hunter certainly had an interesting life. How old were you when you changed your name? That's right, eighteen. And in those eighteen years you did some sick, twisted shit. I suppose that's what the forma- tive years of a serial sadistic rapist look like?'

Harris smiled at Brady again.

But the smile did not quite reach his eyes. He looked at Brady with a chilling coldness, which didn't hide how much he would like to hurt him.

Brady simply carried on.

'Your prior arrests are fascinating: theft, assault, sexual assault, rape of a minor. This was all under the age of thirteen. Quite precocious for your age, weren't you?'

Oliver sighed heavily. 'Really, Detective? I am sure you're aware that my client was not convicted of any of those crimes. There was no evidence to charge him. And as far as I am aware there's no law against changing your name. Especially in such circumstances as my client's.'

Brady shot Oliver a sceptical look. 'And what circumstances would those be?'

'He spent his youth being harassed by the police. He was repeatedly arrested but not once did they have anything concrete to charge him with.'

'Unlike now,' Brady stated. It was enough to silence Oliver.

He then turned his attention to Harris. 'Your mother must have been really proud of you, considering how hard she worked. What was she again, DS Conrad?'

'A prostitute, sir,' answered Conrad, never once taking his eyes off Harris.

'That's right, a single mother who worked as a prostitute so she could put food on the table and pay the rent on the shitty little piss-ridden Tower Hamlets flat you lived in. Bet you saw some action there when you were a kid?'

Brady opened the file and started scrolling down with his index finger. He then stopped and looked up at Harris.

'Ah yes. There it is. You were temporarily removed and placed into social services after a teacher had reported that she had concerns regarding your welfare. Good job she did. Turned out that your mother's boyfriend was abusing you. How old were you? Ten? Bet it started long before that.' Brady stopped as he took a drink of water.

Harris sat back and smiled. The look in his eyes told Brady to do his worst.

Brady put his glass down. He liked a challenge.

'Remember what your mother looked like? Before someone considerately doused her in petrol while she lay pissed in her bed in that rat-infested flat you shared. Whole flat went up. Only made the local news, though. Pity that. Then again, most people don't give a shit if a prostitute gets set on fire.'

Harris didn't respond.

'Why did you do it, Harris? Did you watch her wake up screaming after you'd soaked her in petrol and struck the match?'

Oliver sighed in exasperation.

'Really, Detective Inspector! Is this necessary? You know my client wasn't charged with any involvement with his mother's death.'

'Sorry. You're right. My apologies, Mr Harris. Bit of a coincidence that you disappeared around that time and resurfaced a year later with a new identity, though.'

Brady sat back and looked at him. He was starting to agree with Oliver. This was a waste of police time. He should charge him and just go to the pub.

'The only question I have is why were we able to recover items from your childhood that should have gone up in flames. Bit of a coincidence that they survived when the whole flat was destroyed. Unless of course, you cleared your possessions out before torching her and the flat?'

'Detective!' Oliver interjected.

Brady ignored him.

'We found your secret box. The one you kept in Lisa Sanderson's flat. Photographs of you and your mother and other pathetic pieces of paraphernalia. You even kept the newspaper cutting that reported her death. Just like you did with your rape victims.'

Oliver made an exaggerated gesture of pointing at his watch.

Brady nodded.

'I tell you what was clever, befriending Chloe Winters on Facebook. Why didn't you do that with Sarah Jeffries or Anna Lewis? Or did you become more confident by the time you decided on Chloe Winters? You stalked her, didn't you? Followed her statuses and even made comments on them. But not as Lee Harris, as James Hunter. You see, when you came in on Saturday I had my team run a check on all three rape victims' Facebook pages to see if you were there. But you weren't, were you? We even checked to see if there was a name that matched all three of their accounts. But no. You had only befriended Chloe and that was in the name of James Hunter, with a photograph of you as a small boy with your mother on the beach playing happy families. Chilling really,' Brady said as he looked Harris in the eye. 'As disturbing as cutting off Chloe Winters' tattoo and Anna Lewis's right nipple and drying the skin out. What did you do with them when you were locked away in your attic playing by yourself? Did you touch them? Did they get you all aroused?'

Harris was smiling at Brady in a way that told him he was right. The look in his brown eyes said he was impressed that Brady could even understand something so personal.

It took Brady all his power not to lean over and knock the stomach-turning look of enjoyment off his face.

Conrad hastily gave the time of 10:01 p.m., calling an end to the interview.

He could see the look on Brady's face and had a fair idea what was coming next.

'You're one fucking sick bastard, Harris. I hope you like your new inmates. A pretty boy like you? They'll be fighting over who gets you first! At least it will be familiar, eh? Like the good old days with your mam's boyfriend,' Brady stated, his voice cold.

If Brady had wanted a reaction, he got one. Some dark, forgotten memory sparked inside Harris just long enough for the arrogance and assurance to slip. For a second Brady saw a glimmer of something closely resembling pain. Then it was gone. Replaced by the cold, unnerving smile of a psychopath.

Brady watched him. The look of such pleasure on his face made him feel sick. He suddenly scraped his chair back and stood up. He couldn't stand another second in the same room as Harris. He turned and walked out, leaving Conrad to charge him.

Chapter Forty-Four

'Another pint, Jack? It's your money after all!' laughed Harvey as he slapped Brady on the back.

Brady had handed over 200 quid for the team to celebrate. They deserved it. It had been a gruelling two months with some serious fuck-ups along the way, but they had somehow managed to turn it around. He was now leaning over the bar in the Fat Ox nursing a pint and not much in the mood for celebrating.

He turned to Harvey and gave him a weak smile.

'If I start I won't stop.' It was an honest answer.

'Doesn't sound too bad to me. It's not as if you've got to be back in at the crack of dawn tomorrow, is it?'

Brady shot Harvey a look as if to say: 'How the fuck did you know?'

'You're not serious?'

'Gates has demanded to see me. His office, eight thirty a.m.'

'What a tight-arsed bastard! You turn three bloody cases round in five days, I mean five fucking days, and he's calling you in the morning after you've maybe closed the biggest investigation of your career? To what? Congratulate you?'

'Yeah.' There was nothing more Brady could say.

'Surely he knows that the team . . . no, make that most of the station are here tonight getting bladdered?' Harvey asked, incredulous.

'Yeah, I think that's his point.' The last thing Brady needed right now was Harvey reminding him.

'What the fuck is that about then?' Harvey asked as he signalled to Gaye for two more pints.

Brady shrugged. But he knew exactly what it was about. He had kept his head down and had somehow managed to avoid Gates. He had no idea how, but he had. Then Conrad had walked into the pub with the news that Gates wanted to see him at 8:30 precisely.

'There you go, pet. You look like you need it,' Gaye said as she handed Brady a fresh pint.

'Thanks, Gaye,' he muttered.

He liked her. She always had time for a chat when it was quiet. She was a small woman in her early fifties with short blonde hair and a smile for every customer. Despite her size she had a way of handling trouble when it came in. Brady had witnessed her successfully bar four skinheads who were on the lash and out to wreak mayhem. He still didn't quite know how she did it.

'You want to talk about it?' she asked, concerned at the state he was in.

She had known Brady for over ten years. The exact length of time she had run the place.

'No,' Brady answered with a weak smile.

'Ignore him, Gaye. He's just being a miserable bastard for the sake of it! Likes the job too much. That's his problem. Look at the rest of the team, eh? Celebrating because we've closed an investigation and what's this miserable sod doing? Looking depressed! Some people are never happy!'

Harvey laughed as he clapped Brady on the back again before walking off towards the raucous crowd shouting and cheering at the back end of the pub. The troublemakers belonged to Brady. It was a collection of his team members and other officers who had been called in to help work the serial rape case.

Brady looked over for Conrad. He seemed to be having a good time. He was already on his third pint. Conrad had worked up quite a thirst – they all had. But for some reason Brady was struggling to drink. He swilled the dregs at the bottom of his glass around. He couldn't shake his mood. It was the knowledge he had to face Gates in the morning.

Shit . . .

Brady had no idea what he was going to say. Let alone how he was going to excuse his actions. He would just have to wait and find out what Gates wanted. But he knew that the outcome wouldn't be good.

'Hey, penny for them?' Amelia said as she joined Brady.

'You'd want your money back if I told you,' he replied.

He turned and looked at her. She was leaning over the bar trying to catch one of the bar staff's attention.

She looked as stunning as ever.

'What? What's wrong? Have I smudged my lipstick or something?' Amelia asked, realising he was staring at her.

'No . . . You look perfect,' Brady answered without thinking. 'I mean . . . no you . . . you're fine. Your lipstick's fine.'

He suddenly focused his attention on the dregs in the pint glass in front of him. He picked it up and drained it.

Brady's awkwardness made Amelia feel embarrassed.

She turned away and tried to catch the eye of one of the bartenders again. She failed.

'Large white wine, please, Gaye?' Brady called out as the proprietor walked past.

'Thanks,' Amelia said.

'Doesn't say that much about me though, does it?'

Amelia didn't get his drift.

'That I'm on first term names with the bar staff?'

She broke into a smile. 'I see.'

Brady handed over a tenner to Gaye as he gestured that the wine in her hand was for Amelia. 'Keep the change.'

Gaye shot him a winning smile in return but handed him his change back.

'Keep your money, Jack. You've already spent enough tonight on that lot,' Gaye said as she looked over at the group of rowdy drinkers.

289

'So, who's this lovely young lady, then?' Gaye asked, turning her attention back to Brady. It had been a long time since she'd seen Jack Brady with an attractive young woman. The last woman who actually suited Brady had been Claudia, his ex-wife. She hadn't seen Claudia since they'd separated but in a funny way this woman reminded her of Claudia.

Brady's face became flushed. 'No one,' he quickly answered. Too quickly.

He felt Amelia's eyes on him. 'I mean . . . Yes, this is Amelia. She's a work colleague. Amelia this is Gaye – who likes to embarrass me. And Gaye, this is—'

Gaye smiled at his discomfort. 'Amelia,' she cut in. 'I know. Don't you just love him?'

Amelia turned to Brady. She bit her bottom lip, getting red lipstick on her teeth. 'I don't know. Is he worth loving?'

Gaye laughed. 'The jury's still out on that one, pet.'

Brady had his head bent down and focused on the second pint Harvey had ordered for him.

'It's OK. I'm going now. I'll leave you two lovebirds alone.' She shot Brady a mischievous smile before walking off to serve another customer.

'She seems to know you well,' Amelia commented.

'Knows everything about me. So if there's anything you want to ask, Gaye's the woman.'

'I'll keep that in mind,' Amelia replied as she watched Brady.

He still had his head bent down, staring into his pint.

'You all right, Jack?'

He shrugged. 'I dunno. Depends what happens tomorrow with Gates.'

'Oh . . .'

'Yeah. He wants to see me first thing.'

'That's shit.'

Brady turned and looked at Amelia. It was the first time he had heard her swear.

'Yeah,' he agreed. It was shit.

'What do you think he'll say?'

'You're the shrink. You tell me,' Brady answered as he looked at her.

Her brown eyes were filled with genuine concern. 'I wish I had the answer. But I don't.'

He dropped her gaze and turned back to his pint.

'Jack?' she asked as she touched his arm.

It was gentle and reassuring.

'Jack?' she repeated, wanting him to look at her.

Reluctantly he turned.

'Look, you're not really in the mood for this are you? This whole end of investigation celebration thing?'

Brady looked at her, waiting for her to say it. From the look in her eye he had an idea of what was coming.

She faltered. Not sure whether she should.

But there was something in Brady's face that told her he already knew what she was about to say – and that he was receptive.

'Why don't you come back to mine? I'll open a bottle of wine and cook us some supper,' she said.

'You sure?' Brady asked. 'I don't want to be some sad charity case.'

Amelia smiled at him. 'Believe me, you'll never be that.'

'OK. If you're sure,' he answered, returning her smile.

Brady knew it was time to move his life on. So much had happened to him in the past eighteen months and now . . . He had no idea what the outcome of tomorrow would be. Let alone tonight. But he was willing to take a chance.

'Great. Give me two minutes while I go to the—' she gestured towards the toilets.

Amelia seemed nervous. As if she didn't quite trust her luck.

'Go on. I'll still be here,' Brady said, picking up his pint.

'Two minutes?'

Brady nodded. His dark brown eyes filled with amusement.

He watched as she turned on her heels and walked over the uneven flagstones to the Ladies. He couldn't quite believe his luck. That after all this time she was still interested.

Amelia was thinking exactly the same thing as she went to the bathroom to compose herself. She spent a few minutes reapplying her lipstick, checking her eye make-up and her hair. Then she readjusted her black woollen dress. She wished she had gone home and changed into something more seductive instead of coming straight from work.

She stared at herself in the mirror as she went through a mental check-list.

Was the apartment tidy? Shit! What about the bedroom? It looked like a bomb had gone off. Were the sheets clean? Shit!

Amelia bit her lip as she tried to steady her nerves. The last thing she wanted was for Brady to see her in this state – like some nervous teenager on her first date.

By the time she had composed herself and come back out into the pub, Brady had gone.

Amelia walked over to the bar, ignoring the sickening, ominous feeling she had.

He's gone to the Gents. No big deal.

The empty pint convinced her that was the case.

She took a sip of white wine as she waited anxiously for him to return.

When Gaye saw her she came straight over.

Amelia smiled, trying her best to look relaxed.

'I'm sorry, pet, Jack asked me to pass on his apologies. Some call came in. Said it was an emergency.' She gave Amelia a sympathetic smile before walking off.

It took a couple of seconds for Amelia to absorb the information.

She looked at the glass in her hand, resisting the urge to drink it in one go. She didn't hear any of the cheering and clapping coming from the bottom of the pub. All she could think about was whether Jack Brady often brought women in here. And how often he had humiliated them.

Amelia put the glass down firmly on the bar and walked out.

Chapter Forty-Five

When he returned home he found Claudia in the kitchen with a large glass of Sancerre in her hand. She had conveniently let herself in and helped herself to the contents of the fridge. It had never crossed his mind to change the locks when she left.

'You weren't saving that, were you?' she asked, pointing at the wine bottle.

Brady looked at the open bottle on the worktop. It was nearly empty.

She already had a glass poured for him. Brady picked it up.

'Thanks,' he said, raising the glass at her.

She wouldn't look at him. And he knew why. She'd been crying. He knew Claudia – had known her . . .

'I'm sorry . . . I shouldn't have rung you. I shouldn't have come back here of all places. I . . . I . . . God! . . . don't know any more!' Claudia said as tears escaped down her face. She had been trying to rein it in; hold herself together.

Brady remained silent. He was resisting the urge to take her in his arms; to hold her wild, unruly curly red head of hair against his chest and just . . . *Just what?*

Claudia no longer existed in his life.

So why the fuck was she here? But crucially, why was he?

She'd rung him while Amelia had been in the toilets. She'd been desperate. Claudia was never desperate. He knew then that something serious was wrong. She only had to say one word. One name and he left. Without hesitation.

Claudia took a large mouthful of wine. Anything to stop her crying.

It took her a few moments before she could actually look at him.

'Shit, Jack! What happened to your face?' she asked, momentarily forgetting her own troubles.

'It's nothing,' Brady answered as he shook his head.

This wasn't about him. It was about her. And the reason why she was standing barefoot in his kitchen, drinking his wine.

Claudia's emerald green eyes were filled with sadness. Usually they were filled with intense irritation when she looked at Brady.

'Claudia?'

She shrugged, still unable to get the words out.

Brady took a drink. He needed one.

He had a feeling it was going to be a long night.

He couldn't stop himself looking at her. He hated himself for thinking it. But she was perfect to him in every way. As he stood there, mesmerised by Claudia's presence, Amelia and his promise to go back to hers melted into the background.

She was the perfect height for him. Her figure was shapely – sexy. She was the antithesis of the fashion fascists' prepubescent ideal. She was what the average bloke found desirable; rounded hips, full breasts and a narrow waist that accentuated her voluptuousness. She even had perfectly symmetrical features. High cheek bones complimented by delicate, pale naked lips. The wild, curly red hair and vibrant green eyes just added to everything else. Then there was her searing intellect, which at times had caught Brady out. Even hurt him. She was everything he was not: middle-class background, University educated and ultimately privileged.

'Nicoletta . . .' Claudia began. She dragged her fearful eyes up to meet Brady's.

He nodded. This was the reason she was here. Why he'd agreed to meet her. He had too readily dismissed Claudia's initial call about Nicoletta being denied residency. Too preoccupied with Lee Harris to even think about the consequences.

'Let's take another bottle through to the living room,' Brady suggested. He had a feeling she would need it.

Claudia nodded. Despite the amount of wine she had already drunk she still felt sober. She wanted to get drunk. Anything not to think about what might have happened.

Brady went over to the large black fridge and pulled out another bottle from the chilled wine rack. He had his back to her but he knew she was scared. Terrified. It was Brady's job to find out why.

'Shit! I don't know what to say,' Brady stated.

He got up from the couch and walked over to the bay window. It was black outside. He could hear the North Sea churning away relentlessly against the cliffs below. He stood there staring out but all that was thrown back to him was his own troubled reflection against a bleak backdrop.

'Jack?'

Brady turned and looked back at Claudia. She was on the couch with her legs curled under her. She had nearly finished her third glass of wine.

'I . . .' she faltered, the expression in his dark eyes stopping her.

'Why me?'

She shook her head, not quite understanding what he meant.

'Why bring this to my door? You've got someone. Shit! He even works for your team. He's part of Newcastle's armed response unit. So why not share this with him?'

Claudia looked at him. He was angry. He had every right to be.

'I did. He didn't think there was anything in it,' Claudia answered.

Brady nodded. He appreciated her honesty, even if he didn't like the answer.

He turned back to the window. He couldn't bear to look at her right now. He was second best. She had just said as much.

'Jack – don't do this.'

'Do what?' Brady asked as he stared out into the blackness. There was one thought racing through his mind.

Had they returned? And if so, did they have Nicoletta?

'Please, Jack? Don't shut me out. Not tonight . . . I . . . I don't want to go back . . .'

Brady turned round.

'What are you saying?'

'I'm scared. I'm scared that they've abducted Nicoletta and that they . . . the Dabkunas brothers are back.'

Brady watched as thick tears ebbed down her cheeks.

'I don't want to be on my own. Not tonight.'

'What about James? Where's he?' Brady asked, trying to keep the cynicism out of his voice.

This wasn't his problem. She wasn't his problem any more. She had left him. Or had she forgotten that part?

Claudia looked at him and shook her head. 'He left. We had a big argument about Nicoletta's disappearance and he left.'

Claudia took another drink.

As she did so she caught Brady's eye.

'I kicked him out. All right? And . . . and he went. Took his bags and went,' Claudia said, not quite believing that it had actually happened. That James had gone.

'So let me get this straight. He leaves you alone knowing that there's a possibility that those bastards have returned to the North-East?' Brady demanded. 'What the fuck is he thinking?'

'That's my point. He's not. He thinks that I'm over-reacting. That because the Home Office turned down her application for residency Nicoletta decided to take her chances and disappear. But she wouldn't do that without telling me first,' Claudia said, shaking her head. She looked at him, wanting some kind of assurance. 'I mean I . . . I've worked with her for six months now. I set her up in a flat, organised money for her. She wouldn't just leave without letting me know where she was going.' Claudia faltered, the reality too jarring to continue.

Brady looked at her. He realised being mad at her was not helping the situation. He walked back over to the couch and sat down next to her.

Without thinking, he automatically put his hand on her knee. 'Come on . . . Maybe James was right? Maybe she's just cut ties and disappeared. Better that than being deported back to her own country and falling back into their hands again.'

Brady knew the odds as well as Claudia. When trafficked women and children were deported back to their home country their chances of falling back into sex slavery were extremely high.

Claudia looked at him, her green eyes burning with the belief that something terrible had happened to Nicoletta.

'I know that they've taken her. She's been gone since last Thursday. There's been no sightings of her and no one's heard from her. That's nearly a week . . .' She paused as she searched his face for something. Anything.

Brady said nothing. He couldn't give her reassurance when there was none to give.

'Why didn't she take anything with her? No money, no clothes. Not even her mobile phone,' Claudia asked, her eyes desperate for him to come up with an answer.

'Claudia . . . I can't—'

But before he said it she stopped him. She took his hand from her knee and placed it on her cheek. She leaned against it, momentarily closing her eyes. She just wanted him to touch her. Make her feel safe again.

Brady swallowed hard. He didn't want this. Not this way.

He knew that she had a tumult of emotions misdirecting. Not to mention a bottle of wine.

'No . . .' Brady began. But he didn't get a chance to finish.

Claudia leaned into him and brushed her lips against his face. It was an inquisitive, hesitant touch that rekindled everything he had been trying his damnedest to forget.

Whatever objections he had quickly evaporated when her soft, lingering lips found his own.

Chapter Forty-Six

When Brady awoke the next morning he knew that she had gone before he even opened his eyes. He lay perfectly still for a moment breathing in her scent just to convince himself that last night had been real. That he had not imagined her there.

He missed her so much it ached. The memory of her soft, supple skin beneath him was unbearable. The way she touched him . . . kissed him.

He buried his head in his pillow. The torture of having had her one more time was too much to take. He wished it had never happened. Better that than being thrown back into the torment of the past eighteen months.

Why, Claudia? Why the fuck would you do this to me?

He wondered whether it was payback for the hurt he had caused her when she'd found him in bed with his junior colleague, Simone Henderson. If it was, then she had succeeded. The agony he felt ripping through him was so intense he wanted to punch something, anything to stop the pain.

Claudia had already told him that it wouldn't happen again. That it had been a one-off. Otherwise she would be here with him now.

He wondered whether she'd left a note. But he knew that would not be the case. That wasn't Claudia's style.

He suddenly remembered that he was supposed to be in Gates's office at 8:30 sharp. He turned and looked at the bedside clock. It was already 8:13 a.m.

So? Who gives a fuck?

He rolled back over and buried his face in the pillow that Claudia had used.

Not that they had slept much.

He lay there for what felt like an interminable amount of time just breathing in her smell and remembering.

He ignored the phone when it rang. First his mobile. Then the landline. Someone left a garbled message. He didn't listen. What was the point? It wasn't her voice.

He ignored the phones when they rang again and again. He lay there refusing to move. Refusing to acknowledge that she had actually gone.

Then he heard it. The belligerent sound of someone banging on his front door. After a couple of minutes of listening to it he resigned himself to getting up. He looked around the floor for his clothes, not sure where they had ended up amidst the frenzied desperation of last night. He found his jeans by the bedroom door and his T-shirt in the hallway. Hurriedly pulling them on he made his way down the flight of stairs ready to punch whatever bastard was intent on putting a fist through his door.

It was Conrad.

'I'm busy,' Brady answered, his face filled with menace.

'Sir? Gates needs to see you,' Conrad said in an attempt to stop Brady slamming the door in his face.

'Yeah? Go tell it to someone who gives a damn!'

Conrad had no idea what had happened to Brady last night. He had seen him talking to Amelia at the bar and then they had both disappeared. He assumed something had happened between them. But whatever it was, Amelia had turned up at the station and had, without a word, started clearing her desk out. Her stony-faced silence was enough to tell Conrad that things had not quite gone to plan between her and Brady.

It was only the news of the car crash that had stopped her in her tracks. Or to be more precise the news of who owned the car that had been rammed over the cliffs in Tynemouth. No survivors. It had been reported at 6:39 a.m. The station was reeling. And there was only one person who still didn't know – Brady.

'Sir? Please? You have to come with me,' Conrad insisted.

Brady wasn't listening. He was already swinging the door shut.

Conrad threw his body against it, jamming his foot inside.

'For fuck's sake, Conrad. What's wrong with you? I'm not going in to work today! So you can tell Gates from me that he can go fuck himself!'

'Sir, I'm afraid that—'

'Now get your foot off my property before I break your fucking leg!' exploded Brady.

'It's Claudia,' Conrad said in a last-ditch attempt to get Brady to listen.

'What?'

'Claudia, sir. Something's happened . . .'

It didn't take Brady long to get into the station. He didn't care that he looked like shit. He hadn't showered or shaved. He was still wearing the same clothes as last night. Not that it mattered. Nothing mattered any more. The shock of what he had been told made everything else seem insignificant. He wanted nothing.

No, that was a lie. He wanted Claudia.

He walked through the station like a leper. No one would look at him. Let alone talk to him. Even Charlie Turner was lost for words. The only person talking to him was Conrad. And that was only because he'd been under strict orders to deliver him to Gates ASAP.

Conrad knocked on Gates's office door.

'Come in,' Gates ordered.

Conrad opened the door and walked in. He turned and looked expectantly at Brady, who refused to move.

Gates stood up from behind his desk and walked over to Brady.

'Jack? I'm really sorry. Believe me.'

Brady had nothing in him to say. Nothing. It felt too unreal.

Gates walked Brady over to one of two seats in front of his desk.

He waited until Brady sat down and then gestured for Conrad to leave them alone.

Which he did.

Gates sat back behind his desk and looked at Brady.

He was a wreck. No two ways about it. He steeled himself for a moment. He was about to have a very different conversation with Jack Brady than the one he had anticipated yesterday evening.

'It's definitely her car?' Brady asked, breaking Gates's thoughts.

Gates nodded. 'I'm sorry.'

Brady looked at him. It was genuine. Gates had always had a soft spot for Claudia.

Who didn't? She was so unique. So fucking special that it hurt. It hurt so bad . . .

Brady stood up. His hands were clenched by his sides. His face rigid as he tried not to get emotional. Not here. Not now in front of Gates. He still had some pride left.

'I . . . I can't do this, sir. Sorry,' Brady said, turning to leave.

It took all his self-will not to break into a run.

'Jack? There's something you need to know,' Gates called out after him.

Brady continued walking. There was nothing left to interest him. He reached the door and was about to open it when Gates threw him a lifeline.

'Jack! Wait! It's not her. Claudia wasn't in the car. I found out just before you got here,' Gates explained. He wanted Brady to hear it from him first. Soon enough it would spread like wildfire around the station. Everyone was desperate for news about Claudia.

Brady spun round. His expression a mixture of disbelief, hope and anger.

'What? What did you say?'

'They've just recovered her car from the rocks. Bentley's team's there.'

He felt sick at the thought of Bentley overseeing the crime scene. But he wasn't surprised. Tynemouth came under the jurisdiction of North Shields police station.

'I thought there were no survivors?'

Gates nodded his head.

'There aren't any.'

Brady walked back to his chair. He needed something to hold on to.

'Who was in her car then?' Brady asked, not quite believing what he was hearing.

'DCI James Davidson.'

'What?' Brady questioned. 'Why would he be in Claudia's car? I mean ... she stayed at mine last night and ...' Brady stopped himself.

The look in Gates's eye told him he wasn't surprised by this revelation.

Everyone knew about his failed marriage. Worse still, they knew why it had failed. They also all knew that she had moved on. That she had left Brady in the rear view mirror. Until last night. So why did Gates not look surprised?

'Her mobile phone was stuffed into DCI Davidson's mouth. The last call she made was to your mobile at 11:02 p.m. last night. The details of that call were left on the screen. Whoever did this to DCI Davidson wanted us to know that.'

'Did what? What did they do to him?'

Brady felt like he had a noose around his throat. And then he realised why.

Gates was weighing Brady up. He was determining whether Brady already knew what had happened to Davidson or if he was lying.

'Sir?' Brady asked.

'Davidson was found bound and gagged. It appears that he had taken quite a beating. His ID badge had been shoved into his mouth, along with Claudia's mobile phone before he was gagged.'

Brady's shoulders slumped forward as he gripped the back of the chair.

'What happened? How did he die?'

'He either drowned or the impact of the crash killed him. We can't say until Wolfe has carried out his autopsy.'

Brady weakly nodded. He felt sick. His mind was in turmoil. He clung on to the fact that Wolfe was carrying out the autopsy. He was a cantankerous old bugger who drank too much, but he knew his job. He was the best Home Office pathologist the force had ever had, and they'd had a few. Even Chief Superintendent O'Donnell was aware of Wolfe's foibles, but since he was the best pathologist around, everyone turned a blind eye.

But Wolfe was also a personal friend of Brady's – of sorts. He knew that if push came to shove Wolfe would talk to him. Brady was certain about one thing: the shit was about to hit the fan. Gates had not said it yet. But it was coming.

'I'm sure you agree that it's not a pleasant way to die. Bound, gagged and beaten and then locked in the boot of your girl-friend's car, which is then rammed by a second car until it plummets over the cliffs.'

Brady was speechless.

'No driver. Just Davidson's body in the boot. The water and cliffs are currently being searched by the Coast Guard and the Marine Unit. But so far, there's no sign of Claudia's body.'

Brady felt winded. Gates had said that she was not in the car. That she was still alive.

Or had Brady just imagined it? Fuck ... please let her be alive?

'I thought you said she wasn't in the car?' Brady asked, his voice shaking.

'I did. All the doors were locked and the windows were fractured but intact. She couldn't have been in the car when it went over the cliff. But Bentley is looking at the possibility that she might have been thrown or jumped into the water.'

Brady breathed out. It was too much to take in.

He dragged his head up and was met by Gates's cold, clinical gaze. He was watching Brady. Studying each reaction as if he were a suspect.

'You don't seriously think . . .' Brady stopped himself. He couldn't even put it into words. It was too ridiculous.

'What? That you're a suspect in your ex-wife's partner's brutal murder? A man you made no attempt to hide your hatred for? Because he was sleeping with your ex-wife. A woman who even a fool could see you still loved.'

Brady just stared at him. Unable to comprehend what he was implying.

'You admit that she spent the night with you last night?'

Brady nodded.

'She . . . Yes, she stayed the night. But when I woke this morning she had gone.'

'So, Claudia just vanished, did she? What time was that?'

Brady shrugged. 'I don't know. When I woke up it was around eight. Her part of the bed was cold so I assumed she'd been gone for a while.'

'Her car was seen being rammed over Tynemouth cliffs on the corner by the Gibraltar Rock pub shortly after six thirty. And you say you didn't wake up until eight o'clock?'

'Yes,' Brady answered, unable to keep the anger out of his voice.

'Look, Jack, I'm only trying to get the facts straight in my head. All right? I'm sorry if you don't like what I'm asking. But you better prepare yourself because DI Bentley will want to interview you,' Gates informed him.

It took a second for Brady to realise the magnitude of what Gates had just said.

'Why?' he thundered, unable to rein in his anger.

'Because he is the SIO in charge of this murder and missing person investigation. You were the last person to see her before she disappeared. You, better than anyone, should know the significance of that.'

Brady thought about Bentley. He would crucify Brady. He had a score to settle, as Gates had pointed out. Brady had closed Bentley's investigation without even consulting him. Now Bentley had a chance to do some kicking of his own where Brady was concerned.

'I want you to go home. Wait until Bentley contacts you. But as of this moment you are suspended, DI Brady,' Gates informed him.

'What?' He looked at Gates in disbelief. 'You can't be serious. Claudia is missing, for fuck's sake! You can't expect me to go home and wait for a phone call. God knows who has her but if they murdered Davidson I don't hold out much hope of her coming back in one piece. Not if Bentley's in fucking charge! You need me. You need me here working on this. She needs me.'

Gates said nothing. Instead he waited for Brady to finish his tirade.

'You can't just sit there. She's been abducted!'

'By who, Jack?'

Brady shook his head. His eyes were wild.

'I don't know! No . . . last night,' he paused as he remembered. *How could he have been so stupid?*

'That's why she came to see me. She was scared. No. Terrified that the Dabkunas brothers were back in the North-East. Marijuis and Mykolas Dabkunas. Claudia said that Nicoletta had gone missing. That nobody had seen her since last Thursday. She feared that the brothers had kidnapped her and that they would kill her for giving information to the police about their sex-trafficking operation.'

Gates nodded but there was nothing in his expression that told Brady he believed him.

'Very interesting, Jack. I'm sure Bentley will want to hear all about your theory.'

'Why don't you fucking believe me?' bellowed Brady.

He didn't care if he lost control. After all, Gates had just suspended him.

'Two reasons. Firstly, why did Claudia not report her fears about Nicoletta?'

'She did. To Davidson,' Brady fired back, cutting Gates off.

'But he's dead, Jack, so he can't substantiate that. Also, Intelligence have no further information on the Dabkunas brothers. If they did, we would be the first to know. But they're clear that the brothers haven't returned to the UK.'

'That's if they ever left the UK in the first place,' said Brady.

'Come on, Jack. You're clutching at straws.'

Brady was dumbfounded. He couldn't believe what he was hearing. Did Gates really believe he was making all this up?

'Get Conrad to take you back home. And stay put. I don't want you doing anything stupid. Understand me? Bentley will find Claudia. That is . . . if she's still alive.'

Brady didn't respond. He just stood there trying to get a grasp on what was happening.

She was with me last night . . . She was with me . . . How? How could he say that? 'If' she's still alive? This is Claudia he's talking about . . . Claudia!

'Jack? Are you listening to me?'

Brady looked at Gates.

'Fuck you, sir, and fuck Bentley!' he replied as he turned and left.

He had nothing to lose. Not now.

'Don't make this any more difficult than it already is!' Gates called out after him.

But he was too late. Brady was already slamming the door behind him. Gates hadn't expected Brady to take it well. He just hoped that Brady did as instructed, kept his head low and Bentley sweet. It wasn't a lot to ask. But he knew, where Brady was concerned, it would be impossible. His ex-wife had gone missing, presumed abducted, and her ex-SAS officer boyfriend had turned up dead after being beaten, bound and gagged. Davidson was a man who had hands-on combat skills. It would have been no mean feat to overpower him. Never mind murder him.

Whoever had done this was dangerous and well-organised.

Precisely the reason why Gates had wanted Brady to lie low. The last thing he needed was him becoming a casualty of something that Claudia and Davidson's team had uncovered. Gates was sure it was connected to one of their covert investigations into sex crimes against women and children. They dealt with a lot of dangerous criminals making money out of this kind of business. Gates had already talked to Claudia and Davidson's boss and had been told enough to know that much.

Chapter Forty-Seven

Brady stormed out of Gates's office and headed straight for his own. He needed some time to calm down and collect his thoughts.

He opened the door and then just stood there, unable to move. This office had been an integral part of his life for so long. The bulky old wooden desk that was his workspace. The leather couch by the window that many a night had doubled up as his bed. He looked over at the large Victorian sash window with its dusty Venetian blinds. Below it was a leaky cast-iron radiator that religiously clanked and clunked its way through winter. It had always irritated the hell out of him but right now he would give anything for things to return to normal. For James Davidson to still be alive and for Claudia to be safe. He would have given anything for that to happen. Anything.

He breathed in slowly, trying to steady the waves of crippling nausea that had been coursing through him from the moment he had heard. What panicked him the most was the fact that he had no idea what was going on. Why had they taken Claudia? For that was what he was counting on. Every atom in his body prayed that this was the case. That she had been kidnapped and was being held hostage somewhere. The alternative was unbearable.

Brady nervously dragged a hand through his hair. He needed to figure out what to do. But Gates was right. First he had to get out of the station. The day would soon disappear and with it Claudia's chances of survival.

He walked over to his desk and picked up his Che Guevera mug. He pulled open his top drawer and took out two framed photographs that used to sit on his desk – both of Claudia. He collected a few other personal effects and put them in a cardboard box.

He cast his eyes one last time around his office before going to find Conrad.

Instead he found Amelia.

She was walking along the corridor. When she looked up and saw Brady it was too late to change direction.

'I'm sorry—' Brady began.

'Forget it. I have,' she interrupted him.

But her face told Brady she was lying. That she would never forgive him for running out on her. Regardless of the reason. And Brady knew that Claudia was not the best reason to give.

At the thought of Claudia's name panic welled up inside him. A sudden reminder of what he'd had so briefly and what he stood to lose: everything. Sure, he felt bad about DCI Davidson. But he was the least of Brady's concerns right now. His only focus was on finding Claudia.

'Leaving?' Amelia asked, gesturing at the cardboard box in his arms.

Brady automatically covered the contents with his right arm while he supported the box with his left.

'DCI Gates has suspended me temporarily,' Brady said, deciding that she might as well hear it from him. Soon the news would be all around the station, as well as the other Area Commands.

'I see,' Amelia replied, her voice flat.

She could barely bring herself to look at him.

'Amelia, if I had time to explain I would. But . . .' he faltered, not knowing what to say next.

'Don't let me stop you.'

'See you around. Yeah?' Brady asked, wanting some kind of confirmation that things would be all right between them again.

But Amelia wouldn't give him the answer he wanted. She simply looked away.

He could see the hurt in her, despite the fact she wouldn't look at him.

He sighed heavily. He felt bad enough without feeling like a total bastard to boot.

'Take care,' he said, before walking away.

Amelia turned and watched him. His head was down and his body slumped over the box he was carrying. He looked like a man with the weight of the world on his shoulders. And he effectively was; he had just found out his ex-wife was dead. She realised that she was being childish letting her personal emotions get in the way of something so devastating.

'Jack?' she called after him.

He stopped and turned around.

She ran up to him. 'I'm sorry . . . about Claudia.'

This time it was Brady who could not look her in the eyes. He dropped his gaze to the box he was holding protectively.

'Thanks,' he muttered.

She gently touched his arm.

'Really, I'm genuinely sorry, Jack.'

He knew he didn't deserve her sympathy. If she had known that he'd left her standing for Claudia, she wouldn't be feeling sorry for him. Not to mention the fact that he had spent the night with his ex-wife, instead of her.

In that moment Brady wondered if the outcome would have been any different if he had not responded to Claudia's call. If he had ignored it instead. Where would he be right now? He was sure he wouldn't be feeling as if the world had exploded around him and he was the only one left standing – with a box of memories.

'Thanks, Amelia. But I don't deserve it,' Brady said.

With that he walked off and left her wondering what he meant.

Brady had gone voluntarily to North Shields police station to make a statement. He had no choice. Rather that than Bentley turning up at his door with an arrest warrant. But for what? Nothing. He had done nothing. But that was the problem. That was the bit that was killing him inside.

Claudia had come to him terrified and what had he done? He'd taken advantage of her. Then she'd left without a word, leaving him to wake up in a world that he did not know, or trust. A world that had no meaning without her in it.

Brady got Conrad to drive him home afterwards. Conrad had tried to insist on staying but Brady was adamant that he needed to be on his own. He had spent the last few hours pacing up and down like a sane person locked inside a mental sanatorium. But the worst part was he felt that this was his doing. That he had a part to play in all of this. He didn't understand what or why. But he couldn't shake the feeling that he was somehow involved.

He looked at his mobile phone, willing it to ring. He had it clutched firmly in his right hand. There was only one person in the world he trusted to help him find Claudia, to understand what was happening, but he couldn't get hold of him.

Where the fuck are you when I need you, Nick? Where?

Then it hit him. The sickening reality. That he was deluding himself that Nick would hear the voicemail that Brady had left on his mobile – the only means of contact he had. Why had he left the message when he had a really bad feeling something had happened to Nick as well? That he had disappeared, just like Claudia?

Why? Nick, what the fuck's happened to you? Was Claudia right? Have those Dabkunas bastards come back to the North-East? Had they ever really left?

If they had Claudia then what about Nick? What about him? Oh shit . . . They would slowly torture him before . . .

Brady couldn't bring himself to think about it.

Fuck! Fuck! Fuck!

He threw his phone on the ground. He couldn't stand this any longer.

He walked over to the bay window and looked out. It was 8:33 p.m. and pitch black outside. But the time was all he noticed. He had been counting it down since he got back to the house.

Brady sighed heavily and crouched by the window. He cradled his head in his hands as he tried to think straight. He knew from Conrad that Claudia's house in Jesmond had been ransacked. Conrad had made use of his contact at North Shields. The police had established that Claudia had gone back there after she had left Brady's. The house had been turned upside down. Forensics had found blood, lots of blood, mostly in the bedroom. It was clear a struggle had taken place. Whether the murderers had turned up there looking for Claudia and had instead found Davidson, Brady had no idea. Had Davidson calmed down after his argument with Claudia and returned home to find himself overpowered by whoever it was that Brady was about to meet? They would have held Davidson and tortured him to find out where Claudia was. Brady assumed that would have taken place in the bedroom, accounting for all the blood. But Davidson would never have talked. Even if he'd wanted to, he would have had no idea where Claudia had gone. The last thing he'd have assumed was that she was with Brady. If he'd known that, they would have turned up on Brady's doorstep. It would have made things a lot easier for them. They would have captured Brady and Claudia without the complication of murdering Davidson. Brady hated to imagine Claudia returning to the house with them waiting for her and Davidson beaten within an inch of his life.

Brady had managed to talk to Wolfe, the Home Office Pathologist, after he had made his statement. The autopsy on Davidson had unsurprisingly been prioritised. Wolfe had been able to confirm that Davidson was still alive when he had been locked in the boot of the car. That he was still alive even after the car had plummeted over the cliffs to the sea and rocks below. That he had died a painful and excruciating death, slowly drowning, trapped in a small, dark, enclosed space. Bound so tight he couldn't move, let alone get free, watching as water slowly started to fill up around him. Worse still, he would have died knowing that whoever had done this to him had Claudia. That he had not been able to save her. That as he lay there, fighting against inevitable death, Claudia could be suffering a similar fate.

Brady fought the compulsion to get a bottle of whisky and blot it all out. Anything was better than this tortured, manic state. But he'd been there once before when Claudia first left him. Six months on the sick with a crippled leg, a lapful of divorce papers and a bottle of whisky permanently in his hand. Life had been a dark, miserable existence then, but at least he had been so drunk he didn't remember most of it. It was tempting. So very tempting.

No! Don't go there. Not again. He sat there repeating the words over and over in his mind.

At 9:58 p.m. his mobile rang. Brady was still on the floor beneath the window. He pulled himself together and scrambled along the polished wooden floorboards for the phone. Grabbing it, he looked at the caller – unknown.

'Brady,' he answered, trying to sound calm. He was anything but.

'Drive down to the end of Davy Bank towards the Tyne. You're looking for an empty warehouse. You can't miss it. Twelve thirty a.m.'

'What do I bring?'

'Yourself. Anyone else and she's dead. Understand?'

'Is she all right? Can I talk to her?' Brady asked, trying to keep the desperation out of his voice.

'Nick. You tell us where he is. Then we let her go.'

Before Brady could ask anything else the line went dead.

He sat there, not moving as he absorbed what had just been said. The caller's accent wasn't local, he was from the South. Brady automatically thought of Johnny Slaughter and then he remembered Weasel Face – Madley's hired gun. He was from the East End of London.

Was it him? I don't know ... I don't fucking know.

Brady tried to calm himself down. He had to focus. He was meeting them at 12:30 a.m. He knew the location; Davy Bank was in Wallsend. The road led down towards the Tyne River. It was filled with warehouses, workshops and factories. Most of them in disuse now. In other words the ideal place to do an illegal trade. Brady's life for Claudia. Brady was only worth keeping alive until they got the information they wanted on Nick. He was under no illusion. They would put a bullet through his head as soon as he talked. Brady accepted that. He had no choice. But he would make sure that Claudia was released before he said a word.

Brady thought about calling Gates. But as soon as he did he discounted it. If he passed on this information to his superiors he knew the chances of being allowed anywhere near the kidnappers would be nil. They would hand the situation over to a hostage negotiator and an Armed Response Team. The outcome? Claudia would end up dead. The kidnappers would shoot her as soon as the police showed up instead of Brady. He had no other option than to follow her abductors' instructions and not report it. Not that he saw it as a problem. He had been suspended from duty so at this precise moment he was a civilian.

Then he thought about calling Madley. He knew he could help him. Madley had the kind of back-up that Brady needed – ruthless. But something in him warned him against turning to his old childhood friend. Too much had happened in the course of the past few days. He didn't trust Madley any more. He had no idea whose side Madley was on. Brady realised Madley was on Madley's side, always had been. Thoughts of Jake Munroe and what he had done to Trina McGuire to extract information about Nick's whereabouts was enough for Brady not to turn to Madley. After all, Munroe was on Madley's pay, as was Weasel Face. Brady couldn't discount the evidence. He had seen Weasel Face in Durham prison's visiting room talking to Munroe. What more proof did he need? Would Madley really hire men to kill Davidson and kidnap Claudia so he could get Brady to trade his brother's life for Claudia's? Brady wasn't sure any more. And that was what worried him.

Why kill Davidson? Why not? Maybe he was just a casualty. Maybe it was that simple.

Brady breathed in. He needed to clear his head. He had to think straight. The last thing he wanted to do was walk into a hostage situation and end up not only losing his own life, but also Claudia's. Davidson's life had already been wasted. Brady would be damned if Claudia became another casualty in this search for Nick.

Chapter Forty-Eight

Brady parked his car. It was Friday: 12:25 a.m.

He had made one call. He was not expecting to walk out of this situation alive. So he had called the only person left – Nick. Whether it was for himself that he left the message explaining exactly what was about to happen, he didn't know. But he had said where he was going and what was about to follow – his life in exchange for Claudia's. Maybe it was his way of mentally preparing himself for what was about to happen. Because if he was honest, he held out no hope of Nick hearing it. He hadn't responded to the other messages that he'd left over the past few days, so why this one?

He switched the headlights off and cut the engine on his car. The place was desolate, the streetlights broken, adding to the feeling that he was in no-man's land. He got out of the car. There was no point in waiting any longer. He looked around the deserted area. There was nobody around. But then, what was he expecting? No one in their right mind would be down here at this time of night. It was well and truly off the beaten track. The place was no longer used. The buildings scattered around him were empty. The factories and warehouses had been abandoned when the shipping industry had disappeared.

Brady headed for the warehouse right at the end of Davy Bank. He was sure he'd seen a torchlight stabbing around in the blackness.

He had resigned himself to his fate, so he had no fear. Not for his own life at least. The fear that he did have was for Claudia.

He had no idea how this would turn out but he would do everything in his power to make sure she survived.

He approached the wasteland in front of the warehouse. He saw two cars parked up. Expensive black 4x4 Land Rovers. What else did he expect? He continued walking past them heading towards the door.

'Brady?' a voice said behind him.

The accent had a heavy Cockney twang.

'Yeah?' Brady answered, his voice steady, despite the cold pressure of the barrel of a handgun now pressed against the side of his head.

Brady wasn't surprised. After all, they'd been expecting him.

'Get down on the ground!'

But before Brady had a chance to follow the order he had his legs taken out from beneath him. He lay in as much surprise as pain, face-down in the dirt as his arms were forced back behind him and his hands quickly handcuffed. Before he even realised it something connected with his left calf.

FUCK!

His leg exploded with pain.

It took him a few moments before he realised he couldn't move it without excruciating pain. It had to be broken. He raised his head off the ground to see who had attacked him. There were two men wearing black balaclavas and black military-style combat trousers and jackets. One held a gun, the other a crowbar. Both had attitude.

Before he had a chance to do anything one of the masked men bent down and yanked his head up by his hair.

'Time to get up,' he ordered.

His friend joined him. Between them they dragged Brady to his feet. They were about Brady's height but heavy set and muscle-bound. He had no chance against them, with or without their weapons.

One moved ahead and opened the warehouse door while the other one kept his gun to Brady's head as an encouragement to make him walk forward. Brady had no idea who they were but he knew that they meant business. These men were not your local hard nuts or criminals. They were trained militia.

A third militia type appeared out of nowhere carrying a semi-automatic rifle.

Brady had to remind himself that this was Wallsend, not some war-torn country ruled by despots.

'He's alone?'

'Yeah.'

The man holding the semi-automatic looked around the bleak, dark landscape for confirmation before turning his eyes onto Brady.

All Brady could make out were the slits of his eyes through the black balaclava. It was enough to unnerve him. They were cold and detached. Brady was purely a business transaction. Nothing more. Nothing less. His life was what they were paid to take.

'Move it!'

Brady did as instructed, despite the crippling pain as he dragged his left leg along. The cold metal at the side of his head was enough incentive to make him move.

The warehouse was a huge, dark, empty space. Parts of the concrete floor were covered in water from where the rain had come in through the leaking roof. Brady looked up at the rotting wooden rafters overhead. There was no first floor, it was just one large cavernous room. But what struck Brady was the fact that it was empty.

Where the fuck is she? Where the fuck is Claudia?

Brady tried to keep calm, keep his wits about him. If he ended up dead then Claudia would inevitably die.

If she's not already dead . . .

The only item of furniture in the room was in the centre. It was a chair. A gloomy light bulb hung down from the ceiling above it casting an eerie, pale glow over the middle of the warehouse. Just enough to illuminate the seat and presumably the occupant.

'Go on,' instructed the masked militia guard behind him as he poked the gun into the side of Brady's head. 'Take a seat.'

Brady did as he was ordered and limped over to the seat. He sat down, wincing as he tried to straighten his left leg out. All he could do was edge the leg out at an angle that caused the least pain. He looked at the two masked guards in front of him. The third guard had taken his handcuffs off and was busy securing his wrists to the arms of the chair with black duct tape. He then wrapped it around his chest, restraining his body to the back of the chair.

It was ludicrous. He was obviously unable to put up a fight. His wrists were already secured to the chair and there was a good chance his leg was broken.

'What are you waiting for?' Brady asked, unable to disguise the thick contempt in his voice.

The reply was swift. A crack to the left side of his face with the gun.

The pain was horrific. It took him a moment to come back to his senses. The gun had struck his jaw in the exact same place as Munroe's fist.

'Fuck!' cursed Brady as he spat out blood.

He knew this was just the start of it.

Before he had a chance to talk again the guard carrying the semi-automatic rifle disappeared. Brady realised now that there was a door at the back of the warehouse. Where it led, he had no idea.

He sat and waited for whoever was in charge to show.

Minutes later heavy, echoing footsteps signalled the armed guard's return. Brady looked up. He was dragging something – someone. He realised then that it was Claudia. It had to be. She had a bag over her head but it was her. He recognised her clothes. Her body.

'What the fuck have you done to her?' Brady shouted.

The answer was another heavy, resonating crack to the side of the head.

320

The pain was blinding.

'Fuck you!' Brady spat.

But he knew they were just playing with him. This was nothing.

He struggled in vain to get free as Claudia's body was thrown unceremoniously down at his feet.

'Claudia? Claudia?' he asked, desperate for a response.

The guard who had dragged her in bent over and yanked the black bag off her head. Her face was badly swollen and bruised but it was her. It was Claudia. Relief coursed through him. She was still alive. He could feel his eyes stinging. The reality too much to accept.

Then it hit him. Her damaged face. The bruises and cuts on her arms and around her neck. Even though she was gagged he could see that her lip was bleeding. There was a nasty two-inch split that needed stitches. He felt sick as he looked at what they'd done to her. He didn't want to think about what else they might have done. The thought was too repulsive to even wonder whether it had happened. But he knew animals like this were capable of anything.

Why? There was no fucking need to touch her. Why the fuck did they touch her?

Claudia looked up at Brady. He tried to hide the shock he felt. One eye was completely swollen shut. But the other one was filled with absolute terror as she stared up at him.

Whether it was at seeing Brady there, unable to move, unable to save her, he didn't know. All he knew was that her chances of survival were low. The kidnappers had removed the bag from her head. That wasn't a good sign. It meant she could identify them. Brady tried to talk himself down. They were all wearing black balaclavas so maybe he was over-reacting.

'I'll fucking kill you if you touch her!' shouted Brady as he attempted to stand up.

The guard with the rifle turned it onto Claudia.

'Don't move.'

Brady resisted.

The guard jabbed hard into her lower back.

She moaned, her eyes filled with tears.

Brady sat back, his hands clenched tightly around the arms of the chair.

'Why don't you give us what we want, Jack?' asked a voice with a heavy Eastern European accent.

Brady couldn't see the speaker.

But he saw Claudia's reaction. It was enough. Her eyes were wide and filled with fear as she looked up at the man standing behind Brady.

He felt sick inside. She recognised him. He could tell. She could see his face.

No, Claudia! Fucking no! Don't look at him!

He could feel the adrenalin coursing through his body. He had to get her out of here. But he didn't know how. He was trapped. Tied to a chair with a shattered leg. He couldn't save himself, so how the hell did he think he could save her?

All he could feel now was blind rage. At his own stupidity for walking into this situation. How did he think it was going to end?

They would have no choice but to shoot her. Bastards like this lot were too organised. They wouldn't leave any loose ends. Anything that could tie them to the atrocities they carried out. Claudia was a liability. A witness who could identify them.

A hand was placed on Brady's shoulder.

'I have been looking forward to meeting "the" Jack Brady for some time now. You caused us a lot of problems. And wasted us a lot of time and money. But I am sure you know that,' he said as he slowly removed his hand.

Brady couldn't help but notice the gold signet ring with a diamond-encrusted 'N' emblem on one of the manicured fingers. This had to be one of the Dabkunas brothers. It made sense. Ronnie Macmillan's killing in prison to silence him. Trina McGuire's beating and rape to force her to reveal Nick's whereabouts. Kidnapping Claudia so they could lure Brady in. Their ultimate goal was revenge. Brady had exposed their lucrative sex-trafficking business venture with Ronnie Macmillan. And Nick? Nick had betrayed them. They hadn't known that he was only on their payroll to infiltrate them. Not until the end did they realise that Nick was undercover.

Brady looked down at Claudia. She was trembling as the tip of the rifle rested in the small of her back.

'Let her go. Then I'll talk.'

'If we do not?' he questioned.

'Then I won't talk.'

His captor laughed. It was cold and detached.

'You really think we cannot make you talk?'

'Try me,' Brady said.

'Take her out,' the man ordered.

The guard standing on Brady's left went round and dragged her to her feet.

Brady looked at her. He wanted to reassure her that everything would be all right. But she was petrified. He could see it in her eyes and there was nothing he could do. She was going to die and she knew it.

Her eyes fixed on him, wild with panic, as she was taken away.

Brady attempted to lunge forward, anything to stop them. But he was hit in the face. This time with a rifle butt. The chair fell backwards, taking Brady with it. He crashed to the ground, cracking the back of his head against the cold, uneven concrete.

The next thing he remembered was being doused in cold water. He came to, gasping for air. He looked around. Two expensively suited dark-haired men were standing in front of him – the Dabkunas brothers.

'Where is she?' Brady cried.

No one answered him. He looked around at the two remaining masked guards.

Where the fuck is the third one? Where is he? Where's he taken her?

323

Then he heard the gunshot outside, the sound ricocheting through the silent night.

'NOOO!' Brady shouted.

He tried to move. To get his arms free from the tape that restrained him to the chair.

A swift crack to the side of his head stopped him.

'Where is Nick?' asked one of the brothers.

'Fuck you!' answered Brady. His dark eyes were filled with hatred.

There was nothing they could do to him. It was over.

He couldn't remember how long he had tried not to scream. To hold the pain in. Eventually he did.

The crowbar had come in handy. Every bone in his right hand had been obliterated. His left leg was definitely broken now. He had heard the sickening snap of the bones under the weight of the crowbar as it hit again. Then again. And again.

Still he didn't talk.

They had used pliers on him. He passed out cold after the sixth fingernail had been pulled out.

Again they threw water over his face. Dazed and exhausted, he came to.

'Bring the girl in. Maybe that will make him talk.' one of the brothers said.

'If not, then cut his tongue out,' ordered the other.

Brady had only one thought racing through his mind: Claudia.

Is she still alive? God . . . please let her be alive?

But he had heard the gunshot outside.

Brady watched as one of the two remaining guards left. Minutes later he returned with a young, brutally beaten woman. It took Brady a moment to recognise her. When he did his heart sank.

Nicoletta . . .

Claudia had been right. They had abducted her. They were back in the North-East tying up loose ends. Silencing ex-business partners and punishing those who had acted against them. Nicoletta – trafficked by the Dabkunas brothers and handed over as a gift to Ronnie Macmillan to seal their business deal – had talked to the police.

Brady couldn't look at her. Her bedraggled long blonde hair hung as limp as her bony arms. She had no fight left. Whatever they had done to her had killed her on the inside. She was just waiting for them to show mercy and execute her.

'Nicoletta?' Brady whispered, his throat hoarse.

She looked at him. Recognition briefly flickered in her large brown eyes. Then it was gone.

'If you do not tell us where your brother is we'll kill her,' said one of the Dabkunas brothers.

One of the hired militia raised his semi-automatic rifle and pointed it at her head.

Before Brady had a chance to talk a shot was fired. It was deafening. He watched as blood sprayed and her body collapsed to the ground.

After that, everything turned black.

Chapter Forty-Nine

'Jack? Can you hear me?'

Brady blinked.

'Oh God, Jack! Jack?'

It took Brady a couple of moments to realise he had no idea what had happened to him. Or even who was talking to him.

'Nurse!' a voice screamed.

Blackness came before the nurse.

Two days passed in a morphine-induced blur. Brady had seen countless faces – most of which he didn't recognise. Or want to recognise. Two days of not knowing where he was or why. All he felt was pain, despite the morphine drip. Every part of him ached. It was unbearable. But most of all it hurt to breathe.

It was only when he realised that he had survived that pieces of the jigsaw started falling into place.

When he next opened his eyes he saw her – Claudia. She had her head on his stomach. Even though he couldn't see her face he knew it was her. The wild, unruly red hair a giveaway. He knew she was asleep. Could feel her chest rising gently against him.

Relief coursed through him.

She's alive ... Fuck, she's alive ...

As if aware, she stirred. Half asleep, she raised her head and looked at him.

'Oh God, Jack!' Tears spilled down her cheeks as she reached out to his face and touched him, as if making sure he was really there.

Brady stared at the damage to her face. At what they had done to her. He could feel the pain and anger inside start to build as he took it in. But she was alive.

Thank God she was alive.

'Harry?' Claudia cried out suddenly.

Brady watched as she turned and looked expectantly at the open door. For some reason he couldn't move. Nor could he talk.

Conrad ran into the room. He stopped when he saw Brady. 'Sir?'

The word hung in the air.

Brady wasn't sure what was going on or why Conrad was looking at him as if he'd come back from the dead.

A few more days passed by in a drug-induced blur. But Claudia had stayed. She had refused to leave him. Too scared.

'I . . . thought they had . . .' Brady couldn't bring himself to say it.

'Killed me?' Claudia asked.

He attempted to nod his head but it hurt too much. Everything hurt.

Claudia closed her eyes as if blocking out the memory.

'It's OK. Tell me when you're ready.'

She opened her eyes and looked at him. They flashed emerald green. She was a fighter. Always had been.

'When he took me outside . . . I thought . . . I thought I was going to die. That he would shoot me and then . . . Then they would kill you. I knew they had Nicoletta. I hadn't seen her but I'd heard her screams when those bastards had tortured her. I heard her beg . . . I didn't understand what she was saying but I knew the desperation in her voice. She was begging for her life . . .' Claudia faltered, unable to continue.

She turned her head away for a moment, unable to look him in the eye. 'I knew they wanted you to see her die. I understood that much. And then . . . then they planned on killing you.'

Tears escaped down her bruised and swollen face. The fight had left her eyes. Replaced by a pained sadness.

Brady attempted to smile at her. Reassure her. But he couldn't. After all, he had seen them shoot Nicoletta in front of him. He had watched as her body had crumpled and fallen to the ground. Then he had no memory of anything else.

'I'm sorry . . . I . . .'

'Take your time,' Brady said. His voice was gentle. Paternalistic even. He resisted asking her what had happened to Nicoletta. Resisted asking the crucial question – was she dead? He had to let Claudia tell him in her own time. After all, he wasn't going anywhere.

'It happened so quickly. One minute I had a gun to my head and then the next thing I knew he'd been knocked to the ground and someone else had a gun pointed at that bastard. There were two of them. One scrawny guy and another one who was tall with muscles and long dreadlocks. They forced the guard onto his knees with his hands behind his head.'

Claudia didn't need to tell Brady who they were. He already knew that they were Madley's men – Weasel Face and Gibbs.

'The one with the dreadlocks grabbed me and made me walk. There was a car down by the water. I didn't know who they were or what they wanted. All I knew was that they had saved my life. The next thing I heard was a gunshot.'

Brady had heard the same shot, believing it had been aimed at Claudia.

'The other guy who stayed behind?'

Claudia nodded as she swallowed slowly. 'He shot him.'

Brady realised it must have been Weasel Face. Gibbs had taken her to a waiting car – Madley's – and Weasel Face had stayed behind and shot the kidnapper. He knew it would have been execution style. Gun to the back of the head. He expected no less from Weasel Face. Despite all Brady's reservations about Madley's employee, he now accepted that he was indebted to him.

But why? None of it made sense.

'I know ...' Claudia said, seeing the confusion on his face. 'I didn't understand it at the time either. I still don't.'

'The car?' Brady asked.

'We get to this black car and I'm forced into the back. Inside there was a man ...' she paused. 'Well-dressed, handsome?'

Brady didn't react. But he recognised the description.

'He never told you his name?'

'No. He instructed me to follow his exact orders. That under no circumstances was I to mention him or his two men.'

Brady nodded.

'Then the scrawny guy came back. He opened the back door and handed the gun to me. I ... I didn't know why.'

But Brady knew exactly why. 'They wanted you to say that the guard took you outside to kill you. Realising you were going to die you struggled with him and managed to get the gun. That you shot him in self-defence before he shot you.'

Claudia nodded, surprised.

It didn't take a lot to figure out. The question Brady wanted answering was how Madley knew what was going on. How the fuck did he know to turn up when he did?

'What happened next?' Brady questioned.

'The thin guy who gave me the gun then hands me the dead guard's mobile phone. I'm told to call 999 if I want to save your life.'

Brady was taken aback by this comment. He couldn't say why. But he understood perfectly why Madley would have instructed Claudia to use the dead guard's mobile phone. Madley wanted no connection to the scene. He had turned up, saved Claudia's life, then Brady's and left. No questions. No police investigation – nothing.

'I did as instructed and called 999. I explained what was happening and then ...' she looked at Brady and shook her head. 'It's all a blur now. It happened so fast, it's like it never happened. You know? The two men turning up like that. The third one in the car calmly telling me what I had to do. Then they drive off, leaving me holding a gun and a dead man's phone.'

Brady looked at her. He didn't know what to say. He was still trying to make sense of Madley's actions.

'I never mentioned them to the police.' She looked at Brady. 'You know him, don't you? The man in the suit? The one who gave the orders?'

Brady thought about telling her the truth. Just for a brief moment. But he knew it was better this way. The less she knew the better. He gave her a non-committal shrug.

She frowned at him. It was clear that she didn't believe him.

'So, they left, and—' Brady asked, ignoring her questioning eyes.

She sighed heavily. 'Within minutes the police turned up. Or should I say the Armed Response Unit. It was them who saved your life and Nicoletta's . . .'

Brady stared at her in disbelief. He wasn't sure he had heard correctly.

'Nicoletta? She's . . .?'

Claudia nodded. Her eyes had lit up. 'Yes, she's alive. But she's in a bad way . . .'

'Where? Where is she?' Brady said, expectantly looking at the door.

'She was transferred to the RVI in Newcastle. I don't know the exact details but I know it's still touch and go.'

Brady sank back as relief took hold. 'I thought . . . I saw them shoot her. I saw her fall to the ground.'

'They stormed the building. It was so fast. It was over within seconds. From what I was told they shot the kidnapper holding Nicoletta. He went down, taking her with him.'

Brady realised the spray of blood he'd seen when Nicoletta had collapsed must have been from when one of the Armed Response team had shot the man restraining her.

330

'Do you remember anything of what happened next?' Claudia asked.

He shook his head. 'Nothing. The next thing I remember is waking up in here with you asleep on me,' Brady said, smiling at her.

He realised her eyes were filled with tears.

'You got shot . . .' she whispered. 'Not by our lot. By one of them. DCI Gates said one of the kidnappers had a rifle aimed at Nicoletta's head. So one of our officers shot him before he had a chance to shoot Nicoletta . . . or you. But when the bullet hit the guard, his body jerked forward, causing his rifle to go off. The bullet went straight through you.'

Brady wasn't surprised. It accounted for the pain in his chest – and the fact he couldn't move.

'DCI Gates?' Brady asked.

'He turned up with Conrad shortly after. He was really worried about you . . . we all were. When I heard the shots go off inside that warehouse I had no idea whether you were still alive . . . I . . . I . . . thought that they had . . .' Claudia faltered, unable to say it.

Brady wanted to touch her. Reassure her that everything was all right now. That it was over. Then he remembered. There was one last detail missing. The most crucial part to the whole piece.

'The Dabkunas brothers?' Brady asked, unable to hide the fear from his voice.

'Oh, Christ! I'm sorry . . . I should have told you,' Claudia said. 'They were shot. Killed when the Armed Response Unit stormed the warehouse.'

'You're sure?' Brady asked, not quite believing it.

She nodded. 'Nobody needed reassuring more than I did that they were dead.'

Brady was exhausted. He still couldn't quite figure out how he'd survived. All he knew was that he was tired. Too tired to talk any more. For the first time in six months he could close his eyes with the reassurance that it was finally over. That those bastards were dead. Nobody else would get hurt by them. And Nicoletta? He wanted to see her. He had to. He needed to be sure. He had to be certain that what he thought he'd witnessed had not actually happened.

Chapter Fifty

'Jack?'

Brady opened his eyes.

'They're calling again. This is the sixth time today. Do you want to answer it?'

Brady looked at the nurse. 'I can't . . .'

'I know, pet. Why don't I hold the phone to your ear? Promise I won't listen,' she reassured him.

Brady trusted Janice. He knew her life story. She had shared every detail of her painful divorce, her three adult children and her latest grandchild. She was a large woman in more ways than one and had a voracious appetite for everything – including taking care of him.

Brady nodded reluctantly. He knew who it was and knew they wouldn't stop until they'd talked to him.

'Here you go,' Janice said as she picked the phone up and placed it by his ear.

'Yeah?' Brady muttered reluctantly.

'Jack! You took your fucking time!' Madley replied.

Brady didn't respond.

'So? When do you get out?'

'In a week or so . . .'

'Good.'

There was an awkward silence. Both lost for words.

The nurse looked at Brady. 'Listen, I'll wedge this pillow here. OK? It should hold the phone in place so it'll give you some privacy.'

Before Brady had a chance to object she had gone, closing the door behind her.

Brady sighed. There were so many questions he wanted to ask. But whether or not Madley would be forthcoming was another matter.

'How did you know?'

'Know what? That you'd been shot? It's been all over the news. You even made national headlines for a week.'

Brady should have expected as much. Madley wasn't the sort to talk.

'Can I ask you something?'

'Depends,' Madley answered.

There were only two questions that bothered Brady now.

'That morning when I turned up unannounced?'

'Go on,' instructed Madley.

'It was Mayor Macmillan, wasn't it?'

Madley didn't answer. But his silence was enough.

It didn't make any sense. 'Why?'

'Business. He offered to buy me out.'

'What did you say?'

'I told him I wasn't interested.'

It was simple but honest. Enough to quell any doubts Brady might have had. He had known Madley long enough to tell when he was lying. But there was still one more question Brady needed answering – Weasel Face. Brady had seen him visiting Jake Munroe in prison hours after Munroe had stabbed Ronnie Macmillan to death. Why?

'Jake Munroe had a visitor when he was in prison,' Brady ventured.

'Really?'

'Yeah. It was the same day Ronnie Macmillan was killed.'

Silence.

Brady waited. Madley knew what he was asking and why.

'Maybe there were some questions that he needed to ask Munroe.'

'Like what?' Brady replied.

'Who he was working for and why.'

Brady accepted what Madley had said. Why not? Madley had saved his life. And in doing so, he had saved Claudia's and Nicoletta's. Brady could never thank Madley enough. He had been in trouble and Madley had come to his aid – no questions asked.

'Thanks,' Brady said.

'For what?'

'You know for what.'

A week later, Brady was being discharged. He looked at the wheelchair in the corner of his room and wondered how the fuck he was going to cope. But before he got a chance to get overly maudlin there was a knock at his door. A tentative knock.

'Yeah?' Brady called out.

The door opened.

It took Brady a moment to realise who was standing there. She was the last person he had expected to see.

She looked at him nervously.

Brady wasn't sure whether she was awkward because of his physical condition or if it was the on-going effect of what she'd endured.

'Hey,' Brady said.

'Hi . . .'

'It's great to see you,' Brady replied, smiling.

'I . . . asked DC Kodovesky if I could visit you. She said that you're going home today?'

Brady nodded. 'Yeah. They're kicking me out. Too much trouble, they said.'

She looked at him and smiled weakly. But it was enough. He hadn't ever imagined Chloe Winters smiling again – let alone at him.

'Do you want to come in?' Brady asked.

She shook her head. 'No . . . I can't stay. I . . . I just wanted to say thank you. Thank you for getting him.'

With that she turned and left.

'Chloe?' Brady called out. But to no avail. She had gone.

Chapter Fifty-One

A month later, Brady still couldn't believe what had happened. Let alone the fact that he had survived. He'd been hit in the chest with a bullet. The one that had been intended for Nicoletta. Luckily for her, it had hit him instead. He had the exit wound on his back to prove it.

Nicoletta survived against the odds. He didn't want to think about the catalogue of injuries that she'd sustained. They were brutal, nasty and sadistic, typifying the men who had exacted them.

'Jack?'

Brady turned to Nick. They were both sitting in his black 1978 Ford Granada 2.8i Ghia parked up by St Mary's lighthouse. Nick had driven him here at Brady's behest. He had just got back from some private covert job in Europe and had jumped on his Ducati 848 sports bike as soon he docked at Portsmouth and ridden straight up to Newcastle.

Brady knew exactly what Nick did for a living; but he never asked questions. Nick hired himself out as a bodyguard; at least that's what he had told Brady. At six foot three, muscle-bound but lithe, he was never short of work.

'You know if I could have got there in time, I would have?'

Brady nodded. Nick didn't need to state the obvious. The loyalty between them was unquestionable.

'The bastards really roughed you up,' Nick said as he looked at Brady's face. It still bore the scars a month later. His right hand and fingers were in a cast. As was his left leg. The smashed bones in both his hand and leg were now held together with pins. But he'd live.

337

He had spent three weeks in hospital recovering from his chest wound and the other injuries he'd sustained. It had been enough to worry even DCI Gates.

'Have you seen Martin yet?' Nick asked.

Brady shook his head.

'Shit, Jack!'

Brady shrugged. 'I talked to him on the phone.'

Nick looked at him. His green eyes were serious. 'If it wasn't for Madley, Claudia would be dead. No two ways about it. And so would you.'

'I know,' Brady muttered.

He owed Madley his life. He owed Madley for Claudia's life.

Nick had told him that he'd eventually picked up his voice-mail messages just in time to act. He had called Madley and asked for help.

Madley had listened and then acted under Nick's instruction.

Brady had been wrong about Madley and was still struggling to come to terms with the fact that he'd doubted him. He now knew that Munroe had been paid by the Dabkunas brothers to get information on Nick and kill Ronnie Macmillan. It was just coincidence that Munroe had worked for Madley. Then again, the Dabkunas brothers might have been trying to frame Madley – just as they had done before. Madley had been a problem. He had refused to go into business, so in return they tried to force him out.

But the Dabkunas brothers were dead. Ronnie Macmillan was dead and Munroe was locked up indefinitely. Madley's problems had disappeared. It was a satisfactory conclusion for him, as much as it was for the police.

DCI Gates and Detective Superintendent O'Donnell were both more than happy with the outcome. They had the infamous Dabkunas brothers and their armed guards, albeit dead.

Brady, on the other hand, felt cheated. He'd wanted the brothers to pay for the extensive crimes they had committed in the UK and Europe. He'd wanted to see them convicted so the women they'd trafficked and held hostage as sex-slaves could have some kind of justice. Death was too easy an out for them.

'What about you and Claudia?' Nick asked.

Brady thought about it for a moment. He had told Nick about everything; including Claudia.

'She said she needs time to come to terms with everything that's happened,' Brady said simply.

'Will you wait?'

Brady turned and looked at Nick. He already knew the answer.

'For as long as it takes.'

Acknowledgements

I would first like to thank all my family and friends. Especially Francesca, Charlotte, Gabriel and Ruby, who are without a doubt my inspiration. Thanks to Eliane and Professor Pete Wilson and Dr Barry Lewis for their constant encouragement and kindness. Thanks also to Richard Dykes Brown who was kind enough to answer whatever questions I threw at him and for sharing his invaluable experience as a Crime Scene Manager and police officer. I would especially like to thank Keshini Naidoo for all her help. Thanks also to Clare Usher whose skill and expertise enabled me to keep writing this book. Thanks to Pamela Letham and Gill Richards and Suzanne Forsten for their endless support. Also, thanks to Elaine Marr and Gillian Penman for just being there. Thanks to Stef Richards for her time and patience. A heartfelt thanks to Michelle and Keith Murphy for their friendship and for offering me the perfect writer's retreat in France – I am forever indebted to you. And, as always, thanks to Re.

I am eternally grateful, and always will be, to my literary agent, Jenny Brown.

Special thanks to all at Mulholland Books and Hodder & Stoughton for being such an incredible team. Finally, I am truly indebted to my editor, Ruth Tross – thank you.

You've turned the last page.

But it doesn't have to end there . . .

If you're looking for more first-class, action-packed, nail-biting suspense, join us at **Facebook.com/ MulhollandUncovered** for news, competitions, and behind-the-scenes access to Mulholland Books.

For regular updates about our books and authors as well as what's going on in the world of crime and thrillers, follow us on **Twitter@MulhollandUK**.

There are many more twists to come.

A
Girl's Best
Friend

JULES WAKE

SPHERE

First published in Great Britain in 2018 by Sphere

1 3 5 7 9 10 8 6 4 2

Copyright © Jules Wake 2018

The moral right of the author has been asserted.

*All characters and events in this publication, other than those
clearly in the public domain, are fictitious and any resemblance
to real persons, living or dead, is purely coincidental.*

A CIP catalogue record for this book
is available from the British Library.

ISBN 978-0-7515-7107-3

Typeset in Caslon by M Rules
Printed and bound in Great Britain by
Clays Ltd, Elcograf S.p.A.

Papers used by Sphere are from well-managed forests
and other responsible sources.

MIX
Paper from
responsible sources
FSC® C104740

Sphere
An imprint of
Little, Brown Book Group
Carmelite House
50 Victoria Embankment
London EC4Y 0DZ

An Hachette UK Company
www.hachette.co.uk

www.littlebrown.co.uk